Tengoku

Also by Rae D. Magdon

Death Wears Yellow Garters

Amendyr Series

The Second Sister
Wolf's Eyes
The Witch's Daughter
The Mirror's Gaze

And with Michelle Magly

Dark Horizons Series

Dark Horizons
Starless Nights

Tengoku

by
Rae D. Magdon

Desert Palm Press

Tengoku

by Rae D. Magdon

© 2016 Rae D. Magdon

ISBN-(trade): 9781942976271
ISBN-(epub): 9781942976288
ISBN (pdf): 9781942976295

All rights reserved. No part of this book may be reproduced in any form other than that which it was purchased and without the express permission of the author or publisher. Please note that piracy of copyrighted materials violates the author's right and is illegal.

This e-book is licensed for your personal enjoyment only. This e-book may not be re-sold or given away to other people. If you would like to share this book with another person, please purchase an additional copy for each recipient. If you're reading this book and did not purchase it, or it was not purchased for your use only, purchase your own copy. Thank you for respecting the hard work of this author.

This is a work of fiction. Names, characters, places, and incidents are the product of the author's imagination or used fictitiously and any resemblance to actual persons, living or dead, businesses, companies, events, or locales is entirely coincidental.

For permission requests, write to the publisher, addressed "Attention: Permissions Coordinator," at the address below.

Desert Palm Press
1961 Main Street, Suite 220
Watsonville, California 95076
www.desertpalmpress.com

Editor: Kellie Doherty (http://editreviseperfect.weebly.com/)
Cover Design: Rachel George (http://www.rachelgeorgeillustration.com/)

Printed in the United States of America
First Edition — December 2016

Acknowledgments:

During the writing of this novel, more than any other work I have ever written, I relied so much on the help of my friends and colleagues. Without them, I never would have been able to finish it, let alone ensure its quality and honesty.

First, I must thank my friend Lex for his expertise on Japanese culture. It was a rough road at times, but he never gave up on me despite all my mistakes. Tengoku wouldn't exist at all without him, and I hope he knows how much I appreciate his hard work. He is incredible, and he poured hours and hours of his personal time into this manuscript in order to bring valuable, accurate minority representation to a lot of people.

Secondly, I need to thank Sarah. Not only did she guide me on how to write a believable trans lead, but she also served as a second adviser on Japanese culture. Although I tried to write Kaede's relationship to her gender with as much care as I could, she helped me reach another level of authenticity.

I also need to thank Kristin, who offered her valuable insight at several opportunities. It was incredibly important to me for a woman of color to read the manuscript and point out my (inevitable) errors, which she did with kindness and gentleness.

Lastly, I need to thank the fantastic team at Desert Palm Press: Kellie, my editor, and Lee, my publisher. They have always believed in me, and I appreciate them every time I sit down to write. I love working with them so much, and hope to do so again many, many times in the future.

Table of Contents

Prologue..1
Chapter One...3
Chapter Two...15
Chapter Three...23
Chapter Four...31
Chapter Five..39
Chapter Six..49
Chapter Seven...59
Chapter Eight..69
Chapter Nine...77
Chapter Ten...87
Chapter Eleven..103
Chapter Twelve...113
Chapter Thirteen...127
Chapter Fourteen..139
Chapter Fifteen...151
Chapter Sixteen...165
Chapter Seventeen...177
Chapter Eighteen..193
Chapter Nineteen...213
Chapter Twenty..225
Chapter Twenty-one..237
Chapter Twenty-two..249
Chapter Twenty-three..261
Chapter Twenty-four...273
Chapter Twenty-five..291
Chapter Twenty-six..303
Chapter Twenty-seven...313
Chapter Twenty-eight..327
Glossary of Terms and Places..345
About Rae D. Magdon...349
Other Books by Rae D. Magdon..350
Note to Readers..355

Prologue

LONG AGO, BEFORE THE age of fire and steel, the lands of Tengoku were young and filled with wonders. The untamed forests and soaring mountains were home to the yokai, spirits of the wild. These gigantic beasts dwelled side by side with humans, taking their first steps, with the Great Spirits of the Sun and Moon watching over them all and smiling from their place in the sky.

For a time, humans and yokai lived in harmony. But as the humans aged, they lost touch with the land they had sprung from and the yokai who lived with them. They built large, gleaming cities that sparkled like jewels and their rice fields stretched from one end of the continent to the other.

Three kingdoms rose in this new age. First was Akatsuki Teikoku in the northeast, forged around the honorable samurai with a wise and just Emperor leading them into a new dawn. To the west was the Kingdom of Tsun'i, where science, art, and music blossomed. To the south was Xiangsai, a small nation of warriors who guarded their borders fiercely. These three nations grew together, and though they sometimes fought, they remained connected through the branching rivers that fed them and the common souls of the Ancestors, who found peace beyond the Roaring Ocean.

And yet, even as the human world grows and changes, ancient magic still lives on. A chosen few maintain a strong connection to the yokai and the land of Tengoku itself. These few serve to remind the kingdoms of their past and guide them safely into the future, a future where humans and yokai are not divided, but live in harmony, two halves of the same whole.

This is Tengoku: the land of sword, magic, and beast.

Rae D. Magdon

Chapter One

THE FOREST HUNGERED. SNARLING branches tore at Kaede's kimono, catching the hem as if to drag her back. She huffed in frustration, fighting her way through the undergrowth, but as soon as she kicked aside one curling limb, another took its place. The thick roots sent her stumbling, and she caught herself against a nearby tree trunk, rough bark grazing her palm. She hissed in pain, but didn't stop. Instead, she straightened, ignoring the sharp sting and ran into the darkness.

The lonely howl of a wolf cut through the night air, covering the sound her sandals made as they crunched across the ground. She turned left, heart racing. *Did the call come from that direction? Who did it come from?* After a moment of indecision, she decided to take a risk. Alone, she didn't stand much of a chance. She needed to find Rin.

She plunged back into the thick of the forest, heading in the direction she thought the noise had come from. The wolf's cry didn't echo again, but a flash of white in the trees made Kaede's frantic heartbeat pound slower. "Rin, please tell me that's you."

"Stop!"

Kaede skidded to a stop, her small supply bag slipping perilously down her shoulder. Pulling it up, she squinted at the uneven twilight of the undergrowth, trying to locate the voice. A pair of ice blue eyes peered out from a patch of shadow, and she could just make out a white whiskered muzzle. She breathed a sigh of relief.

"Get down and stay out of sight," Rin growled. "We won't be able to outrun them."

Kaede began to protest, but another piercing howl changed her mind. She flung herself to the ground, scrambling beneath the overhang. Shivering with fear and cold, she tucked herself into the giant wolf's side, curling up as small as possible beneath the thick tree branches.

The sound of rapid footfalls came closer and she caught sight of swaying branches several yards away. A tall, broad-shouldered figure dressed in black stepped up to the same tree she had fallen against. His katana was drawn, and moonlight glinted from its sharpened edge.

Hayate. Kaede would have recognized her cousin even if she hadn't glimpsed his stony face. *But where is Kaze?*

Her question was answered a moment later. Another dark figure padded up to the tree, this one on all fours. The black-furred wolf was huge, standing high enough for his muzzle to reach Hayate's shoulder. They whispered together, words Kaede couldn't make out. She could barely concentrate on anything but the pleading chant circling through her head. *Please don't see us. Please don't see us. Please don't see us.*

After what felt like an eternity, Hayate relaxed. He sheathed his katana back into his saya beside his shorter wakizashi before starting off in another direction. His strides were swift and purposeful, but he made a great deal of noise as he disappeared into the depths of the forest. Kaze didn't follow. He lifted his nose into the air, sniffing the wind. When his eyes locked onto her, Kaede's blood went cold.

Kaze didn't lunge for them. Instead of howling in triumph, he padded off after his companion, swift and silent as an owl's wing.

Once they were alone, Rin hauled herself out of her makeshift burrow, shaking off dirt and twigs. The coarse fur on her back still bristled. "Come. We need to leave before Hayate finds us."

Kaede pushed down her fear. The forest was dangerous, but she knew it far better than her cousin did. If he thought he could catch her, he was mistaken. She started off again, away from the clumsy path Hayate had left in the brush, heading toward the river. Sharp pants of breath spilled from her mouth as she ran, hanging before her in coiling clouds of silver mist. She had no idea where she would go when she left the forest, but she did know one thing—she couldn't stay in Kousetsu, or anywhere in the province of Yukimura for that matter. She couldn't even go to the neighboring province of Aozora, where her father was daimyo. Everything that had happened back at Setsuna's cave was her fault.

Once more, her ears reverberated with a haunting echo. *Your fault. Your fault. Your fault.* It drowned out even the murmur of the blue-black river travelling through the trees. She blinked her watering eyes, trying to banish the ghostly images. The flashes refused to go away: mangled bodies bleeding onto the snow, gleaming black claws rending flesh, and hungry, gaping mouths. *The yokai aren't always like this. I know they aren't.* She glanced over at Rin who was still hovering close to her side, nose pointed into the wind. *Setsuna is the one who made them violent. And I helped her do it.*

"Kaede, slow down. We're safe for now."

It took Kaede a moment to notice the familiar clearing. The riverbank they had been following branched off into a small pool, its starlit surface smooth as glass. The pool held special memories, and Kaede slowed her run to a stumbling stagger as she approached its edge. There didn't seem to be anyone else nearby, but Kaede remained silent, listening. She couldn't hear anything apart from her own breathing, but Rin's ears perked high. Trusting her companion's senses better than her own, she reached for her katana, but Rin stopped her. "Don't worry. It isn't Hayate and Kaze."

Rin turned her head and Kaede followed the motion, catching sight of more large shadows weaving through the trees. She still didn't hear anything, but she did sense the prickling aura of a nearby spirit's ki on the back of her neck, rolling down like beads of sweat. Yokai were close.

When she removed her hand from her blade, the presence made itself known. Another wolf stepped into the clearing, a fierce-looking grey creature even larger than Rin and standing slightly above Kaede's head. A scar slashed down one side of her muzzle, and Kaede's left cheek ached in sympathy. The crescent-shaped scars she carried there had healed surprisingly well over the past several days, but they still bothered her.

"Haruna," she said, making a polite bow.

"Kaede. I thought I might find you and my daughter here." Haruna's voice was smoother than Rin's gruff bark, serving to put Kaede at ease. She glanced at the shining pool, and then her one good eye fixed on Rin. "Where is your brother?"

"With Hayate," Rin growled. "He didn't engage us."

Something unspoken passed between the two wolves and Kaede stayed respectfully silent. Rin's family struggles were private, just as her own were.

"He is loyal," Haruna said, and Kaede thought she saw a hint of pride on the wolf's face. "And what about you? Are you leaving the forest with your human?"

Rin inclined her head and Kaede felt a wave of relief. She had assumed her childhood friend would accompany her wherever she went, but it was still good to hear it. The forest was Rin's home, and she easily could have chosen to stay there

"I ask your blessing to leave the pack, mother. Kaede is my friend. I want to protect her, as I have always done."

A lump formed in Kaede's throat. She bit her lip, still unsure what to say. Rin seemed to understand, because the white wolf turned and nudged affectionately at her cheek, touching it with the tip of her nose.

"You have my blessing, but if you return, you will not find us here." Haruna's lips peeled back to reveal the sharp points of her teeth. "Setsuna has gone too far. We will not allow ourselves to become drawn into her ill-thought plans. The balance between yokai and humans is delicate enough as it is. Her attempts to twist it to her own purposes will only end in disaster, for her and many others."

"If you believe that, then we should stay and fight." Rin took an aggressive posture, her tail sticking straight up from her bunched haunches. "We can't allow Setsuna and Hayate to continue with this. You agree, don't you, Kaede?"

Kaede lowered her eyes to the ground, swallowing down her shame. "The best way for me to help is to get as far away from Setsuna as possible. She was using me, Rin. Those samurai who died could have been me, my family, and friends. Those yokai she killed could have been either of you. We have to get out of here."

Rin looked as if she wanted to object, but there was little time. Another piercing howl broke through the silence of the night, and as Kaede turned toward the sound, she thought she saw the water of the small pool ripple.

"You should leave." Haruna gazed past the clearing to where the forest led on. "Kaze let you go once, but he may not be able to delay Hayate for long. One day soon, he will have to make his choice and decide where his heart lies."

"If he tries to harm Kaede, I won't go easy on him," Rin said.

"I'm sure you won't." Haruna padded forward, touching her muzzle to Rin's. "I wish you luck and safe travels. Turn your anger to strength. My intuition tells me you're going to need it. If you wish to find your pack again, venture beyond the west snows and trust your instincts. And you, Kaede." Kaede looked up as Haruna approached, lowering her massive head and bringing them nose-to-nose. "May Tsukine, Goddess of the Moon, and the spirits of your ancestors watch over you. Remember your compassion for the yokai. We have given you many gifts. Someday, I hope you will repay that kindness."

Kaede could only nod. After all, Haruna and the other yokai who lived in the forest had done for her, the least she could do was make sure she wasn't responsible for any more killing. "I will. Goodbye, Haruna." She flung her arms around the grey wolf's neck, burying her face in the soft fur.

Haruna allowed the embrace, but after a moment, she stepped back. She disappeared into the forest without another word, slipping off to rejoin her pack. "Come on," Rin said, giving Kaede a light bump with her shoulder. "Kaze's call wasn't too far away. He's trying to warn us."

Kaede spared one last glance at the pool. She picked up her jog again, heading off into the night and trying to ignore the weight of guilt as it settled back over her shoulders. She still had no idea where she was going, but she needed to get far away from here.

***

A grunt of exertion burst from Imari's lips as the tip of her sparring spear scraped across Takeshi's. The carved wooden blades of their yari clacked together, ringing through the courtyard, but she didn't pull back. Instead, she strengthened her stance and prepared for the next strike. She won the last two matches, but she wouldn't be satisfied unless she went three for three.

Takeshi's second lunge came lightning fast. Imari met it with her left forearm, leading the blow to the side with the protective padding of her kote. The block forced his weapon to skid, but Imari knew from the jolt racing along her shortened left arm she had not been precise enough to redirect all the power behind the thrust. Takeshi had more upper body strength and two hands to her one. If she was going to win this match, she needed to do so with skill, not brute force.

When he came at her again, she was ready with a different tactic. She shifted her weight from front to back, moving her yari in tight circles to avoid his. Takeshi was fast, but she was faster, dodging with subtle steps. Her eyes moved more than any other part of her body, searching for the perfect opportunity.

Her chance came a few seconds later. Takeshi overestimated his next thrust. She took a step toward him, letting his spear miss her side by an inch, and twirled. With one quick motion, she struck at Takeshi's unguarded stomach, driving the blunt end of the spear right into his gut.

"Oof!"

Takeshi stumbled, dropping his weapon and landing flat on his backside. As he hit the ground, Imari's eyes widened. She had wanted to win but not quite that dramatically. She set aside her spear and rushed forward, kneeling in the dust beside him. "Takeshi, are you all right?"

Takeshi coughed, struggling to regain his wind. The maroon edge of his sleeve caught his dark hair as he wiped the sweat from his brow.

"It's all right, Homura-dono. I'm fine."

Imari stared at him for a few moments, but other than a few streaks of dirt on his kimono, he seemed none the worse for wear. Hopefully, his pride was the only thing she had wounded. "Are you sure?" She reached for his fallen spear, passing it back to him as he climbed to his feet. "I wasn't trying to knock you back like that."

A smile brightened Takeshi's serious face. He took the offered weapon and bowed. "I'm just glad we were using sparring weapons. Otherwise, I'd have been skewered."

Imari sighed in relief. She returned Takeshi's bow and fell into a more casual pose. "Takeshi, you know I'd never stab you. But thanks for the practice."

"I'm not sure you needed it," he said, straightening his clothes. "Why did you want to train with yari today, anyway? We could have been using daishō."

Imari retrieved her own weapon, folding the fingers of her right hand around the grip. "Spears are what our soldiers use. I won't be much of a leader if I can't fight with the same weapons as the people who follow me." She grinned. "Besides, I like to stay on my toes. Beating you with a sword is too easy."

A blush spread across Takeshi's cheeks and he rubbed the back of his neck. "Guess that means I'm on your good side again, huh?"

With a soft sigh, Imari averted her eyes, staring at the rest of the barracks courtyard. None of the guards were about, but the privacy only unsettled her more. She and Takeshi had been close for years, but lately, it was hard to talk to him. The distance between them almost certainly had something to do with the abrupt end of their romantic relationship.

Her father had approved of the match, and initially, so had she. Takeshi was her best friend, and he wasn't half-bad to look at either, with his sturdy build and angular jaw. But the reality of being with him hadn't lived up to the fantasy. Too often, she worried he was deferring to her wishes and ambitions in an effort to please her instead of being himself—and that wasn't even getting into his maddening protective streak. He had become stiff, formal, and nearly intolerable to be around until she had called things off.

"You were never on my bad side, Takeshi," she said, adding a little reassurance to her voice. As often as he annoyed her, he was still her best friend.

Takeshi seemed to understand what she wasn't saying. He took a step back, giving her more space. "Of course not, Homura-dono."

"And stop calling me that when we're alone," Imari insisted with a friendly roll of her eyes. "Just because we aren't engaged anymore doesn't mean you can't use my first name when no one else is around."

A brief look of hurt crossed Takeshi's face, but he recovered quickly. "Sorry, Imari. It's just hard when…" His voice trailed off abruptly, and he tilted his head to one side. "Wait, do you hear that?"

At first, Imari could only hear the distant nickering of horses and the usual steady hum of people moving through the markets, but after a few moments, something caught her attention: raised voices. The decision to train in the courtyard of the guards' quarters placed them not a dozen yards away from the plaza, with only one wall in between. She couldn't make out what was being said, but the tones were clear. Blades were about to be drawn.

"I'll bet you twenty circles it's Naoki causing trouble again," Imari muttered. She placed her wooden spear next to the wall, electing to replace it with a real weapon just in case. She was partially responsible for dealing with any conflicts that arose in Mirai, especially petty squabbles not worth her father's attention.

Takeshi followed her without being told. "I know better than to take that bet. I'm not made of money."

"What do you think set him off this time?"

"Who knows? Someone probably looked at him funny. For a samurai, he doesn't have much patience."

A sizable crowd had already gathered by the time Imari and Takeshi arrived at the small plaza at the city gates, but one tall woman stood out from the rest. She had planted herself in the middle of the ring of onlookers, her chin tilted at a proud angle. Her hair was a dark, striking red, piled on her head in a messy topknot, and her brown skin glistened in the sun. Her simple clothes of deep blue wrapped tight around her, but she had the lean muscles and powerful stance of a warrior. She also had two slashing, crescent-shaped scars across her left cheek, a somewhat recent looking injury that reminded Imari strangely of clawmarks.

A samurai? Her eyes moved lower, to the daishō in the stranger's belt. *But what province is she from? The stitching on her clothes has seen better days. She's not wearing the mon of her family or master. Without an emblem she can only be—*

"I already told you I was sorry," the woman said, averting her eyes and lowering her head. Somehow, she managed to convey a sense of remorse without appearing entirely submissive. The line of her shoulders remained tense, as if she was still expecting a fight. "It was an accident. I didn't see you passing by."

As Imari had suspected, Naoki stood on the other side of the open circle. "You bumped against my blade," he sneered, his upturned nose wrinkling in clear distaste. "Your clanless sword shouldn't have even been near it. I don't want it dirtied."

The woman abandoned her attempts to be polite. She pursed her lips and let out a clear whistle. The silver noise fluttered through the air, and murmurs rippled through the crowd. Several let out gasps of fear and awe as an enormous white wolf padded up to the woman's side.

Although the wolf stood taller than a person's shoulder, its body was all muscle and bone, and its muzzle was curled in a snarl even more frightening than Naoki's. Imari's breath caught in surprise and delight. The creature must be one of the yokai. No ordinary wolf could match that size and its face held a feral kind of intelligence.

"I might be clanless, but I still have my honor." The woman met Naoki's gaze as the wolf hovered beside her, a silent white shadow. "Accept my apology, and Rin and I will leave you in peace."

Imari exchanged a nervous glance with Takeshi, and the expression on his face reflected her own worry. If this strange samurai really had bumped into Naoki's sword, there was no way he would allow the slight to pass. Fights were common when a samurai's weapon was involved.

Takeshi stepped forward to settle the argument, but Imari stopped him with a soft shake of her head. She wanted to see the result of the duel. Naoki was an excellent swordsman, but she had a feeling he was going to lose—badly.

"I don't want your apology," Naoki spat. He seemed wary of the spirit wolf, but it wasn't enough to quell his pride. "I want your blood. Draw your sword, ronin."

The unsworn samurai's hands bunched into fists, and her expression hardened. The wolf beside her growled, but she gave a soft shake of her head. "Please, don't interfere, Rin. I can handle this myself." At her request, the giant wolf sat on its haunches, still gazing at Naoki with slitted blue eyes. The strange woman's eyes narrowed, lips pressed tight together. "If you're determined to fight, I'll defend my honor, but I did try to resolve this peacefully."

Naoki reached to his hip, drawing his katana. "My name is Kato Naoki, samurai in the service of the great daimyo Homura. My sword is Ōkami-kiba, Wolf's Tooth. I challenge you to a duel of retribution."

Despite the seriousness of the situation, Imari couldn't help but snort at the irony. Naoki's sword-name seemed ridiculous, especially since there was a flesh-and-blood wolf sitting at his opponent's feet. She could have sworn the white-furred beast huffed at the name.

The woman reached toward her obi. Sunlight glinted off metal as she drew the longer of her two swords. "My name is Iori Kaede." She paused, deliberately leaving out the name of her master. "My sword is Mizu-no-Hamon, Blade that Ripples on Water."

Imari's eyes widened. Sword-names were rare, and most samurai, let alone ronin, didn't have named katana. She herself had chosen not to name her blades, although that was partially because she enjoyed a certain amount of versatility when selecting her weapons.

"I accept your challenge, but you're going to regret it."

Imari couldn't be sure, she thought she saw the hint of a smile tug at the stranger's mouth. Both bowed, Naoki reluctantly, and silence settled over the onlookers. Imari's breath burned in her chest, and her eyes remained fixed on the mysterious woman's blade as it hovered in the air. The stillness shattered as Naoki thrust his blade forward, aiming straight for Kaede's throat.

Kaede didn't hesitate. Her katana flashed in a circle, knocking Naoki's aside. Imari caught the slight widening of Naoki's eyes when he realized he had missed, but he recovered quickly. He lunged again, grunting with rage as he tried to strike at her shoulder. Once again, the woman's blade slid along his, angling it away from her body. It slipped with a hiss of metal on metal.

"Stop playing, clanless." Naoki lunged again but not quickly enough. The woman grabbed his wrist with her free hand, catching him in mid-thrust. While he struggled, her katana sliced through the air. The blade never met flesh. Instead, she whipped it around, changing her grip, and jabbing the pommel directly into Naoki's face. It met his nose with a sickening crack. He cried out, reeling back as blood poured down his chin.

The woman let go of his wrist and stepped away, allowing him to keep his sword but remaining well out of reach. "First blood is mine."

"But...but you didn't." Naoki blubbered, sniffing to keep back the river of red.

"Why should I waste my blade on you? I drew first blood. It doesn't matter how I did it. Let me pass."

Naoki lifted his sword again, but the look in his eyes made Imari step forward. She had no doubt the strange woman would kill him if he continued to attack, and as much as she disliked Naoki, the waste of life seemed senseless.

"Enough," she said, passing her spear to Takeshi. He took it without question, although she didn't miss the protective way he followed her into the ring.

Naoki seemed to notice her presence for the first time. He straightened and sheathed his sword, bending into a deep bow. "Homura-dono, I didn't know you were here. I was just—"

Imari narrowed her eyes at him. "I saw what you were doing. We don't fight strangers here, Kato-san, even ones who are rude to us. Mirai welcomes people from all provinces of the Empire, including those without allegiances. It's why this city was built in the first place."

"But she bumped my blade, my lady! Saya-ate!"

"No disrespect was intended. She apologized for bumping your sword. Accept it and move on."

Naoki grimaced and grunted, sniffing against the stream of blood, but eventually, he spat out an insincere, "I apologize. My conduct was unbecoming of a samurai in your presence."

Good enough. I won't get anything more out of him until he's had a chance to calm down. Satisfied, Imari turned to the stranger. Up close, she was surprised to realize the woman couldn't be much older than twenty. From a distance, Imari had thought her to be a much more seasoned warrior, but the soft edges of her face gave her away. *She is also remarkably...beautiful? Perhaps. Or maybe striking is a better description.*

Imari realized that everyone was waiting for her to speak. She cleared her throat, trying to sound as official as possible. "Everyone is welcome in Mirai, stranger, but we don't start fights without cause here."

"It wasn't without cause. He challenged me."

Surprised by the woman's boldness, Imari found herself intrigued instead of offended. She fought a smile as she shook her head. "And you bumped his sword. Regardless, I'm afraid you will have to come with me."

Imari saw the moment realization dawned on the woman's face. First, the stranger's eyes darted toward the emblem on her training gear—a bronze hexagon, with a striking white yamayuri inside. Then, they flew up to the matching banners placed around the plaza, a whole fluttering field of lilies backed with bronze and red. Her expression shifted from surprise to panic before finally landing on guilt. "I apologize, my lady. I didn't know."

Imari smiled. It wasn't the first time someone had taken a moment to place her. She could play the part of the aristocrat well enough, but most people didn't expect to see the lady of the house in dirty training clothes carrying a weapon, let alone missing a hand.

"Don't worry about it," she said, in a slightly less formal voice meant to put the other woman at ease. "Come with me. I promise you won't be judged too harshly." She glanced over at the spirit wolf, who watched her warily. "If anything, I'm interested to find out why a wanderer with a spirit wolf as her companion has come to Mirai."

Many travelers came to Mirai every day, but none had ever caused quite such a scene, or shown such an affinity for the yokai. Despite herself, Imari couldn't help being curious. *Hopefully, I'll get a chance to find out more soon. If she could help me.* She shook that thought away. It was too soon for such a request, and she still didn't know enough about this mysterious stranger. *First things first. I need to find out how much she really knows about the yokai.*

"Hibana-san, please take care of the crowd," she said, gesturing at the curious onlookers. "I wish to speak to our new arrival alone."

Takeshi looked as though he wanted to protest, but under the power of her gaze, he bowed his head. "As you say, Homura-dono. Please, be safe."

"I always am." Imari offered a smile before turning back to the woman she was truly interested in. "Iori Kaede, you and your wolf-clan companion will follow me."

Chapter Two

KAEDE STUDIED THE DAIMYO'S castle from a distance, staring at the magnificent building in awe. Its white layers stretched up to the sky like a mountain shrouded in mist and the trim around each curved red rooftop glittered gold in the afternoon sun. She and Rin, led by Lady Homura, had already climbed a few levels up from the gates, but the castle stood even higher above the city. It was different from the castle she had once called home and certainly a large departure from the dense forests and oceans of tall grass she had traveled through over the past several weeks. Impressive though it was, the bustle of Mirai didn't put her any more at ease. This city felt no safer than the abandoned countryside.

Rin noticed her conflicted emotions. "I don't like it," the wolf growled. "This place smells like fire and smoke. Sweat. Too many humans."

Kaede aimed an apologetic glance at Lady Homura. Rin's voice hadn't been soft, and she could tell by the slight stiffening of their guide's shoulders the words had carried. Lady Homura turned toward her, looking intrigued instead of angry. Her dark eyes glittered and Kaede's stomach did a nervous flip.

Come on, Kaede. Stop staring like an idiot! The last thing you want to do is offend the daimyo's daughter. Her entry into the city had already been messy enough, and she couldn't afford to ruin her chances. She was an outcast, and if Mirai wouldn't accept her, nowhere would. "Don't talk like that, Rin. I think it's amazing."

A smile crossed Lady Homura's face like a patch of light breaking through the clouds. "I'm glad you think so. My father built this castle. He built most of the city, in fact, with my grandfather's blessing. It's hard to believe, but when I was born, Mirai was mostly farm country." She turned to Rin and gave a small bow. "I'm afraid it's the factories on the eastern side of the city that are offending your nose, wolf-clan. Mirai is the most industrialized city in the Homura province, and ours is the fastest-growing province in the Empire."

Rin let out a low huff, but to Kaede's relief, she didn't continue complaining.

"So, how did you come to travel with a wolf spirit, Iori-san?" Lady Homura asked. "We live in harmony with the spirits here in Mirai, but not many yokai are willing to travel among humans."

Kaede grinned. She didn't mind discussing Rin at all. "I've always liked the yokai, and they seem to like me, but Rin is special. She's my best friend." She reached out to pat Rin's neck, tangling her fingers in the wolf's thick fur. "I found her lost in the forest when I was a child. I kept her company until we found her pack again, and she's been my friend ever since."

"The forest?" Lady Homura's dark eyes brightened a little. "Your accent sounds northern. Which province are you from? Aozora or Yukimura? Or perhaps one of the smaller ones?"

Kaede averted her eyes as they continued walking. She felt guilty for lying, but it was a matter of self-preservation. "I'd rather not talk about it, if that's acceptable to you, my lady."

"Of course."

They lapsed back into silence, and Kaede took the opportunity to study her escort more closely. At first, she had only noticed Lady Homura's missing hand. It had been a struggle not to stare. But the longer Kaede looked, the more she saw aside from the obvious. Lady Homura was curvy and graceful, with fine pale skin and smooth black hair that lay over her shoulder in a braid like spilled wet ink. But Kaede remembered the confident way she had gripped the spear earlier as she strode into the circle of onlookers. This was no soft princess. To treat her as such would be a mistake. Despite her missing hand, she had the bearing and dress of a warrior. Perhaps this woman could even help her.

"I'd like to apologize for earlier, my lady." It galled her to apologize for a fight that wasn't really her fault, but she needed all the allies she could get while she was on the run. "I wasn't trying to cause any trouble."

To her surprise, Lady Homura laughed. "But trouble found you. I know the man you offended. He isn't known for his patience or hospitality, especially with newcomers. Don't take it personally."

"Is it because I don't have a mon to show?" she asked, with a tinge of apprehension. "I know most cities aren't exactly welcoming to those without a clan or a master, but I thought Mirai was different."

"Mirai is different. You wouldn't be the first to come here for that reason." The smirk on Lady Homura's face grew bigger. "But I have to admit, you're the most memorable visitor I've met so far, and not just because of the wolf-clan who travels with you. That's why I wanted to talk to you."

Kaede gulped. The castle drew nearer, and she feared Lady Homura would lead her there. When she had come to Mirai, she certainly hadn't planned on visiting its daimyo, especially not in dirty clothes and smelling like the countryside. "You aren't taking me to see Lord Homura, are you? Surely a daimyo of his status doesn't need to concern himself with petty scuffles."

Lady Homura shook her head. "I would hardly call it a petty scuffle, but no, I'm not taking you to see my father yet. I think I'd like to keep you to myself for a while longer. This way." She gestured ahead of them, not at the castle, but to a wide street running along the outer wall of the daimyo's residence.

Once they turned, the branches of the ume trees lining the road closed above their heads. The dark-rose and pastel-pink petals placed a curious shade upon the ground, blocking some of the sunlight and carrying a sweet scent. Walled-off houses stood on either side, curving with the street. The bustle of the market faded away, leaving a peaceful sort of silence.

Lady Homura moved to one of the first houses with its own moderately raised wall some short distance away. "I've decided to put you up in the Hibana household for a few nights. The Hibana brothers are two of my closest friends. They won't mind hosting you as a favor to me."

Kaede took a closer look. Past the bending boughs of the overhanging trees that skirted the top of the wall, she could make out a large, three-roofed house beyond. With a wall like that, and so close to the castle, these Hibana brothers had to be important. "That's incredibly kind of you, Lady Homura, but it isn't necessary. I'm just glad you didn't have me thrown out of the city. I know I don't have a mon at present, but I can afford to pay for my own lodgings."

Lady Homura waved her off. "Nonsense. As of right now, you're officially my guest. Think of it as repayment for the rude welcome Kato-san gave you. One of my father's samurai really should've known better. Please, allow me to correct his mistake."

Kaede started to protest once more, but Rin spoke up first. "Say yes, Kaede. It's the polite thing to do, and you need at least one proper night of rest."

"All right." She sighed, giving Rin an affectionate scratch behind her ears. "Thank you, Lady Homura. Your generosity is appreciated, and I'll be sure to extend my thanks to the Hibana brothers for housing me when I have the pleasure of meeting them."

"You've already met one of them, in a way," Lady Homura said. "Hibana Takeshi, the older of the two, was standing beside me while I watched your duel. He has a protective streak, but he isn't as unreasonable as most karo."

Kaede remembered the tall, dark-haired samurai who had acted as Lady Homura's escort. Takeshi had looked awfully young to be an adviser to Lord Homura, but it wasn't her place to question. He couldn't have been more than a few years older than she and Lady Homura were.

Her musings were cut short when they arrived at the entrance to the house, a grand affair with an impressive square archway that led into a lovely green garden. "This way," Lady Homura said. "Hibana Kenta should be around. I'll introduce you."

When they passed through the entryway into the courtyard, a man hurried out to greet them. He was tall, with broad shoulders and large muscles, but his bright eyes and slightly chubby face made him seem anything but intimidating. From his clothes and blades, Kaede could tell he was a samurai like his brother.

"Imari!" he said, offering Lady Homura a wide smile on his way.

Kaede glanced over at the daimyo's daughter in surprise. *Imari? So, that's her given name. Pretty.*

Noticing the two other figures, Kenta stopped, giving one of the most energetic bows Kaede had ever seen. "I mean, Homura-dono! I saw you coming up the path. Who is this? A wolf?" He gaped at Rin, not even trying to conceal his stare.

"You're happy as ever, I see," Lady Homura said with a laugh. "This is Iori Kaede, and her companion, Rin. If it's no trouble, I'd appreciate it if you'd let them stay in your household for a few nights. They're new to Mirai, and in need of a friendly atmosphere."

"Well, friendly is my taken name!" Kenta said, resting a flat palm against his chest. "Nice to meet you, Iori Kaede. I'm Hibana Kenta, but my lady probably already told you that." He resumed gawking at Rin, who faced him eye to eye. "So, how long have you been traveling with a wolf-clan yokai? How did you get him to stay with you?"

"You mean she," Kaede said.

"And she can speak for herself." To Kaede's relief, Rin didn't appear threatened by Kenta's enthusiasm. In fact, she seemed amused by his interest in her. "I think I like you, human. At least your greetings are friendlier than some of the others we've received in this city."

"I'm sorry if I offended you. Some yokai live in the mountains around the city, but they usually don't come close enough to talk to the humans here. I knew some of you could speak, but...it's just...you're a talking wolf! You're so lucky to have such a strong connection with spirits, Iori-san. Have they always followed you around, or is Rin-sama special?"

That question hit a bit too close to home. Kaede fumbled for an answer, unwilling to reveal too much. Kenta seemed friendly, but the last thing she wanted to do was talk about the mess she had left behind. "Rin's special." Kaede gave the wolf a fond look. "I've never met another like her, yokai or otherwise." That statement was true enough, even though it wasn't an entirely honest answer.

Thankfully, Kenta didn't pry. "So, Rin-sama, what do you eat? Do yokai even need to eat? I can show you where the kitchen is if you're hungry."

As Kenta continued rambling, Kaede's gaze wandered back to Imari. She had stepped back, observing the lively conversation with interest. The sight made Kaede strangely uncomfortable, although she couldn't put her finger on why.

"Thank you, Homura-dono," she murmured, in a softer voice so Imari would know the words were meant only for her. "You could've thrown me out of the city or had me arrested after what happened, but instead, you've been nothing but welcoming. I don't know why you've taken an interest in me, but I'm grateful. If there's any way I can repay your kindness."

"There might be," Imari said, studying her with sharp eyes. "The two of us can discuss it in private tomorrow. For now, I want you to eat and get some rest. You will be well taken care of here until I can meet with you again."

Kaede's heart sank at Imari's words. The two of them didn't know each other, and she had suspected Lady Homura's interest in her wasn't idle curiosity but hearing it confirmed was strangely disappointing. *I guess it's always the same. Every time someone shows me kindness, they always want something from me in return. Hopefully, whatever Lady Homura wants is something I can easily give.*

***

Hayate approached the mouth of the cave with slow, steady steps, his eyes tracking along the ground. The crisp layer of snow should have been white, but instead it was stained with sluggish rivers of red and black. Droplets fell from the point of his katana, hissing as they hit the top layer of frost and leaving a dark, dotted trail alongside his footprints.

From a short distance away, a patient set of eyes followed his progress. Kaze had slipped away as soon as the fight had begun, but he hadn't wandered far. Hayate could feel the wolf watching, as well as his friend's disapproval. It weighed heavily on his shoulders. Kaze was his beloved companion, but Setsuna held his fate—the fate of the whole kingdom. His loyalty to her had to come first.

He arrived at the black mouth of the cave but didn't enter immediately. Instead, he looked back over his shoulder at the battlefield he had crossed. The few Yukimura samurai who hadn't been hurt tended the injured, but the "lucky" survivors didn't look well off. Some were missing limbs, and others sat in fresh pools of blood and snow—and those were the ones who weren't dead. One of the banners had been broken in the fight, and the painted piece of cloth lay crumpled atop the snow. Three pinecones in a white circle on a green field, one of the most ancient mons in Akatsuki Teikoku, the Empire of the Dawn, had been stained red. Not a good omen.

Hayate squared his shoulders. Any pity he felt was worthless. A distraction. Their deaths were regrettable but necessary. There was nothing he could do. With a slow blink to regain his focus, he turned his attention to the other corpse on the ground. The bear's massive form lay heavy and crumpled against the cold grey stone. Life had already left its body, but its great head and the giant cudgels of its paws were a reminder of the power it possessed. The open wounds slashing across the creature's belly and sides still smoked, and thick, oily trails of black blood leaked onto the cave floor.

He made to move past it, wincing as the gashes along his arm stung in response. The fangs of the bear-clan had ripped through his sleeve, and he could feel the bite of cold air on his wounds. Not too high a price to pay for the final blow that had spared many of his warriors. He would need some heavy bandages once he arrived back at the city, but more importantly, he would need to cleanse the wound.

"Another failure." The low voice made Hayate's head jerk up. Setsuna stood at his shoulder, staring down at the bear with similar intensity. The dim light filtering in through the mouth of the cave made the angles of her gaunt face look sharper than usual. Her kimono was a dark shade of blue and her hair was done up in an older, more traditional fan. Pinned to one side was a kanzashi, flower-shaped, and its light blue petals protected a milky-white pearl at its center. It gleamed, drawing Hayate's eyes as she spoke again. "This one was too weak."

Hayate pursed his lips. "The men or the yokai?"

"Both, perhaps." Setsuna knelt to study the butchered bear more closely. "The process corrupted this one. Maybe your warriors weren't strong enough, or maybe the yokai was unwilling."

The words made Hayate falter. He understood the importance of sacrifice, but that hadn't made watching such destruction any easier. He sighed, exhaling a stream of breath from his mouth. "There has to be a better way to do this. Not a single yokai has survived the trial so far, and we lose more men each time we try."

"Then we haven't been using the right methods." Setsuna turned toward the mouth of the cave, and Hayate thought he saw something like sadness on her face. The expression strengthened his own resolve. If Setsuna saw something worthy in this despite the sacrifices, surely she had to be right.

As if she could read his mind, she stood and put a hand on his shoulder. "I know watching these failures is difficult, Hayate, but this goal is too important to give up on. The yokai have always served humans they deem worthy. If our entire society could benefit from their powers, just think of the possibilities. As the shogun of the northern provinces, it is my duty to harness that power for our betterment."

Still, Hayate couldn't forget the body lying on the ground or those of his men outside. "I understand, but what if it isn't possible? Only legends exist of humans bringing yokai under their control. What we're trying to accomplish is important, but with just stories to go on—"

Setsuna pressed her lips together in agitation. She was not an emotive person, and the rare display of impatience gave Hayate pause. "I know these past few weeks of failure have been difficult, but that doesn't mean our goal is impossible. Perhaps it is time to seek out my prodigal niece again and put her back on the right path. She may be the key to our success."

Once again, Hayate's doubts crept in. His failure to capture Kaede during her escape from Yukimura weeks ago, weighed on him, but he was nervous for other reasons as well. "You don't know for certain that Kaede can do this." He pointed at the spirit's corpse. "And even if she can, do you really want to see her like that? She was precious to you once." *Perhaps even more precious than me.*

"Spirits are drawn to her like no one else I have ever seen. I know she has some power over them. But then she grew short sighted. The first failure left her shaken. After the second, she ran. She was immature, incapable of understanding the importance of what we're doing."

From Setsuna's tone, Hayate could tell it was a warning. For what felt like the thousandth time, he forced down his doubts. "Of course, if you think Kaede is vital to our success, perhaps I should retrieve her."

He received a pleased nod, yet Setsuna's gaze remained focused on something far away. "I was just about to suggest that. You're right in that we can't afford to sacrifice any more people or waste any more time."

Hayate turned away to conceal his frown, removing the cloth tucked in his obi to wipe away the blood dripping from his katana. The slight movement aggravated the open wound along his arm, and he flinched, fighting away the stinging memory of the bear spirit's teeth.

A strong hand clasped his other shoulder, urging him to stop. "Come. Let me cleanse your wound before it gets infected." Hayate tensed, preparing to argue, but Setsuna continued. "I will not allow my son to be put in danger because of careless, unnecessary bravery." Her face wasn't gaunt anymore, but tender. "You will leave in the morning, after a good night's rest."

He bowed his head, obeying her as he always did. "As you wish, Okaa-sama."

Chapter Three

TAP. SCRRRRAPE.
"IMARI!"
TAP. Scrrrrape.
Imari yawned, reaching up to rub her blurry eyes before she realized she was using the wrong arm. With a sigh, she lowered it and switched. Sometimes she still forgot, even three years later. Her dreams had been of dragons and fire, but they filled her heart with hope. If she was lucky, Iori Kaede's arrival in Mirai might lead to several interesting possibilities, and perhaps even a solution.
Tap. Scrrrrape.
"Imari, wake up!"
Although alone, Imari recognized the noise and the voice calling out to her. She left her futon, tightening the sash of her soft sleeping yukata. It was a little looser than she would have liked, but tying it properly with only one hand would take more effort than she cared to put in. "Coming," she called. The balcony door was open, and although the sun hadn't risen, she could make out a figure in the garden below.
Unfortunately, it didn't seem as though her early-morning guest had seen or heard her. A pebble flew by her head, and she barely managed to duck out of the way in time. "Kenta, stop throwing pebbles. The door's already open."
Kenta cleared his throat in embarrassment. "Oops. Probably should have checked first, huh?"
"Probably." Imari scanned the gardens below. From the looks of it, Kenta appeared to be alone. "Takeshi isn't with you, is he?"
"Nope. He's back at the house to keep an eye on things."
Imari sighed. By "things," Kenta surely meant Kaede. She had known Takeshi wouldn't approve of Kaede's presence in his home, but she also knew he was far too polite to object. At worst, his behavior would be slightly stiff and formal. "That's no surprise. He hates the thought of anything that could put me in danger."
"That's exactly what he said this morning." Kenta pushed a hand

through his hair to make it stand up more like Takeshi's. "'I don't see why Imari is paying attention to this ronin.'" He jutted out his jaw in pretend annoyance as he imitated his brother. "'What do we know about her, anyway? She could've been thrown out of her clan for failing her last master, or worse. And that wolf spirit. Its jaws are bigger than Imari's head!'"

It was a fairly good impression, and Imari laughed. "I'll talk to him."

Kenta gave an apologetic shrug. "Better you than me. For an adviser, he isn't always the best listener, especially when it's his younger brother talking."

"He doesn't always listen to me either, you know," Imari pointed out with a snort of sympathy. "I'm lucky he agreed to stay behind and calm the crowd yesterday afternoon instead of following Iori-san everywhere, trying to look intimidating."

Kenta shrugged. "If you need a break from the whole 'protective older brother' thing, you can always train with me. You know I've got the time."

"I did train with you," Imari reminded him. "The day before yesterday, as a matter of fact."

"I know, it's just...you're always so busy lately." His smile faltered, and Imari caught a glimpse of sadness in his brown eyes. "I miss how it used to be, you know? Just the three of us, before the engagement ended and you started acting like a proper heir, spending all your time in the library."

Imari bent further over the railing so Kenta could see more of her face. As much as she enjoyed the library, she did feel a pang of wistfulness for the days before her injury, when she hadn't been quite so devoted to her studies. "I miss it too, Kenta, but at least things are getting a bit more exciting around here, huh? Between Iori-san and Rin, I have a feeling the next few days are going to be entertaining."

Kenta seemed to brighten at the reminder. "Yeah. Do you think wolf yokai play fetch? Or do you think Rin-sama lets Iori-san ride her? She's definitely big enough."

"You'll have to ask them," Imari laughed. Although she had long since accepted the responsibilities that came with being the heir apparent to Mirai and was eager to take on more of her father's duties, she knew Kenta felt differently. He was much more of a free spirit, and preferred playing his shamisen or tending his garden to most other activities.

"And you'll get the chance, too. I'm taking you off guard duty for the next few days. Your new job is to keep Iori-san company and get her accustomed to Mirai."

"Friendly tour guide!" he said with a grin. "Got it. You can count on me. But what about you? You could use a break, too. Being in the library so often, sometimes I wonder if you ever sleep."

"Books are good for you," Imari said. "You should try reading one sometime."

"I read my share of Bushido wisdom, but you don't see me buried under a mountain of manuscripts taller than me. Now, get dressed and come on down here." Kenta waved toward the gate. "The sun's coming up."

Imari followed the gesture, looking over the garden trellis toward the sky. A soft pink line stretched across the horizon, although the sun's rays hadn't quite peeked over the mountaintops. It was still early, and she didn't think it would be polite to wake her guest at such an hour.

"Tell you what, Kenta. Go back to the house while I get ready and make sure Kaede gets a nice breakfast. Then, ask Takeshi to escort her here. Tell her to bring her daishō. She's going to need them."

***

"I don't like this, Kaede," Rin growled. The wolf-spirit paced the length of the wall, whipping around before she reached each corner of the room. Kenta had provided them with a comfortable place to sleep, along with several hearty meals and plenty of blankets and bedding, but Rin hated being kept indoors. Kaede knew her companion had only agreed to remain confined to the room because the city smells made her even more uncomfortable.

Sitting cross-legged on the tatami floor, Kaede leaned back on her arms. "I know, but I already told you, I'm not leaving. This is my chance to start over somewhere new. Besides, you were the one who told me to accept Lady Homura's invitation and get a decent night's sleep."

Rin whirled again at the mention of Lady Homura, nearly upsetting the decorative centerpiece on the table with her tail. It was filled with lilies, the same white blossoms that graced Mirai's mon. "You don't know this city's humans well enough to trust to them. They could try to hurt you, like that stupid one yesterday. Or if they find out you are not who you appear to be."

Kaede let out a loud puff of air. Rin's protective instincts had saved her life more than once, but they were off the mark this time. "No one's going to hurt me, and I'm not staying in Mirai forever. If I need to, I can move on. Lady Homura's been nothing but kind to us."

But niggling doubts remained, doubts Rin immediately picked up on. "Exactly. A little too kind, in my opinion." Rin stopped pacing and padded across the room, ears tipped low over her head. "Don't you find it odd that a daimyo's daughter would be so eager to take in two strays? A samurai without a mon and a wolf yokai? She looked at me with fascination, the same look I've seen all too often on Setsuna's face."

Kaede looked away, trying to hide the hurt in her eyes. Deep down, she suspected her friend was onto something. Imari was obviously interested in them, but comparing her to Setsuna was harsh, not to mention paranoid. "That's not fair, Rin. We don't even know what she wants yet. Some people are interested in the yokai because they respect them. Like me."

"You're different," Rin said, but having stated her piece, she didn't seem to want to argue any further. "Just remember not to trust this Lady Homura blindly simply because she has a pleasing face. You've already put your faith in the wrong person once before."

Thanks for the reminder, Kaede thought glumly. It was still difficult for her to admit her aunt had taken such a dark path. They had been close since her childhood and had become even closer when she'd chosen to live her life as the woman she was instead of the boy her parents had thought her to be. The fact that they were both attuned to the yokai had only enhanced their bond, and she had looked to Setsuna as a mentor as well as a parental figure, especially since she had never been close with her own father and mother.

All of that is gone. She was the most important person in my life, and now I don't have anyone but Rin. My parents don't even know I've left Yukimura. They have no idea what Setsuna is doing.

"I'll keep my guard up," she mumbled, not wanting to dwell on the subject. "At least now that I'm here, Setsuna can't use me to find the yokai anymore. She'll have a harder time tracking them down and capturing them for her experiments without my help." She reached up to touch her face just beneath her left eye. The scars there were still tender, although some of it might have been her imagination. A few centimeters higher, and the owl spirit's attack might have left her blinded.

Rin padded closer and lowered herself to the floor, placing her chin in Kaede's lap. "It wasn't your fault."

Kaede closed her eyes, resting her cheek on top of Rin's head. "I know. But I can't help feeling like it was."

They remained that way for several moments, holding still until the sun's rays crept in through the window.

"I guess it's time," Kaede said, reaching out for the bag slouched against the wall. She had packed as light as possible for her journey, and that included only three outfits, one of which she hadn't worn since leaving Kousetsu weeks ago. Her fingers traced the delicate stitching on the best dark blue silk, a silhouette of an icy mountain in a light blue circle. Sighing and shaking her head, Kaede folded the kimono and put it at the bottom of her bag. After examining the other two, she chose a faded blue kimono with the least amount of wear before fastening her obi at her waist. Finally, she put on her hakama and secured her daishō in their proper places.

A knock on the door interrupted her, and she turned to Rin. The wolf spirit seemed alert but not afraid as she sniffed the air. Whoever was waiting for them outside wasn't a threat.

"Yes?"

"It's Hibana Takeshi. May I enter?"

"Of course. Hold on a moment."

Kaede pulled the screen aside, allowing the dark-haired samurai she had met yesterday to enter the room. He was dressed in full formal kamishimo, a maroon kimono and a wide-shouldered gray kataginu jacket with white threading over it. He bowed, but not before she caught a glimpse of mistrust in his eyes. "Good morning, Iori Kaede. I've come to escort you to the castle. Lady Homura wishes to see you."

His manner, cold and businesslike, reminded Kaede of the way Imari had spoken of him the day before. From her description, combined with some information she had gleaned from Kenta the evening before, she suspected it wasn't personal.

"Nice to meet you under better circumstances, Hibana-danna," she said, giving a bow. "Thank you for letting me stay in your household. I know Lady Homura made the decision, but I appreciate your hospitality." As she suspected, he didn't respond, although the furrow in his brow smoothed out a little at her politeness. "So, where am I supposed to go, exactly?"

From the look on Takeshi's face, he clearly didn't approve of his mistress's decision to summon her. "I'll show you the way."

Rin began to rise as well, but Kaede held up a hand. "I'll be fine on my own. Stay here and guard our things, okay? I know you don't like it out in the city, and we don't want to cause a commotion."

The white wolf's eyes narrowed in clear disapproval, but she curled up on the floor, resting her head on her front paws in a sulking pose. Kaede reached down to scratch her ears in apology, then turned to follow Takeshi out of the room.

To Kaede's surprise, her escort started the conversation as they travelled out of the house and through the large archway. Based on the chill of his initial greeting, she hadn't expected him to be the talkative type. "That duel yesterday was something. A little unconventional, maybe, but impressive."

"Thank you. That's a high compliment from a skilled samurai like you."

Takeshi seemed surprised. He turned to look at her, and his face softened ever so slightly. "What makes you say that? You don't know anything about me."

"I know if you're in the daimyo's service as his karo at such a young age, you must be steady-handed and skilled with a blade." She gave Takeshi a sidelong look. "Besides, I saw you and Homura-dono arrive together right before my duel. Both of you were in training gear, by the looks of it. I doubt Lord Homura would let you spar with his daughter unless you were good."

"You're observant. Good. If you're staying here, you'll need to be."

It wasn't an unfriendly statement, but it made Kaede slightly uncomfortable. Being on the run for the past month had taught her caution, especially about revealing her future plans. "What makes you think I'm staying?"

They stepped out into the samurai district, and from the road, Kaede could see the roof of the castle once more, gold trim glittering in the early morning light. Takeshi turned toward her at last. "You've caught Homura-dono's interest. You're no prisoner here, but I suspect she will want you to stay a while."

Kaede waited, but he didn't offer any further explanation. At last, she gathered the courage to ask, "Do you have any idea what she wants with me?"

A shadow crossed Takeshi's face, one that revealed he did know something and wasn't happy about it. "That is for you to discuss with her. I will remind you that any requests she makes of you are strictly voluntary. You aren't obligated to offer her your help just because she was kind to you on your first day in the city. Don't take this the wrong way, but she would've stepped in for a peasant. You don't owe her anything."

Well, I don't know whether that makes me feel better or worse, she thought with a shiver. It was nice that Imari made a habit of standing up for the innocent, but Kaede suspected the daimyo's daughter wanted her for something—wanted her help, even—and that didn't bode well. She thought back to what Rin had said just a few minutes before. *The last time someone was interested in my connection with the yokai, it all went wrong. I can't let something like that happen again because of me.*

Soon after, they arrived at the castle itself. It was even more beautiful up close, and Kaede craned her neck in awe as they passed through the stone archway, trying to take in everything at once. As the daughter of a daimyo herself, she had grown up in relatively luxurious surroundings, but Lord Homura's castle was something else. The red peaks of the roof were trimmed with gold, and the high white walls were lavishly decorated. The courtyard was even more impressive. Plum trees stretched their blossoming arms out over the soft green grass, filling the air with the same sweet scent as the day before, and a small stream trickled over piles of shining rocks.

A little bridge crossed the water, and just beyond stood Imari, waiting for her with a smile. Her dark hair was pulled back in a braid, and she wore a pair of twin blades sheathed at her waist. When Takeshi nodded for her to approach, Kaede took a deep breath and prepared to cross the bridge. Hopefully, whatever Imari wanted wouldn't get her into yet another mess.

Chapter Four

IMARI WAITED PATIENTLY BENEATH the shade of the ume trees as Kaede crossed the bridge, trying to get a handle on her racing heart. She wanted to step forward and meet her guest halfway, but she restrained herself, adopting a relaxed pose. She needed to calm down if she wanted to get anywhere.

Kaede was clad in a blue kimono, but she carried herself proudly, with the bearing of a noble warrior. Once more, Imari found herself wondering where Kaede had come from. She seemed to be of humble origins, but something about the way she moved and talked was familiar. Kaede had probably spent a fair amount of time among nobility, if she wasn't a disgraced noble herself.

Finally, Kaede came to a stop, dipping in a brief but formal bow. "Good morning, Homura-dono." She rose again, and Imari found herself trapped in the samurai's dark eyes. "How may I be of service?"

Imari shook herself, embarrassed she had stared at Kaede's face so intently. She bowed in return, smiling to offset the moment of awkwardness. "Good morning, Iori-san. I hope your stay at the Hibana household last night was pleasant?"

"Yes, for me." Kaede looked back over her shoulder at Takeshi, who was observing them from the other side of the garden. Imari sighed with fond exasperation, motioning for him to leave. After a moment of hesitation, he bowed and disappeared.

"Don't worry about him. He's a good man and a good friend. He just takes a little while to warm up to people. I hope his brother was friendly, at least?"

"Very friendly, but Hibana Takeshi wasn't rude. I understand why he might be suspicious of me. A samurai without a master is unusual, even in a city like Mirai."

"Yes, and you can't exactly walk into a strange city with a giant white wolf and expect everyone to trust you, either, but it was quite the impressive entrance." Imari gave Kaede another long look. "You certainly caught my attention."

Kaede grinned, her face brightening. "Oh? Well then, I must have been doing something right."

"Not that I recommend fighting someone during your first five minutes in every city you visit, but I must admit, your skill with a katana is impressive. I don't suppose you'd be willing to give me a demonstration? One that doesn't end with a bloody nose, I hope."

Kaede's eyes widened, but she recovered quickly. "I'm sure you'll try to restrain yourself, my lady, but are you sure the daimyo would approve?" An uncertain crease formed in her brow, and Imari felt a shiver of disappointment at her doubtful expression.

"Don't worry about my father. I've been training as a samurai since I was a child, at his insistence. True safety involves knowing when and how to fight."

"But what about..." Kaede's eyes darted toward Imari's missing hand, but then she seemed to think better of it. "My apologies, Homura-dono. I'm not going to finish such a rude question. You wouldn't be carrying swords if you couldn't use them."

Imari smiled in what looked to Kaede like relief. "It's nice to have someone come to that conclusion on their own instead of having me spell it out for them. Thank you for that."

"Of course, I know what it's like to have people make assumptions about you based on your appearance."

It was a cryptic statement, but one Imari sensed Kaede didn't wish to talk about any further. The warrior's expression was polite, but somewhat guarded once more, and Imari's instincts told her not to press. "Then the two of us have something in common. So, do you want to do some forms with me?"

Kaede still didn't look entirely convinced, but she dipped her head. "If that's your wish, I would be more than happy to run some partnered forms with you. I assume you're familiar with Aizu teachings?"

Imari nodded. "Northern style? Good choice. Let's stick to the katana for now. Single sword technique, some traditional kata?" On impulse, she threw in a little dig, just to see if Kaede would react. "I'm sure you can keep up."

Kaede's shoulders straightened, and a look of determination fixed on her face. She gave another short bow and took a few steps back, withdrawing a white cord from her kimono and using it to tie the sleeves out of the way. Despite the samurai's earlier hesitation, Imari could tell that Kaede was prepared to take this seriously.

As they approached each other, Imari straightened to her full height, making her bow at the same time as her opponent. They faced each other, unsheathing their swords, the steel glinting. Imari narrowed her eyes, focusing intently on Kaede's movements. She had a feeling the samurai would choose a slow pace, but she had other plans. If Kaede wasn't sweating by the time they were finished, she hadn't done her job.

The kata began a breath later. As one, they drew their blades in an arc above their heads, lowering them until the points nearly touched. Kaede moved like water, fluid and graceful, and only years of training prevented Imari from being distracted. Her shoulders loosened, and she let all the tension melt from her body. Kaede might be the current of the ocean, but she was the fire of the sun.

They moved slowly at first, trading smooth slices back and forth. As soon as one blade came down, the other rose. One step forward matched another step back. Sometimes they moved in contrast, parrying each other's pantomimed blows. Other times they were in sync, mimicking each other. As they grew used to each other's reach, the tempo sped up, becoming less like a drill and more like a dance. They twirled toward and away from each other, blades whispering a breath apart but never actually striking.

A smile spread across Imari's face. She had found a worthy sword-partner and was eager to test the limits of their new relationship. The sweeps of their blades came closer and closer to flesh as their bodies rolled through the familiar motions, and Imari felt a jolt in her chest. She couldn't remember the last time she had enjoyed practicing her kata so much. Not since she and Takeshi had been engaged, at least. *No, not even then. Takeshi always held back. Kaede wants to push me.*

Kaede sped up, and Imari shifted seamlessly to match the new rhythm. Her body began relying on instinct instead of deliberate movements, and she relaxed into a state beyond thought. Even when relying on pure muscle memory, Kaede's strikes always matched hers. During the last stance, Kaede swiped down so quickly Imari was certain she heard the air split beneath her blade. But she brought her own sword up, slipping it away with only a sliver of space between them.

At last, it was over. They lowered their katanas and stared at each other, both too awestruck to remember their bows. Imari couldn't even recall how to breathe as she watched a thin line of sweat run down from the corner of Kaede's forehead and past her ear. The back of her neck tingled, and her face burned with heat.

She snapped out of the stare and dipped forward, finally prompting

Kaede to do the same. Despite her embarrassment, she couldn't help stealing another glance as Kaede sheathed her katana. The muscles in her arms were almost as entrancing as the way she moved her blade. Imari had hardly noticed when Kaede had used her tasuki to keep the sleeves of her kimono up, but now she could not look away. The white cord lifted her sleeves more than high enough to offer a tantalizing view of her biceps.

"Not bad, Homura-dono."

Imari blinked, returning her gaze to Kaede's face. Judging by her expression, she could tell that the samurai was teasing. "If this is your way of trying to get me back for my comment earlier, you'll have to try harder."

She slid her own blade back into its saya and matched Kaede's crooked grin with a smirk. "If that was a sincere attempt at complimenting me, I'm afraid there's no hope for you at all."

Kaede laughed, and Imari's chest fluttered. "My parents always told me I was hopeless, at least when it came to social interaction. If it wasn't for them smoothing over most of my mistakes, I would have died in a duel long ago."

Shock ran through Imari at the mention of Kaede's parents, but she didn't let on. Apparently, a blade was the best way to earn Kaede's respect and trust. Instead of putting the casual conversation at risk by asking questions, she snorted. "You mean like you almost did at the southern gates when you first arrived?"

Kaede gave a dismissive roll of her eyes as she pulled on the knot of the cord holding her sleeves up. "Someone as skilled with a katana as you should've known I would outmatch that other samurai as soon as we drew our blades. Admit it, my lady. You called the result of our fight from the sidelines before it even started, didn't you?"

"I won't admit to anything." Imari headed toward the edge of the garden, feeling strangely happy when Kaede followed close by her side, remaining a respectful pace or two behind. "And by the way, thank you for not holding back. Between being the daimyo's daughter and this—" She held up the stump of her left hand. "it's hard for me to find good partners to train with. Most people are reluctant to give me their all, even though I can take it."

"That must be upsetting."

"More like annoying." Imari sat down on a curved stone bench beneath the shade of the trees, motioning for Kaede to join her. Kaede appeared surprised and reluctant at first, but eventually sat beside her.

"Honestly, people's assumptions about what I can and can't do have caused me more problems than losing the hand itself."

Kaede nodded. "What other people think of us is usually the problem, isn't it?" She paused, as if considering something deeply, and then continued. "Please forgive me if I'm wrong, my lady, but I don't think you invited me here to tell me about your hand, or because you wanted to run forms. You've been kind to me, but ever since I came into the city yesterday, you've looked at me like a woman who wants something. Am I wrong?"

A heated flush spread across Imari's face. It wouldn't do to keep Kaede in the dark any longer, and she didn't want to come across as manipulative.

"I want my hand back. I know I'm capable without it, but not everyone agrees. Some people don't think a broken girl can rule a province this large and prosperous, or do anything at all. I've spent the past several years trying to prove them wrong, but some of the older samurai and the daimyo of the neighboring provinces are stuck in their ways. If they think I'm weak, I won't be able to continue what my father started."

"And what does your father think?" Kaede asked. "He isn't disappointed in you because you're missing a hand, is he?"

Imari relaxed against the back of the bench. "Not at all. He's always been supportive of me." She turned away, gazing up at the patches of blue sky peeking through the ume branches. "Everyone who matters understands, but when you're next in line to be daimyo, you have to care what everyone thinks, even the idiots."

"I see. So, what do you want from me?"

Imari turned back at the offer, looking at Kaede in surprise. The samurai's face was closed off once more, and her cheerful grin had vanished. She looked guarded, perhaps even mistrustful.

"I must have said something wrong," Imari said, trying to salvage the moment. "I apologize if it felt like I was pressuring you, Iori-san. I do have a request to make of you, but it isn't a demand. It's simply an offer, and I won't think any less of you if you say no, although I will be disappointed. You're still welcome to all the hospitality I can offer while you choose to stay here." She knew she had read the situation correctly when Kaede relaxed. Her smile didn't return, but some of the worry lines in her forehead disappeared.

"Thank you, Homura-dono. That's kind. Please, tell me what you need."

"Have you heard the legend of Kurogane?"

Kaede shook her head.

"They say he was a mortal once, somewhere in the westlands, but his life changed when he happened upon the dragon yokai. He stole the source of their power, or it was given to him, and he used it to forge all kinds of magical objects. Some people think he's dead, or that he isn't real at all, but I've done my research, and I'm sure there's some truth to the tale. He made the enchanted black spears that Empress Tomoyo's imperial guards carry, and he's credited with forging the magical iron soldiers that guard Tsun'i's borders with Xiangsai in the south."

"That does sound familiar," Kaede said with a nod. "So, you want this mystical blacksmith to make some kind of new hand for you? If he's real?"

"I know he's real. I've spent the past three years in my father's library, using every spare minute I could to search for information. When I ran out of scrolls and maps, I bought more." She sighed, remembering Kenta's earlier complaint. "I've gotten quite the reputation as a bookworm."

"And did it pay off? Did you figure out where this mysterious, magic-hand-making blacksmith lives?"

Imari shrugged. "That depends. I have a strong suspicion that he lives near Mount Aka. The Tsun'i name for it is Hongshan, and even though the River Go runs right by it, no humans have settled there in over a century. Pretty suspicious, if you ask me, and that's not even considering the reports of dragons flying overhead."

Kaede's eyebrows arched. "And you found all this out by spending some time in the library?"

"It's a nice library," Imari said, smiling wistfully. The smell of wood and silk-bound books was almost as nice as the flowering trees of the garden. "The continent might be big, but there are only so many mystical, isolated dragon mountains to choose from."

"So, you want to go all the way around the Jade Sea and through the Kingdom of Tsun'i in search of a magical legendary blacksmith who stole power from dragon yokai?" Kaede's tone wasn't skeptical, but it was definitely surprised and, Imari hoped, intrigued. "And you think I can help you?"

"Yes. I've seen the way you interact with Rin. You have a connection to the spirits, and that's exactly what I need. What am I supposed to do if I meet a dragon yokai? Wave my katana at it?"

"Personally, I'd suggest running, my lady," Kaede said with a smirk.

"It's what I'd do."

"Somehow, I doubt that." She studied Kaede's face, peering deeply into the samurai's eyes even though she knew the over-attentiveness might be mistaken for rudeness. "Most people would run from a wolf yokai, too, but you befriended one. Most people would have called me crazy for even suggesting this coming from a stranger, but you haven't. When I mentioned dragon yokai, your first reaction was to make a joke about them. If anyone could guide me up a dragon mountain safely, it's you. You're the best prospect I've found in all the years I've been tossing this around in my head."

"If I'm your best prospect, you must have slim pickings," Kaede muttered. She seemed to be considering something deeply, and at first, Imari was certain she would say no. But at last, Kaede nodded. "I'm in, my lady. Your quest sounds interesting, and..." She hesitated, as if she wasn't certain how much she wanted to share. Imari could see the uncertainty in her eyes before it solidified into a decision. "To be honest, there are some dangerous people who don't like me here. Mount Hongshan is far away and far away sounds like a good idea right now. You'd be doing me a favor, assuming I don't get eaten by a dragon."

Imari's heart leapt with hope, but she managed to restrain herself to a smile. "Then it's a deal. You help me find Kurogane, and I'll make sure whoever doesn't like you can't find you." *Although who wouldn't like you, I have no idea.*

Chapter Five

"ARE YOU SURE YOU want to do this, Hayate?"

Hayate didn't look at the large black wolf crouched beside him. He kept his attention trained forward on the cheerfully glowing fire of the caravan ahead. It had stopped in the middle of a grassy clearing, and several people milled about, preparing dinner and setting up camp for the night. Men, women, and children sat clustered together, talking and laughing as the sun set.

"No harm needs to come to them," Hayate whispered back, refusing to meet Kaze's gaze. He could feel the guilty scorch of his friend's disapproval. "If they tell me what I need to know."

"And what if they can't help you? They're simple travelers. They might not have seen Kaede at all."

Hayate frowned. It was possible these people hadn't seen Kaede, but it was also possible they had—and he needed leads if he was going to find her. His cousin had run with hardly any supplies. She must have stopped to barter for food and shelter somewhere along the way. Even she couldn't have survived out on the plains for a month just by foraging.

"Let's hope they have." Hayate rose from his hiding place, bringing his hand to the hilt of his katana.

Kaze remained behind in the shadows, but Hayate didn't bother trying to convince him. He knew his friend was conflicted, but they had no choice. Setsuna's experiments had to continue for the benefit of the Empire and she needed Kaede. He steeled himself, straightening his shoulders. *I can't let her down.*

The moment Hayate stepped into the small camp, all heads turned. Some smiled and waved, mouths opening to call friendly greetings, but as soon as they saw his hand hovering near his sword, an eerie silence swept over the crowd. Mothers pulled their children closer. Even the fire seemed to grow dimmer. Twenty people camped here in total, all different ages, but as Hayate scanned the caravan for any possible threats, he found none. The young, able-bodied adults in the group didn't seem to be armed, and most were looking at him with wide eyes.

"My apologies for interrupting your dinner," he said, a stiff formality rather than a reassurance. It only seemed to make the small crowd uneasy. "I won't intrude long, but I'm looking for someone. Have any of you seen a young woman, dark skin, red hair, a little over twenty? She dresses as a commoner but carries daishō, and she is accompanied by a great white wolf."

He knew he had stumbled upon a lead. Several of the frightened people shared glances. "So, you have seen her," he said, focusing on the nearest young man who sat by the fire. When the stranger didn't answer, Hayate reached down, gripping his kimono and hauling him upright. "Tell me where she went. Now."

"I—I haven't seen her," the man stammered. His lips trembled, and his eyes darted everywhere, obvious signs of a lie. "No one like that has come across our camp."

"No one?" Hayate drew his sword with a soft hiss, aiming the sharpened point at the man's neck. "Are you sure?"

Someone else shouted from further back. "She was headed to Mirai!"

Hayate glanced over the man's shoulder. It was a young woman, huddled by the fire with a worn shawl around her shoulders and a child in her lap. Hayate lowered his sword, although he didn't place it back at his hip. Instead, he stared at the woman. "And how do you know this?"

"She asked for directions," the woman said. "She was headed southwest toward the city when she left. It's where most wanderers end up. Please."

Hayate released the man's shirt, pushing him back toward the fire. "There." He put away his sword, and the whole camp breathed a sigh of relief. "That wasn't so hard, was it? Thank you for your assistance." He disappeared back into the darkness, not stealing a single backward glance.

Once he was a fair distance away, the rice stalks around him began to rustle and sway. Hayate stopped, waiting patiently until Kaze appeared from the shadows. "We need to work on your people skills. Was that really necessary? There were children in that camp."

"I didn't harm any of them," Hayate said, continuing onward into the darkness. He could see the road in the distance, and he headed toward it, following its curve.

"It doesn't matter. Threatening innocent people is against the way of the warrior. I thought you were more honorable than that."

Hayate clenched his teeth, jaw hardening. "I can regain my honor by bringing back what was lost. Setsuna is counting on me to find Kaede. It's the right thing to do."

"And that excuses your methods?" Kaze's muzzle nudged his shoulder, and Hayate turned to look at him at last, struggling not to react to the disappointment he saw in his companion's eyes. "I stay with you because you're my friend, Hayate, and it's as a friend that I say this—you are losing your way."

Though Hayate managed to keep his face smooth, he felt a nagging sense of uncertainty in his chest. It came upon him whenever Kaze spoke, and it was growing increasingly difficult to ignore. "I'll try not to frighten or disturb any of the people in Mirai," he promised, trying to ease his own guilt as well as Kaze's fears. "If Kaede comes quietly, there's no reason anyone else needs to get hurt."

***

"I told her I'd help her find the magical blacksmith so he can make her a new hand." Kaede looked up from the washbasin in her room as she finished her story, unsurprised to see doubt on Rin's face. Her blue eyes narrowed, and her tail stood high, bristling behind her like a spiky branch.

"I know you admire our host, Kaede, but signing up for a quest? You barely know this woman. You've only been in Mirai for a few days, and this kind of decision—"

"It's a smart decision," Kaede interrupted. In truth, she was half-certain she was crazy for saying yes, but since she had already given Imari her answer, she didn't want Rin to bring her own doubts back to the surface. "Homura-dono intends to travel all the way to Tsun'i, across the Jade Sea. That's about as far from home and Setsuna as I can get. We'll be safe there."

She finished swiping the damp cloth over her arms before moving down to her stomach, cleaning away the light coat of sweat that had formed during her kata. She didn't feel comfortable enough in Mirai yet to visit the communal bathhouse. At home, she had been allowed to bathe with the other women after choosing to live as one herself, but in a strange city, she feared the sight of her naked body might draw unwanted and unfriendly attention. For now, she would have to make do in private.

"And what of your family?" Rin lowered her haunches to the

ground and sat, but from the stiffness of her spine, she wasn't pleased. "What about their safety? They're your pack, Kaede. You can't simply abandon them."

Kaede frowned. Rin knew exactly how to tap into her guilt. She turned away again, refusing to meet Rin's eyes as she dipped the cloth back into the basin. "They'll be safer without me. Besides, you left your family."

"To make sure you stayed safe, not so that you could get wrapped up in some foolish nonsense over a pretty girl."

"She's not pretty," Kaede insisted, bending over to scrub angrily at her legs. It was only a few strokes in that she realized what she had said. "I mean, of course she's pretty. She's gorgeous, a vision of loveliness," she said, with just a hint of over-exaggeration to show she was joking. "But that's not why I'm going. I'm doing it for my own reasons."

"Of course, you are." Rin huffed loudly through her nose.

Instead of arguing further, she continued her crude bath, finally moving between her legs. A few years ago, she might have hesitated, but this time, she simply went about the regular business of cleaning herself. Her mind drifted back through time, recalling the moonlit night when Haruna had urged her to bathe in the forest pool. She had been so young then, barely twelve, disgusted with the changes her body was going through. She had pleaded with the yokai for help, and to her immense gratitude, they answered. The yokai's magic had given her some of what she wanted—smoother, hairless skin on her face and a slightly higher voice, a hint of hips and small but visible breasts—but it hadn't been able to change everything.

She had been disappointed at first, but over the years, she had learned to deal with it. This was her body, and while it wasn't everything she had hoped for back then, she had become accustomed to it. Fond of it, even. At least now, living in it felt like home.

"You're free to go back home if you want," she said, finishing her wash and setting the cloth aside, "but I don't want to be responsible for anyone else getting hurt." She hung her head, closing her eyes and drawing in a deep breath as the cool air dried the water droplets on her skin. "Setsuna isn't going to use me again. I won't let her."

Rather than chide her, Rin padded over to the table and nuzzled gently at her shoulder. "I know she hurt you, Kaede, but what happened wasn't your fault. Those deaths are hers to carry, not yours."

Kaede opened her eyes, placing an affectionate hand on top of Rin's head, but she turned toward the mirror hanging on the nearby wall. Her eyes darted to the scars along her cheek, and she winced with a pain that was more emotional than physical. The wounds of guilt ran deeper than the scars.

"It's not that I don't want to go back," she murmured. "I miss home. I just...I can't be Aozora Kaede right now. I can't be the daimyo's daughter who ran away, the shogun's niece who got a band of good samurai killed because I couldn't..."

Rin nudged her again and spoke slowly, softly. "Perhaps, a trip to Tsun'i might not be such a bad idea? As long as you don't intend to stay there forever."

Kaede sighed. She had no idea what she intended to do, but at least if she was helping Imari, her life would have some sense of purpose. *I guess you can only run away from something for so long before you start wanting to run toward something instead.* Imari's smiling face and dark eyes flashed to the front of her mind again, and she smiled.

"Don't worry, Rin. Everything's going to be okay. You'll be with me, right?"

Rin's nose pressed into the top of her arm, snuffling gently. "Of course, Kaede. Always. But what about this Imari? How much have you told her about your past?"

Kaede resisted the temptation to flinch. With all that had happened over the past few days, she hadn't had much chance to feel guilty, but in the safety of her room, a huge wave of it came crashing down over her. Imari had been nothing but kind to her since her arrival in Mirai—and not just that, but she had revealed something deeply personal to Kaede in the garden. It felt wrong to keep her true identity from her host, even if it was for self-preservation.

"Barely anything," Kaede said. "It's safer for her if she doesn't know."

"But you feel guilty nonetheless. Don't, Kaede. You've only known this woman a few days. You don't owe her your life's story."

"I could at least tell her my real name," Kaede mumbled, but she knew that wasn't true. Imari couldn't find out about her past. If she did reveal her family name and the reason she had fled, Kaede was certain she would be disinvited from Imari's quest, and even though she had her doubts about going, she needed to do something with her life. She couldn't simply run from town to town, waiting for Hayate to catch up with her.

This is the right thing, she told herself, even though she didn't really believe it. *For me and for her.*

***

Imari stood behind the byōbu at the library's entrance, keeping out of sight behind its edge. The painted screen was mostly blue, a moving landscape of ocean and sky, only a little faded from years of sunlight and handling. The color made it impossible to see his shadow, but judging by the stream of glowing golden lantern light shining from within the room, Imari could tell her father was still awake and hard at work—just as she had both hoped and feared he would be.

The library was usually her domain, the place where she felt most at home, but for once, she didn't feel comfortable entering. Her father had always been her champion, but she feared asking for his support on this would only lead to disappointment. She lowered her eyes to her sandals, but her stubborn feet refused to budge. She felt like a coward.

What are you so afraid of, Imari? That he'll say you're too weak to do this? That he'll resent you for abandoning your family duties? That he'll think you're crazy? She could be crazy. Surely Takeshi and everyone else would think so once they found out about her plan…at least, almost everyone. Kaede hadn't seemed to think she was insane for wanting to go chasing a magical blacksmith.

Imari straightened her shoulders. She had dreamed of this for years, and somewhere along the way, it had become more than regaining the hand she had lost. It was about proving herself—proving her own strength and resilience, proving that she would be a strong leader for Mirai, and proving her worth to all their neighbors.

They might look down on her now—*missing hand, too young, only four noble generations in her family*—but they wouldn't be able to once she got back. She would be a woman reborn: the leader with the dragon-forged hand, guiding Mirai into the future. She would be worthy of maintaining the legacy her great-grandfather, her grandfather, and her father had worked so hard to create for her. No one would dare to question her authority or her capability again.

That gave Imari the push she needed. She slid the screen aside until the painted blue ocean disappeared and all that remained was the twisted trunk of the bonsai tree on the end. Even though it was only a painting, it possessed the illusion of movement, almost as if it reached out toward the waves and tried to grasp them. *I won't be like that tree, stuck with my roots in the ground. I can go anywhere I want. I will go anywhere I want. I just hope father will understand.*

As she entered the library, Imari took comfort in the familiar surroundings. A little light filtered in through the open-square-frame of the window, but the beautiful rows of silk-bound books were still illuminated by the light of the evening lanterns. It even smelled the same, like paper and ink and dust mixed with the faint fragrance of the summer air drifting in from outside.

"Imari?"

She broke out of her haze. Her father, Seishirou, sat on a cushioned mat in the most comfortable corner of the room, one of the places she usually liked to occupy. Several scrolls were spread across the low bench beside him, and it looked as though he had been in the middle of sorting through them.

Correspondence, Imari thought. *Always correspondence.* As much as she wanted to follow in her father's footsteps, there were some things about the job she wasn't looking forward to.

"Good evening, Father," she murmured, inclining her head respectfully. She held the pose for a beat longer than usual, probably out of guilt. Even though her mind was made up, seeing his face added a touch of sadness to the excitement of leaving.

To her relief, Seishirou smiled when she rose. He seemed different sitting there in the dimmed light, less rigid and imposing than usual. There were only the two of them and Imari could see the softer, familiar side of her father he showed only to her. With her, he was always just Homura Seishirou, a father—rather than Lord Homura, the honorable daimyo, though the weight of responsibility never truly left his eyes.

"Come here," he said, gesturing to one of the spare cushions beside him. She approached the bench and sat, taking the paper he passed over to her. "Read this for me and tell me what you think."

Imari scanned the paper up and down, brow furrowing as she read. It was a trade agreement with the neighboring province of Furuyama, but judging by the details, it wasn't a fair offer. 'They want reduced payments again? And instead of coin, the only offer is of rice shipments in exchange for our steel? What kind of price agreement is this?"

"One that comes from a mind stuck in the old ways, when rice was everything," her father said. He took the paper back from her, placing it on the bench again. "To some of our neighbors, rice isn't merely food to fill hungry bellies. It's money and power."

"So is steel and iron," Imari insisted with wounded dignity. "We're the most industrialized province in the kingdom. Where will they get their metal if not from our factories? And their textiles? Old women can't spin enough wild silk with their bare hands to meet the needs of an entire nation."

"And this is why we must remind them," her father said with a look of approval. "Homura might be a new province, but it provides for many people's needs. Rice can't make clothes and houses and weapons, and that contribution deserves to be recognized, too."

"Two thirds of the previous price, and not a circle less," Imari said after a moment's thought. "Personally? I'd push for two and a half in addition to the rice to cover the rest before settling."

Her father nodded, a subtle gesture of agreement that made Imari's face glow with pride. "That was my thinking as well. But why are you here so late? Not to talk about rice or trading with our neighbors, I assume."

"Not to read either." Imari felt her father's searching look, and she couldn't stall any longer. "I've told you about my research, my studies of the old legends."

"About Kurogane, yes. Do you think you've found your mysterious blacksmith?"

"Yes, a while ago—but more importantly, I think I've found someone who can take me to him. A ronin arrived in the city the other day, a woman by the name of Iori Kaede."

Seishirou's brows arched with interest, but he didn't interrupt, nodding for her to continue.

"She dresses modestly, but I can tell from her movements and her manner of speech that she's spent time as part of a noble household," Imari said, falling back on her memories. They were surprisingly easy to conjure, especially when she thought of Kaede's face. "She's been trained as a samurai, and she also has a close connection with the yokai. A great white wolf spirit accompanies her wherever she goes."

"A wolf spirit?" he asked, clearly intrigued. "That is unusual."

"Unusual, and potentially useful," Imari said. "I haven't left before now because I couldn't ensure my safety on the journey. Who better to protect me than a woman who can control the yokai?"

Seishirou's look of interest shifted into one of concern. Imari could tell he was revisiting an old memory and she could guess which one without being told. "You know yokai are not meant to be controlled by humans, Imari. Some are friendly, but others are not, and most of them only look out for their own interests, just as humans do."

"Fine, control was a bad word, but the rest of your statement isn't true. There are lots of yokai who help humans." She held up her left arm, letting the sleeve of her kimono slide down to reveal the stump of her wrist. "I would have died in that rockslide if it wasn't for the yokai. I never once resented them for cutting off my hand to get me out of the mine. They did it to save my life."

"And you're willing to risk that life again, just to get your hand back?"

Imari's first instinct was to be angry, but as her father's words settled between them, she could tell he was genuinely asking. It was a serious question, and his tone didn't imply her choice was foolish. He was trying to get her to think, not giving her the answer outright but leading her to find it herself—just as he had during her childhood.

"It's about more than my hand," she said, considering her words carefully. "It's about proving myself. It's about showing I can be a strong, capable leader, just like you are and grandfather was. The other nobles..."

He shook his head, frowning once more. "The other nobles either respect you already or their opinions are worthless."

"You don't understand." Imari reached for the trade agreement, brandishing it with her right hand. "This offer is basically an insult. People already think they can take advantage of you because I'm all you've got for an heir. I make you look weak. How do you think they're going to treat me when I become daimyo? I can tell you, it won't be with the respect I deserve."

"There is more than one way to gain respect, Imari. You don't need to find a magical hand to earn it."

"What if I told you I was doing it because I wanted to fight with two hands on my katana again? Or because it's really annoying trying to tie a knot or pour a glass of water without a second hand to steady the cup? What reason would make this quest seem worthwhile to you?"

"You misunderstand me." Her father's eyes softened and he placed a hand on her shoulder, squeezing gently. "I have no idea what missing a hand is like. Your reasons don't have to be good enough for me. They only have to be good enough for you. If you have made your decision, I will do everything I can to support you. Tell me, which route are you planning to take to Tsun'i?"

"Through Hyewang," Imari answered. Most travelers to Tsun'i chose to pass through the border city at the northern tip of the Jade Sea, since it was far away from the restless southern kingdom of Xiangsai.

Seishirou frowned, shaking his head slightly. "I'm afraid you may need to consider other options. Hyewang has been in a state of unrest since their daimyo crossed the Roaring Ocean. The political situation there is tense, and several skirmishes have already broken out. I fear it will get worse before it gets better."

"What about Empress Tomoyo?" Imari asked. "If the situation is unstable, shouldn't she do something?"

"I expect she will, but you know how these things go: always far too slowly."

"I'll look into different routes," Imari agreed. "I don't want to drag my friends into the middle of a dangerous political scuffle."

"Speaking of friends," Seishirou continued, "I expect to meet this mysterious woman who will be guarding you before I give your journey my blessing."

For several moments, Imari didn't know what to say. As always, her father had come through for her, and he hadn't once implied she was crazy or foolish for feeling the way she did. She leaned into his open arms, giving him the tightest hug she could manage. "Of course, I will, Otou-san. Thank you. I promise, I'm going to be smart about this."

"I'm sure you will," he said, running his hand up and down her back in a soothing gesture. "You always are. That's why I'm proud of you."

Chapter Six

KAEDE SLOWED HER PACE before heading up the steep castle steps, staring intently. She craned her neck in every direction, struggling to take everything in. She had grown up in beautiful surroundings herself, but Lord Homura's castle was something else entirely. The red roof shone like the peaks of a flame and the large bronze statues standing at the bottom of the stairs were incredibly detailed, almost lifelike. She could even see the texture of their armor.

"Come on," Kenta called, waving for her to catch up. He was a few steps ahead, grinning at her from over his shoulder. "Shake the lead out of those feet, Iori-san. You don't wanna keep Lord Homura waiting, do you?"

"Sorry," Kaede said as she stole one last glance at the impressive entryway. "And I've told you, Kaede is fine. I don't mind if you want to use my given name, since I'm staying in your house and all."

Kenta's grin widened and he nodded. "All right, Kaede, but when my brother yells at me for being rude, it's your fault."

Kaede hurried to join him, skirting around other people on the way up. The castle was breathtaking, but also crowded. Several strangers passed by, bustling about their daily business, but Kaede only attracted a few stares. Blending in was a lot easier without Rin by her side.

Rin had elected to stay behind once more, much to Kenta's disappointment. The two of them had taken a strong liking to each other—a fact Kaede was grateful for, especially with Takeshi around, staring stone-faced at her over dinner and keeping suspicious eyes on her wherever she went. Rin and Kenta's companionable interactions made things much less awkward in the Hibana household.

"How did you convince Hibana-danna to let you escort me to the castle, Kenta?" she asked as they arrived at the lavish front doors. They were framed by four sturdy columns, the same red as the rooftops and painted all around with winding bronze serpents. The door handles were stylized white lilies, and the guards pulled them open as she and Kenta approached. They were inside and out of earshot before she spoke again. "He barely lets me out of his sight except when I'm in my room, or Lady Homura makes him."

"She would do that, wouldn't she?" Kenta attempted what Kaede suspected was a long-suffering look, but his chubby face and bright eyes made it difficult for her to take it seriously. "Anyway, I had nothing to do with it. Homura-dono must have insisted, because Takeshi looked pretty annoyed before we left."

"Tell me about it. How can someone so good-looking seem so grumpy all the time?" Kaede asked. "What a waste of a handsome face."

"Oh?" Kenta's eyes widened. "I like to think I got the best looks in the family, but if you want me to put in a good word with him."

Heat flashed across Kaede's cheeks, and she shook her head as she realized her mistake. "No, that's not what I meant at all." She took a chance, deciding to reveal a little more of herself. Her romantic inclinations weren't really any of Kenta's business, but he seemed friendly enough, and living in a big city like Mirai, surely, he had encountered others who preferred their own gender. "I'm a lady of a different court."

Kenta didn't seem surprised by the statement. "Then you'll fit right in here with us," he said, smirking. "I happen to be a member of your court too, and Homura-dono is a lady of both."

That tidbit of information caught Kaede's attention. She blinked in surprise, flushing as she remembered the kata she and Imari had performed the day before, as well as their conversation on the garden bench. It had been a rather intimate thing for two strangers to do, now that she thought about it. *Did I miss something? I've never been good at this. Was she flirting with me? If she was, this has the potential to get really awkward fast.*

Fortunately, Kenta didn't seem to notice her staring. "Don't worry, I won't tell Takeshi you said he was handsome. But truthfully, it might do him some good. He's been sulky ever since Imari called off their engagement."

Kaede didn't know how to respond to that shocking revelation. Instead, she studied her surroundings more closely. The inside of the castle was just as impressive as the outside. The walls and screens were painted with beautiful landscapes and the sunlight streaming in through the windows made the rooms glow. Still, Kaede couldn't help feeling a little uncomfortable as she gazed around at all the finery. It reminded her too much of what she had left behind.

"Are you ready for this?" Kenta said, stopping short in front of a tall shoji screen and nodding politely to another pair of armored guards. "Don't be too scared. Lord Homura's a kind, wise man. He takes after Imari."

"I think you mean she takes after him, since he's her father and all," Kaede joked, but it didn't help loosen the knots in her stomach. She wasn't afraid, not exactly, but she was nervous. If Lord Homura didn't approve of her presence here, or her new association with his daughter, she was in for a lot of trouble. "Sorry," she mumbled, aiming an apologetic glance at Kenta. She cleared her throat, brushing out the creases in her kimono. "I'm ready. I've visited noble houses before. I won't embarrass you."

"I know you won't." Kenta gave her a friendly nudge. "Go on in. I'll be waiting for you out here."

After a gesture from one of the guards, Kaede stepped past the shoji screen and into the room. The first figure her eyes lit upon was Imari, even though she wasn't seated front and center. Her hair was done up in an ornate fan with a red comb perched on top. Her lips carried a subtle smile, and Kaede smiled back before she caught herself and averted her gaze.

Somewhat embarrassed, she turned to Lord Homura. The daimyo sat on a low platform, legs crossed. He stared at her thoughtfully. He looked younger than Kaede expected, and his beard and mustache only had a few touches of grey at the edges. She studied him for as long as she dared while she moved to sit, surprising herself as she tried to search for similarities between his appearance and his daughter's. Aside from the fine clothes and the same coloring, Imari and Lord Homura didn't seem to have much in common.

Behind the daimyo were the banners of the House, fluttering down toward the floor in long stripes. The design was familiar: a bronze hexagon seated in a field of red, bearing a white lily in the center. "My Lord," Imari said, rising from her seat and giving her father a deep bow, "I apologize for interrupting your work, but an important matter has come to my attention."

Lord Homura's eyes still fixed on Kaede. "So, I see. I assume your guest has something to do with this important matter?"

Imari turned to Kaede, who hurried to make her own bow, trying not to scramble as she touched her forehead to the ground in the lowest posture. "Honorable Lord, thank you for allowing me entrance to your House and granting me an audience. My name is Iori Kaede." She held her breath, waiting for a response. She had used her false surname before, but she still felt nervous about lying to a daimyo.

"You're welcome here, Iori Kaede," Lord Homura said, and she took that as her cue to exit the bow. "My daughter has already told me of her intentions to leave Mirai in the next week. She has also told me that you have agreed to accompany her. Is this true?"

"Yes, Homura-dono," Kaede said, "with your permission, of course."

Lord Homura studied her with shrewd eyes, and for a moment, Kaede felt as though he were peering through her skin. The intense scrutiny made her uncomfortable, but she tried to hold still nevertheless. "That remains to be seen. She has also told me that you have a connection with the yokai."

"Yes, Homura-dono," Kaede said again. "I'm from the north, and many yokai inhabit the forest near my home. I don't know if Lady Homura told you, but one of them is my companion."

"The white wolf," Lord Homura said. From his tone, Kaede suspected Rin had been the subject of several conversations at the castle. "And what is your opinion of the yokai, Iori-san? I'm curious."

Kaede could tell this was a test, but for the life of her, she couldn't figure out what kind of answer Lord Homura wanted. In the end, she went with the truth. "My opinion of the yokai is no different from my opinion of people, Lord Homura. Some are helpful and kind, some are mischievous or even dangerous, and others simply wish to be left alone. I respect all of them, but I can't generalize about them. I can only hope to understand the ones I encounter."

From the look that crossed Lord Homura's face, she could tell she had given a pleasing answer. "And what about your former clan? What made you leave?"

Kaede had been hoping he wouldn't ask, but when confronted with the question, she couldn't avoid it. "I left because my duty demanded it, but I left with my honor. I did nothing to bring disgrace upon my ancestors." *Only disgrace upon myself for my own foolishness.*

Apparently satisfied with that explanation, Lord Homura turned to Imari. "You witnessed this ronin's skills for yourself, daughter. Do you wish to bring her with you on your journey?"

Imari looked at her, and Kaede's stomach did a flip. "Absolutely."

"And have you planned your route? It is a long way to ask a stranger to travel." He looked at Kaede, letting her know the question was for her.

Imari answered nonetheless. "We will go south, across the

narrowest part of the Jade Sea. With the unrest in Hyewang, it would be better to avoid the province entirely."

Kaede tried not to show her surprise. Crossing the Jade Sea wasn't the easy task Imari made it sound. Still, she didn't take back her offer. Hayate would be hard-pressed to follow her that way. "I'm up for the challenge, Homura-dono," she said with another bow. "I've already travelled a long way from home. I have some experience."

Lord Homura seemed to make up his mind. "Then it shall be as you wish, Imari. Iori Kaede will accompany you as your yojimbo as you travel to Mount Aka. If she proves to be a valuable bodyguard, we can discuss granting her a permanent place here in Mirai upon your return."

Imari gave her father another bow. "Thank you, my Lord. I'm sure this is the right decision."

No, thank you. Kaede made her own bow. She was incredibly grateful for Imari's support, especially since they had only known each other such a short time. If she stayed, hopefully she would get the chance to return the favor many times over.

"Very well," Lord Homura said. "You will give your oath at dawn, Iori Kaede. I'm sure my daughter will be grateful for your services."

***

"I humbly receive." Kaede unclasped her hands and shifted on top of her mat, shooting an uncomfortable glance at Takeshi from across the table.

The heavy silence between them was growing unbearable, but she had no idea what else to say. He had obviously known about Imari's plan, and it wasn't a stretch to read the disapproval in his stony face. His food sat untouched in front of him, and Kaede didn't feel comfortable enough to reach for her own chopsticks until he started.

"So." Kenta broke the silence first, stealing a nervous, pitying look at her before turning toward his brother. "These radishes look good." He popped one of the strips into his mouth, chewing thoroughly and making sounds of approval—although, thankfully, with his mouth closed.

"Mmm." Takeshi remained noncommittal, continuing to stare. His eyes burned, and Kaede felt the back of her neck prickle. In an effort to avoid his gaze, she reached for her hand towel. In moments like this, she almost wished she could be rude and wipe her face, because she was starting to break out in a light sweat thanks to Takeshi's glare.

"And these pickled plums," Kenta said, inserting even more forced cheerfulness into his voice. "They're so red. And...red?"

Takeshi closed his eyes, hanging his head in exasperation. "They're plums, Kenta. They grow everywhere around here. We have plums at least five times a week. We have so many plums the cooks don't know what to do with them."

Kaede swallowed. Although he wasn't shouting or gesturing, this was the angriest she had ever seen her host. "Hibana-danna, with all due respect, I didn't mean to offend you. If I have overstepped, perhaps I should apologize."

To her surprise, Takeshi let out a long breath and gave a short bow of apology. "Forgive me, Iori-san. You haven't offended me. And forgive me, Kenta, for speaking harshly to you. I simply worry for Homura-dono's safety. She has spoken of this quest of hers on and off for years, but I wasn't prepared for her to make such solid arrangements."

"If she's spoken about it for years, why didn't you think she'd do it?" Kaede asked. "Does she have a habit of coming up with grand ideas and not following through?"

"Quite the contrary," Takeshi said. "When she sets her mind to something, she'll go to the ends of the earth to make it happen. But she is also a reasonable, methodical person. She isn't the type to go forward without a proper plan in place."

"Or a proper guide," Kaede finished. Her presence allowed Imari to take the next step forward, and although he wasn't rude enough to say so outright, she suspected Takeshi held her responsible for Lady Homura's sudden enthusiasm.

"Don't blame yourself, Kaede," Kenta said, offering her a smile. "You didn't do anything wrong. Imari—Lady Homura—was going to do this eventually, with or without you. And I'm glad it's with you. If we're going all the way across the Jade Sea, I'll feel better knowing a girl who makes friends with spirits is coming along with us...especially with the rumors of dragons. Do you think you could teach a dragon to play fetch?"

Instead of indulging the question, Takeshi picked up his chopsticks, much to Kaede's gratitude. As he dipped a bite of food into the sauce beside his bowl, she did the same. Her stomach was still tied in nervous knots. Even the fish and rice couldn't tempt her.

"Hopefully, there won't be any dragons," she said. "Are the two of you coming with us? Lady Homura didn't say."

"I should hope we are," Takeshi said. "Your skills are considerable from what I've witnessed, but Lady Homura needs more than a single yojimbo to attend her."

Great. Although she didn't object to Kenta's presence, the thought of Takeshi coming along on the journey wasn't a pleasant one. She remembered Kenta's earlier slip all too clearly, and the last thing she wanted to do was put herself between Lady Homura and her overprotective ex-fiancé.

"Honestly, I'm not even sure she needs me," she said, trying to sound modest. "When she invited me to perform kata with her, she was going so fast I could barely keep up. I think she could handle a dragon all on her own." At Takeshi's disapproving look, Kaede backtracked. "But, of course, I'm sure she will be glad of your company."

"It won't be so bad, Takeshi," Kenta said, skillfully dulling the edge of tension once more. "It might even do you some good to get out of here for a while. You can see more of the world, fight a few bandits, flirt with pretty merchant girls."

"No bandits," Takeshi said with a firm shake of his head, "and definitely no merchant girls."

Kenta stuck out his lower lip in a pout. "But—"

"For their sake, of course. I wouldn't wish you on any of them as a brother-in-law."

It was such a deadpan delivery it took Kaede several seconds to realize Takeshi had actually made a joke. She snorted then bent back to her food, sharing a slightly less antagonistic look with him before she did. Takeshi still didn't seem happy about Imari's decision, but at least he wasn't glaring holes through her head anymore. However, she got the distinct impression that, if she failed in her duties as Imari's bodyguard, he would be a foe far more fearsome than any dragon.

***

Imari leaned back against the wall she had placed her futon beside and stared down at the silk-bound book in her lap. A smile crept across her face as she traced her fingertips over the tapered black lines, following the path of the River Go. It started in the mountains at the top left hand corner of the page, winding down diagonally through the heart of Tsun'i. It looked small, a crease in the paper, but in reality, she knew it would be much larger—larger than anything she had ever seen. Despite her privileged upbringing, she wasn't particularly well traveled.

Her finger continued east until it arrived at a dark patch near the center of the map—the Jade Sea, a place she had read about extensively but longed to see in person. It had been frozen in stone for centuries, but her books said the waves in the middle were as high as hills, and the bodies of fish and other sea creatures were trapped beneath the clear green waters, perfectly preserved.

Near the northernmost tip of the Jade Sea was Hyewang, the province most people passed through when entering Tsun'i. However, with the turmoil there of late, she didn't feel comfortable taking that route. Even less appealing was the option of skirting the Jade Sea's southern edge, which would take them dangerously close to the Kasai Mountains and the tightly guarded kingdom of Xiangsai. Instead, it would be better and faster to cut across the narrowest part of the sea itself on foot. It wouldn't be an easy journey, but she had heard of guides who would escort travelers across for the right price.

She tapped her finger against the bottom of the sea, where a single lonely mountain was sketched in ink. It was labeled "Mount Aka" in scratchy characters, but Imari preferred the Tsun'i name for it. Her knowledge of the language was only fair at best, but there was strength to "Hongshan." Both names meant Red Mountain, but from the way the characters looked to her, "Hongshan" spoke of the red fire of a forge, while "Aka" was more of a rosy red sunset. It was dragons she was looking for—or, more accurately, the man who had managed to master them.

She returned her attention to the map, cutting across the Jade Sea and continuing northeast. There, not too far away, was Mirai. It was in the middle of the plains, built into a small mountain range near the center of the kingdom. Once, the lands around her province had been a bountiful bowl of rice paddies, but Mirai had moved into the future. The neighboring provinces could take care of the farming, as far as she was concerned.

With some curiosity, her eyes continued up to the northern forests and mountains of Aozora and Yukimura. If she didn't miss her guess, Kaede had come from one of those two places. Judging from her speech and manners, perhaps she even had some association with one of the large noble households.

A distant knock startled her from her studies, and she closed the book, setting it aside on the mattress. At this late hour, having a visitor was unusual. Still, she had a good suspicion who it was. *I'm surprised he didn't come to check on me earlier. Surely Kenta has told him the news by now.*

With a sigh, she stood and checked the sash of her yukata, making sure she was presentable. The crimson, black-threaded robe hung loosely, and she struggled to tighten it one-handed. After an awkwardly long fumble and some breathy mutters, she managed to make a clumsy knot at the small of her back. Working with her remaining hand was more difficult when there was a time limit involved.

She crossed the living quarters outside in a few strides, sliding open the screen to reveal exactly who she had expected: Takeshi, standing awkwardly out in the hallway and looking unhappy. "Forgive me, Homura-dono—"

"Imari," she interrupted, correcting him so she wouldn't have to do it later. "Come on, Takeshi. If you're going to come to my bedroom this late, the least you can do is use my given name."

The corner of Takeshi's eye gave a noticeable twitch, but he bowed nevertheless. "Of course, Imari. I'm sorry to bother you this late, but I think the two of us need to talk."

"Well, I don't particularly want to." A furrow creased Takeshi's forehead, and Imari stepped back into the room so he could enter. "But I'll humor you. Come in. And before you ask, I'm going to Hongshan, and you aren't going to change my mind."

"But are you sure you know what you're getting into?" Takeshi asked. "Tsun'i is far away. Not all the people there think highly of Akatsuki Teikoku, its daimyos in particular. And what about Iori-san? Kenta tells me you're going to take her on as your yojimbo. Are you sure a stranger is the best person to protect you on a mission like this? You hardly know anything about her."

"Well, there will be plenty of time to learn about her on the trip, won't there?" Imari kept her voice deliberately cheerful, partially because she knew it would grate on Takeshi's nerves. His overprotective routine was getting exhausting, and she didn't have the patience to deal with it any longer. "Besides, do you have any idea how to talk to a dragon yokai without getting eaten? Because if you do, I'm all ears."

Takeshi frowned but didn't argue the point. "I see how she could prove useful," he muttered, grudgingly, "but I still don't think you should go."

"Then it's a good thing I don't care what you think."

A look of hurt flashed across Takeshi's face, and Imari regretted her rudeness. She bowed in apology, keeping her gaze lowered. "I'm sorry, Takeshi. I shouldn't have said that. You're one of my closest friends, and I do care a great deal about what you think."

"It's all right." Takeshi rubbed the back of his neck. "I guess I should've known better than to barge in here and tell you what to do, huh?"

"Yes, you should have, but I should've had the courtesy to hear you out, too."

"I'm worried about you," Takeshi said, staring at her with dark, intense eyes. "No awkward romantic feelings implied, I promise. As your friend, I'm scared about what might happen if you do this. You want to travel halfway across the known world so that a legendary smith can give you a magical hand? You know you're perfectly capable with one, don't you? I've got two, and you still beat me more often than not."

"Tell that to the other daimyos," Imari muttered, but she offered a slight smirk to let him know her bitterness wasn't directed at him any longer. "This isn't just about the hand. I want to see what's out there, and when I come back, I want to have so many amazing stories to tell that not a single noble can question my competence. And even if they give me dirty looks and whisper behind my back, I'll know I've done something great."

After a long pause, Takeshi sighed and nodded. "I understand. If you're determined to do this, it isn't my place to stop you. But you will let me come, won't you?"

"I won't just let you," Imari said, reaching out to pat his forearm. "I insist. How am I supposed to travel all the way across the Jade Sea without my best friend?"

"I hope you mean around," Takeshi said, but Imari shook her head.

"Across. I want to avoid Hyewang."

"You can't be serious. Crossing the Jade Sea? I haven't heard of anyone doing that in at least the past ten years." Takeshi's brow furrowed. "What about Xiangsai? If we go further south…"

"Going south would take months. Crossing the Jade Sea will save us so much time. We'll manage."

"Oh, I'll manage," Takeshi said, with a slight note of pride. "Now, that yojimbo of yours…let's hope she can keep up."

Imari thought back to the kata she and Kaede had performed the other day and smiled. "Don't worry about Iori-san. She'll be able to keep up with us just fine."

Chapter Seven

STICKY POOLS OF BLACK LIQUID dot the ground, carving rivers through the wrinkled white sheet of snow. The entrance to the cave is littered with bodies, severed limbs, torn chunks of flesh and feathers. The left side of her face burns, and her eyes water so badly she can't see anything but blurry streaks. But she can hear. She can hear the sizzling hiss of hot blood on cold ice and the echoes of screams.

"Kaede."

She knows that voice. She knows the hand that caresses her arm, helping her sit up. Setsuna has been like a mother to her these past few years, but this time, the grasp is like a bite. She jerks away, kicking up clods of wet snow and scrambling backwards, trying to stand up on her own. "What...what have we done? What have I—"

"Kaede, listen carefully." Setsuna's voice is meant to be soothing against her ear, but all she hears is a serpent's hiss. "This was not your fault. I know you're afraid, but this is your destiny. You were meant for great things, my precious girl. This is simply the price that must be paid first."

Kaede swipes the sleeve of her kimono angrily over her eyes, smudging away tears and sweat and worse, careless of the crimson stain she might leave behind. "Price, Yukimura-sama?" She gazes around the battlefield, fighting off waves of nausea. Her head swims with fear. "This isn't a price. It's a massacre."

Setsuna hovers over her, offering a hand once more. Her expression is open, worried. Somehow, her concern is more frightening than any sadistic mask of glee. "Come. I'll fix your face. It will get infected if we don't—"

An infection. All this death, this butchery, and Setsuna is only concerned for her. "No!" Without another word, or another look at the corpses—human and yokai—littering the ground, she runs. She runs until she can't run anymore, until she's deep within the forest where no one can find her. Only then does she slump to her knees, hands scraping against the bark of the tree where she has caught herself, bitter tears *streaming down her face. They make the open wound burn more, but she doesn't care.*

Her pain is worth nothing. She is still alive, so it is hers to bear.

Kaede opened her eyes, tears smeared her cheeks and the futon beneath her head. They had left a stain, and she sniffed, doing her best to rub it dry. The dreams had become almost routine over the past month. Waking up crying was normal rather than an unusual occurrence. At least according to Rin, she didn't scream and thrash as much anymore.

Instead of sitting up, she pulled the covers around her shoulders and huddled beneath them, nuzzling into a dry patch of fabric. She had gone to bed full of excitement and hope, ready for the sun to rise so she could swear her oath to Imari, but it all had been sucked out of her. Leaving home had been the right decision, but guilt still followed her like a shadow. Setsuna had been the one to put the horrible experiments into motion, but that didn't make her any less complicit. She had summoned the yokai to be bound, and she had sealed the fates of the humans and spirits unlucky enough to witness her failure.

Her current situation wasn't much better. She hadn't caused any death, but she still hadn't told Imari the truth about her past or parentage, and as her oath drew closer, she felt increasingly worse about keeping it a secret. Every time Imari said something kind to her or talked about her own past, Kaede's stomach churned.

"Kaede?"

The sound of soft breathing and the feel of a cold nose nuzzling against her hair made her peek out beyond her pillow. "I know, Rin," she muttered, her voice muffled by the quilted top sheet. "Just give me a minute. I need to breathe."

"You can't breathe under all those covers, and you don't have a minute," Rin growled, nudging her again. "It's almost sunrise. If you're going to swear your oath, you need to get dressed."

Reluctantly, Kaede sat up. From what she could see out the window, the sun hadn't risen yet, but there was a faint pink glow on the horizon.

"Do you still think I shouldn't do it?" she asked as she climbed out of her bedding and crawled in search of her clothes. She didn't have much to choose from, and she could only hope the least stained and wrinkled of her traveling kimonos would be formal enough. The blue one with her mon on it was the nicest garment she owned, but she couldn't wear it for obvious reasons.

Rin curled her tail around her haunches, observing Kaede with bright blue eyes. "It isn't my decision."

"That's a no," Kaede mumbled, continuing to dress. "If you've got something to say, say it."

"It isn't the oath I object to. Being under the protection of a daimyo's daughter might save your life if Hayate or any of Setsuna's forces come after us. It's your infatuation with Lady Homura that frightens me."

The words stung. Kaede stopped in the middle of fastening her obi, glaring sharply at Rin. "I know better than that. I'm not infatuated—"

"Infatuation or friendship or simple service, it doesn't matter." Rin raised her back paw, scratching at one ear and looking decidedly bored. "You are starting to trust her, and the last person you trusted betrayed you. You would do well to remember."

"I do remember." Kaede clenched her teeth and dug her nails into her palms. "I remember every night. But just because Setsuna went down a dark path doesn't mean every human is untrustworthy, Rin. There are good people in this world. You've always stood by me."

"Yes," Rin said, "but I'm not human."

"Well, I am," Kaede snapped. "Don't you trust me?"

Rin exhaled through her nose, the canine version of a sigh. "Yes, Kaede, I trust you. And I will trust you today. I'm only reminding you to be cautious. You can't afford to give your loyalty blindly or freely again. If Lady Homura is worthy of it, she will prove that on the journey."

"Noted." Kaede didn't want to discuss the subject any further, and hopefully, Rin would read her reluctance in her tone. She finished dressing and picked up the bronze hand mirror beside the bed, gazing at her reflection. Her face looked clean, at least, and the bags under her eyes weren't too noticeable, but her hair was in a sorry state, tangled and stringy with a few strands clinging to her neck. She grabbed a comb from among her supplies and brought it into some semblance of order.

By the time she finished her topknot, she looked humble, but presentable—pretty much what she had been going for. When she turned away from the mirror, it was to see Rin giving her a slow, affectionate blink. "You look fierce," she said, and Kaede smiled. She had known Rin long enough to translate the compliment from wolf to human.

"Thanks. Are you coming to watch, or do you want to stay here?"

"Of course." Rin's whiskers quivered, and her nose twitched with offended dignity. "Where you go, I go. I can handle this foul-smelling city for a few hours."

Kaede stood, flipping the mirror over and staring at the intricately designed relief on the other side. Birds soared around the mirror's edges, and the sight of them weighed on her heart. They weren't dissimilar from some of the spirits she had brought to Setsuna the night she had gotten her scar.

"Come on," Rin said, nudging her hand. "Finish getting ready. Your new master is waiting for you."

She set the mirror down, smoothing the wrinkles out of her kimono. *If Imari is going to be my new master, it won't do to be late. This is supposed to be a fresh start, after all, even if it isn't an honest one.*

***

"She's late," Takeshi muttered from the corner of his mouth, staring impatiently at the courtyard gate. He was far too refined to leave his position in line, but Imari could see a glimpse of his pose: shoulders stiff, eyes narrowed, mouth pressed into a tight diagonal slash of disapproval.

At first, Imari thought she shouldn't say anything. Arguing with Takeshi or attempting to reassure him wouldn't do any good, and although she hated to admit it, she was worried herself. The sun was starting to rise over the garden walls, and in the back of her mind, she was beginning to fear Kaede wouldn't come.

"Hey, I'm sure she'll be here," Kenta said from behind her other shoulder. "She seemed pretty excited at dinner last night. Maybe she just overslept? I could always go and get her if..."

Imari shook her head. "No. I don't want her to feel obligated to swear an oath to me. If she has any doubts, she hardly needs someone breathing down her neck." But to her shame, she realized she hadn't really thought of it as Kaede's choice before now. Since their last conversation, she had viewed it as a promise, and she was swiftly realizing it had been a mistake. She stared at the ume blossoms, watching the delicate pink and white petals sway in the light morning breeze.

"Looks like she made the choice fine on her own," Takeshi said, distracting her from her worries.

Imari sighed with relief as Kaede entered the courtyard. The morning glare cast the samurai's tall figure mostly into shadow, but her smile was still visible from a distance. Though they had only known each other for a few days, Imari could tell it was the sort of smile that rarely wavered. She couldn't help returning it as the line of samurai on either side of her stood at attention.

"Look," Kenta whispered, "she brought Rin with her."

Imari remained transfixed as Kaede crossed the short bridge that led over the courtyard's brook. Kaede held herself with such confidence her faded blue kimono hardly mattered, and she didn't seem to have any doubts about her purpose.

Once the small party crossed the bridge, Rin sat beneath the shade of a nearby ume tree and Takeshi took his proper place in line. That left Kaede standing alone. Though her smile had disappeared, her eyes were focused, bright with determination. She looked ready to take her oath, and Imari was eager to have it. She saw something in Kaede, something interesting and valuable her curious mind wanted to examine closer.

As Imari watched, Kaede stopped in front of the small tatami mat. She broke eye contact, staring respectfully at the ground as she knelt. Her hands were steady and slow as she removed her swords, placing her katana and wakizashi to the right. Once they had been set aside, she pressed her hands to the mat and lowered her head.

Imari's eyes flicked over to her father, who observed the proceedings from a nearby balcony. He sat on his platform, posture straight and regal. She took a deep breath. It was only recently that she had started to take an active role in ceremonies like this. Public speaking didn't appeal to her the way running the city from behind the scenes did, but she knew how to fake it well enough. In all things, she strove to do her best and behave in a way that would make her father proud.

"Iori Kaede," she said, projecting so she would be heard throughout the courtyard, "you are here to place yourself into my service and that of my father. Are you free in your wish to stand between me and any danger?"

Kaede's eyes lifted to meet hers, and Imari felt a hard jolt in the center of her chest. Such an unwavering gaze had to be sincere. "I am."

"Do you swear by the code of the samurai to serve and protect me until the end of your contract?"

"Yes, my lady. I swear to shield you from any danger. I swear that my hand shall be just." Imari couldn't help studying the shape of Kaede's hands as they rested on her thighs. They were graceful and thin, but also calloused. "My words shall be true, and my heart loyal to your cause. Until the day I am free of this contract, I swear to commit myself and my sword to your safety. As long as the contract is due, Mizu-no-Hamon will only be drawn in your honor, and if the need arises it will spill blood in your defense. As my will is free to choose, I have chosen."

"Then stand, Iori Kaede. I accept your service."

Kaede bowed again, lingering in the lowest stance before she stood. She threaded the sheathed blades through her obi and turned toward the balcony, making her bow to Lord Homura. Imari looked toward her father's platform and bowed as well, awaiting his judgment.

Lord Homura nodded. "The contract is made. I, the ruler of this land, bear witness and affirm it. Iori Kaede shall serve as my daughter's yojimbo until her return to this city. So shall it be."

The wind seemed to sigh as the ceremony ended. Imari relaxed, and she saw Kaede do the same as she put a hand on her swords. They smiled at each other, stealing a shared glance while everyone else looked toward Lord Homura. Imari still wasn't sure why this woman fascinated her, why she had requested her services so quickly, or why her eyes couldn't seem to leave Kaede for more than a few moments. But now that Kaede was bound to her, she had all the time she needed to find out.

***

It took a few weeks to prepare for their journey, much to Kaede's impatience. Although Kenta's company was pleasant as always and Takeshi slowly seemed to be warming to her, Kaede couldn't relax. Mirai was larger, louder, and faster paced than the cities in the north she was used to. The city never seemed to shut down and lanterns burned all through the night.

Even during the quiet moments Kaede stole for herself, her thoughts filled the void. Each day, she got to know Imari a little bit better, and each day, she felt worse and worse about keeping her identity a secret. The lie ate away at her, and logic could only assuage so much of her guilt.

That was why she found herself late to meet Imari at the market one morning. She'd been up in the middle of the night with bad dreams and dismal thoughts, and she had lost herself staring into her bowl at breakfast, unable to drag herself out of her chair. Eventually, though, her fear of being rude had forced her to go in search of her master, and the smile that spread across her face upon seeing Imari wasn't all forced.

"You know, I almost thought you weren't coming," Imari said, raising her voice to be heard in the busy marketplace. Vendors and their pushcarts lined both sides of the crowded thoroughfare, shouting their prices. The smell of food, smoke, and burning charcoal lingered in the air, and Kaede's stomach rumbled. Thanks to her lack of appetite, she hadn't eaten breakfast, and lunch was fast approaching.

"I had a few doubts," she admitted, trying not to crane her neck too far toward a cart displaying salted meat and vegetable skewers. "But a samurai always keeps her word. It is my honor to join you on your quest, Lady Homura. I'm yours to command."

Imari smiled, and to Kaede's surprise, she stopped at the cart, exchanging a few whispered words with the merchant. A few coppers changed hands, and Imari turned back toward her with two sticks of beef and vegetables. "Here," she said, passing one over. "Eat. I bet you skipped breakfast this morning, didn't you?"

Kaede bowed before accepting the stick. "Yes, I did. I have a nervous stomach."

"Nervous? Because you were coming to the market with me?" Imari laughed, and Kaede's heart fluttered at the sound. Despite Rin's warning, she found her eyes lingering in places they shouldn't, especially near Imari's lips. "I assure you, Iori-san, I'm harmless."

"Based on the kata we've been doing, I must respectfully disagree," Kaede said. "Thank you for the meal, my lady." Once Imari took a bite, she did so as well, moaning as the salt hit her tongue. Before she knew it, she was half way through the skewer, with a trail of juice running down the corner of her mouth.

Great job, Kaede. Make a mess of yourself in front of your new master. Your attractive new master. She's going to think you're a complete slob with no manners.

Kaede reached into her kimono, fumbling for a cloth to wipe her chin, but before she dug it out, Imari touched the side of her hand, passing over one of her own. "Here."

Kaede's face burned in embarrassment, but she took the offered cloth so as not to be rude, dabbing at the corner of her mouth. "I'll purchase you a new one," she muttered, averting her eyes.

"No need. Besides, we're here to outfit you for the journey as payment for your services, of course."

"Of course, my lady," Kaede said. "And if you'll permit me to return to our earlier conversation, I do find you impressive, but you don't make me nervous." *It's the fact that I'm lying through my teeth to you that makes me feel sick.*

Unfortunately, Imari drew the wrong conclusion. "Takeshi," she sighed. "If he said something to you. . ."

Kaede hastened to correct her. "No, it's nothing like that. Hibana-danna has been a gracious host."

"Good," Imari sighed. "I'd expect nothing less from him. We've been friends since we were children, and we were even engaged for a year."

"So, I've been told," Kaede mumbled before realizing her slip. Her face heated up again, but it was too late. Imari had already stopped, turning slowly toward her. "I'm sorry, my lady, if you didn't wish for me to know."

Imari waved her apology away, continuing through the market. "It's all right. The truth is, I turned him down because he was starting to get on my nerves."

Kaede was surprised by Imari's candor, but also relieved. It seemed the subject of their broken engagement wasn't taboo after all. She trailed behind Imari, coming to a stop at the same time she did near a stall with hanging displays of hitatare. The matching jacket and trousers weren't ostentatious, but they were well made—far better than most of the kimonos Kaede had brought with her, and in the city's colors too.

"What do you mean, Homura-dono?" she asked as she studied the stitching. "Didn't the two of you get along?"

Imari sighed. "Somewhere along the line, he stopped treating me like a friend and started treating me like a stranger he had to protect at all times. I got sick of it, and we fought. We patched things up, but I know him too well to try for anything more than friendship. Maybe someday he'll learn he doesn't have to treat the woman he's interested in like an untouchable Goddess, but I don't have the patience to teach him. I want a partner, not someone I have to fix." She hesitated, offering Kaede what appeared to be a thoughtful look. "You aren't asking because you're interested, are you?"

"What?" Kaede sputtered, dropping the sleeve of the jacket and taking a step back. "No! I mean, not in him." She cleared her throat and tried again. "I'm actually a lady of a different court. Kenta said that wouldn't be a problem?"

"Not at all," Imari said. She turned to the merchant, and more coppers changed hands. A few moments later, Kaede held the hitatare in her arms. "Disapproving of you would be a bit hypocritical."

Kaede's head spun. Although Kenta had let slip that Imari was a lady of both courts, the way Imari had brought it up made her wonder. Her tone had almost sounded...flirtatious? Kaede was so surprised it took her several seconds to realize she had forgotten to thank Imari for the gift. "Thank you again, Homura-dono, but this really isn't necessary. I can afford to outfit myself."

"Nonsense. This is my quest, and as an important member of my party, your safety is imperative to my safety." Imari shot her a look that could only be described as playful, and Kaede almost choked on the nervous lump in her throat. "Besides, I don't want you getting any more scars. One or two are dashing on a samurai. More is a sign that you aren't good at your job."

Kaede had already been blushing, but at those words, her cheeks burned like fire. She coughed, struggling awkwardly until she was able to tuck the new clothes more securely over her arm. It wasn't until Imari merged back into the crowd that she realized someone had mentioned her new scars, and it hadn't upset her. The usual surge of guilt and shame hadn't come.

"I'm still getting used to them," she confessed, hurrying to catch up. "They're fairly recent, I'm afraid. A minor disagreement with a family member."

"The reason you left home?" Imari asked, speaking softer. "You don't have to answer if you don't feel comfortable."

"Yes," Kaede said, but she didn't explain further. Though part of her wanted to, she knew the full story would have to wait until later, when she and Imari knew each other better. *When. Not if. I'm already in deep, aren't I? Rin was right. I should be more cautious. I'm still in hiding.* She glanced over her shoulder, not expecting to see anything, but made nervous all the same by the direction her thoughts were taking.

To her surprise, her eyes landed on a strange figure. Someone, probably a man from the breadth of his shoulders, stared at them from beneath a shadowed hood, trailing a few yards behind and keeping close to the edge of the street. Kaede couldn't make out his face from a distance, but something about his movements set her on edge. She glanced at Imari, debating whether to say something, but decided against it. There was no proof this man was following them, and until she was sure, there was no reason to sound an alarm.

"My lady," she said, leaning in to whisper closer to Imari's cheek, "would you indulge me? If it's all right with you, I'd like to look at the carts down that way." She gestured around the next bend, to a side street slightly less crowded than the main thoroughfare.

A wrinkle of confusion marred the middle of Imari's brow, but she nodded. "Of course, what were you hoping to find?"

Kaede didn't answer. Instead, she turned the corner, pausing and waiting. As she both expected and feared, the hooded man followed, ducking down the side street behind them. The new direction sent more sunlight spilling onto his face, and he came into clearer focus. *Hayate. He's found me.* A cold shiver of fear shot down Kaede's spine, but she placed herself between Imari and Hayate, hand hovering near her katana.

"Homura-dono, we need to return to the castle at once," she said in a low murmur. "What's the fastest way to get there?"

Imari frowned with concern. "I suppose we could go down to the end of this street and turn left to head back the way we came, but why? What's going on?"

"I promise I'll explain later," Kaede said. Hayate took a step toward her, and he reached for the grip of his sword as well. "Please, trust me. We need to go."

Imari started off down the street at a quick pace, and Kaede followed behind, only glancing back long enough to make sure Hayate wasn't in pursuit. Thankfully, her cousin didn't appear to be following them. The next time she looked over her shoulder, Hayate had melted into the crowd, disappearing from sight.

He made no further appearances, but Kaede didn't allow herself to relax until they arrived at the castle, with several guards at their backs. Once they were through the gates, she stole a look at Imari, who wore a decidedly nervous expression. "What happened back there, Kaede? Am I mistaken, or was that man in the hood following us?"

Kaede winced, then nodded. *If Hayate has found me here, we need to leave as soon as possible. Assuming Imari still wants me to come with her.* "Yes. Is there somewhere we can talk? I owe you an explanation, but I'd prefer to do it in private."

Chapter Eight

IMARI STOOD AWKWARDLY IN the middle of her bedroom, unsure what to do. Her first instinct was to watch Kaede pace the length of the painted wallscreen, but that didn't feel right. Kaede was obviously upset, and being stared at probably wouldn't help. Imari wanted to say something, to offer some kind of comfort, but she wasn't sure it would be welcome. Although Kaede had sworn an oath to her, they were still strangers. She knew almost nothing of Kaede's past, other than the samurai's extreme reluctance to discuss it. *Whoever that man was, Kaede is afraid of him. She's moving like a hunted animal.*

It was an apt comparison. Kaede's muscles were tense and her movements were short and jerking. At last, she came to a stop, squaring her shoulders and making eye contact. It was an intimate gesture, although not one Imari minded. She held the gaze, waiting patiently until Kaede finally spoke.

"That was my cousin back there. He's the reason I left home. Well, one of the reasons."

The room lapsed into silence until Imari realized Kaede needed a response. "You had some sort of disagreement?"

"If by 'disagreement', you mean 'wants to take me captive and possibly kill me,' then yes, we had a disagreement. But Hayate isn't my biggest problem." Kaede looked away as if in shame, striding over to the window and peering out over the courtyard below. "I was never close to my parents. They weren't cruel, but they never understood me either. Because of that distance, I spent a lot of time with my aunt. She was the mother I wished I'd had."

Kaede turned back, reaching up to touch her left cheek, and Imari's heart clenched. The pain swimming in Kaede's eyes was clearly visible in the late afternoon light; a glaring contrast to the playful, joking expression Imari had taken pleasure in over the past few days. Kaede looked away again, and Imari took a cautious step forward, until they were face to face again beside the window.

"Until she caused that?" Imari gestured at the scar.

"Yes," Kaede whispered. "It's a long story, but I caught her doing something dishonorable. When I realized she had been using me to further her own selfish goals, I ran. She must've sent Hayate to come after me. He's her adopted son, and my cousin." Her brows knitted together, and her face darkened. "The two of us were friends before, but now, his loyalties are obviously with her."

Before Imari could think it through, she reached out. She touched Kaede's arm above the elbow, a light stroke of comfort. Kaede took in a soft gasp, but didn't protest the touch or step away. Instead, the worry lines she wore seemed to smooth out.

"Well, I'm not about to let some strange man in a hood snatch you away," Imari said, offering what she hoped was a reassuring smile. "I'll send some guards to look for him." At Kaede's unhappy look, she offered another solution. "Or we can push forward the date of our departure, if you don't want them involved. If we hurry, we could leave as early as tomorrow afternoon."

"Really? That's it?" Kaede said, with no small amount of surprise. "We're just going to leave early? You aren't going to demand more of an explanation, or scold me for keeping secrets, or free me from my oath?"

Imari shook her head. "Of course not, Iori-san. You aren't required to tell me every single detail of your life, although, I am curious about one thing, if you'll indulge me."

Kaede chewed at her lower lip. "That depends on the question. You can try me, my lady."

"What caused the rift between you and your parents? I don't mean to pry, but my father and I are close. I'm not sure I understand parents who don't love and support their children."

Instead of being offended, Kaede seemed relieved. Her shoulders relaxed and some of the lines in her face smoothed out. Imari wondered if, perhaps, she was more comfortable talking about her parents than her aunt and cousin, and filed the possibility away for later thought.

"The situation is a little awkward, but I guess it's something you should know anyway. And I feel like it's something I can tell you, considering our...earlier discussion." Kaede rubbed the nape of her neck, and Imari thought she caught a hint of a blush on the samurai's cheeks. "You see, I'm not just a lady of a different court. I'm also a lady of autumn."

Imari's eyes widened. She hadn't expected such a declaration, and her first instinct was to study Kaede more closely. True, she was tall, with narrow hips and slightly broad shoulders—a lean, wiry body type that, while unusual for a young woman, was quite captivating in its way. But her soft face held no hint of hair, and her kimono clearly concealed curves.

Well, I never would have guessed if she hadn't told me.

When Kaede cleared her throat, Imari stopped staring, realizing her silence could be considered rude. In the end, Kaede's appearance wasn't hers to judge, however pleasing she found it. If Kaede said she was a woman, it was hardly anyone else's place to decide whether she looked the part or not.

Kaede coughed awkwardly. "You know what I'm trying to say, right? Summer to winter, yang to yin. . . " Her voice trailed off, and she winced as if waiting for judgment.

"Yes, I understand. I'm sorry for staring, Iori-san," Imari said, giving a short bow of apology. "I'm as pleased to be in your company as I was before you told me. More so, in fact. I'm glad you trust me."

To Imari's relief, Kaede grinned. "It's all right, Homura-dono. I'm used to people looking at me differently once they know. They always start by searching for a man underneath who isn't there, even the ones who mean well."

A flush of shame scorched over Imari's cheeks. That had indeed been her first instinct, and she wished she could take it back and try again. "I understand. I have no idea what it must be like to live in your season, but I'm used to stares and the judgment that comes along with them." She held up her left hand, letting the sleeve of her kimono slide down. "This often draws the wrong kind of attention. People see it instead of me."

"It feels good to talk about it. I suppose I prefer that most people can't tell by looking, but sometimes it's nice to be seen for who I really am." Kaede gazed out the window once more, but this time, it didn't seem like she was trying to escape from the conversation. Her posture seemed a lot more relaxed, and she no longer looked like a mouse cowering beneath an owl's shadow. "Not just being a lady of autumn, either. All of it. I can talk to Rin, but it's nice to speak about my family to another human."

"Of course. But why would you being a lady of autumn upset your parents?" Imari asked, surprised by how upset the question made her. Her stomach simmered with anger on Kaede's behalf, particularly since she had never met her parents. "I hardly see how they could be disappointed in you. You're a fine samurai from what I've witnessed, and your connection with Rin is astounding. Surely they realize a daughter could bring their family honor just as well as a son?"

"They were never cruel about it," Kaede said, a little wistfully. "They didn't shout or cast me out, and they only made slight efforts to dissuade me. But they didn't understand, either. When some of the forest spirits softened my body's changes as a favor, my parents grew nervous. Afraid, I suppose, that the change would harm me or I would come to regret it. But my aunt was happy for me. I was a confused child when I went to her, but she taught me how to be a woman. At least, I thought she did."

Another cloud covered Kaede's face, and Imari gave her arm another soft nudge. "Thank you for telling me, Iori-san. The trust you've placed in me is an honor. In fact…" A thoughtful expression crossed Imari's face, then she nodded to herself. "I would like you to follow me. There is something I'd like to show you."

"The honor is mine, my lady. And please." The sunbeam of Kaede's smile broke through again, making her look much more like her usual self. "I would love it if you used my given name. If you don't think it's too improper."

Imari smiled back, unable to contain her grin. "I don't think it's improper at all, Kaede."

***

"I don't mean to pry," Kaede said as the two of them crossed over the garden bridge, "but I'm curious. Where are we going?"

Imari smiled, surprised Kaede had lasted this long without asking. Although Kaede could be reserved sometimes, Imari sensed in her new friend a strong streak of curiosity—one that mirrored her own.

"A little further," she promised. "We won't need to go far beyond the castle."

She continued, leading Kaede through the garden where they had first performed kata together and toward the far wall. At first glance, it was smooth and unbroken, but Imari knew where to look. She brushed aside some of the decorative hanging vines, revealing a small wooden door with a metal handle.

"It's well-hidden. I didn't notice this the other times we practiced in the gardens," Kaede said in surprise. Still, a worried wrinkle marred her forehead. "It is a weakness, though. Aren't you afraid someone from the city could sneak in? Someone like my cousin?"

Imari shook her head. "This door doesn't lead back into the city. It goes out into the mountains behind Mirai. Here, let me show you." She unbolted the door, letting it swing outward and passing through. Kaede followed close behind—close enough for Imari to feel a warm puff of breath beside her ear. She didn't mind, although she stepped to the side as soon as she could give Kaede a chance to come through after her.

The door led out onto a short, steep path that climbed the foot of the mountain. It was rocky, showing few signs of travel or human disturbance other than the short lantern-capped poles lining its sides, but Imari knew the best places to put her feet. She climbed up the uneven surface, looking back once to make sure Kaede followed. "Come on. It's not far up."

After a few yards, the path turned a corner, disappearing behind a rocky outcropping. Imari stopped once she reached it, waiting for Kaede. Before them was a small shrine, only a few meters high. It stood on four posts, with a steep roof to keep out the rain, and the mountain's stone made the floor. The red torii gate leading through to the entrance cast a midday shadow across the ground, and behind it sat two statues, both in the shape of foxes with their tails curled around their haunches. They were cast in iron, which had grown darker with weather, and each had a red yodarekake tied around their necks.

"This is what I wanted to show you," Imari said. "I had this shrine built a few years ago, and I've taken care of it ever since."

Kaede spent several long moments examining the shrine. A smile crossed her face, and she seemed much more relaxed. "I see why you aren't worried about someone breaking in this way. They'd probably upset the yokai the shrine is for." She looked over at the guardian statues. "You made it for the kitsune, didn't you? Or are the foxes an artistic choice?"

"Good guess," Imari said. "You do know a lot about spirits. Not that I ever doubted."

Kaede gestured around at the mountain. "This is a good place for foxes. They usually like forests, but a mountain offers plenty of places for them to hide too. But why?"

Instead of answering, Imari led Kaede further into the shrine itself. She paused to dip her hands in the small pool beside the entrance, and then removed her shoes, passing respectfully around the gate instead of through.

The shrine's interior was well tended. Four straw ropes hung with paper streamers stretched in a square around the simple wooden altar, and a few plates with fried tofu wrapped in leaves were placed upon it as an offering. Once Kaede had entered too, Imari spoke in a whisper. "I built this shrine because the fox spirits saved my life. I was checking in on a mining expedition in the mountain. We gather all our own metal for the products we produce. We made sure to get permission from the yokai who lived here before taking anything, and we all got along."

Old pain welled up inside Imari as she explained, and she resisted the temptation to rub the stump of her missing hand with her good one. "I'd been near the entrance to the tunnels many times before to see how the miners were doing. It pleased them to see the daimyo's daughter taking an interest in their work. It reminded them what they were doing was important, but I picked a bad day to visit. There was a cave-in. Half the miners died. The other half fled." Imari looked over to Kaede, waiting for a reaction, but the samurai gave none. She simply listened with an open expression.

Imari took a deep breath to continue. Telling the story wasn't easy, even all these years later. If she wasn't careful, she found herself drifting back into the darkness. Back to dust clogging her lungs. Back to the panicked sweat soaking through her clothes and the tears that had streaked down her face, leaving her trembling and cold. Back to the pain that stretched the seconds into hours.

"I ended up trapped with my arm pinned under a big boulder. I drifted in and out of consciousness for a while thanks to the pain and shock. When I came to, it was dark. No one was left to help me. I screamed for what felt like hours with no answer. At least, until the foxes came."

She paused, letting out a soft breath. Thinking of the foxes was comforting. Their warm tongues had licked her tears and their white-tipped tails had been just about all she could see through the dim and despair.

"There were three of them. One stayed by my side to tell me it would be all right. The other two...well, it sounds disgusting, but they bit through my wrist until I was free and breathed fire over the wound. I don't remember what happened afterwards, but they must have carried me out to the rescue team trying to make their way up the mountain. Without them, I would've died."

There was a long silence after the story ended. All Imari could hear was the soft hiss of the wind rustling the paper strips above her.

"I see now why you weren't afraid of Rin," Kaede said after a while, "and why you're not afraid of the yokai like so many are. You learned spirits can be good."

Imari nodded. "If it weren't for them, I wouldn't be here."

Kaede stepped toward her, standing by her side and gazing at the statues near the small altar. "Well, I'm glad you're here, Homura-dono. And I'm glad you told me. You must have been strong to survive something like that."

"Thank you," Imari said. "For listening. And for saying kind things."

They drifted into silence again, but this time, it was a comfortable one. She stood contentedly at Kaede's side for several minutes, thinking about everything and nothing. With some sadness, she realized this was probably the last time she would see the shrine for several months. Although her stays weren't usually long, she visited regularly, especially when she tired of the library.

Her thoughts and feelings settled once more as she bowed deeply twice before the altar. She breathed out, closed her eyes, slowly put her arms together, resting her injured one against the bottom of her palm, and bowed again. This was all she could do instead of the required clap. *I want to come back here again. With a new hand, and with Kaede as well. Ancestors, that's what I wish.*

She opened her eyes just in time to see and hear Kaede doing the same. Two bows, two claps, one bow. Kaede grinned softly, a little embarrassed, and Imari couldn't help wondering what she'd wished for. She knew it wouldn't be polite to ask. They left the shrine together, retrieving their shoes, passing between the guardian statues, and once more circling the gate. As they descended toward the garden again, Imari spoke. "So, are we even now? A story for a story."

"Friends don't need to be even, my lady," Kaede said. "But yes, we are."

Imari smiled. She wasn't against that possibility one bit.

Chapter Nine

THE NEXT MORNING BROUGHT clear skies and plenty of warm sun. It was perfect traveling weather for which Kaede was grateful. After being on the run in the cold mountains of yukimura, riding across the hills would be a pleasant change. Rin seemed to be enjoying the weather too. The white wolf sat in a large sunny patch beside the gate, watching their party prepare with casual interest.

"Is that everything?" Kaede asked Kenta, gesturing toward the small wicker baskets on either side of the stocky brown horses. All their communal supplies were stored inside, and each member of their party carried a pack as well, with a tatami mat rolled up on top for sleeping. Thanks to the new clothes and supplies Imari had bought for her, Kaede's bag was considerably heavier than it had been before entering Mirai.

"It should be." Kenta closed the baskets and came to stand beside her, offering a friendly grin. "Why, is that pack too heavy for you? I thought samurai were supposed to travel with all their worldly possessions?"

"Hmph. I'd like to see you try to travel with all your worldly possessions, Kenta," she huffed with mock indignation. "Unless you can carry your entire house on your back."

"You underestimate my strength, Kaede." Kenta gave his biceps a playful flex. "It leaves men staring and ladies sorely disappointed. Besides, I'd only have to carry half the house. My brother would take the rest."

They looked over at Takeshi, who stood a short distance away. He was conversing with Imari and Lord Homura, but he didn't seem angry, merely focused. From his behavior, Kaede suspected that with Imari determined to leave, he had turned his attention from discouraging her to making her journey as safe and successful as possible.

"Hibana-danna looks downright perky by his standards, doesn't he?" Kaede whispered under her breath, but her attention only lingered on Takeshi for a moment. As usual, her eyes drifted over to Imari and stayed there.

Imari's sleek black hair was woven into its tight braid, and she wore well-made but practical travelling clothes, with her mon displayed on her chest as well as in the middle of her back. Kaede couldn't help but smile as she caught sight of the white lilies, and her own chest swelled with pride. They adorned her clothes as well, and she had to admit that it felt good to be wearing a mon again, even if it wasn't her family's.

She was so lost in gazing at Imari she almost missed Kenta's response. "Don't let the constant frowning fool you. Takeshi can be funny if you give him the chance, although his humor's a bit dry for my taste."

"Homura-dono told me the same thing," Kaede said. "Not about his humor, but that he has hidden depths. Hopefully, I'll get to see that blossom if I'm patient."

"Speaking of patient, how long are we going to have to wait?" Kenta said, on the verge of a whine. "What are they even talking about over there?"

As Kaede watched, Imari rushed into her father's arms, giving him a fierce hug. It was unusual, especially in such a public situation, but Kaede found herself strangely touched. The deep love between them was obvious, especially in what she could see of Lord Homura's smile from over Imari's shoulder. He held her as if he never wanted to let her go, but eventually, he took a step back, allowing her to stand on her own. Imari lifted her sleeve, probably to wipe away tears.

She's lucky to have a father that loves and supports her so much. He must be worried about her, but he's letting her go on this quest anyway. I wonder what that's like, having someone who only wants the best for you without expecting anything in return.

The sound of light panting distracted her from her envious thoughts, and she turned to see Rin standing beside her. *I do have someone like that.* She reached out to scratch the special spot behind Rin's ears. *Rin might not be human, but I can always trust her.*

"We should be careful as we leave," Rin whispered, staring at the castle gates. "Hayate and Kaze are likely watching."

"Probably, but I don't think they'll interfere." She nodded toward Imari and the Hibana brothers. She and Hayate were evenly matched, and he would be unlikely to come after her while she was accompanied by three other samurai.

"What?" Kenta asked, trying to listen to the conversation. "Who won't interfere?"

Footsteps approached, and Kaede breathed a sigh of relief as Imari, Takeshi, and Lord Homura came to join them beside the horse. Kaede made a polite bow, and to her surprise, Lord Homura did the same—toward Rin.

"You have honored me by staying in Mirai these past few days, Rin of the wolf-clan. It comforts me to know you will be accompanying my daughter on this journey, and your presence speaks well to your human companion."

Rin inclined her head, fixing Lord Homura with a stare. "Your daughter has treated my friend well. As long as she travels with Kaede, she is under my protection."

Imari bowed deeply, and Kaede shot Rin a grateful look. It was a generous thing to say, especially since Rin had been mistrustful of Imari at the beginning.

"And you, Iori-san," Lord Homura said, turning toward her at last. "Serve my daughter well and keep her safe, and I will be proud to let you continue wearing my mon for as long as you wish."

"Thank you, Homura-dono, for your faith in me," Kaede said. "I'll do my best to show I'm worthy of it."

"I'm sure you will," Imari said, giving her a big smile. "All right, enough goodbyes. We should get moving before the sun rises." She mounted her horse, using her good hand and part of her other forearm to steady herself. It wasn't the most graceful motion, but Kaede couldn't help being impressed...until Imari started to slip. Fortunately, she landed back on her feet.

Kaede sidled up to her. "Need a...um. Need any help?"

Imari snorted, but when she turned she was smiling. "You were going to say 'need a hand,' weren't you?"

Kaede grinned sheepishly. "Only by accident. But do you need a lift?"

"No, I've got it."

On her next attempt, Imari was more successful. She swung up and onto the horse and settled herself into place without any further difficulties. "Thanks, though. I might need to take you up on it at some point."

"Any time." Kaede managed to settle on her own horse without too much trouble, although she noticed it giving Rin nervous glances. It seemed to know she was a spirit and not a real wolf, but Rin's presence unsettled it nonetheless, and Kaede had to tug the reins to keep it from backing up.

With one more gesture of farewell to Lord Homura, Imari started toward the gates that led from the enclosed samurai community to the rest of the city. To Kaede's relief, Lord Homura's guards had cleared the way so they could leave in relative privacy.

"So, Imari, you know which way we're going, right?" Kenta asked as they made their way through the city. It was still early morning, so the streets were sparsely populated, with only a few vendors setting up their carts and the occasional sleepy watchman.

"Don't call her by her given name, Kenta," Takeshi said, with a look of disapproval. "Just because we aren't in the presence of Lord Homura anymore doesn't mean you can—"

"Takeshi," Imari said. "I know respect is important to you, but this trip will get tedious fast if we stick with formal etiquette the entire way. As long as we're on the road, you and Kenta should call me by my given name. That goes for you too, Kaede."

Kaede's eyes widened. She hadn't expected for Imari to give her such permission in front of the Hibana brothers. "Me? Well, my lady...Imari...I'm flattered. If that's what you wish."

"It is." Imari smiled, and the sky overhead seemed even brighter.

Takeshi sighed, but after a moment, he grinned as well. "All right, Imari, you win. I'll try to restrain myself."

"Good. And to answer your question, Kenta, yes. I know where we're going. I haven't been staying in the library just to avoid you and your brother, you know."

She and Kenta picked up what sounded like a friendly, chattering conversation after that, but Kaede didn't pay much attention. Instead, she scanned her surroundings, making sure none of the people they passed were watching too closely. They attracted a few stares as they exited the city, but none that set her on edge.

No sign of Hayate. I wonder if he's waiting outside, or if he doesn't know we're leaving? Just in case, she kept her hand near the grip of her katana. She was responsible for Imari's safety now, and she wouldn't be taken by surprise again.

***

Kaede raised her chin, letting the sunshine wash over her face. It was past midday but still warm, with only a faint breeze to relieve them of the heat. Still, she didn't mind the light coat of sweat that broke across her forehead. It was a nice change from the snow of the northern mountains.

Her companions were less comfortable. Takeshi's temples glistened, and Kenta kept wiping his face with his sleeve. It helped that all four of them were on horseback. Kaede wasn't sure how they would be able to carry all their supplies otherwise, but Imari didn't look much happier for it. It was obvious from her wincing expression that her backside was getting sore.

I hope she brought comfortable sandals. Kaede glanced at Imari's dangling feet. *If she plans on walking a little later to spare her rear, her feet will pay the price.*

Unfortunately, Imari noticed her looking. "Is something amusing to you, Kaede-san?" she asked with a wry smirk. "Or are my sandals fascinating for some secret reason that has escaped me?"

Kaede's face flushed, and she suspected it wasn't merely because of the heat. "Just gazing aimlessly. Your feet happened to be in the way." She sighed, turning into what little breeze there was. "It's a pretty view. The landscape, I mean. Not your feet."

"It's a bunch of hills," Takeshi pointed out. "The same hills we've been riding along all day. Before that there were rice fields. And before that some more hills. I'll be happy when we get to that forest up ahead."

Kaede glanced ahead. If she looked closely, she could see a smudge of what looked like trees on the horizon. Part of her was disappointed. The forest reminded her uncomfortably of home, while the hills were new and different. "Maybe it's monotonous to you, but I'm from the north. No hills there, just mountains and forests. No rice fields either, our winters are too cold. Until a few weeks ago, all this was new to me."

Takeshi seemed somewhat chastened, because he dipped his head. "I suppose I shouldn't take it for granted simply because I see it every day."

Kaede nodded back, but not before Kenta jumped into the conversation. Unlike his brother, he was full of good cheer. "You're from up north, huh? Whereabouts?"

After a brief inward debate, Kaede decided on a tastefully edited version of the truth. She had to tell the Hibana brothers something about herself if they were going spend the next several weeks together. Kenta was harmless, and perhaps it would go a small way toward easing Takeshi's mistrust. "I've lived in several provinces, including Yukimura and Aozora. And since we're talking about my past, I suppose I should explain something else."

"You don't need to," Imari said, giving Takeshi and Kenta a pointed look that told them not to press. "Only if you're comfortable."

Kaede smiled, grateful for the out. "I appreciate that, Imari." She ignored the twitch at the corner of Takeshi's eye as she used the given name, especially since Imari's face lit up with approval. "But it's all right. I was going to tell them some of what I told you the other day."

"Are you sure you want to ruin the mystery?" Kenta teased, aiming his usual wide grin in her direction. "A good-looking samurai with a shrouded past, you're probably very successful with the ladies."

"Good looking?" Kaede rolled her eyes. "Pfft. And trust me, my past isn't romantic, just depressing. I was close to my aunt back home, but the two of us had a disagreement. I chose to leave before the situation escalated."

"Your aunt?" Takeshi's brow furrowed with concern. "And what did your parents think when the two of you fell out? Did they side with her?"

"They didn't side with anyone. I didn't tell them. My parents and I aren't close."

The Hibana brothers looked at her curiously. Kaede hesitated, feeling the usual spike of fear. She doubted Kenta would think differently of her, and Takeshi would be far too polite to say anything rude, but revealing herself always came with some risk. There were those who didn't approve, though they were in the minority, and more still who had no idea who ladies of autumn and gentlemen of spring were despite their presence in some of the old legends.

At Imari's encouraging glance, Kaede took a deep breath and gathered her courage. "I'm a lady of autumn," she explained, hoping they would know what she meant. "My parents didn't know how to feel about that."

She needn't have worried. Takeshi didn't look surprised. He simply gave Kaede a subtle nod of what she assumed was acceptance. Kenta's reaction was more pronounced. His eyebrows lifted almost to his hairline, and his jaw dropped a little. "Really? I never would've guessed! You look—wait, that's rude to say, isn't it?"

"A little," Kaede said, without any sting in her tone. Kenta's statement was clumsy, but not ill intentioned. "Not all of us look a certain way, but I know you didn't mean any harm. So, that's it. My big secret." *Just not the one that got a dozen Yukimura samurai killed.*

"I'm sorry." Kenta turned on Imari. "You knew about this, didn't you?"

"Yes," Imari said.

"And you didn't think to tell me?"

Imari shrugged. "It wasn't my place to tell."

"Okay, okay," Kenta said, although he continued pouting a little. "But why were your parents upset about it, Kaede?"

Kaede pressed her lips together, rolling them in a little to lick the edges. "All parents make plans for their children. They can't help it. Their plans for me weren't what I wanted. In their eyes, they've lost something."

"They didn't lose anything," Takeshi said, surprising Kaede with his vehemence. "They never had a son to begin with. It was their mistake to assume."

"I was thinking more of their vision for my future. They weren't prepared for it to change so drastically. " Kaede gave him a hesitant smile. "But thank you." Their eyes met and an understanding passed between them.

"What did Rin think about it? And where is she, by the way?" Kenta squinted, glancing over the hills and swiveling his head from side to side. "She was here a few minutes ago."

"Oh, she does that," Kaede said unconcerned. "She's probably scouting ahead." *Or helping to cover our trail so Hayate and Kaze will have a harder time following us.* "She'll turn up eventually. Anyway, yokai don't think about gender the same way humans do. It's barely relevant to them. Some choose not to have one at all."

"So, she didn't care?" Kenta asked.

Kaede shook her head. "Only for my happiness and comfort. In fact, she was kind enough to ask her mother for a favor. It's how I got these." She tugged at her top, clearing her throat awkwardly.

"You're saying a spirit wolf gave you breasts?" Kenta snickered. "That's one I haven't heard before."

"A pool with transformative powers, actually, and that's enough discussion of my body for one day, thank you," Kaede mumbled, regretting her openness just a little. "It's making me uncomfortable."

Kenta held up his hands in surrender. "Okay, okay. I'm not going to interrogate you or anything, but you did bring it up."

"He's right, Kaede-san," Imari said, smirking. "You did bring it up first." Her eyes wandered to the area in question, and Kaede's face flushed even hotter than the sun beating down above them.

To her immense relief, Takeshi cleared his throat, causing Imari to look away from her chest. "Right. So, what did you and your aunt argue about, Kaede? It must have been bad if it made you feel you had to leave home."

Kaede's mood darkened. She didn't mind the curiosity about her gender, but the probing into her past felt like an invasion of privacy. She prepared to dismiss the question, but the sound of rustling from beyond the crest of the next hill made her pause. They had come to the edge of the forest at last, and though the trees offered some shelter from the sun, she suspected they were also an excellent hiding place. She shot her companions a warning glance, holding up her hand for silence.

Footsteps somewhere nearby. Rin? She doubted it. Rin could move across any landscape like a ghost despite her glaring white pelt, and she wouldn't have hesitated to rejoin the group. Whoever or whatever was waiting for them in the forest didn't want to be seen or heard, but they weren't doing a good job of concealing themselves. Kaede's hand drifted toward the hilt of her katana, and beside her, she saw the Hibana brothers make the same motion. She didn't have much experience fighting on horseback, but if danger was lurking nearby, she didn't have much of a choice.

"I'm sure there's no need for daishō," Imari said, but she spoke in a low voice that wouldn't carry, and her eyes revealed her worry.

"I hope you're right, my lady." Kaede glanced at Imari, silently asking for instructions. "But maybe we should stay mounted, just in case?"

"I'm not sure we should," Kenta said, frowning. "The path gets narrower here. We should probably lead the horses through two at a time so they don't feel boxed in."

Takeshi sighed. "Perhaps the hills weren't so bad after all."

"What do you think, Imari?" Kaede asked. "Should we go on?"

Imari frowned in thought, but eventually nodded. "What else can we do? We can't go all the way around. This is the only path. We'll have to stay alert." She dismounted from her horse, taking the reins in her good hand and leading it toward the trees.

Together, the four of them entered the forest, Kaede in the lead, Imari behind her, and Takeshi and Kenta bringing up the rear. The road was wide enough to ride down, but far narrower than the plains they had left behind, with trees closing in on either side. She shuddered as a long branch snagged against one of her sleeves, reminding her all too clearly of the night she had left home. Then, it had almost felt like the trees were alive, trying to drag her back.

The rustling came again, and Kaede whipped her head around,

searching for what had made the noise. It didn't take her long. Her eyes caught a slip of shadow here, a flash of metal there. As she approached, a medium-sized group emerged from the depths of the forest to block the middle of the road. There were five at first count, all carrying weapons. Two wielded swords, two spears, and one giant bear of a man carried a tree trunk pretending to be a mace against his broad shoulder. He was larger even than Kenta, and Kaede braced her feet a little firmer on the ground. One hit from that monstrosity would be enough to send any normal person flying—assuming they weren't impaled first.

Imari, however, didn't seem intimidated. She passed the reins of her horse back to Takeshi, giving the men and women a short bow. "Good afternoon. I assume you're collecting tolls on this stretch of road?"

One of the figures snorted, a bulky man with a considerable gut. "Tolls," he spat, knuckles flexing around the grip of his yari. "What a pretty way of putting it."

"Be quiet."

The man turned, making way for one of his female companions. She was a thin, wiry woman with a narrow face and quick eyes, but she stood a head taller than the man. She wielded a well-made katana, already removed from its saya.

"My apologies, my lady," she said politely, although her eyes never left Imari's face. It was a rude gesture that made the hairs on the back of Kaede's neck bristle. "We do, as you say, collect tolls, although not for the Empress, I'm afraid." She gestured at her clothes, which were somewhat ragged and noticeably missing a mon. "But today, I sense a much more lucrative opportunity. I see you wear the mon of Homura."

"I don't like where this is going." Takeshi had drawn his weapon, and Kaede did the same, taking a risk and hoping her horse wouldn't bolt. "If you're looking for someone to ransom, look elsewhere. We don't do business with bandits."

"Bandits?" the woman said, arching an eyebrow. "What a disagreeable term. I prefer to think of myself and my friends as entrepreneurs."

"Entrepreneurs?" Imari repeated, without the healthy dose of skepticism Kaede thought such a statement deserved. "Then I'm sure you and your friends won't want to pass up an easy business opportunity." She rummaged around in the lining of her jacket, withdrawing a small pouch. "I have several silver coins in this purse. Plenty to keep you for a while, I assume. Take them and let us pass."

"Really? We're just gonna pay them?" Kenta said, shaking his head in disbelief. "Come on. We can't leave people like this on the road to bother some other poor travelers."

"Yes, we can," Takeshi muttered, shooting Kenta a sidelong look.

For once, Kaede agreed with him. She wasn't fond of bandits either, but any opportunity to avoid a fight was one she was willing to take. "He's right. Homura-dono's safety is our first priority."

That caught the bandit's attention. "Homura?" she said, glancing again at the lily set in bronze on their clothing. "How interesting that you should share a name with Mirai's daimyo?" She smirked, motioning her band of warriors forward. "My apologies, Lady Homura, but I'd rather have a chest of gold for your ransom than a single pouch. You understand, don't you?"

Imari sighed. "Please, miss..."

"Ishikawa," the bandit said. "Ishikawa Gin."

"Seriously?" Imari said, giving Gin a skeptical look. Kaede recognized it as well. The name was familiar to anyone who listened to the old stories. "Ishikawa, the hero-thief Ishikawa? That's not original, I'm afraid."

"But appropriate nonetheless," Gin said with a shrug. "Besides, if all goes well, our acquaintanceship won't have to last long. I'm sure your father will be more than happy to compensate me for your safe return."

Imari reached for the longer of her two swords. "I will ask you one more time. Allow us to pass."

"I'm afraid I can't do that. Ichi?" She nodded to the giant, who stepped forward with a smirk. "Bring her to me."

Chapter Ten

IMARI DREW HER KATANA, but Kaede got to hers first. She brought her glittering blade level with her head, aiming at Gin's throat. "My lady asked you to let us pass. I suggest you listen."

Gin wasn't intimidated. She stared down the edge of Kaede's katana without fear. "I suggest you put that away. We have you outnumbered and surrounded. You might get me, but are you fast enough to dodge arrows?" She glanced to the side without moving her head, and Imari followed the look, drawing in a sharp breath. Two more bandits were tucked into the foliage, obscured by leaves and brush, but Imari could make out the curve of a bow. The thought of an arrow piercing Kaede's flesh turned the bottom of her stomach into a sucking pit.

Kaede merely smiled. "And are your archers fast enough to dodge a wolf?"

Gin's brow furrowed. "What—" If she had anything else to say, it was drowned out by the sound of screaming. Pained shrieks came from the bushes, and one of the archers stumbled out of position, clutching a bloody, mangled arm.

"She's got a giant wolf with her! Call it off!"

"Oh no," Gin snarled, "I'm not letting this pretty bird fly away. Get them."

The bandits charged, sending the horses scattering, but Imari remained to face one of the spear carriers. She engaged him with a circular strike, and the force of their blades sliding against each other sent a shock along her arm. She ducked in close, near enough to catch the smell of his sweat. By the time he realized she was a threat, he had to take a step back to reach her with the point of his yari. She sent the hurried, half-hearted thrust glancing aside with her kote, slashing toward his chest at an angle. She met flesh, and her blade slid in like silk.

The man gurgled in pain and his kimono blossomed crimson. He staggered back, dropping his spear, and Imari turned, preparing to disarm her next foe. This one held a katana, and she doubted she could take him by surprise. He attacked with a grunt, and she melted back into defensive forms, dodging and parrying with as little movement as possible.

After a few missed opportunities, he grew frustrated. His upper lip peeled back over his teeth, and he huffed, putting a little too much force behind his next blow. It was the mistake Imari had been waiting for. Instead of deflecting his blade, she tilted to avoid it, slipping past his thrust and aiming for his shoulder. His body jerked when her katana scored his side, and he curled in on himself as a river of blood washed out.

Imari slid her sword free of the bandit's flesh. A loud roar jarred her. She whirled to see Kenta locked in a struggle with the giant, barely dodging his mace. Imari rushed to help him, but Takeshi came to his aid, slashing at the huge man's exposed back. His katana struck, but the man barely flinched. He turned on Takeshi, leaving Kenta to take a swipe at the backs of his legs. The giant staggered, missing his next swing.

Satisfied the two of them could handle him, Imari looked for Kaede. She was still locked in combat with Gin, and they traded blows back and forth, taking up a considerable amount of the sloping path. Kaede had slightly higher ground, but it wasn't an advantage. She had been backed up almost all the way to the bend in the road where the skittish horses had retreated, and though she deflected her opponent's strikes, she couldn't find room to maneuver.

Imari's heart throbbed hard in her throat. Kaede and Gin were evenly matched, but she wouldn't leave her friend to fight alone. She scrambled up the hill, kicking down bits of dust and rock in her hurry. When she reached them, they still whirled like a windstorm. Their blades flashed, dancing around each other, turned into gleaming lines of silver light by the sun.

All Imari's fear burst out from between her lips. "Kaede!"

Calling out her name proved to be a mistake. Kaede hesitated, just for a split second, but it was long enough. Gin's sword darted past hers, slicing along her arm. She cried out in pain, and Imari saw red. She threw herself forward, bringing her own katana down in a violent slash toward Gin's neck.

Gin twirled in time. Their blades clashed, two bolts of lightning spitting and hissing against each other. Gin was deadly quick, and Imari strained to keep up with her speed. Her muscles burned as she forced them to work faster, and trails of sweat rolled down from her hairline.

This was nothing like practicing with Takeshi or Kenta, or even Kaede. This was an actual fight, with an opponent of equal skill. For once, she truly felt the absence of her hand. One fault could mean injury or…

She had to trust her instincts. Her training. She relied on muscle memory, letting her body do the work for her. When Gin struck, she dodged. When Gin stepped forward, she stepped back. Soon, she was the one advancing, and Gin was forced to retreat down the sloping road. Walking backwards put her at a disadvantage, and Imari pressed it for all she was worth, letting her anger boil. This woman had hurt Kaede.

Finally, she saw the opening she was looking for. Gin went for her arm, the one strapped with her kote, and instead of dodging, she took the blow. As Gin adjusted to the force of the hit, she spun, bringing herself in line with the bandit's back. Soon, a bloody stripe seeped through the back of Gin's kimono. She dropped her weapon, holding up her hands.

"Enough, my lady," she panted, grimacing with pain. "You've bested me."

"Enough?" Imari repeated in disbelief. Blood dripped from her blade, spattering against the dust of the road. "You and your men almost killed my friends! You tried to abduct me. Tell me why I shouldn't kill you."

"Because that isn't the kind of person you are. And because that chest of gold wasn't just for me."

She lightened her hold on her katana's hilt. "What do you mean?"

Gin's dark eyes met hers, and honesty sparked within them. "There's a village a few miles outside the forest. Poor. Half-abandoned. They're short on rice this year."

Imari gritted her teeth, conscience wavering, until she felt a hand on her arm. She tensed, startled, but relaxed when she saw Kaede. "We won, Imari," she said, nodding back down the hill. "Look."

Imari kept her sword trained on Gin, but she stole a quick glance. The rest of the bandits were limping back into the underbrush, and Takeshi and Kenta seemed uninjured. Rin stood beside them, tail wagging proudly above her haunches, her muzzle stained slightly pink at the edges and chewing on some scraps of fabric. Imari suspected the archers were missing some clothing, as well as considerable chunks of flesh.

She sighed. She was angry for the danger Gin had put Kaede in, but she couldn't bring herself to strike an unarmed woman. She lowered her sword, turning away. "Go." She placed her foot over Gin's sword so the bandit couldn't pick it up as she retreated. "Without your katana. But you can take this." She pulled out the pouch she had offered before, tossing it toward Gin's feet.

Gin looked surprised but bent as best she could with her injury, scooping up the pouch and tucking it into her clothes. "As you wish." She disappeared into the brush beside the road, moving fast, until nothing remained but the rustling sound of her retreat.

Once she was certain Gin was gone, Imari turned to Kaede. The spike of energy from the fight faded, leaving only concern. The feeling squeezed like a knot in the middle of her chest, and she took Kaede's hand in hers, carefully drawing back the sleeve of her kimono.

"It's nothing." Kaede held still, although she remained visibly reluctant as Imari examined the cut on her upper arm. It was shallow; the result of a glancing blow, but it still leaked blood.

"It's not nothing," Imari protested. "That needs bandaging. It probably stings."

"Then I'll bandage it," Kaede said, withdrawing her arm and taking a step back. "You didn't have to defend me, my lady. I can fight my own battles. I was hired to protect you, remember? Not put you in more danger."

"You didn't put me in danger. Danger found us. If the four of us are going to travel together, we all need to protect each other."

Kaede looked as if she wanted to argue, but she said no more. She pulled away and went to retrieve the frightened horses from further down the path as Takeshi, Kenta, and Rin hurried to join them. "Imari, are you all right?" Takeshi asked, leaning over her with a look of obvious concern. "That bandit didn't hurt you, did she?"

"No, I'm fine," she sighed, still looking over at Kaede. "What about you and Kenta?" *What did I do to make her so angry? She's acting like I've done something wrong by stepping in to help her.*

"Just bruises," Kenta said. "The bandits got it worse than we did. And Rin helped."

Rin spat out the piece of fabric she had been carrying at Imari's feet, as if returning an object she had been asked to fetch. "I smell blood. Was Kaede injured when you distracted her?"

"I didn't distract her," Imari insisted. "I was trying to save her."

"Ah." Rin turned her great head, watching from a short distance as Kaede rummaged around in her horse's packs for some bandages. "Kaede doesn't always appreciate interference. Even interferences for her own good. You should have trusted her to succeed on her own. She is your yojimbo, after all. You wouldn't have offered her a place in your party if you weren't impressed with her abilities."

Imari pressed her lips together, hanging her head. She still didn't see what was so wrong about trying to help a friend and she definitely thought she and Kaede were headed in the direction of friendship. *At least, we were.*

"Give it until this evening," Rin suggested, her blue eyes strangely soft. "Kaede is quick to forgive. Perhaps too quick, in some cases."

With a sigh, Imari nodded. If Kaede wanted an apology, then an apology she would get, even if Imari wasn't entirely certain of what she was apologizing for.

***

Kaede tilted her canteen, trickling a thin stream of water over her injured forearm. The wind had picked up since their party had stopped for the night in one of the forest clearings, but she kept from hissing at the cold by sucking on her lower lip. The slash from Gin's blade still stung, but she couldn't decide whether she felt more pain or relief without the old, itchy bandages. They were currently crumpled in a crimson-stained pile by her knee, needing to be washed before they could be reused.

Rin had curled up beside Kaede's other leg, chin resting on her front paws. The wolf appeared to be dozing, but Kaede knew better, and she wasn't at all surprised when her companion spoke. "Well? Are you going over there to get new wrappings for that wound, or are you going to stay here and sulk, bleeding all over yourself?"

"I'm not bleeding anymore," Kaede mumbled, glancing toward the shared supply packs next to the horses. There was a roll of clean bandages inside, but Imari was currently propped against the bags, bent over what Kaede suspected was a map of the border between Akatsuki Teikoku and Tsun'i. Kenta and Takeshi were close by, preparing something to eat over the fire, but Kaede had chosen to sit apart while seeing to her injury. She had mixed feelings about talking to Imari—partly because she was annoyed with her for interfering that afternoon, and partly because she felt guilty for responding with such rudeness.

She shouldn't have put herself in danger like that. I'm supposed to be her yojimbo—not the other way around. Besides, I had a handle on that bandit. But she did help. I didn't have to shout at her for defending me. It's more than anyone else has done for me lately.

Kaede gave Imari another uncertain glance. Half of her wanted to demand an apology and the other half wanted to offer one. In the end, she chose to remain where she was. "If you're trying to get me to talk to her, it won't do any good," she muttered, slumping further forward on the rock she had chosen for her seat. "I don't even know what to say."

Rin cracked open her left eye, and the brush of her tail gave one lazy flick. "Perhaps 'Thank you' is a good place to start, or, even, 'Could I get some more of those bandages'? It's better than pretending not to stare at her."

Kaede's face burned against the bite of the night wind. "That obvious, huh?"

"Pups learning to hunt have more subtlety."

"Hmm." Kaede looked over at the fire again. This time, she caught Imari looking back. Their gazes met, and Imari offered her a small, hesitant smile—a silent question. Kaede smiled back. After an awkward moment of staring, Imari rose from her place by the fire pit and rolled up her map, putting it back in the saddlebag behind her.

"Sun and Moon," Kaede sighed, "she's coming over here. Rin, what do I do?"

"Nothing," Rin said. "Imari is the one who appears to be doing something." With a weary sigh, the white wolf lifted off the ground and padded over to the fire, joining Kenta and Takeshi. That left Kaede all on her own, holding her injured arm against her stomach as Imari approached.

Luckily, Imari spoke first. "I thought you could use some of these," she said, holding out the roll of bandages.

Kaede stood and bowed, taking the new bandages from Imari's outstretched hand and nudging away the dirty ones with her foot so they wouldn't be in plain sight. She doubted Imari would be upset by a little blood, but it felt rude to have them sitting there. "I appreciate the thought, but it's not that bad."

Imari gave her a knowing look. "If it's not that bad, I don't suppose you'd mind letting me take a look?"

It was phrased as a request, but Kaede could tell Imari wasn't going to take no for an answer. "If that's your wish, my lady."

"Imari, please. Don't pull a Takeshi on me. He always gets formal whenever we have a fight. Takes twice as long to get over it."

"We aren't fighting," Kaede protested, but Imari gripped the sleeve of her other arm, the one that wasn't injured, and pulled her back into a seated position.

"Then I suppose I don't need to apologize for stealing your thunder earlier?"

"It's not about you stealing my thunder," Kaede said. "I don't need the glory of defeating an opponent, and I appreciate that you were trying to help."

"Exactly." Imari brought Kaede's arm into her lap for closer inspection. "You looked like you were in danger."

"But I was handling myself. I've always had to."

Imari avoided the statement, glancing down at her arm instead. "This doesn't look as bad as I thought," she said, unwrapping the fresh bandages. "You've already washed it, right?"

Kaede nodded. Obediently, she held out her arm so that Imari could dress it properly. "Okay, think of it this way then. I'm you. You're Takeshi. Now do you see the problem?"

She knew her words got through, because Imari closed her eyes and exhaled through her nose. "Yes. I see the problem. Ancestors, you're right. When did I turn into my overbearing ex-fiancé? I'm sorry, Kaede."

"I'm sorry for yelling at you." Kaede lowered her eyes guiltily, only to see that Imari's fingers were still resting near her wrist, even though her wound was freshly bandaged. "For what it's worth, that was some pretty amazing swordsmanship. You fought well."

"So did you," Imari said. "You're right. I know you didn't need my help. Still I…wanted to give it. Especially after Gin hurt you. Do you think she was telling the truth about the village?"

Kaede shrugged. "She could have been lying, but I'd put coin on the truth. That was my gut feeling. Why else would a bunch of bandits with no armor and old weapons attack four trained samurai, even with a forest to hide in? It's basically suicide."

"My thoughts exactly." Imari looked up toward the sky, while Kaede found herself looking at Imari's face. Her skin looked especially pale in the dark and she seemed tired. "I've never been this far from home before," she whispered, her eyes carrying some of the stars. "Is it always a little sad?"

"A little sad," Kaede whispered. "A little happy, too. A lot exciting. You'll get used to it."

"You think?"

Kaede smiled. "I know. You beat up a bunch of bandits on your first day out. You'll be fine."

"The moon is bigger and brighter without the city lights." Imari's voice trailed off, and Kaede felt a shiver where their arms were still pressed together.

"Here," she said, reaching for the blanket on top of her pack. "It's cold. We can share." She tucked it around both their shoulders, and the two of them drifted into silence again.

"I see Lady Tsukine's face," Imari said after a while, gesturing up with her shorter arm. "See? I can make it out better here."

Kaede sighed softly. "I loved hearing about her as a child. It was one of my favorite stories, although I couldn't decide whether I wanted to be the moon goddess or the mortal man she fell in love with. It took me a few years to figure out I wanted to be both."

"Be a moon goddess and fall in love with a moon goddess?" Imari said, giving her shoulder a friendly nudge beneath the wrapping of the blanket. "You might need to set your sights a little closer to earth, Kaede."

"Hey. I've already changed from a boy into a woman. Who's to say I can't win the heart of a goddess?" At first, Imari said nothing, and Kaede's cheeks grew warm despite the cold. She realized what she had accidentally implied, and her tongue became thick with embarrassment. "I mean—"

Before she could save herself, Imari laughed. "It's okay, Kaede. If a beautiful goddess tried to seduce me, I'd probably be moonstruck too."

"I didn't say anything about seducing," Kaede said, a little offended. "I was talking about love. Storybook love, like the Moon taking a mortal husband. She was willing to sacrifice everything for him."

"Ah, so you're a romantic at heart." Imari flashed her a grin, and Kaede bent down, covering some of her face with the blanket.

"So?"

"So, it's refreshing. Don't change."

The two of them drifted off into another silence, but it was a comfortable one. They sat together beneath the blanket until Kenta called them both back over to the fire, urging them to get something to eat. "Hey, Imari! Kaede! Come get some grub. I think I managed to make it pretty appetizing."

"Let's hope he did," Kaede said. "Otherwise, we're in for a really long trip." She began to rise from her seat on the rock, and to her surprise, Imari rose with her, keeping the blanket around both their shoulders and letting their arms remain touching.

"I'd give it a fifty-fifty shot. Kenta doesn't have to cook for himself often, but when he does, it's always an adventure."

***

Clouds had devoured the stars, leaving the night dark and cold. The moon cast a faint, swirling beam of silver light down from the sky, but it was barely enough to illuminate the path ahead through the thick forest canopy. Still, Hayate rode down it on the horse he had purchased in Mirai, trusting the black shadow beside him to guide the way. Kaze's eyes were far better than his, and his nose keener still.

"Hayate?"

He turned toward the sound of the wolf's voice, hand already hovering near the hilt of his blade. "Did you find the trail, Kaze?"

"Yes." Kaze's sleek black form came to stand beside him. The horse edged away, ears flicking nervously. "Rin has tried to cover their trail, but she couldn't conceal this."

Hayate's brow rose in surprise. "Conceal what?"

"A skirmish." Kaze lowered his great head, snuffling at the dirt of the path. "People fought here. Several. Blood was spilled."

Hayate followed Kaze's gaze, but he could see nothing. "No bodies?"

"None. The injured escaped."

Hayate breathed a sigh of relief. That meant Kaede was alive. He didn't want to consider his mother's disappointment if he didn't bring her back as he'd promised. "And can you tell which way Kaede and her party went?"

Kaze's ears flattened. He circled as if trying to pick up a scent, tail swishing low between his hind legs. "I don't know. Wait, yes." He lifted his head again, nose to the wind. "This way. But Hayate..."

Hayate frowned. He knew what was coming before his companion spoke and snorted in annoyance. "Let me guess. You're going to suggest we turn back again."

"This journey is changing you, Hayate," Kaze said imploringly. "Kaede means no harm to you or Setsuna. She may be injured. Are you sure you still wish to drag her back home as a prisoner? Enough people have already died—"

"And without Kaede, more will die," Hayate insisted. "I am not unaware. If mother says she needs her, then I'll bring her, by any means necessary."

Kaze let out a sigh and continued on into the darkness. Hayate rode close behind as another blue cloud passed over the moon.

***

"I spy, with my little eye—"

"Please, Kenta," Takeshi groaned from atop his horse. He gripped the reins in one hand, running the other over his forehead and through his hair in exasperation. "No more of that game. It's too hot."

Kaede couldn't argue. They had been on the road for a week, but aside from a day-long detour into the forest where Gin's bandits had ambushed them, they still hadn't made it out of the hills. She was starting to come around to Takeshi's point of view. The mornings and evenings were lovely, but after a while, the wavy scrubland did blend into monotony, especially in the afternoons.

The villages they passed were small, not the kind of places that regularly hosted visitors. Most nights, they slept out under the stars—or, more accurately, her companions did. Kaede spent as much of the night as she could manage awake, keeping watch with Rin at her side. There had been no further signs of Hayate since their departure from Mirai, but that didn't mean he wasn't following them.

"Well, do you have any other suggestions, Takeshi?" Kenta asked, distracting Kaede from her thoughts. "You vetoed singing."

"You were scaring the wildlife," Kaede teased, catching Imari's eye. They had chosen to ride abreast, pulled together by an unspoken desire to remain near each other. Today, she seemed to be in good spirits despite the baking sun. Her eyes held a cheerful glint and her lips, a smile.

"I think you mean he sounded like the wildlife, Kaede."

She and Imari shared a look, and even Takeshi snorted in mild amusement.

"Hey," Kenta protested, glaring at them from over his shoulder. "Excuse me. I have a lovely singing voice. It's not my fault you can't recognize talent."

"Maybe," Imari laughed, "but if you have so much talent, why do you waste it on the same two songs over and over again?"

Kenta huffed, deliberately turning his horse away from them as they started up the next hill. "If you wanted a different selection, you could have asked. Or give singing a try yourself."

"I'll pass," Kaede said with a wry smile. "I think you've done enough singing recently for all four of us."

"What about you, Kaede?" Kenta asked, drawing her out of her thoughts. "What traveling games do they play up north?"

"We play 'don't slip over the edge of the mountain and fall to your death.' I'm not sure Takeshi would approve of that one."

"On the contrary," Takeshi said with a slight smile, "I think that sounds like a fun game, especially if Kenta starts singing again."

"You'd really murder me because you're tired of my singing?" Kenta asked, giving Takeshi a wounded look of reproach. "Some brother you are."

While they glared at each other, Kaede found herself smiling. It was nice to see that Takeshi wasn't always a stick in the mud, and his banter with Kenta reminded her a little of how she and Hayate had acted once upon a time, before her natural affinity for the yokai and Setsuna's favoritism put a wedge between them. He had been more like a brother to her than a cousin, at least until they had become rivals.

"Kaede?" She turned, glancing left to where Imari was keeping pace with her. "Are you all-right? You seem lost in thought."

"Homesick," she said, offering a small shrug. "That's all."

Another voice, one that didn't come from Imari or the Hibana brothers, picked up when hers trailed off. "Then perhaps home is where you should return."

Kaede looked up. The horse beneath her stiffened as she did, sensing her alarm, and she brought her hand down to its neck to soothe it. Her other hand, however, flew to the hilt of her blade as she searched for the speaker. The voice was a familiar growl, but it didn't belong to Rin.

At first, Kaede didn't see anything. Then a flash of black caught her eye, passing through the underbrush beside the path like a midday shadow, and an answering tingle ran down her neck. *Kaze? But if he's here.*

"Is Hayate with you?" she asked, bringing her horse to the middle of the path. The rest of her companions came to a halt as well, hanging a few paces back.

"Kaede, what's wrong?" Kenta asked. "Is someone out there? Who is Hayate?"

"Jealous cousin," Kaede muttered. "Let me handle this. If something happens to me, get Imari out of here."

Takeshi nodded, but Imari shook her head, adopting a stubborn glare. "If something happens, I'm staying right here with you, Kaede."

"Please, not now," Kaede pleaded, her eyes shifting between Imari's face and the bushes. She had lost sight of Kaze, but she could still feel the weight of the wolf's gaze on her, sending prickles up the back of her neck. Hopefully, Rin was hidden somewhere nearby too, prepared to leap out if she did end up in a fight.

"Come out, Kaze. You wouldn't have spoken up if you wanted to stay hidden."

The brush rustled, and a moment later, Kaze's long, sleek black body slipped out onto the path. He stood just as high as Rin, his gleaming white fangs bright against his black face. Kenta sucked in a surprised breath. Imari drew her katana from its saya. Takeshi brought his horse closer, preparing to defend her.

Kaze ignored them all. His yellow eyes remained fixed on Kaede. "Hayate isn't far behind. He intends to bring you back to Setsuna."

Kaede hesitated. Kaze had never proven himself to be a liar, but she didn't trust his motivations. He was loyal to Hayate, just as Rin was loyal to her. "And what about you? Are you going to help him bring me back to Yukimura as a prisoner?"

"I will help Hayate however I can."

The statement should've sounded like a "yes," but Kaede knew better. She was familiar enough with yokai, and with Kaze in particular, to read between the lines. "You don't want him to catch me, do you?"

Kaze's bushy black tail flicked. "Not yet. I want him to catch you later, when his anger and resentment has worn itself out and he is more willing to listen to reason."

Kaede heard more, what the wolf wasn't saying. "But you're not going to lie to him either, are you? You're going to keep helping him follow us."

Kaze lowered his eyes. "It keeps him out of trouble and away from his mother. Setsuna no longer acts like herself. I never thought I would say this, but I no longer trust her, especially around Hayate."

Kaede resisted the temptation to flinch at the mention of her aunt. She had to agree with Kaze. It was better for Hayate to keep himself busy chasing her than return to Kousetsu. There, he would either be forced to command more men to their deaths in the name of Setsuna's corrupted cause, or sacrifice his own life in vain. Despite their differences, she didn't want him to suffer either fate.

Kaede gave a small bow. "He's family, Kaze. So, thank you. You understand."

"He does," another voice said, and Rin emerged from the

underbrush. She stood a few yards away from her brother, facing him down with a stiff, protective posture. "At least, I hope so."

Kaze kept his place, although the fur along his back bristled and his tail rose higher above his haunches. "I protect and defend my human as you protect and defend yours, Rin. I still believe there is good in Hayate. Time away from Setsuna may help him to see the error of his ways. Until then, I will keep him safe."

"If he does catch us, I won't go easy on him," Rin warned with a low growl. "If he harms Kaede, I'll kill him."

"Let us hope that doesn't come to pass."

The two of them continued staring at each other in silent understanding, and a shiver raced down Kaede's spine. *If Hayate attacks me, Rin will step in. If Rin hurts him while protecting me, Kaze will go after her. My best friend might be forced to fight her own brother, all because of this mess I caused.*

"We'll travel fast," Kaede said to Kaze. "Keep working on him. He wasn't always like this."

Kaze almost seemed to sigh, regarding her with sad, tired eyes. "I know."

Without a goodbye, he melted back into the brush, disappearing and blending in with the rest of the shadows.

Reluctantly, Kaede turned back to the rest of her companions. The Hibana brothers gazed at her with matching expressions of confusion and worry, but she noticed a distinct sparkle of curiosity in Imari's eyes.

"I promise I'll explain all of this later, but right now, we need to go. If Hayate is on our trail, we don't have much time. Once we find a spot to make camp—"

"No," Takeshi said, in a sharp voice that made Kaede want to snap to attention. "I need an explanation now. Why did you sign on as Homura-dono's yojimbo if you knew you were being followed by someone dangerous? What about her safety? What if this cousin of yours hurts her simply to get to you?"

"I—" Kaede fumbled, unable to come up with a suitable answer. She was supposed to be protecting Imari, but instead, she had exposed her to more danger.

"I knew her cousin was following us," Imari said. Kaede aimed a hesitant look in her direction, but Imari wasn't speaking to her. She was talking to Takeshi; whose face was still a stone slate of anger. "She told me back in Mirai. I asked her to come anyway."

"But why?" Kenta asked. Unlike Takeshi's fury, his face read concern.

Imari straightened her shoulders, and when she spoke, it was exactly as a daimyo would. "Because I need her, and because I like her," she said, in a tone that allowed no room for argument. "She wants to help me in my quest, and if I can help her by keeping her away from her cousin, all the better. Everyone wins."

"Assuming we don't get killed," Takeshi said. "Homura-dono, I have to protest—"

"Your protest is noted. For now, we continue on. Unless you want to wait around here for this man to find us?"

Takeshi obviously wasn't satisfied, but eventually, he gave a stiff bow from atop his horse. "Very well, Homura-dono. We'll continue."

They spent the rest of their ride in silence as afternoon faded to evening. For once, Kaede actually found herself missing Kenta's singing. It was better than the icy emptiness that echoed between the four of them now.

***

The sun had sunk past the pink-blue line of the horizon by the time they stopped for the night. The moon hung high in the sky, but the beams of silver light didn't comfort Kaede as much as they usually did. She sat slumped against her pack a considerable distance from the fire, trying to listen to the sounds of birds and nighttime insects instead of harsh voices.

Imari and Takeshi argued. They were obviously trying to keep it to a whisper, but judging by the snatches Kaede could overhear, both were speaking harshly.

"Reckless, stupid."

"I'm not helpless! I knew when I asked her—"

"But she put you in danger."

"All choices come with risks. Why do you get to decide which ones are safe enough for me to make? My father would never dictate—"

"Please, my lady, don't bring your father into this."

"Then don't bring yourself into this! And don't call me that, Takeshi. I've told you a hundred times."

Kaede sighed, resting her cheek against the pack, using it as a pillow to muffle the argument in at least one ear. She didn't want to watch the violent hand gestures, or the glimpses of anger the firelight brought from both their faces.

I ran away to avoid causing any more trouble, but it seems trouble has followed me. I spread it wherever I go. Maybe I'd be better off alone after all.

"Kaede?"

It was Kenta's voice calling to her, not Takeshi's or Imari's. She turned, flipping over to the other side. He had crouched down beside her, one hand extended, as if he wanted to grasp her shoulder in friendship but wasn't sure he should.

"You're not going to ask me to get involved, are you?" she asked, aiming a quick glance past his shoulder to the fire. Takeshi and Imari were still involved in an intense-looking conversation, although they had tried to lower their voices again. "I'll only make it worse if I do."

"This has nothing to do with you." Kenta seemed to come to a decision, sitting down beside her and propping himself against one of the other packs. "These two go at it all the time. I'd say they fight like an old married couple, but all the sexual tensions burnt to ash at this point."

Kaede grimaced. "That doesn't really make me feel better. I don't want to be the excuse two ex-lovers use to argue, either."

"I understand." Kenta placed both hands behind his head, leaning further back and gazing up at the stars. "I promise it'll get better after this. Give it some time. Takeshi will get over himself, he'll apologize to Imari, and we can concentrate on getting to Tsun'i as fast as possible."

Kaede pulled her bottom lip between her teeth. Her stomach was still in knots, although Kenta's soft voice slowly untangled some of them. "But should he get over it? He's right. I did put Imari in danger by agreeing to come along. My cousin thinks I betrayed my aunt by leaving after our disagreement. It was bad. He's going to try and bring me back home, and if I don't go, he could use force. You saw how Imari could've gotten hurt with those bandits. She's a great fighter, but if she tries to step in for me—"

"You know what?" Kenta turned to meet her eyes, offering a soft smile of reassurance. "You sound like a person who hasn't had many friends before, aside from Rin, of course. And trust me, because I know from experience: Imari's one of the best, most loyal friends you could have. If she wants to start acting like a friend to you, you should go with it. And if that means she wants to step in when you're in trouble, that's her choice to make."

"But what if I don't want her to make that choice for me?" Kaede sighed, glancing over at Imari once more. She and Takeshi seemed to have calmed down, but they were turned away, so she couldn't see their faces. Instead, she studied the loose braid falling down the middle of Imari's back, running through the middle of a white lily. "She's got plenty of her own problems. If she starts trying to fix mine, too, it gets awkward. She barely knows me."

Kenta's smile became a smirk. This time, he made contact when he reached out, giving her shoulder a friendly nudge with his fist. "Oh, she's getting to know you, Kaede. And she likes what she's getting to know. I haven't seen her look at someone the way she looks at you in a long time."

A sliver of moonlight finally broke through Kaede's shroud of gloom. "What? Really?" *She likes getting to know me, and what did Kenta mean, "the way she looks at me"?* Her heart did a flip in her chest, and a good deal of the tension finally eased. "So, this arguing..."

"I'm not saying my brother's jealous, but I think he's concerned about more than just a possible threat to Imari's safety. Trust Imari to tell him to back off. He's not stupid. He'll get the message. In the meantime, sit tight. Things will get a lot better." He sat up and stretched his arms up to the sky, preparing to stand.

"Kenta?"

He paused in the middle of getting up. "Yeah?"

"Thanks."

"You're welcome. And for what it's worth, if that lame cousin of yours comes around, I'll help you kick his ass. Okay?"

Kaede laughed. If this was what having friends was like, maybe it wasn't so bad. "Okay. You've got it...friend."

Chapter Eleven

THE CITY OF YIN had once been great. The sweeping jade roofs, the great tiered towers, and the broad staircases leading to the upper levels of the city told Imari that much. As they led their horses past the outskirts, however, she began to understand why some referred to it as the City of Ghosts.

Faded green banners flapped in the breeze, but they seemed worn and old, as if someone had forgotten to replace them. Any mon they had once held was no longer visible. The edges of the street had crumbled, and the horses' hooves echoed eerily on the broken road. The glittering green roofs needed a thorough patching, and Imari caught the occasional whiff of garbage and manure from the alleyways. Strangest of all, there were hardly any people. The marketplace should have been packed to the brim at this time of day, bustling with merchants, craftsmen, and even samurai. Instead, only a few lonely stalls sat on the sides of the road, and a good number of those weren't even occupied.

Her companions were similarly unsettled. "It's the middle of the day," Kaede murmured, eyes narrowed in suspicion. "Where is everyone?"

"Maybe they heard you were coming and went to hide," Kenta teased, but even his voice had lost some of its brightness. Takeshi gave him a look but didn't comment. He had been somewhat withdrawn and cold the past three weeks, although true to his word, he hadn't brought up the subject of Kaede's cousin again. At least, not directly. Imari had caught him circling the camp in the middle of the night more than a few times and had thought it better not to bother him about it.

"I'll admit it's creepy," Imari explained, "but from what I've read, it makes sense. Yin used to be a thriving port before the Jade Sea solidified, but when the ships stopped coming—"

"The people stopped coming too." Kaede nodded. "That explains why the buildings look so old. It's like stepping back a hundred years in time."

It was an accurate description. Fine as they had once been, the architecture did seem outdated—a politer word would have been "picturesque." It was nothing like Mirai, with its solid shapes and firm foundations. There was a handmade quality to these buildings that would have been charming if not for the lack of people.

"So, what do we do?" Kenta asked. "This place doesn't exactly seem to give warm welcomes."

He craned his neck, looking around. A few vendors waved, trying to catch his attention, but their efforts seemed halfhearted at best. They had passed desperation and slipped into lethargy, just like the city itself. The ones who noticed Rin recoiled in fear and ducked behind their stalls, a fact the wolf didn't seem to mind. The city didn't bother her like it did the rest of the group. Her tongue lolled and her tail stood up proudly, the tip wagging slowly back-and-forth.

Imari frowned. They did need supplies, and someone in this city was bound to be grateful for a few gold coins, spirit wolf or not. "First order of business is to find a place to stay, preferably one that serves food. There has to be an inn around here somewhere, right?"

"Right," Kaede said. "Should we check on the other side of the square?"

"We can try." Takeshi aimed a sideways glance at Rin. "But I wouldn't be surprised if some of the innkeepers bolt their doors and pretend not to be home. Our party is a little strange, you have to admit."

Kaede gave him a frown, and Imari stepped in to cut off the brewing confrontation. "I'm sure we'll find someplace, Takeshi," Imari said, in a tone that implied he should shut his mouth. "Not everyone is afraid of the yokai. I welcomed Rin into Mirai, didn't I? And you and Kenta allowed her into your home."

"Besides, Rin is cute," Kenta added.

"I am a wolf spirit," Rin growled, the picture of offended dignity. "We are not cute." Still, Imari had been observing Rin closely enough along their journey to catch a sparkle of amusement in her blue eyes. If she'd been human, she would've been smirking.

"Fine, you're not cute," Kaede said. "You're fierce." But the way she reached over to scratch Rin's ears belied her statement.

Maybe Rin isn't cute. Imari's mood perked up when she saw Kaede's smile return. *But you definitely are.* She stuck to admiring Kaede's grin at first, but gradually, Imari found her eyes slipping lower without her permission. Even though she'd had several weeks of close contact to drink the vision in, something about looking at Kaede still made her heart skip a beat and her breath quicken. Her arms were strong, but also lean and graceful, and her hands—

Imari blinked. She didn't have time to consider how rough or soft different parts of Kaede's palms might be. But still, her instincts told her the looks she offered weren't entirely unwelcome. Kaede had caught her a few times in the past, only to blush and look away while hiding what Imari hoped was a smile.

"There," Takeshi said, pulling her from her thoughts. They had crossed the marketplace only to arrive at a building slightly less run down than the others. It was two stories, and judging by the siding, someone had made repairs recently, even if they were a bit shoddy. An ornate sign hung above the door, older than any other around the square, but it was clear that someone had been doing their best to maintain it. Nonetheless, the green wood had grown dark with humidity, and the golden edges had long since lost their shine. Several bronze Tsun'i characters—Zhong An Inn—had been etched in the middle. Perhaps a long time ago, that name would have been widely known, but Imari couldn't place it.

"This is probably our best bet." Kaede glanced at the window screens, studying them closely. "Second floor? No trees or balconies to make breaking in easy."

Takeshi nodded. At least they agreed on one thing: keeping her safe. Even she saw the sense in their decision. "Okay, second floor it is. Let's see if they have any vacancies, shall we? And before you ask, Takeshi, I won't flash my circles around. The fact that we came in on horses will attract enough attention."

"Oh, don't worry about it," Kenta said cheerfully. "Thieves aren't going to mess with us while we have Rin on our side, right?" He scratched her ears, a gesture Rin had graciously given him permission to perform, and her tail wagged back and forth.

"Good point," Imari said, glancing thoughtfully at the door. Still, we shouldn't bring Rin in yet. I'll go check it out."

Kenta nodded. "And I'll keep an eye on the horses."

"Need some help?" Kaede offered, but Imari looped an elbow through hers, urging her to hand off her reins to Takeshi.

"Nope. You're coming with me, Kaede." She leaned in, brushing aside a loose strand of Kaede's auburn hair and whispering beside her ear. "Please, don't leave me alone with Takeshi. I need to see a smile once in a while or I'll go nuts."

Kaede didn't smile, but a crimson blush did bloom across her cheeks. Her lips moved soundlessly, as if she wasn't quite sure what to say, and Imari felt the ticklish wings of butterflies flutter in her stomach. The flush was even better than a smile, in her opinion. She only hoped she wasn't wrong about what it might mean.

"I'll...you and Rin can handle it, right, Kenta?" Kaede mumbled, patting his shoulder in passing and heading toward the door. Imari was pleased to notice Kaede didn't attempt to unlock their arms, either. Together, they entered the inn, with Takeshi a step behind.

The inside wasn't quite as depressing as the outside. Clean and warm, there was enough light to bring a little life into the place. Imari stepped out of her sandals and loosened her grip on Kaede's elbow in order to put on the slippers provided.

Kaede looked up and saw a plump, smiling woman dressed in Tsun'i fashion hurrying across the mat to greet them. She wore a qipao dress, orange and purple, and although it had seen better days, not a thread of the floral stitching was torn or frayed, speaking to a certain fastidiousness. Her hair was pulled back from her temples and knotted together in a horizontal bun on top of her head, with a rose ornament pinned to one side and a brooch to the other. *They must be family heirlooms*, Imari thought as the woman clasped her hands in front of her and bowed.

"Good afternoon, dear guests. Welcome."

Imari gave a shorter bow back. "Thank you for allowing us to trouble you. Do you have rooms available?"

"Oh yes, my lady," the woman said. "It would be our honor to take care of you. How many would you like?"

"Two, please," Imari answered, before Kaede or Takeshi could say anything else. "We have a party of four, so two futons in each one. Is that possible?"

That got Kaede's attention. Her eyebrows rose and her mouth dropped open a bit until she seemed to realize she was gaping. Her jaw snapped shut, and she looked away, clearly embarrassed but showing the edges of a grin.

Imari smirked as well. It was far too soon for that kind of thinking, but that didn't mean she couldn't enjoy a few minutes alone with Kaede in their room, either.

"Of course," the innkeeper continued. "And if I may be so bold, is your party planning to visit the Jade Sea? It is quite beautiful this time of year."

Takeshi's brow furrowed. "With all due respect, that isn't your business."

"My deepest apologies," the woman said, bowing again. "I wasn't trying to pry into your personal affairs. It's just that most travelers to Yin come here for that reason, and I was going to make a suggestion."

"Please, go ahead," Imari said, aiming a silencing look in Takeshi's direction. "We would love to hear any advice you have."

"Most of the guides who escort travelers such as yourselves along the edge of the sea gather at the pier during the day, waiting for customers. If you would like to leave your things and go in search of a guide, I will be more than happy to prepare your rooms."

Imari nodded. "Thank you! That sounds perfect." She looked to her companions, stifling a giggle as Kaede reached back to rub the base of her neck.

"Just one other thing, ma'am. How do you feel about a wolf spirit sleeping in your stables?"

***

"So, what did the innkeeper say we were looking for?" Kaede asked as she descended the steps to the pier, shielding her eyes with her hand. It was late afternoon, going on evening, and unfortunately their group of four faced directly into the setting sun. "Not that I can see anything. Ugh, my eyes are watering."

"Should have worn your hat," Imari sang from a short distance ahead. "Let's keep going. If this is their profession, I'm sure the guides will find us. Oh, Sun and Moon!"

Imari's exclamation didn't sound upset, but Kaede stiffened anyway, hurrying to close the gap between them. When she came to a stop at Imari's shoulder, she saw what had caught her friend's attention and couldn't help gasping too.

They had reached the middle of the wide stone steps, and from this vantage point, she had a clear view of the Jade Sea. A brilliant green, it sparkled as brightly as the Empress' jewels in the low light. Its surface seemed to shift and stir like any other ocean, but Kaede knew it was an illusion. It had been frozen for hundreds of years, and all that remained were remnants of the ancient waves.

"It's beautiful," she murmured, staring in awe. The longer she stared, the more shades of green she saw: bright ones that glowed almost yellow at the peaks of the waves, and darkening to deep hues that bordered on blue.

Imari reached out to take her hand, giving her fingers a warm squeeze. "Yes. It is."

The awkward sound of a throat clearing made Kaede pull her hand back, although she found she missed the feel of Imari's palm against hers. She turned to see Takeshi staring at them with his usual blank, serious expression, while Kenta wore a smug, knowing look on his face.

"We should..." Kaede mumbled, hurrying down the steps at the head of the group. On the way, she shot Imari a look of apology. She hadn't really wanted to withdraw her hand.

When they arrived at the bottom of the steps, Kaede felt the same eeriness that had come over her in the marketplace creep back in. The harbor had been beautiful once, judging by the buildings and the grand wall separating the city from the shipyard, but it was in a depressing state of disrepair. Parts of the wall were old and crumbling, and no one had seen fit to fix them. The buildings seemed mostly abandoned, as if their inhabitants had fled into the city itself. There were only a few carts around, and some of those didn't even have merchants.

"Our adventure in the ghost town continues," Imari said, taking it all in.

"Ghost town is right. Look." Kenta pointed out toward the sea, and Kaede followed the gesture. There, a few yards out from the docks, were ancient looking ships. Or, more accurately, the bottom halves of ancient looking ships. The tops had rotted away, but the sections under the water remained, preserved as if in amber. The waves were clear enough to see through, and Kaede could make out the bottoms of the boats perfectly.

"Wow. I don't know whether that's creepy or cool."

"Cool," Kenta said.

"Definitely cool," Imari agreed.

Even Takeshi looked intrigued. "It is fascinating."

"Guides," Kaede reminded them, after a moment. "We have to find one who's actually willing to go across the sea with us instead of just hitting the tourist highlights."

"If you're looking for that kind of guide, perhaps I can be of assistance?"

Kaede stiffened in surprise. The voice came from just a few centimeters behind her, and she whirled around, instinctively reaching for her katana. When she caught sight of who had spoken, however, she breathed a sigh of relief. The person was standing uncomfortably close, but they were only a small figure in a hood. She couldn't tell much about them, not even gender, but she did suspect the stranger was old from the way their back bent and the wrinkles on the visible part of their face.

"Excuse me," she said, taking a step back to regain some personal space. "We are in the market for a guide. We have to get to the other side."

"Then you've found the right person." The stranger bowed and Kaede bowed in return. "You may call me Bo. I'm the most experienced guide in this city."

"The most experienced?" Imari placed her good hand on her hip as she rose from her own bow, studying Bo. "My name is Homura Imari, and did this just become a job interview?"

"Perhaps," Bo said. "Where does your journey take you?"

"To Hongshan," Imari said. "Ever heard of it?"

Bo paused, lifting a hand to their chin. Upon closer inspection, Kaede could see a little more of their face, but not much. They still hadn't lowered their hood, and aside from pale skin and dark eyes, their features seemed soft and nondescript. "Hongshan. That is an unusual destination. I know where it is, but few travelers wish to go there. If you don't think me rude for asking, don't you find the rumors of dragons frightening?"

"It's not dragons we're looking for," Imari said, "but a certain person we believe may be living there. Will you help us?"

Bo nodded. "I will take you there for thirty golden circles, half to be paid in advance. You will buy your own supplies. We leave in two days' time. Are those terms agreeable?"

Imari gave Bo a shrewd look. "Fifteen circles," she said, lips pressing together. "The innkeeper did say we would have our pick of guides if we came to the harbor."

"Oh, Ancestors," Kenta sighed, as Takeshi muttered, "Not again."

Kaede aimed a sidelong look at Kenta. "Does she haggle often?" So far, they had mostly used their own supplies, so she hadn't had a chance to witness Imari's bargaining prowess in action.

"Unfortunately, yes," Kenta whispered back. "For a wealthy daimyo's daughter, she really can be a cheapskate unless it's for charity."

Bo did not seem intimidated. "Twenty-five circles. I guarantee you, none of the other guides have been to Hongshan before. Few bother venturing to the dragon mountain these days. You won't find anyone who knows the area better than I do."

"Twenty," Imari countered. "Final offer."

Kaede waited with bated breath, but thankfully, Bo nodded. "You drive a hard bargain, Homura Imari, but I agree to your price. Twenty circles it is, although that is a fairly cheap price for a new hand."

Imari's eyes widened. "What?" She cradled her left arm against her stomach, letting the sleeve of her kimono conceal the stump almost self-consciously. "But how did you—"

Bo gave her a mysterious smile. "People only search for Kurogane when they need miracles. And why else would you be going to Hongshan but to find them? I will give you a piece of knowledge, though, as an apology for startling you: finding the blacksmith will not be easy. Kurogane only reveals themselves to those who have proven themselves worthy."

Imari got over her shock and peppered their guide with questions. "What do you know about Kurogane? Can you tell us how to find him? Where around the mountain does he live?"

"Those are difficult questions that would take longer than I have to answer. Before we reach the end of our journey, I will give you some advice on finding Kurogane. But first, I have business to attend to, and you must purchase supplies for the journey. You will need to carry three days' worth of food and water, and your horses must be left behind. Nothing grows in the middle of the Jade Sea. It's like walking on glass."

"Water, got it," Kenta chirped. "Anything else?"

Bo glanced at Kaede. "Be sure to bring a hat and mask," they said with a hint of a smile. "You'll need to protect your face from the sun. I will meet you at the Zhong An Inn tomorrow morning. Until then, farewell." Bowing low, Bo departed, heading back down the steps at a surprisingly fast pace for someone of their apparent age. They disappeared near the foot of the staircase, leaving the stunned party behind.

Once she got over her surprise, Kaede caught Imari's eye. "Do you think Bo overheard you teasing me earlier, or are they just really perceptive?" she asked, running her hand awkwardly through her hair. A few strands had slipped free of her topknot and clung to her forehead.

"I'm more interested in how they knew where we were staying," Takeshi muttered, his brow furrowed.

"Clever guesswork," Imari reassured him. "There weren't many suitable inns still up and running between here and the harbor. We're wearing nice clothes, even if they're a bit dusty at the bottom. That rules out the shabbier establishments. It was probably a well-reasoned deduction."

Still, Kaede wasn't convinced. She found herself looking in the direction Bo had left, hoping to catch another glimpse of them. The short conversation with Bo had raised questions instead of providing answers, but one thing was certain: their guide seemed almost uncomfortably familiar with them.

***

"You're sure they came this way?" Hayate muttered. He peered around the edge of a decaying building, scanning the street beyond. From the alley, he had a perfect view of the buildings and people. The smell was of damp rubbish and rotting food, but he ignored the stench. His nose wasn't the one that mattered.

Beside him, one of the deeper shadows of the alleyway moved. "Positive," Kaze said, and Hayate caught a brief flash of white teeth as he spoke. "I'd recognize Rin's scent anywhere, not to mention Kaede's. We've finally caught up to them."

Hayate fought a scowl. *Finally is right.* The nose that never struggled to track game in the forest or sniff out missing people from the villages wasn't up to his usual standards. Over the past several weeks, Kaze had often complained of losing the trail, and although Hayate couldn't prove it, he suspected his companion occasionally led them in circles on purpose.

Maybe Rin is just clever at concealing Kaede's tracks. Or maybe Kaze doesn't want me to find them.

"No offense, old friend, but I'd like more reassurance than your sense of smell. I won't believe Kaede is here until I see her."

Kaze gave Hayate an inscrutable look, as if his bright yellow eyes could see right through the comment, but he didn't say anything. Hayate also waited in silence. There was little more to say. Either Kaze would come through, as he always had, or he would be left chasing yet another ghost.

Just as his hands began to clench into fists of frustration, Hayate saw movement. A group of four was coming down the street, and he pressed himself closer to the wall to avoid being seen. From his hiding place, he could make them out: two women and two men, wearing fine clothes with...*Yes. The mon of Homura. And that red hair. It seems as if*

I've found you at last, cousin.

To his surprise, the expression on Kaede's face did not seem haunted, fearful, or tired. Instead, she seemed to be laughing at something her companion had said. Upon closer inspection, Hayate recognized her as well: beautiful dark hair, smooth but ample curves, and most telling of all, a missing hand. This was the woman he had seen with Kaede in Mirai, Lord Homura's daughter. *So, this is what you have chosen to waste yourself on since leaving home. Not helping Setsuna, not using your powers for the greater good, but making a fool of yourself over a pretty face. Well, that ends now.*

He watched as Kaede and Lady Homura disappeared into one of the buildings on the street, ducking further back into the alley as they entered through the front door. From what he had glimpsed, the place appeared to be an inn. "They're probably spending the night," he told Kaze, feeling his confidence grow. "Once night falls, we'll look for a way inside."

"I don't recommend it," Kaze said. "Sneaking into someone's bedroom in the middle of the night isn't the best way to start a conversation."

"This isn't a negotiation, Kaze," Hayate replied. "I'm here to bring Kaede back so she can finish what we all started. That's all. Either she will see reason and come willingly, or I will bring her by force."

Kaze's voice lifted from a growl to more of an urgent yelp, and his tail hung downwards with worry and concern. "Have you really thought this through? Kaede is every bit the warrior you are. If she doesn't want to go, you won't be able to make her. Even if you manage to drag her from the inn, how are you going to keep her under your control for the weeks it will take to return to Yukimura? And what about Rin? If we do take Kaede, my sister will try to stop us."

"Let me worry about Kaede. I know how to deal with her. Rin will be your concern." There was more Hayate wanted to say, but he thought better of it. He turned, resting his hand affectionately behind Kaze's tilted ears. "Thank you for tracking them, old friend. I knew I could trust you."

Kaze closed his eyes, and a little more of the light in the alley went out. "Yes," he said, but the hesitation at the word was obvious. Hayate could hear the sentence finish in his head, and it unsettled him more than he wanted to admit: *But I'm not sure if I can trust you.*

Chapter Twelve

"HEY, THIS IS PRETTY comfy," Kaede said, flopping back onto the futon the proprietor of the inn had laid out for her. It was one of two, and she had taken the one closer to the door before Imari could object. For once, she was thinking like Takeshi, putting herself between Imari and anyone who might enter the room.

Fortunately, if Imari noticed, she didn't seem to mind. She placed her pack beside the other futon and went over to investigate the closet instead. "Seems more than nice enough for one night," she said as she stuck her head in. "Better than sleeping out in the open, at any rate."

"I dunno." A grin spread across Kaede's face, and she placed her hands behind her head. "I kind of liked seeing the stars. It'll be strange to be back inside again. A lot safer, though."

"I'm sure Takeshi will be grateful for that." Imari stepped back from the closet, carrying a fresh green yukata draped over each arm. "Here." She tossed one in Kaede's direction, and Kaede sat up as it landed on her lap. "Change into something comfortable. I'll step behind the screen."

Kaede's face heated up, and she couldn't help following with her eyes as Imari slipped into one of the screened-off areas. Thanks to the warm glow of the paper lantern in the middle of the room, she could see a perfect silhouette even after Imari closed the door. She looked away, clearing her throat awkwardly.

"I was surprised you wanted to share a room with me," she said, stripping out of her own clothes. She went about the process as quickly as possible, setting the clean yukata on the table and shedding layers onto the floor to be gathered later. She had to admit, it would feel good to put on some fresh clothes for the night.

"Why?" Imari asked. The screen was still open a crack, enough for her voice to carry. Instinctively, Kaede turned toward the sound, and she felt a ticklish flutter in her stomach. Imari had also shed most of her clothes, and the shape of her shadow against the door was much different without her kimono and harder to look away from.

Kaede managed to look away. "I don't know," she said, trying to blink the image away. It stuck stubbornly in her brain, generous curves and surprisingly full breasts and things she was definitely not supposed to take notice of, especially since they belonged to her master. "I figured you'd want me to room with Takeshi and Kenta next door since we're all your bodyguards and all. Not because—"

"Good," Imari said, "because the thought never crossed my mind. Besides, is it so strange that I'd ask to share a room with you? I enjoy your company."

"I actually think Takeshi approves." Kaede busied herself by shrugging into her own yukata and fastening the sash, making sure to fold it extra tight to conceal as much skin as possible.

"That's nice," Imari said, in a tone that suggested she didn't much care. She let out a low sigh, and once more, Kaede couldn't help turning. This time, she found herself staring even longer than before. Imari had removed her hair from its braid, letting it flow around her shoulders, and even though she only had a silhouette to go on, Kaede felt a tug deep in her gut.

"Look, I haven't meant to make things awkward between you two the past few weeks," she mumbled, trying to change the subject.

Imari stepped out from behind the screen, and despite the nervousness Kaede felt, she smiled. Somehow, Imari looked even lovelier with her hair down in a simple yukata than she did in her fine kimonos. "You haven't, but please, let's talk about something besides Takeshi and Kenta."

"Like what?" Kaede said, unsure whether she was nervous or excited to hear what Imari had in mind.

"Like this." Imari returned to her pack and rummaged through it for a moment, fishing out a sizeable scroll. She then headed over to the table in the middle of the room, and Kaede followed, taking one of the cushioned seats. While Imari spread the scroll across the table, Kaede stretched her legs all the way out beneath it.

"The map?"

Imari nodded. "Yes. Look how far we've already come." She trailed her finger from a dot near the middle of the map down and to the west. "This is where the bandits tried to rob us," she said, tapping against a small patch of loops that looked like trees.

"It looks so small," Kaede said, shaking her head. "But we spent at least two days in that forest."

"And here." Imari continued following their path, stopping at the edge of what was clearly the Jade Sea. "This is where we are now."

Kaede studied the spot beside Imari's fingertip. "I see why Yin is the way it is. There's nothing else nearby."

Imari nodded, her voice tinged with obvious regret. "It's sad, isn't it? It must have been beautiful once. A little bit of Akatsuki Teikoku and Tsun'i mixing together everywhere you look. There aren't any other cities like it."

"No," Kaede said, her mind wandering back to earlier in the day, "but you do have to admit, it still holds some interesting people."

Imari laughed. "You're talking about Bo. They were quite interesting. I just hope they meant it when they said they could give me advice on finding Kurogane."

"You will. You've come this far already, haven't you? You've fought bandits, explored a ghost city, and hired a strange and mysterious guide for ten circles less than they quoted you." Without really thinking about it, Kaede placed her hand on top of Imari's, giving it a light squeeze. It was soft and warm beneath hers, so soft and warm that Kaede realized what she had done and began to second-guess herself.

Imari's hand turned beneath hers, facing up so they could link fingers briefly. Instantly, Kaede relaxed. "If those are the most exciting things that happen to us, I'll be fine with that."

"You liar," Kaede laughed. "You wanted an adventure, and you're getting one. Don't try to pretend otherwise."

"All right, all right. I did want at least one adventure to brag about before I took my father's place as daimyo. So far, it's been worth it." Her dark eyes took on an inquisitive look, asking a question, and Kaede returned it.

"For me, too. These past few weeks have helped clear my head. It's nice to be going toward something instead of running away."

"I think it's a sign of inner strength, searching for purpose so quickly after you were forced to leave home." The edge of Imari's thumb ran along the side of Kaede's palm, and a pleasant shiver raced down her spine. "It can't have been easy. But here you are: helping me and making new friends instead of hiding. You're a survivor, Kaede. It's admirable."

The corners of Kaede's cheeks grew warm, but she resisted the temptation to keep her eyes on the map. Instead, she took a risk and gazed into Imari's to show her sincerity. "Thank you. That means a lot, especially coming from you."

"I'm only telling the truth." Imari released her hand, turning back to the scroll. "Just a little further to go," she said, tapping the lonely mountain on the other side of the Jade Sea. "The distance looks so short here, but it won't be easy to cross."

"Easy? Probably not," Kaede said. "But impossible? No way. I know the five of us can do it."

"I don't have any doubts." Imari folded up the scroll, standing up and tucking it beneath her arm. "But for now, we need a good night's sleep. We don't know how early Bo will show up tomorrow."

"Sleep. Right." Kaede stood as well, tugging the overlapping part of her yukata a little further open. She knew it was improper, but she needed to let a little more air in. For some reason, she felt unusually warm even though the sun had set and the room was cool. She returned to her futon as Imari retrieved the basin of water and clean cloths set out for them.

"You don't have to wait for me, you know," Imari said, carrying the bowl over so they both could use it. "I'm sure you want to clean up too." She dipped one of the cloths into the water, but instead of bringing it to her own face, she wiped the cool fabric across Kaede's forehead. Kaede's eyes widened, but she allowed the intimate action, holding still as Imari brought the cloth down the side of her cheek—the left one, with the slashing scars beneath her eye. "These don't still hurt, do they?"

Kaede shook her head. "Not anymore. I'm getting used to them. They still surprise me whenever I catch a glimpse of my reflection, though."

"I like them," Imari replied.

"So you've said before. I'll take your word for it." Kaede gently plucked the cloth from Imari's hand and finished scrubbing her face, partially to break the tension, and partially because her heart hammered so hard her ears thundered with it. Imari's face was incredibly close to hers, and Kaede didn't want to think about how if she leaned in a few more centimeters, she could kiss her.

Thankfully, or perhaps disappointingly, Imari didn't try for more intimacy. Instead, she picked up the other cloth and began washing her own face. Kaede stole a few glances, amazed at how such a simple action could capture her attention so thoroughly. *How does she make something as simple as washing her face look beautiful? Or maybe that's just the way she is. Everything she does is beautiful.*

"Kaede?"

"Huh?" She blinked, only to realize Imari was smirking at her.

"Is something wrong? You're staring at me like I have two heads."

Kaede sighed, draping the wet cloth over the back of her neck. "It's nothing. Just tired."

Imari didn't seem convinced, but she didn't say anything. She did, however, keep smiling as she finished washing up. Kaede stole a few more glances, committing each glimpse to memory until the light in the middle of the red paper lantern finally went out.

***

Despite the darkness, sleep didn't come easily. Kaede tossed and turned long after the lantern went out, unable to find a comfortable position. Her body ached with exhaustion, but her mind continued to race, jumping from one thought to the next. She thought of the hills and forests she had already crossed, the wide green expanse of the Jade Sea, and the snowcapped mountains of home. She thought of Imari's beautiful face, but whenever she tried to focus on the details, it sharpened into memories of Setsuna and Hayate.

Even though she hadn't seen him in several weeks, she knew her cousin still followed her. It was an eerie feeling more than anything else, a churning in her gut she couldn't dismiss. Hayate had never been the type to give up, especially where she was concerned. Her presence only seemed to make him more determined.

With a heavy breath, she sat up and rolled her shoulders. She knew where her thoughts would wander next if she remained in bed, and she had no desire to remember what the corpses of Setsuna's soldiers looked like bleeding out into the snow. If she wasn't going to sleep, there was no reason for her to stay in bed, shifting and sighing and possibly waking her companion.

Before she left, Kaede glanced over at Imari. Her eyes were closed, but her brow seemed drawn as if in concentration. *Dreaming?* Kaede wondered, watching Imari's eyes dart beneath their lids. *Well, I hope yours are more peaceful than mine.* For a moment, the corners of Imari's lips pulled up, as if she had heard the thought. The wrinkles on her face smoothed out, and she gave a low moan.

Satisfied, Kaede crossed the mat and, ignoring the set of guest slippers by the door, toed into her sandals instead. Then, she hesitated. After a little thought, she decided to take Mizu-no-Hamon. She doubted she would need her sword, but with the way the past few weeks had gone, it was better to be safe than sorry. Besides, if she had to leave the room for her own sanity, she could at least put the time to good use. A quick patrol around the inn would help ensure Imari's safety and her own peace of mind.

Removing the blade from its resting place, she tucked it against her side and slipped silently out into the hallway. She hesitated, glancing back over her shoulder, but sighed and continued after a moment of silence. Imari would be safe with Takeshi and Kenta in the room next door. She left the second floor behind, only sparing a brief glance to make sure the Hibana brothers' door was open a crack.

She didn't meet anyone on the stairs, and the first floor was similarly abandoned—not surprising, considering the time of night. One of the room's far windows caught her attention, and she looked past the partially open screen that led outside into a small interior garden.

Kaede smiled. Although this ryokan was humbler than some she had seen in larger cities, the owner had obviously tried to make it beautiful for guests. She headed through the door and out into the night, stopping to admire the artfully clipped shrubs on the way. They descended in a soft cloud pattern, leading down toward a small koi pond ringed with decorative stones. The moon's reflection danced on the dark, sleek surface of the water, and lilypads floated around its edges.

As she approached the pool, she caught a glimpse of her own face staring back at her. It wavered on top of the water, rippling and indistinct, but she could still make out the scars beneath her left eye. She forced herself to look, but to her surprise, the usual pain never came. Instead of thinking back to how she had received the scars in the first place, she remembered the way Imari had touched them with the wetted cloth before they'd gone to bed.

We're going to have to talk about it eventually, how she goes out of her way to make contact with me.

Kaede's thoughts were interrupted by a curious prickling sensation along the back of her neck. Though she couldn't hear any noise or sense movement nearby, some deep-rooted instinct told her that someone was watching—someone close. She started to tense her shoulders but resisted the impulse, remaining precisely where she was. Instead, she continued gazing into the pool, pretending she hadn't realized that she wasn't alone.

After a few heartbeats, she did pick up something: a slight rustling in the shrubs behind her. She reached for Mizu-no-Hamon, drawing it from its saya with less than a whisper. "Please, come out," she said in a calm voice. "I'm armed and I don't like being spied on."

Kaede turned to see two black shadows emerge, one on two legs and one on four. Some part of her had known who it was, so she wasn't surprised, merely wary as Hayate and Kaze stalked toward her. Hayate's blade gleamed, but Kaze seemed almost hesitant. He held his tail tucked low between his legs.

"I'd hoped you had given up trying to find me," Kaede said to Hayate, shaking her head in disappointment. "I made it clear I wasn't going to interfere in Setsuna's business anymore. She has nothing to fear from me."

Hayate took another step, bringing his sword into an offensive stance—both arms up, blade held diagonally across his chest. His expression darkened even further at the mention of Setsuna's name, and a muscle in his face twitched. "This isn't about her. This is about me and you, and the duty you refused."

"If this is about me and you, why did you bring Kaze?" Kaede asked, thinking quickly. She could read the wolf's reluctance in every movement, and she knew he didn't want to be involved in this fight.

"He's here for insurance," Hayate said. Loose strands of dark hair had fallen out of his topknot to frame his face, but the rest of his muscular body was sharp lines of tension. Besides, you have Rin."

"Not with me." Kaede took a defensive posture, knees bent, holding her body sideways to make a smaller target. She breathed slower, trying to calm her heartbeat.

"Don't be so sure," a low voice growled. There was more rustling, from the opposite side of the garden this time, and Kaede saw a flash of white out of the corner of her eye. She felt a flicker of annoyance, but a wave of relief drowned it.

"Rin, you're supposed to be asleep."

Rin loped toward her, coming to stand at her side. "How can I sleep when you're always getting into trouble?" She and Kaze met eyes, giving each other nods of greeting. Instead of growling or snarling, they stood off to the side, content to observe the proceedings rather than fight.

"Sister," Kaze said, sniffing in Rin's direction. "I see your human is causing you trouble."

"Yes," Rin said, "but much less trouble than yours is causing you."

"This wasn't my fault," Kaede protested. "I'm trying to get as far from trouble as I can."

"Is that what you call your responsibilities? Trouble?" Hayate glared at her, his brown eyes every bit as sharp as his sword. "I don't understand why Setsuna always catered to you. It's clear you have no appreciation for what she gave you."

That touched a nerve. "What about all those soldiers?" Kaede's arms tensed and her fingers clenched tighter around the hilt of her katana. "What about what she gave them? They're dead, Hayate, and so are the yokai who killed them. I won't be part of that. I won't have that stain on my conscience."

"You think their deaths don't bother me? I feel them, Kaede. I fought alongside those soldiers. But Setsuna—"

"Forget Setsuna," Kaede snapped. "Whoever she was before, she's someone different now, and she's hurting people. If you really loved her, you'd go home and stop her from doing this."

For a moment, Hayate faltered. A look of uncertainty, perhaps regret, passed over his face.

* * *

Her hand burns. Pain sears along her arm, all the way from the middle of her wrist up into her throat, and she screams, her eyes blurring with tears. For a moment, the edge of agony fades, although she can still feel her blood seeping into the earth. "No, keep going," she sobs to the shimmering figure beside her. "Please. Please help me."

A long, coiling shadow passes above her, and a great roar shakes the heavens. Fire crawls up along her forearm, but this time, there is no pain. Instead, her flesh glows golden, wreathed in beautiful light.

She curls her fingers—I have fingers!—and the glow intensifies, swallowing her body. She is whole again. She shines like one of the brightest stars in the sky. She throws her arms open to the dragon sailing above her, tilting her head back and laughing with pure joy.

Imari jerked awake, sucking in a stabbing breath. Disoriented, it took her a moment to realize what was wrong. She couldn't hear the sound of Kaede's steady breathing any longer. She frowned and rubbed her right hand across her eyes, but froze in mid-motion. The futon beside hers was empty, and the screen door leading into the room had been left open a crack.

She stood, checking beside the door, but only one pair of sandals remained. Kaede's sword was missing from the table. With a frown, Imari fastened her yukata tighter and took up her own blade, unsure whether to be comforted or worried by the fact that Kaede was armed.

Either way, I can't let her wander around at night alone, especially with her cousin following us.

Imari had only seen him once, but the memory of the hooded man who had followed them through Mirai still made her uneasy—uneasy enough to go in search of Kaede. She put on her sandals and crept out into the hallway, tiptoeing past Takeshi and Kenta's partially closed door so she wouldn't wake them.

There was no sign of Kaede on the second floor, so Imari made her way down the stairs, listening. If she strained, she could hear raised voices coming from somewhere. *Could they be outside?* More than one person was speaking, and their tones didn't sound friendly.

As Imari reached the first floor, she saw a pair of shadows moving past one of the screen doors. She hurried over, pulling it open. Starlight illuminated a small walled garden and bounced off the edges of two naked blades. Kaede held one, and a dark, broad-shouldered figure held the other. The two of them had locked eyes and seemed prepared to lock swords as well. Rin and Kaze watched like silent statues.

Fingers of ice squeezed Imari's stomach. "Kaede!"

Kaede whirled around. "Imari?"

"Do not interfere," the man said. As he turned, Imari recognized his face. This had to be Hayate, the same man who had been trailing them the past few weeks. She hadn't gotten a good look at him in Mirai, but some part of her knew. "This doesn't concern you."

"Please, Hayate, leave," Kaede said. "You don't have to do this."

Hayate didn't answer. He leapt for Kaede, his sword a flash of silver slicing through the air.

Kaede raised her own sword to meet it. Their blades clashed, ringing out through the courtyard. The deflection didn't slow Hayate down. He recovered and struck again. The two of them danced along the path, twin blurs dipping in and out of the column of light streaming from the open door.

"Aren't you going to do something?" Imari shouted to the wolves. Rin and Kaze watched the fight with unwavering concentration, but neither seemed inclined to interfere.

"No," Rin said.

Kaze nodded. "This is something the two of them need to work out for themselves. We can't get involved."

"Well, you two might be able to watch Kaede fight alone, but I can't!"

Imari hurried to catch up to the two combatants, drawing her katana from its saya. As she rushed toward them, Hayate pivoted, taking notice of her. He struck, and she dropped to one knee, ducking out of the way. The air above her head whistled—she dodged the edge of his blade by no more than an inch.

"Hayate, stop this!"

Imari straightened and planted her feet to continue fighting in time to see Kaede shove her way between them.

"Your fight is with me, not her."

"Fight?" Hayate stepped back, warier now that he had two opponents to face. "This isn't a fight. This is a retrieval mission."

"She isn't going back," Imari said. Just the thought fed a hungry flame of anger deep inside her chest. "I won't let you abduct her."

"Abduct?" Hayate shook his head, laughing bitterly. "Is that what she told you? She ran away from home. I'm just bringing her back so she can fulfill her duties—the duties she abandoned because she was too much of a coward to accept them."

"Hayate," Kaede said, sadness in her voice, "please, just go home. I can't be a part of Setsuna's plans anymore."

Hayate looked utterly disgusted. "You will do your duty, Kaede. You will make this world a better place, whether you want to or not."

Their blades hissed as they swept against each other, and the fighters' bodies moved so quickly that Imari could barely see the forms they used. She waited, watching carefully, but she couldn't find an opening. If she struck at Hayate, she ran the risk of distracting Kaede as she had during the fight with Gin—or worse. *But I can't just stand here! I can't let her fight him alone.*

Her mind made up, Imari rushed around the two twisting bodies, positioning herself behind Hayate. She brought her sword down in a diagonal slash, but he spun to meet her. Their katana clashed, and the shock ran up her arm.

"Stay out of this," Hayate snarled, using their crossed blades to shove her back. "It doesn't concern you!"

"I've already involved myself," Imari panted, struggling to regain her footing. "You're going to have to deal with both of us."

Hayate lunged for her, but Kaede was there to block him like a gust of wind, whirling between them so fast Imari hardly had time to move out of the way. Their swords screamed against each other, and Imari flinched as the edges met near her shoulder. She wove out of the way, backing up to look for another opening.

Kaede engaged Hayate with a swift sideways strike toward his ribs, but he was ready. He met the blow instead of retreating, and sparks spat from the edges of their blades. Hayate recovered first, and he swept at Kaede's legs, trying to throw her off-balance. Imari went for his arm while it was extended, but there was no need—before she could connect, Kaede sprang up and over Hayate's sword, moving backwards through the air. When she landed, it was on the rocky edge of the koi pond, both feet balanced on the decorative border.

"Come on, Hayate," Kaede called, holding her katana in front of her. "You're holding back."

The words were a hollow taunt at best and Hayate knew it, too. He turned on Imari, and she spun to the side just ahead of his sword. She tried to keep up with his strikes, but they came fast and constant, and she found herself stepping backwards. Panic surged through her, and the fluid motions of her training became hard and jolting. Compared to Hayate, she felt sluggish. His forms moved faster than her eyes, and when she looked for the perfect opening as her father had taught her, there wasn't a gap to be found. She was outmatched.

With little choice left, she gave into recklessness, throwing herself straight into Hayate's guard. He saw the desperate move coming from a mile away. He caught her elbow, jerking her sword-arm back and spinning her around instead. The next thing she knew, his sword dug into the front of her neck, pressing deeper with each hammering thud of her heart.

"Imari!"

Her name sounded distant with her blood pounding in her ears, but Imari could see the expression on Kaede's face all too clearly: complete and utter terror. As their eyes locked, Imari tried to send her a silent apology for losing, but something hot and bright blazed back at her. Anger. Kaede was angry, and when she moved, it was to spring from the edge of the pool like a wolf leaping onto the back of a deer. She spun through the air, higher than any human should have been able to jump, soaring up and over both of their heads until Imari lost sight of her.

A moment later, she felt Hayate stiffen and heard him suck in a sharp breath. Kaede had to be behind him, holding him at sword point.

"I still have my sword on your girlfriend's throat," Hayate said in a low voice, right beside Imari's ear. "Are you willing to risk her life to kill me?"

"It's not a risk if I sever your spine first."

The three of them held still for what felt like an eternity, not moving, not even breathing. Then, the silence shattered. The screen door flew open. Takeshi and Kenta burst into the garden, still wearing their yukata, but with their blades drawn.

"Imari!"

"What's going on?"

Their voices spurred Hayate into action. He removed his sword from Imari's throat and shoved her forward, ducking beneath Kaede's katana and sprinting toward the wall. He was up and over in an instant, scaling the flat stone surface with incredible agility and speed. If Imari hadn't just witnessed Kaede flying, she would have been even more astounded. Before she could even close her mouth, Hayate had vanished, disappearing into the darkness. Moments later, Kaze was gone too, melting back into the shadows. Rin still sat beside the path, her tail curling around her haunches as if nothing remarkable had happened at all.

Takeshi and Kenta rushed the rest of the way into the garden, wearing identical expressions of concern. "What happened?" Kenta asked, stopping short in front of them while Takeshi headed over to the wall.

"He's gone," Takeshi muttered, staring out into the darkness. "That was Hayate, wasn't it?"

Imari ignored him. She turned to look at Kaede, who stood silently where Hayate had left her. Mizu-no-Hamon hung limply in her grasp, and her face was more shadow than moonlight.

"Promise me, Imari. Promise me you'll never do that again."

Imari winced at the darkened tone. Kaede was upset, and not just because Hayate had tried to attack them. Once more, she had stepped in to do what she'd thought was right and defend someone she cared for, and just as before, her assistance hadn't been welcomed.

"You were handling him," she said. "But I wanted to help."

"It's my job to defend you," Kaede insisted again, stepping past Kenta until they were face-to-face. "I don't need someone to die for me, okay? Especially not you. And if you can't stand back and let me handle my own problems, this—" she gestured between them "isn't going to work. So, you need to promise me, right now, that you'll let me handle Hayate next time. If there is a next time."

Imari began to protest, searching for the words to explain the conflicted feelings in her chest, the affection and the fear, but before she could, Takeshi returned. In a rare display of physical affection, he placed a hand on her shoulder. "Listen to Kaede, Imari. She's right. If you got hurt while fighting one of her battles, she would have to carry that guilt. That isn't fair."

"You're assuming I'll lose," Imari muttered, but she saw the truth in what her friends said. Kaede already carried many heavy burdens from her past. If Hayate did return, and if she did step in to defend Kaede and end up getting injured or worse, Imari knew Kaede would blame herself. They had only known each other for a little over a month, but Imari could see it all playing out in her mind's eye.

"All right," she said, giving Kaede a short bow. "I promise. Next time, I'll let you do your job and protect me."

"Thank you." Instead of bowing back, Kaede surprised her by seizing her in a tight hug. It was awkward, especially since they were both still holding their swords, but they managed somehow, and Imari melted into the embrace. She hugged Kaede back, cheek resting against her hair.

"I'm sorry."

"It's okay. You did help me. Just don't do it again."

"I won't," Imari murmured, but somewhere deep inside, she wondered if she could really keep that promise when the time came.

Chapter Thirteen

KAEDE WOVE THROUGH THE waves, making her way carefully across the uneven landscape. From a distance, the Jade Sea's surface had looked easy to cross, even with smooth waves rising and falling on the horizon. Up close, it was quite different. The polished green stone waves near the docks didn't reach that high, but her feet threatened to slip if she didn't watch where she placed them. Worse still, the sun's glare fell straight into her eyes. The wide-brimmed straw hat she had brought along only offered so much protection.

Bo had spent the previous day helping them prepare for the treacherous journey. The only way to cross the Jade Sea was to travel at night and sleep the boiling days through in a special black tent. The Jade Sea reflected the sun's light, heating the still air to dangerous temperatures. To avoid the worst of it, they had left at midnight under a cloudless night sky. Still, the flickering stars and the full moon provided enough light to make the landscape gleam as far as the eye could see.

"I see why Bo said this would take three days," Imari muttered. She had similar troubles, Kaede noticed, moving without her usual grace and struggling to find the best footing. "It's like walking on ice, and we can't ride."

Kenta heaved a sigh. He hadn't been thrilled at the thought of walking the whole way, as he had declared several times that morning already.

"Don't make that noise," Takeshi said. He seemed to be making do, but his forehead furrowed more than usual in concentration. "The horses couldn't carry all the supplies, enough water for the trip, and us."

"Hey, I just don't want to fall," Kenta protested. "This stuff is more like glass than stone."

Kaede shot a grin over at him. "Trust me, we should stick to walking. At least this way, you won't fall with a horse on top of you."

Kenta snorted, but he did smile back, looking a little more cheerful.

"And I thought you were the clumsy one, Kaede," Rin said with a playful growl. She had less trouble on the slippery surface than the humans in the group, although Kaede could hear her claws scrabbling a little in search of purchase.

"Well, we can't all be as graceful as wolves. For a human, I think I do all right." She turned away from Rin and faced forward once more, sliding down the edge of the next wave in a controlled skid. She managed to make it without losing her balance, and she looked at her companions in triumph. Unfortunately, none of them seemed to notice. Imari, Kenta, and Takeshi worried about their own paths, Rin rolled her eyes at the unnecessary display, and Bo was much further ahead.

Like Rin, their guide seemed to have little trouble keeping their footing. Bo climbed up and down the rolling waves with the agility of a person far younger than they appeared to be, only looking back to make sure the rest of them were following. "Come on," Bo called, motioning for the group to hurry. "We have a long way to go before the sun rises too high."

"I'm not looking forward to that," Kaede whispered as Imari came to stand beside her. They fell into stride together, cautiously picking up their pace to catch up with Bo. She couldn't tell exactly how their guide was moving so quickly, obscured as they were by their heavy, dark robes, but it was impressive nonetheless.

"Me neither." Imari gestured past the long shadows their bodies cast with the moon directly behind them. "Look ahead of us. It's a whole lot of nothing. No trees, no mountains, no place to get any kind of shade."

"Stop it," Kaede laughed, "you're making me sweat just thinking about it."

"Oh?" Imari's brows arched, and Kaede flushed as she realized her friend was studying her face with obvious, intense interest. Something unspoken and suggestive hovered between them until Kaede cleared her throat and looked away, back toward where Bo waited for them atop one of the waves.

"We should—"

"Yes." Imari continued stealing glances at Kaede as they picked their way forward, and Kaede continued pretending not to notice. Sometime soon, they would have to address this tension between them, both their mutual attraction and Imari's infuriating insistence on fighting battles that didn't involve her, but for now, contentment washed over her. *It's actually kind of nice. Scary, but nice.*

It wasn't often that women took notice of her. Men, sometimes, but most women didn't show their interests so brazenly. Many were content to wait for her to make the first move—something Kaede wasn't comfortable doing, especially since she was a woman herself and didn't want to create an uncomfortable situation for a lady who didn't belong to her court, or one who didn't understand her situation as a lady of autumn. But Imari was different. Imari wasn't at all shy about showing her interest, and Kaede got the sense it was only a matter of time before the two of them discussed it more openly. *And what then? If she does bring it up, what am I supposed to say?*

There were many reasons she and Imari shouldn't take their relationship beyond friendship. She was on the run from Hayate and Setsuna and her lack of experience with romantic relationships. *But still, would it be so bad?*

She had plenty of time to ponder the question as they made their way out to sea. Its surface flattened the further they went, and Kaede was able to walk a little faster. She looked over at Rin, who returned the glance with a knowing one of her own.

Somehow, I don't think she approves and I can see why. Hayate almost killed Imari last night, all because of me.

Despite the promise she had extracted, Kaede had a feeling that convincing Imari to stay back next time would be impossible. Imari had wanted to tail Hayate and Kaze through the city after their escape over the garden wall, but Kaede had managed to talk her out of it. With any luck, they wouldn't find themselves in a similar situation again. Kaze wouldn't be able to track them as easily across the sea—or, at least, he would pretend he couldn't.

That did remind her of something, though, and she cleared her throat, speaking up to get Bo's attention. "This is probably a stupid question, but where are we supposed to use the bathroom?"

Bo turned to look at her, and Kaede thought she saw their guide smile beneath their hood. "Pick a place," they said, gesturing at the open space. "Any place."

"Great," Kaede sighed, wrinkling her nose in distaste. *This is going to be a really long three days.*

By the time afternoon arrived, Kaede's calves were stiff from picking her way up and over the waves, and her face dripped with sweat. They stopped to take a brief rest, but it didn't do much good—without any shelter, the heat from the waves and the absence of any breeze was wearing her down.

"If enough people crossed the Jade Sea, it would become an ocean again," Imari said during the worst of it, wiping a hand across her brow.

Kaede laughed between pants. Although she and Imari walked together, neither of them had much energy to waste on talking. Every breath made her mouth dryer and the stitch in her side worse.

Eventually, relief came. A tall shadow began to take shape against the fuzzy horizon, offering a dark triangle of shade on top of the sea's glittering green surface. "That almost looks like a mountain," Kaede said to Imari and Rin.

It was Bo, however, who answered. Their ears must have been very keen, because they responded to her whisper from several yards ahead. "Not a mountain, Iori-san, but a wave."

"A wave?" Kenta said. From his expression, he seemed skeptical. "That big?"

Bo slowed down to match the rest of the group's pace, and Kaede thought she caught a hint of a smile under their hood. "It's the kind of wave that can only be found in the middle of the ocean; the sort you hear about in sea stories. That one is fourteen meters high."

Kaede squinted, trying to get a clearer look, but the monster wave stood fuzzy and indistinct against the sky. It did seem to be as huge as Bo claimed. Beside her, she noticed Imari grinning. "This will definitely be a story to tell my father when I get back home."

Bo seemed to approve. Their eyes lit up, and they turned back to look at her. "So, you're a storyteller, Homura-dono? One of the noblest arts, to be sure."

Imari nodded. "Not a storyteller so much, but a story collector, certainly. I read and listen to any stories I can get my hands on."

"Do you, now?" Bo seemed to lose themself in thought for a moment, and then come to a decision. "And do you know the legend of Lady Tsukine?"

Kaede frowned. Everyone in Akatsuki Teikoku was taught the legend of the moon, practically since birth.

"Yes," Imari said, similarly confused. "Why?"

"Oh, not the children's story," Bo said, waving their hand dismissively. "I mean the legend. The real thing."

"The real thing?" Kenta skipped a few steps ahead to catch up with them and Takeshi followed.

"There is only one true story," Takeshi insisted. "Are you saying Lady Tsukine wasn't real?"

"Oh, she was real," Bo told them. "But she wasn't a beautiful white-haired goddess who descended from the heavens. You see, Lady Tsukine was a dragon."

Kaede's eyes widened. This was certainly not like any telling of the tale she had ever heard. She leaned in, eager to hear more. "A dragon? You mean a dragon yokai? The kind that flies around and breathes fire and everything?"

"Tsukine was not a member of the kasai clan, but she was indeed a dragon. And of course she could fly." Bo tilted their head up to the sky, where the moon was just coming into view. "Back then, dragons had little to do with humans—even less than they do today."

"They still don't have much to do with us," Kenta added, only for Imari to shush him.

Bo smirked, but continued without complaint. "The dragons had their lives, and humans were not part of them until one day. Tsukine was the wisest of them all—"

"And the most beautiful?"

Before Imari could chastise Kenta again, Bo laughed. "Dragons do not think of beauty in the same way humans do, but yes, I suppose you could consider her to be beautiful. One day, she was sleeping in the shadowed forest beneath Mount Hongshan when she heard a noise. It was the cry of an injured deer, and she followed the sound to see what the matter was."

"I know this part," Kaede said. "That's where she met Yama."

"Yes, although he did not let the deer go from the hunter's trap, as some versions of the legend say. It was he who had caught it, because everyone needs to eat to survive. But unlike the other hunters who took from the forest without a thought for their greed, Tsukine saw Yama give thanks to the deer he had taken. When he took what he needed, he buried the rest, so its antlers could become trees and its bones could become the hills outside of the forest. Tsukine had never seen another hunter treat the animals of the forest with such reverence. Yama understood an important piece of knowledge only the dragons had possessed before: life is precious, no matter its form." Bo paused, and Kaede felt the weight of their eyes fall on her. "Perhaps it is because his own life was not easy. And yet, he still treasured it. Tsukine was impressed. She revealed herself to him, and Yama was amazed."

"He would be, if Tsukine was a dragon," Takeshi muttered. Even he seemed to be getting into the story, and apparently hadn't found it too blasphemous.

"She presented herself as a woman at first," Bo explained. "The legend is not all wrong. As some of the most powerful yokai, dragons can take many shapes, including human forms. As a human, she spoke to Yama and asked him what he had done."

"And then they fell in love?" Kenta asked.

"Not quite," Bo said, "but they did become friends. Tsukine came to him at night, when the world slept and her powers were at their strongest. She was a dragon of the water, you see, and her abilities were tied to the moon."

"I guess she was a moon goddess after all," Imari said, with more than a little breathless awe. "She was just a dragon, too. I wonder why most versions of the legend leave that part out?"

Bo smiled wide enough to show their teeth. "You haven't seen a dragon before, have you, Homura-dono? Most humans find them terrifying."

"Not me," Imari insisted. "I find them fascinating."

"Of course, you do," Takeshi muttered, but Kaede saw that his smile was more indulgent than she had expected.

"More than anything, dragons are powerful," Bo explained. "They are capable of great good, as well as great evil."

"Like us, then," Kaede said.

Bo nodded. "You understand the yokai well, Iori-san. Dragons and humans are much more alike than most humans think. Both have transformed the world more than any other living creature, for better and worse."

"Finish the story," Kenta begged. "Please? I want to hear the part where they fall in love." A look of worry crossed his face, and he bit his lower lip. "Wait. They do fall in love in your version, right?"

"They did indeed," Bo said. "It is extremely rare for a human and a yokai to fall in love, but that is what happened in this case. Each night, Tsukine lingered a little longer by Yama's side, and each night, they parted with more reluctance."

"That's beautiful," Kenta sniffed, but Kaede ignored him. Instead, her eyes drifted over toward Imari.

"But that wouldn't have worked," Takeshi said. "Yama was human. Tsukine was a dragon. She would have lived a lot longer than him."

"Yes, but dragons are not without their resources." Bo gestured up toward the sky where the stars still shone, beautiful, winking white diamonds across smooth black velvet. The falling moon brought out a different, softer color in Imari's face, one that almost seemed to glow.

"Ancestors," Kaede sighed, looking up. "The sky's even clearer out here than it is at home." Warmth surrounded her left hand, and she looked down to see that Imari had grasped it. Despite her surprise and the slight jolt of her heart against her ribs, she didn't let go. She merely squeezed to let Imari know she welcomed the touch.

"When Yama reached the end of his life, as all humans do, Tsukine placed his face in the moon. That way, he would always be with her."

For a moment, the whole group looked up at the sky, seeing the familiar shadow anew.

"You mean it's his face up there?" Kaede asked. "Not hers?"

Bo chuckled. "Think about it. Why would Tsukine want to see her own face? Whose face would you put in the moon, Iori-san, if you had that power?"

Kaede struggled to stop her eyes from sliding left, but they did so without her permission. When Imari met her gaze, she glanced away, blushing furiously.

Thankfully, Bo didn't seem to expect a verbal response. "Some say Tsukine is still alive, working to make the world a better place. The spirit of Yama still burns within her, and for him, she watches over humanity, because she knows the good they are capable of."

"You know, I think this is my favorite version of the legend so far." Imari adjusted her grip, and Kaede sucked in a soft breath as their fingers laced tighter together.

"What did you think of it, Rin?" Kaede asked, searching for a distraction so she wouldn't make quite so much a fool of herself. She glanced over at her friend, who was padding softly beside her. "You've been awfully quiet."

Rin snorted. "That's because, unlike the rest of you, I know it's rude to interrupt a good story." She bowed her head to Bo in obvious approval. "You have told the legend well. It is refreshing to hear my own clan's version of the tale for a change."

"Wait," Kaede said, brow furrowing, "you mean the wolf clan tells the same story?"

"Almost all yokai clans tell the same story," Rin said. "We haven't added flourishes and embellishments the way you humans have because the story doesn't need them. The truth is beautiful enough."

"And you've never thought to tell me any of this before?" Kaede asked, shaking her head in disbelief. She wasn't sure whether to be amused or mildly annoyed.

Rin gave her a blank look completely free of guilt. "You never asked."

"She's got a point," Imari murmured.

"That's not fair, though," Kaede protested. "How am I supposed to get a true answer if I don't even know which questions to ask?"

"Well, now you know," Rin said. "And although you haven't asked, I will tell you that I have remained your friend for so many years because you exemplify the traits that made Tsukine fall in love with Yama. You respect all life and are open to living in harmony with animals, yokai, and every living thing."

"Oh? This isn't a love confession for Kaede, is it, Rin?" Kenta said. "Because I think you might have some compete...ow!"

A sharp nudge from Takeshi silenced him, but Kaede flinched anyway. She tried to remove her hand from Imari's, but the grip on her fingers tightened. Eventually, she sighed and let it be. She didn't want to stop holding Imari's hand anyway.

"Don't worry," Rin said, and Kaede recognized a glint of amusement in her blue eyes. "I have no desire to take any mate, let alone a human, but you should be honored by the comparison to Yama, even more so since he was a gentleman of spring."

That got everyone's attention.

"What?"

"Really?"

"Wait, but didn't they have children?"

Kaede didn't say anything. Instead, she looked at Bo. Thanks to her smooth face and breasts, few people recognized her as a lady of autumn. But to her immense relief, Bo's face read acceptance. She breathed out a sigh, her worry evaporating before it really had a chance to take hold. It was unlikely a mysterious person like Bo, who seemed to have no discernable gender themself, would have a problem with her, but it was nice to be sure.

"So, he was," Bo said. "And Hibana-san, there are many ways to have children besides the usual one. Theirs were adopted, and all went on to become great daimyos, leaders who exemplified their mother's kindness and their father's respect for the balance of life." A small smile pulled at their lips. "Some even say their descendants have a special connection to the yokai, passed down through the generations."

"Hey," Kenta said with a note of excitement, "that could be you, Kaede!"

"I don't think so," Kaede said, but she did feel Rin's muzzle nudge affectionately against her shoulder. She laughed, draping an arm around the wolf's thick neck. Tiredness aside, this felt good—travelling with Imari on one side and Rin on the other, on a beautiful moonlit night, listening to a magical story.

***

Nothing. Hayate had spent hours walking the coastline, waving off beggars and would-be guides, searching every grimy, rotting dock in the harbor, and still: *nothing.*

No signs of Kaede and her companions since early that morning. He had returned to the inn just before dawn to watch for their departure, but he'd been too late. According to the proprietor, Kaede and the others had left the night before. He hadn't even bothered threatening her for more information, although it might have made him feel better. He'd been in too much of a rush to get to the harbor in the hopes of catching her.

But Kaede had vanished, and no one had seen her leave. Even mentioning a giant white wolf had brought only confused stares from the people he asked. That had led him to where he was now, stuck staring out over the Jade Sea from the harbor with no idea where to go next. As the light faded, so did his spirits. He hung his head, ignoring the sticky, warm wind that blew into his face. Kaze still hadn't returned from his latest search, but his other attempts had been fruitless. Why would this one be any different?

What am I supposed to do now? Hayate wondered, peering down at his sandals. *Just give up? Setsuna would never accept me back without Kaede. I promised I would find her, and I've as good as failed. Even after everything Setsuna has done for me.* Old pain opened in his chest, and he swallowed thickly. Yet again, he was a disappointment to his mother. Yet again, Kaede had bested him.

"Hayate?"

He looked up, recognizing Kaze's voice, but from the look on the black wolf's face, Hayate suspected there would be no good news. "You didn't find her trail, did you?"

Kaze shook his head. "I'm afraid not. There are no prints to track, and the wind has long since blown their scents away."

Hayate's jaw clenched, and he glared into Kaze's yellow eyes, enunciating every word. "So, that's it? You're prepared to give up, after all we've gone through?" Anger boiled in the pit of his stomach, threatening to bubble up and out of his mouth despite his efforts. "The five of them can't have disappeared!"

Kaze was not in the least intimidated. He stood his ground, tail lifted proudly above his haunches. "I never claimed they disappeared, but I meant what I said. Their trail leads to one of the docks, as I told you before, but I can follow it no further."

Hayate turned away, crossing his arms tight over his chest. The sparkling green waves of the Jade Sea stretched out before him, glowing almost insolently in the low light. *Hours of searching, all for nothing. They must have left some trace, some clue. I can't return to Setsuna a failure. She's counting on me.*

"There must be a way to follow them," he muttered, his fingers clenching into fists. "You aren't trying hard enough."

Kaze let out a low, warning growl, showing the sharpened points of his fangs. "I love you as a brother, Hayate, but I will not allow you to speak to me this way. I have followed you against my own conscience simply because I care for you and want to keep you safe. It is because I love you that I am telling you this, even though you do not want to listen. Your loyalty to Setsuna has blinded you to your moral code. You have abandoned your warriors at home, threatened innocents, attacked your own cousin, and insulted me. This isn't the way of the samurai. It isn't your way."

Hayate started to speak, but something in Kaze's eyes made him swallow his words. Silence stretched between them, broken only by the low groan of the wooden docks in the wind.

"I understand that you do not want to disappoint your mother," Kaze looked at Hayate with stinging sympathy he knew he didn't deserve, "but chasing Kaede across the sea is not the way to win Setsuna's approval. If you truly want to make her proud, go back and stop her experiments. I respect her, but she has also taken a dark turn. Perhaps with your knowledge of the yokai, you can set her on a better path—one that helps her achieve her dream of a better world while preventing her from harming spirits in the process."

"You don't understand," Hayate said, with sadness rather than exasperation. His shoulders slumped, and his fists fell open. "Kaede is the one who walks with the yokai. I tagged along. They never accepted me the way they did her. They even changed her body because she asked. I'm not arrogant enough to think I can march back home and tell Setsuna she doesn't need Kaede because she has me."

Kaze padded over to him, nudging his shoulder. "Kaede doesn't matter in this. This competition is all in your head. I am wolf-clan, and I am telling you that you do have a way with spirits, just like your cousin. Kaede has never thought she was better than you, and I have never thought so, either."

"Then why did Setsuna always act like it?" The words slipped out before Hayate could think them through, but once they hung in the air, he couldn't take them back.

"We all put our parents on pedestals. Part of growing up is realizing they are not perfect. Perhaps she worked hard to build a relationship with Kaede because she knew your cousin had a falling out with her own parents. Perhaps she simply wanted to nurture the talent of someone she cared for. And perhaps she already had faith in your abilities, since she raised you from a pup. If she neglected you, it wasn't because she stopped loving you, or because she wasn't proud of you."

Hayate sat down on the top step, folding his arms around his legs and resting his chin on his knees. He couldn't meet Kaze's eyes, and so he continued staring at the sunset, watching the last of the light fade. "All I ever wanted was to make her proud," he said, blinking back tears. He couldn't remember the last time he had cried. "I was never good enough."

"I disagree." Kaze sat down beside him, his bushy tail curling around them both. "The Hayate I know is good enough. Go home. Tell your mother how you feel. Forget Kaede, lance this wound, and let it heal."

"It can't be that simple, can it?" He turned to look at Kaze once more. "Besides, I thought you didn't want me to help Setsuna?"

"I disapprove of her methods just as I have disapproved of yours lately. But despite that, I trust you. Setsuna might take a gentler course with you at her side."

"I've been awful lately, haven't I?" Hayate whispered, thinking back. He remembered the terrified villager cowering before the point of his sword, the dying men in the snow outside the cave. He had blamed Kaede for their deaths, attributing them directly to her unwillingness to help. *But that's not fair, is it? Kaede never hurt anyone. I wanted someone to blame. Blaming her was easier than blaming me.*

"You know what needs to be done, don't you?" Kaze asked.

Hayate nodded. He closed his eyes, feeling a weight lift from his shoulders despite the painful realization he had just wrestled with. For the first time in months, his path was clear. It would not be an easy one to walk, but at least he knew which direction to travel in.

"Thank you, friend," he said, wrapping his arm around Kaze's shoulders. "I'm sorry. You've been trying to tell me this all along, but I haven't listened. I need to go home and see if I can reason with Setsuna. If that makes me ungrateful—"

"It doesn't." Kaze rested his chin on top of Hayate's head. "It makes you a good son. She raised you this way."

"She did," Hayate agreed. He opened his eyes once more, watching the last of the sunset fade. "Before she became obsessed with the idea of a united world, she would have expected nothing less of me."

Chapter Fourteen

BY THE TIME THEIR party reached the giant wave, stars were scattered everywhere and the moon was slowly dipping toward the horizon. Kaede gazed up in awe, craning her neck to see the top. Its crest curled over on itself thirty meters high, forming a loop that looked as though it were in constant motion. The rippled currents of its body formed overlapping facets, gleaming green in the soft light.

Countless small stones scattered at the bottom, broken-off pieces that formed perfect little teardrops. Without even being told, Kaede could imagine what had happened. The moment the sea had frozen over, these droplets had been spraying from the sides of the wave and had fallen to the ground as gemstones.

"It's amazing," Kenta whispered from a few paces back, sounding as astonished as Kaede felt.

"It's beautiful," Takeshi agreed, with a surprisingly sincere display of emotion.

"It's all right," Imari said. Kaede turned, looking at her in disbelief. Only then did she see that her friend was joking. "But really," Imari laughed, "this is one of the most incredible things I've ever seen."

Only one of the most incredible. Kaede tried not to read too much into it. Instead, she lost herself in the way the stars shone through the wave from behind. In some places, it was almost thin enough to be translucent. In others, it was opaque, a smoky green glass that held hidden depths. On impulse, she placed her palm against the wave. It felt very warm to the touch, and not as smooth as it looked. Her fingers found countless tiny wrinkles her eyes hadn't noticed.

"It is impressive," Rin agreed, snuffling at the jade stone, "but I would have liked to see it before, when it was water and creatures lived in it."

"No, you wouldn't have," Imari pointed out. "You'd be drowning."

"You're assuming I don't know how to swim."

Kaede ignored the playful argument. While everyone else was occupied, she dropped to her knees, sifting her fingers through some of the teardrop pebbles. They glittered in her hand, and she let them fall back onto the surface of the sea with a soft clatter. "These must be worth a fortune."

"Not to anyone around here," Bo whispered back.

Kaede nearly jumped in surprise. Sometimes, their guide was so silent that she forgot about their presence. "I'm sorry," she muttered, sending more of the gemstones scattering back onto the ground. "I didn't realize you were so close."

"Jade carved from the sea is one of the few items the city of Yin has to sell," Bo continued. "Much larger pieces can be taken from near the shore without coming out this far. These little broken pieces aren't as valuable unless one wanted to keep them for sentimental reasons."

At first, Kaede wasn't sure what Bo was implying, but when their eyes slid over to Imari, she got the message. Her face flushed at the realization that Bo knew, but she supposed she shouldn't have been surprised. *They did seem to know other sensitive information about me. Maybe they're just one of those people?*

"That's a good idea." Kaede selected one of the largest stones, tucking it into her fist "I'll keep it in mind."

"Kaede?" She turned to see Imari walking toward her, preparing to kneel beside her. "What are you doing on the ground?"

"Nothing," Kaede said, blushing harder at the concerned crease between Imari's brows. "Just playing with pebbles." She stood up, heading toward the large black tent. "Should we camp here for the day?"

"Way ahead of you," Kenta said as they ducked through the opening. He was already halfway through spreading his bedroll on the ground, and Kaede shared an amused glance with Imari as he flopped down onto it with a long sigh.

"I suppose I'll prepare a late dinner," Takeshi sighed. "Someone has to."

"What about us?" Imari asked, giving Kaede's arm a friendly nudge. "Should we help him, or follow Kenta's example?"

"Help," Kaede murmured. She turned the jade stone over in her hand, running her thumb over its smooth surface. Then, she headed over to where Takeshi unloaded his pack, tucking it stealthily into her kimono on the way. *I just hope Imari thinks it's as pretty as I do.*

***

She is running through the forest again, crunching over frost and fallen leaves. The sound of ragged breathing tells her Hayate is behind her, and the high-pitched howl of a wolf means Kaze is close by. No. She can't let them catch her. She has to get away from the bodies, from the yokai corpses, from the blood on her hands.

She hears the hiss of a blade being drawn and stumbles forward with a fresh burst of speed—only to fall to her knees. A great green wave has risen out of the ground, spraying her face with small flecks of stone. It grows taller and taller, towering over her until she can see nothing more of the moon.

In a panic, she turns back, only to come face to face with Setsuna.

"I knew you would return," her aunt says, extending her hand. "Stop running and join me. Help me build the beautiful future you promised you would."

Before she can answer, Setsuna's face changes. It becomes paler, smoother, much softer and much more youthful. Her eyes are darker now, her lips fuller. "Kaede," Imari says, extending the opposite hand, the one she still has. "Trust me. Just trust me."

"Kaede? Kaede, wake up."

At the sound of her name, Kaede rolled onto her side, propping herself up on her bedroll. *Imari. Thank the Ancestors.*

"Sorry," she said, rubbing the sleep from her eyes. "Bad dream. What is it?"

"Bo is gone."

"What? Gone?" Fully awake now, she climbed to her feet, heading over to the place where Bo had set their bedroll the day before. It was gone, and there were no other signs of their guide anywhere. "How long has Bo been missing? Do you think they ran away?"

"If they did, I don't understand why." Imari came to stand beside the bedroll as well, her brow scrunched in confusion. "When I woke up, there was a pouch of circles beside my head, the same one I gave them. If they'd wanted to rob us, they would have taken our supplies and turned around instead of giving me a refund."

By that time, the Hibana brothers were up and about as well. Kenta seemed sleepy and confused, while Takeshi seemed to share Imari's concern. He came over to join them. "Kaede, are you sure you didn't see or hear anything? A person can't disappear into thin air."

Kaede shook her head. The only thing she could remember was her dream, and even those images faded. She scanned the area beneath the wave before settling her gaze on Rin, who was still curled up next to their packs with her chin on her paws. "You didn't see Bo leave, did you?" she asked her friend.

Rin lifted her head, blinking her blue eyes. "You won't find them nearby. Bo's scent is long gone. They probably left right after the rest of you fell asleep."

"Probably?" Kaede gave Rin a suspicious look, but Kenta interrupted them before she could continue the interrogation.

"What are we going to do?" He sounded more than a little worried. "We can't stay out here. We should turn around and head back for Yin."

"Oh no." Imari shook her head, folding her arms across her chest. "I didn't spend all of yesterday drowning in a pool of my own sweat to turn back now. We've got the moon. We should keep going forward. Hongshan is only another night's walk to the west, right? I bet we'll even be able to see it before too long."

Kenta looked far from convinced, and Takeshi frowned. "We only have enough water for two days. What if we get lost out here?"

"How can we get lost?" Imari said. "All we have to do is walk in a straight line, and we'll get to the other side."

"Let's put it to a vote," Takeshi said. "All in favor of going back?"

"Me," Kenta said. "We can still go to Hongshan, but maybe take a different way? We could ride around the sea..."

"That would take forever. Besides, we don't need a vote." Imari straightened her spine, taking on an imperious, commanding look Kaede suspected she had learned from her father. "This is my quest, and you all chose to come with me. I'm going on."

Despite the seriousness of the situation, Kaede couldn't help smirking. Although she wouldn't describe Imari as bossy, she was definitely stubborn when she put her mind to something. "Well, we can't just let her go on her own," she said to Takeshi, giving him a friendly nudge on the arm. He didn't smile back, but she saw his face fall into a look of resignation.

"No, we can't."

"For what it's worth, I agree with Imari." Rin lifted herself from the wave's shade, striding out onto the sea's glittering surface. "It seems sensible to continue the way we've been going."

"See?" Imari said, shooting Rin a look of gratitude. "It's three-two in favor of going. Thank you, Rin."

"You're not even going to ask for my vote?" Kaede asked, more amused than annoyed.

Imari gave her a soft smile. "Do I need to?"

Kaede sighed. "No." At Takeshi's scowl, she added, "Besides, Hayate might be waiting for us back in Yin. I think we're all agreed that we don't want to run into him again."

"That's true," Kenta said. "I mean, the guy scaled a wall with his bare hands. Let's not get in another fight with him."

"And Kaede flipped over my head," Imari said. "She can take him."

"Wait," Kenta said, "Kaede flipped over your head? When?"

A flush crossed Kaede's cheeks. "Um." She stammered, stumbling for words, but thankfully, Rin picked up on her discomfort.

"She watches and learns," Rin said, looking on Kaede with pride. "She has spent her whole life around the yokai. She was bound to pick up a few things from observing us and feeling our ki. Hayate is no exception."

"Wait," Kenta said, "so you're telling me you aren't just friends with spirits, but have awesome spirit moves, too? Why didn't you use them back with the bandits? I could have used the help when I was fighting off that giant guy with the club, you know."

Kaede rubbed the back of her neck. "Hey, I'm human. Doing that kind of stuff isn't easy on my body. It only happens when my instincts kick in."

"Like when you were trying to save me," Imari murmured. Unlike Kenta, she didn't seem excited by the revelation. Rather, she looked almost guilty. Their eyes met, and they communicated silently for a moment before Kenta began peppering her with more questions.

"So, what else can you do? Can you climb walls too? How high can you jump? What about—"

"Enough," Takeshi said, gripping Kenta's shoulder and pushing him toward their packs. "Get our supplies together. We need to start moving before we lose any more night."

"But—"

"They're having a moment," Takeshi muttered near his ear, so softly Kaede almost didn't hear. "Let it be."

Reluctantly, Kenta slouched over to their bags and began packing, with Takeshi and Rin following. That left the two of them in relative privacy, and Imari drew her lower lip almost nervously between her teeth. "I never thanked you for saving me, did I? Not that I would have needed saving if I hadn't rushed in like that."

"You were trying to help," Kaede said, but her stomach churned thinking about the cold shock of fear that had come over her when she'd seen Hayate's blade at Imari's throat. "You remember your promise though, right? Not to do that again?"

"Well, since you have secret spirit powers you didn't feel like sharing with the rest of us, I guess I won't have to." It was obviously meant to be a joke, but Kaede could still see the hurt in Imari's eyes.

"It's not something I spread around, and it's not something I can use often. Just in really desperate situations. It has nothing to do with not trusting you." She took a deep breath. "I actually trust you a lot more than I've trusted anyone else in a long time. And that's saying a lot, since the last person I trusted was my aunt."

"Who made you leave home," Imari finished for her. "I get it."

From her sympathetic look, Kaede believed her. "Anyway, about Hayate, it's not that I don't think you're capable. You're a great fighter, and you're going to be an even better daimyo. But you don't have to throw yourself in dangerous situations to prove it." She glanced at Takeshi and Kenta, who were waiting for them a short distance away. "We already know what you can do."

To Kaede's relief, Imari seemed to take her words in stride. She gave a short bow, not of formality, but of genuine gratitude. "Thank you, Kaede. I guess I'm so used to people underestimating me I forget real friends know better."

"Do they? I wouldn't know."

"Yes, you do," Imari said with a laugh. "You can't keep pretending you don't have human friends. You're stuck with us now."

Kaede grinned. "To be honest, that doesn't sound so bad."

***

By the middle of the night, Imari couldn't trust her eyes anymore. They had followed the moon west, avoiding the worst of the heat by walking in the shadows of the waves, but with limited water and a whole lot of nothing in every direction, her vision had started to blur. When she first saw a blackened smudge against the glittering green horizon, she thought it was simply her imagination. It was only when she lifted her canteen to her lips and took a few precious sips to clear her head that she started to think it might be real.

"Please," she rasped, ignoring the dryness in her throat, "tell me I'm not the only one who sees that." She gestured at the shadow, which started to take shape into a coastline. She couldn't be sure, but it almost looked like the top of a tree line if she squinted.

The others all looked too. "I think so?" Kenta said, rubbing his hand across his eyes and blinking to check. "Yeah, it's not going away."

"The four of us can't be seeing the same mirage," Kaede said, with growing excitement. "I think we made it!"

"We did," Rin said. "I noticed it an hour back."

Kaede turned on her. "And you didn't think to say anything?"

Rin snorted softly. "I thought you'd seen it too."

"Let's hurry." Takeshi hoisted his pack higher on his shoulders, increasing the length of his stride over the waves. "I'd do just about anything for some shade."

They covered the rest of the distance much faster than expected. The combination of excitement and desperation gave them another burst of energy, and they arrived at the breakers by the shore with sore legs and happy hearts. They slid and scrambled over them sloppily, but with sighs of utter relief. Up close, Imari could see the dark blanket of a forest not too far from the shore, and it looked so inviting she almost wanted to cry.

"Thank the Ancestors," she muttered.

"I never thought I'd actually want to kiss a tree before," Kenta panted beside her. He slid the rest of the way down the wave on his bottom before rising to tackle the next. Imari followed his example, laughing at the feel of wind whipping her face. The air wasn't still and stagnant as it had been over the Jade Sea, but carried a cheerful breeze that cooled the sweat clinging to her temples.

"Come on," a voice said, and she looked up to see Kaede offering her a hand. "We're almost there!"

She accepted it with a squeeze, allowing Kaede to help her to her feet. They finished the rest of the run together, arriving a little after Kenta and Takeshi. The two Hibana brothers were already lying flat on their backs, arms outstretched. Even Takeshi's normally surly face had broken into a rare smile.

"I vote we go back the long way," Kenta said, and Takeshi let out a laugh.

"We can discuss it," Imari said. "But we did it!" She let go of Kaede's hand and brought her canteen to her lips, finally draining the last of her water. She'd been saving it, but now, there was no need. If there was a forest, there had to be lakes and rivers around somewhere. "How about we find a place to refill these and rest?" She shook her empty canteen at the others so they could hear the droplets rattle.

"I'm all for that," Kaede agreed. "I don't know about the rest of you, but I stink. A bath would be good, even if it's in a river."

"You had me at bath," Kenta said, pulling himself up with a groan and retrieving his pack. "And I want to pee behind an actual tree instead of wandering a few yards away and telling the rest of you not to look."

Imari was about to make a comment about how Kenta had it much easier than her, but she noticed the pink flush of embarrassment on Kaede's face and kept the comment back. Honestly, she hadn't given what was between Kaede's legs much thought. Well, not too much thought, anyway. It hadn't mattered to her, although she had found herself curious in private moments. Based on the way Kaede kept to herself while dressing and undressing, and her awkwardness about certain subjects, she could hazard a guess.

I wonder why the spirits didn't change her, like they did with her face and breasts? Or maybe she didn't want to change? I never asked. It was something she would have to bring up eventually, but now wasn't the right time. *First, water, then a long, well-earned sleep.*

The five of them made their way into the forest together, pausing to scout the area once they broke through the outer branches. It was a cheerful, open place that let a fair amount of moonlight in through the gaps in the trees. Imari couldn't hear anything but faint birdcalls and the occasional rustle, Rin's ears perked up as they entered. "This way," she said, turning to the left. "I smell a stream."

They followed Rin's directions, and soon they arrived at water—a river, wide and deep, running through the forest at a moderate pace. The surface glittered blue beneath the patchy moonlight that broke through the canopy, with little white caps leaping up as it rushed over a patch of rocks. Imari studied it, trying to judge how safe it was, but Kenta was far less cautious. He threw his pack to the ground by the bank and began shedding his clothes. "Last one in has to get out first and set up camp!"

"Kenta, wait—" Takeshi tried to protest, but it was too late. Kenta had already kicked off his shoes and unfastened his obi.

Imari laughed, politely averting her eyes. She turned toward Kaede instead, who looked distinctly uncomfortable. Her brow crinkled, and she bit her lower lip. "It's all right," she whispered, taking Kaede's hand. "I'll make sure you get some privacy." To Kenta, she said, "You and Takeshi have fun. I'm going to take Kaede a little further upstream.

"Spoilsport," Kenta said as he fought with his clothes. "I would've kept my fundoshi on."

"I've never understood the human obsession with modesty," Rin added. "I walk around without clothes all the time."

"You have fur," Imari pointed out. "It doesn't count. And you'll have to forgive me for not wanting to lick my own rear in public."

Rin gave her a look of wounded dignity. With a reproachful air, she stalked off into the forest, tail waving high above her haunches. Imari guessed she was amused rather than angry, and this was simply her way of offering them some privacy.

"Don't mind her," Kaede mumbled. "She's probably going to have a sniff around and make sure it's safe." She looked down at their hands, which Imari realized were still joined.

A loud splash interrupted the moment. Kenta had leapt into the river and swam near the bank. His head bobbed up and down, but it appeared as though he had found the bottom with his feet. "It's not too deep here," he said. "Come on, Takeshi!"

Takeshi sighed. "Kenta, I really don't think—" Kenta aimed a wide splash at him, and it hit right on target. Takeshi spluttered, swiping at his face with his sleeve. "All right. Now you're asking for it." His serious demeanor vanished as he began stripping out of his own clothes, and Imari took that as her opportunity to steal Kaede away.

"Come on," she whispered. "Let's go around that bend up ahead."

They went a little ways further into the forest, following the river around a subtle curve and behind another cluster of red and orange maple trees. The bushy leaves offered some privacy, and Imari gasped as she peered around them. "Kaede, look!" she said, pointing excitedly. A small waterfall, no more than three meters high, splashed before them. The river cascaded down in rippling sheets, a shining ribbon of blue.

"Well?" Kaede asked. Now that the two of them were alone, she seemed much more relaxed. "I don't know about you, but I'm getting in." She began unfastening her kimono, and afterwards, Imari accepted Kaede's help with her own. Three hands made the job a lot easier than one.

Soon, they were down to their juban, and it was only then that Kaede hesitated.

"Can we—" she began, and Imari nodded.

"Of course."

Kaede gave her a big smile. Her shoulders finally relaxed, and she ran for the river with the same excitement as Kenta. With a whoop of joy, she leaped in, sending a spray of water high above her head.

Imari remained behind, laughing when Kaede emerged again. "How cold is it?"

"Cold, but good," Kaede said. "Come in with me."

Imari didn't hesitate. After three days travelling across a glass desert, she ached to feel water on her skin. She jumped in too, ducking under the water. The river pulled at her steadily but not hard enough to carry her downstream. She was able to swim around a little beneath the surface, and she caught a glimpse of Kaede's legs kicking a small distance ahead. She popped up out of the water, gasping and shaking droplets from her hair.

"It does feel good," she said. "Ancestors, I needed this."

Kaede paddled over. Her hair was a much darker shade of red now that it was wet, and somehow, her disheveled appearance only made her seem more beautiful. "Thanks for taking me away from the others. I like Kenta, and even Takeshi is growing on me lately, but I don't want them to see me like this."

Imari's eyes widened. "But you do want me to see you like this?"

Kaede drifted a little closer. "That depends on whether you like what you see or not."

Imari smirked. She had tried not to look too closely, all too aware that Kaede might not appreciate such an intense gaze, but the glimpses she had caught of Kaede's figure through her kimono slip had been more than pleasing. "I liked what I saw the first day we met. Imagine my delight when I realized you were excellent company, too."

A flush bloomed across Kaede's cheeks, until she was almost as red as the maple trees that surrounded them. "Uh."

"Hey, you started flirting with me," Imari teased. "I'm just flirting back."

"I know. I like it. It's just...I don't have a lot of experience with pretty girls giving me attention, okay? If you haven't noticed, I'm kind of awkward when it comes to this."

"Oh, I've noticed. It adds to your charm." She began moving against the current, heading toward the waterfall, and motioned for Kaede to join her. "If you don't mind my asking, why are you so surprised that I think you're good looking? Surely someone else has told you before?"

"Not really," Kaede said, gliding along by her side. "I didn't spend a lot of time with humans at home, especially ones who weren't my relatives. Wolf spirits don't care how you look."

"Well, take it from someone who has seen a lot of good-looking men and women. You're much more beautiful than you give yourself credit for."

"A lot of good-looking men and women, huh?" Kaede repeated, a little nervously. "So, you probably know more about this than I do. Tell me, what happens next, because I honestly don't have a clue."

Imari floated closer, brushing Kaede's arm with her fingertips under the water. "Oh, I think you do, but I'll humor you and tell you. Usually, once two people admit they're attracted to each other, there's a kiss."

Kaede's lips parted, and she inhaled a sharp breath. "A kiss? Like...on the mouth?"

"Well, it doesn't have to be on your mouth," Imari purred. "I can think of a few other places I'd like to plant one, but your mouth is probably a good place to start."

Kaede's eyes darted toward Imari's mouth and lingered there. A look of indecision crossed her face, as though she was trying to make up her mind. Instead of leaning forward, Imari simply waited. As much as she wanted to weave her fingers through the wet strands of Kaede's hair, gently grip the back of her neck, and pull her in, she knew this needed to be Kaede's choice.

Finally, it happened. Kaede leaned forward, and Imari felt soft, sweet breath caress her cheek moments before Kaede's warm lips closed over hers. At first, neither of them moved. They both held still, mouths touching gently. Then Imari felt an arm wrap around her waist beneath the water, and she gave into the temptation to sink her fingers into Kaede's hair.

When it became obvious from her lack of movement that Kaede wasn't sure what she was doing, Imari decided to offer some guidance. She opened her mouth a little more, just enough for her tongue to peek out and tease the edge of Kaede's bottom lip. Kaede let out a soft moan, and from the way she shuddered, Imari knew it was one of pleasure. She showed Kaede a slow, gliding way to kiss, one that didn't delve too deep, but allowed them to taste more of each other.

After a while, Kaede seemed to grow bolder. She added a little more pressure, and her hand wandered lower, resting on Imari's hip. Imari's stomach erupted with butterflies. Kaede's moments of shyness were sweet, but her newfound confidence was even more exhilarating. She groaned and trapped Kaede's lip between her teeth, giving it a gentle tug.

"Hey," Kaede muttered. She broke the kiss and pulled back, but not more than a few centimeters. "Since when is biting a part of kissing?"

"Biting is an important part of kissing, if you do it right," Imari said. "But if you don't like it. . ."

To her surprise, Kaede darted in again and did the same to her, following it up with a soft suck. "I like it," she whispered. "Show me more."

Imari was happy to oblige.

Chapter Fifteen

IT TOOK THEM ANOTHER day and a half to reach the base of Mount Hongshan on foot. It was far easier than crossing the Jade Sea, even though they were heading uphill. They stuck to the small river, grateful for a steady supply of water and the cover of the trees. Gradually, as the foliage thinned, the forest shifted from golden maples beneath the shadow of towering oaks to strange foliage Kaede didn't recognize. As they continued forward, a foul smell began to surround them, like rotting fruit after a rainstorm.

"Ugh," Kaede said, wrinkling her nose in disgust. "What is that?"

Kenta sniffed and made a similar face. "Reminds me of Takeshi's tabi—hey!" he said, dodging the light cuff Takeshi aimed at him. The Hibana brothers had been in a much more pleasant mood since their afternoon of rest.

"I know what it is," Imari said, sounding pleased with herself. "And it's not Takeshi's socks, although those are bad."

"We were crossing the Jade Sea," Takeshi replied. "Smelly socks are forgivable."

Imari ignored him. "It's the trees," she said, gesturing all around them. "They're called chouchun, although another name for them is 'tree of heaven'."

Kaede looked up. The tall, green trees had narrow trunks and wide, bushy branches. She sidled up alongside one of them, taking a whiff of a green, star-shaped blossom. "Sun and Moon!" she exclaimed, recoiling. "They don't smell like heaven to me. How do you know this, anyway?"

"I read," Imari said with a grin. "Some accounts of Hongshan mention them. We must be getting close."

"Great," Kenta said in a muffled voice. Kaede glanced over to see that he was covering his nose and mouth with his hand. "How much further?"

"I don't know, but we should stay close to them," Rin said. Instead of being distracted by the smell, her eyes constantly scanned the forest, looking for any signs of movement.

Kaede stared at her in disbelief. "Why? I would have thought they'd bother you most of all."

"They'll cover our scent," Rin explained. "If Hayate and Kaze did manage to follow us this far, they won't be able to track us through this. I wouldn't be able to find them if the positions were reversed. The smell is too strong."

Kaede doubted Hayate and Kaze had pursued them all the way across the sea, but Rin's words did bring her some comfort—or perhaps it was Imari's arm pressing close to hers. The two of them had taken to holding hands since their kisses beneath the waterfall, and her company always made Kaede feel more at ease.

"Do you think any other yokai live in this forest?" Imari asked her.

"Yokai live in every forest," Kaede told her. "They just don't like to be seen much. But I bet if we looked really close we'd spot one." She glanced around, trusting her senses more than her eyes. Spirits had a certain energy about them, a tingling sort of warmth she could sometimes pick up when they were near, if she paid close attention. Finally, she caught something—the sense of being watched and a tingling on the back of her neck, as well as a brief rustle off to the left. She whipped her head around in time to catch a flash of red diving back into the bushes.

"There," she whispered. "A fox."

Imari's face lit up. "Kitsune? Really?" She seemed to drift, almost as if to another time and place. Then, she shook herself out of it. "Do you think it's following us?"

"Probably, although with that display, it probably wanted us to know it was there."

"And you sensed it? I had no idea." Imari looked impressed, but Kaede merely shrugged.

"If you spend as much time with spirits as I have, you get a feel for it. Anyway, a fox won't harm us. Let's keep going."

"Are you sure about that?" Kenta asked. "I've heard the stories about them. They're tricksters."

"If it had wanted to trick us, it wouldn't have shown itself. It won't cause us any trouble." She continued, taking the lead, and the others followed. It felt a little strange, taking charge of the group, but she had more experience with forests and spirits than any of them. In fact, it was flattering they trusted her judgment.

As they made their way further into the foul-smelling trees, Kaede's sense of being watched grew stronger. At first, she wondered if it might be the fox again, but the heated prickle on the back of her neck was too intense. Something else—someone else—was following them, and she hesitated, wondering if she should tell the others. Rin seemed to sense it too. The wolf gave her a suspicious look, one Kaede returned with nervous agreement.

Before she could alert her friends, the rustling sound returned, this time from above. Kaede looked up, but barely had enough time to stumble backwards before a shower of leaves rained down on top of her. Several large shapes hurtled through the canopy of the chouchun trees, breaking branches as they went. Their cries sounded like the screech of a hawk, and the air became alive with feathers. She drew her katana, stepping in front of Imari, but the creatures didn't attack right away. They landed on the forest floor, and Kaede got a better look.

Six enormous birds touched to the ground, as tall as any human. Their wings were as wide as a small ship's sails, black on top and a dazzling white underneath. They had blazing black eyes and sharp, curved beaks, and their feet ended in wicked talons. A name came to her, a yokai clan she had heard about before, but had never seen in the forest at home. These were tengu, hawk-spirits not at all fond of humans.

"You," one croaked, clacking its beak and puffing up its feathers. "What are you doing here? This is our place. Humans are not welcome."

Kaede studied her companions. Imari, Kenta, and Takeshi had drawn their swords as well, taking on defensive postures but looking to her for guidance. She took a deep breath. If there was any chance of talking their way out of a fight, she had to try. "We don't want to stay. We just want to cross through the forest to the mountain."

That didn't seem to please the tengu. They chattered amongst each other, flapping their wings and flexing their talons in the dirt. Kaede gripped the hilt of her katana tighter.

"You will go," another of the tengu said. "Humans are not welcome."

"We want to go," Kaede said as calmly as she could. "If you let us pass, we'll be gone by the end of the day."

"No!" a third tengu squawked. "No humans!"

Rin growled. "Look here, featherbrains. These humans want nothing to do with your forest. They are going to the mountain, and it's no business of yours."

That only seemed to anger the tengu further. The nearest one hissed at Rin, almost like a cat. "Smelly dog! You will go too. No one passes."

Kaede's mind raced. If she didn't do something soon, there'd be a fight. The others trusted her to get them through safely, so she had to do something—and fast. *What do I know about tengu? They're hostile and proud, and they think they're better than everyone else.*

That gave her an idea. She lowered her sword and addressed the tengu again. "What about a riddle? If you come up with one we can't solve, we'll turn around and never return. If we come up with one you can't solve, you'll let us pass, and we'll be gone by evening."

Imari began to protest, but Kaede silenced her with a warning look. *Trust me.*

As she had hoped, one of the tengu puffed up its breast. The largest of all, with ragged edges to its feathers, this one had a scar over one of its eyes. From the vivid coloring Kaede suspected it was male. "I am leader," he cawed. "I say our riddle will be better than yours."

"Good," Kaede said. "So, you agree? Whoever tells the hardest riddle wins."

The tengu circled in on each other, bobbing their heads and conversing rapidly in a language Kaede couldn't understand. While they talked, she gathered her own companions around her.

"Kaede, are you sure this will work?" Kenta asked, aiming a nervous glance over his shoulder. "I don't like the look of those talons. Who's to say they won't attack us anyway if we beat them?"

"Yokai aren't like that," Kaede insisted. "They almost always stick to their bargains, even the unfriendly ones. They're too proud to go back on a wager. We have to come up with a good riddle to stump them."

"It's better than nothing," Imari said. "I'll take a riddle contest over a fight. Want me to give it a try?"

Kaede nodded. "If you know some good ones, go ahead."

Imari left the group and turned toward the tengu, shoulders straight and squared. "Okay, should we go first, or do you want to?"

The tengu looked to their leader. He snorted through the slitted nostrils of his beak, fixing her with a glare. "You first, humans. We will take turns."

"Okay." Imari took a deep breath. "What has an eye, but cannot see?"

The leader's feathers ruffled, as if he was confused and displeased, but then one of his companions whispered to him. He preened himself for a moment, as though he had never been conflicted at all, before answering. "Too easy. A needle."

"How do birds even know what a needle is?" Kenta muttered. "That's stupid."

"Don't call them stupid," Takeshi murmured back. "We want to get out of here with all our fingers and toes."

Kaede cleared her throat to cover up their conversation. "Your turn. Give us a riddle to solve."

Once more, the tengu conversed among themselves, flapping and hopping, but at last, they seemed to come to an agreement. The leader spoke, "If you have me, you want to share me. If you share me, you cannot keep me. What am I?"

Kaede knew the answer. She looked at the others, and from Imari's smile, she could tell she wasn't the only one who had figured it out. "A secret," she said with confidence. "I'm a secret."

The tengu screeched angrily, beating their wings, but they didn't attack. Instead, they merely responded with piercing glares. "Your turn," the leader said. "Another riddle."

"I've got another one," Imari said. "What is as light as a feather, but even the strongest person can't hold it for more than a few minutes?"

The tengu turned to each other again, but this time, they grew more and more agitated, with some breaking off to nibble at their feathers while the others pecked and jabbed at each other. After several tense minutes, the group seemed to arrive at an answer. Kaede swallowed. Her heart drummed too hard in her chest, and she couldn't get enough air. It had been several minutes since the start of the confrontation, and still, the tension hadn't broken.

"A bird," the tengu leader said. "Light enough to fly, but no human can hold us."

Imari shook her head. "No, I'm afraid not. The answer is breath."

At this, the tengu erupted in a great commotion of squawking and hopping, enough to shake the leaves of the chouchun trees and cause several to fall to the ground. Kaede readied her sword, but to her relief, the birds didn't attack. They seemed angry, but inclined to stick to their bargain.

"You still won't win," the leader of the tengu said. "Now, we ask another riddle. What is greater than Sun and Moon, older than the first Ancestors. Poor have it. Rich need it. If you eat it, you die. What am I?"

With a stab of panic, Kaede realized she couldn't think of the answer. She paused for a moment, searching her brain, but nothing came to her. Looking at the others, she was discouraged. Kenta shrugged helplessly, and Takeshi frowned even more than usual. Imari's brow knitted in concentration, but she didn't seem to have a clue either.

Ancestors, this was a bad idea, Kaede thought as the sinking feeling of doubt began to creep in. *I shouldn't have suggested a riddle competition. I can't think of anything, not a single thing.*

"Wait! Nothing."

Imari's head whipped around. "What did you say?"

"Nothing."

"You definitely said something," Kenta protested. "I heard you. What was it?"

"No," Kaede said. "The answer to the riddle is nothing. There's nothing greater than the Sun and Moon, and nothing older than the Ancestors. Poor people have nothing, and rich people want for nothing. And if you eat nothing, you die." She turned to the tengu. "I'm right, aren't I?"

Again, the tengu hopped and flapped and jabbed their beaks and shook the trees, but this time, Kaede wasn't afraid. Breathless and thrilled, she was confident that she had won. When the tengu finally settled and the leader spoke, she could tell from the venomous reproach in his voice that though she had angered him, he wouldn't attack her.

"Go," he crowed. "Leave now, and do not come back this way."

Kaede didn't wait around for him to change his mind. She started off past the tengu at a swift trot, diving back into the forest as quickly as she could. The others were hot on her heels, and none of them slowed back to a walk until they were a fair distance away.

"That was a close one," she panted, waiting for the others to catch up.

"Yeah, but we got out of it all right, thanks to you," Imari said. She was breathless, but her eyes gleamed with excitement and admiration. "That was brilliant! How did you think of it?"

Kaede grinned, pleased with the praise. "I told you, I know my spirits. I knew if we could get them to agree to a wager, they'd let us go by."

"A good trick," Takeshi said, also sounding impressed. "You were clever to think of it."

"Indeed she was," said another voice, one that didn't belong to any of their party members. "Almost, dare I say, as clever as a fox."

Kaede stopped in her tracks, but she didn't have to look around to find out who had spoken. There was movement in the brush ahead, and then a small creature stepped out into the open. It was a fox, the same fox from before, as far as Kaede could tell. It had a fine gleaming coat of orange and white, and nine bushy tails trailed behind it, almost like the plumes of a peacock. Daubed in black with white at the tips, they swished slightly as the fox regarded them.

"Don't worry about the tengu coming after you for revenge, Iori-san," the fox said. "They're horrible trackers. If they can't see you, they won't be able to find you."

Kaede's eyes widened. The fox had addressed her by her ronin name, but none of them had spoken it. "How do you know who I am?"

The fox smiled, if ever a fox could smile. "I have been watching you and your companions for a while, Iori-san. You have been of great interest to me."

"Interest?" Kaede asked. The fox didn't seem to bear them any ill will, but she was still suspicious. Kitsune were tricksters, according to all the legends she had ever heard and the yokai she had spoken to. They weren't usually hostile, but they often had secret motivations.

"Yes. But first, give me a moment."

The fox began to glow with a strange light, and Kaede watched in fascination as its body rippled and shifted. It grew taller, standing on two legs instead of four. Its fur receded, leaving only skin behind. Its tufted ears melted back into its head, and its nose shrank and changed shape. The air around it seemed to blur, and Kaede felt as though she were watching the transformation through smoky glass or the surface of a pond.

At last, a young woman stood before them. Her straight black hair fell down her shoulders, and her round, youthful face reminded Kaede of the moon. She wore a simple kimono the same color as her fur had been, but beneath it, Kaede could still see the tips of her tails curling around her ankles. In this form, she appeared to be about eighteen or twenty, if Kaede had to take a guess, but judging by the nine tails, she had to be at least nine hundred, possibly even older. With foxes, looks were deceiving.

Beside her, Imari bowed. "Hello. My name is Homura Imari. May I ask yours?"

Kenta stared at her. "Really, Imari? That's all you're gonna say?"

"Or maybe ask why she was following us?" Takeshi added suspiciously.

The fox's eyes twinkled. "You say 'following' as if it's a bad thing, Hibana-san." She returned Imari's bow, dipping deeply before all five of them. "You can call me Kyuubi."

Kaede tilted her head. "Isn't that a little bit on the nose? 'Nine-tailed'?"

The fox grinned brighter still. "I find it amusing, Iori-san. And, as I said before, you have been of great interest to me. It isn't often that humans come here."

"We've come here in search of Kurogane," Imari said. "Do you know him?"

Unsurprisingly, Kyuubi's answer was indirect. "Yes and no. However, I believe I can be of assistance to you. I would ask you to follow me."

Kaede looked to Imari. "Should we trust her?"

"I was about to ask you the same question," Imari whispered back. "You're the yokai expert. What do you think?"

Kaede thought about it. Despite what had happened with Bo, they could probably use the help of someone who lived in the forest in case more unfriendly yokai showed up as night fell. "Will you take us to Mount Aka, Kyuubi? You may know it as Hongshan."

"Yes. Just be warned, what you find there will not be what you expect. It never is, with dragons involved."

"So, there are dragons here," Imari said triumphantly. "Forgive me, but our last guide wouldn't confirm it."

"Of course there are," Kyuubi said. "It's not called Mount Hongshan for nothing. Now, come on. We should be off, if we want to reach our destination before dusk."

Kaede noticed Takeshi looking over at her. "I don't like this—"

"But you don't see a better option," Kaede finished for him. "I don't think she means us harm, but keep your eyes open anyway. The tengu were a close call."

He gave her a nod. Once more, the tension between them had receded into mutual respect. Without being told, Kaede could tell he appreciated what she had done, especially since it had kept Imari safe. She smiled. Even Imari hadn't tried to interfere this time. It seemed her companions were finally starting to trust in her abilities.

"We'll go with you," she told the fox, "and thank you for helping us."

"Very well. Try and keep up." Kyuubi headed off through the forest at a spritely pace, barely grazing the leaves with her sandals. Kaede followed, but she let Imari and the Hibana brothers take the lead this time, waiting for Rin to fall into step beside her.

"What do you think of all this?" she whispered under her breath, so only Rin could hear. "You were quiet back there."

"Just because I didn't say anything doesn't mean I wasn't paying attention," Rin said.

Kaede had thought as much. "So?"

"I agree with Takeshi. I don't like this. Kyuubi seems friendly enough, but we should keep our eyes open and our noses to the ground. My mother always told me when I was a pup, you can never trust a fox, especially when they're trying to be your friend."

***

Shortly before sunset, they arrived at the foothills surrounding Hongshan. The chouchun trees thinned out, revealing the open air, and the soft, leaf-covered ground beneath Imari's sandals became rough with gravel. As she picked her way up the uneven slope, she remained near Kyuubi. Normally, she would have walked with Kaede, but their new guide fascinated her. She stuck close as the fox scaled the mountain, putting her feet in the same places.

Although she knew it was rude, she couldn't help staring at the lightly swishing tips of Kyuubi's nine tails. The foxes she had encountered in the past had three or four at most, including the ones who had saved her life years ago. To find a fox with nine was almost unheard of. Kyuubi had to be almost a thousand years old, possibly even older.

And yet, here she is, volunteering to help us. Why? Imari knew she couldn't come right out and ask, so she started with something a little less direct. "So, do you live here in the forest?" she asked, panting lightly as she scurried over a boulder. Like Bo, Kyuubi was far more agile than the rest of them.

Kyuubi paused, allowing her to catch up. "I've lived in many places, but currently, this is my home. I find it quite picturesque, aside from the smell."

"True enough. I'm sure the tengu would have cleared out too, if they'd had noses instead of beaks."

"Probably," Kyuubi laughed. "But what about you, Homura-san? Why are you so far from home, searching for the mysterious Kurogane?"

Imari hesitated. She wasn't certain how much of her story she wanted to tell, but she saw no reason to keep it secret, either. After a moment of indecision, she held up the sleeve of her kimono, allowing it to fall past the stump of her wrist. "I was hoping he could do something about this. I lost it in an accident—one that a clan of foxes saved me from, actually."

Kyuubi's tails perked up and her eyes brightened. "Foxes, you say? Well, that's good to hear. Not all humans trust us, so it's nice to meet someone who's had a pleasant experience with my kind."

"I'd call it more than a pleasant experience. I was trapped beneath a large rock in a cave-in, and the foxes pulled me free. They couldn't save my hand, but I owe them my life. Anyway, about Kurogane. The legends say he isn't an ordinary blacksmith, so I thought..."

Kyuubi murmured low in understanding. "I see. Well, you're right that Kurogane is no ordinary blacksmith. They may be able to do something about your hand, but whether they will choose to help, I cannot say."

"Is there a reason he wouldn't?" Imari asked, eager for information. The thought of coming all this way only to have her request denied was unbearable. "Please, if you know something, tell me."

"I know," Kyuubi said. "Kurogane is a reasonable person, but I don't want you to get your hopes up. There is always a reason to say no."

Imari retreated to her own head for a moment. For all the planning she had done, all the preparations she had made, and all the difficulties she had overcome, the fact that Kurogane might refuse to help had never occurred to her. *And what will I do if he tells me no? Not give up, surely. I didn't come all this way only to return empty...oh. Perhaps that's a bad turn of phrase.*

"If he won't help, I'll ask him to direct me to someone who can," Imari said, full of determination.

Kyuubi smiled. "I admire your spirit, Homura-san. Good things always come to those who are willing to pursue them. If Kurogane will not help you, search the forest for me. Perhaps by then I will have thought of someone else who might replace your hand. My memory is long, you see, and it takes me some time to sort through the older ones."

"Thank you so much, Kyuubi," Imari sighed with relief. "I hope I won't need your help, but the offer is more than appreciated."

"Yes." Kyuubi froze in place, raising her nose to the air. Even though it was human-shaped, Imari had the impression of whiskers twitching as the fox sniffed the breeze. "But now, I'm afraid I must take my leave. I'm sorry to abandon you so abruptly, but I've caught scent of something troubling."

"Troubling?" Takeshi asked. He, Kenta, Kaede, and Rin had finally caught up just in time to hear Kyuubi speak. "What do you mean?" He reached for his sword, but Kyuubi stopped him with a gesture.

"Troubling to me, not to you. I sense someone coming, a friend of yours, as a matter of fact. They have no quarrel with you, but I'm afraid they aren't on the best of terms with me." She gave a sheepish grin. "I played a trick on them a few centuries ago, and dragons are known to hold grudges."

"Wait, dragons?" Imari blurted out. She wasn't sure whether to be eager or wary. "They're a friend? I would have remembered meeting a dragon."

Kyuubi dipped her head. "Trust me when I say that you won't be in any danger. I really should be going. Foxes are good at sensing other spirits, but if I don't hurry, the dragon will feel my ki too." With a final look over her shoulder, she curled in on herself, growing shorter and shorter. Her ears grew tall and pointed, and her kimono melted into sleek sheets of fur. Soon, she was a fox once more, standing only as high as their waists. "I won't be far," Kyuubi told them, black nose twitching. "I'm simply going back down to the forest. Come and see me some time. It was a pleasure to meet you."

Imari began to protest, but before she could say anything, Kyuubi darted off down the mountain, disappearing into a crevice between two large boulders.

"Well, that was strange," she said, turning to Kaede. "What do you think?"

Kaede searched the sky. "I don't know, but I don't see any sign of dragons." She frowned. "And I don't sense anything out of the ordinary either. If there is a dragon here, they're hiding well."

"Good riddance, I say," Rin huffed. Her lips were peeled back slightly, showing the points of her fangs. "Foxes are too clever for their own good. You can't trust them."

Slightly offended, Imari put her hand on her hip. "Is that necessary, Rin? Kyuubi was nothing but nice and polite."

"She ran off," Rin pointed out. "That isn't nice or polite."

"So did Bo," Imari said. "I don't hear you complaining about them."

However, she was prevented from arguing further by the faint sound of footsteps approaching. They seemed to be coming from a little further up the mountain, and Imari squinted ahead, trying to see in the low light. "Do you hear something?" she whispered.

"Yes," Kaede whispered back. "Someone's coming, but it sounds like a person to me." She hesitated, and a visible shudder ran through her. "I'm not sure though. Something feels off."

Rin's ears flattened against her head, and she pointed her muzzle at a boulder a few meters ahead. "There."

Imari drew her sword. She wasn't sure what good it would do if there was a dragon nearby, but she didn't want to be caught defenseless. However, the creature that emerged wasn't a dragon at all. It was a thin human figure in a familiar brown robe, one that shielded their face except for a slight, mysterious smile.

"Thanks for the refund, Bo," Imari said, recognizing them at once. They were dressed in the same clothes they had worn to cross the Jade Sea. She lowered her katana, although she didn't sheathe it quite yet.

Kenta stared at Bo. "Why did you leave us stranded in the middle of the sea?"

Bo smiled. "I do owe the five of you an explanation, and perhaps an apology."

"Perhaps?" Kaede repeated with raised eyebrows.

Rin growled, her nose wrinkling in anger. "Make it a fast one. And show us what you really are while you're at it. I knew you didn't smell human from the beginning."

Suddenly, the pieces clicked in Imari's head. She stared at Bo in newfound awe, more certain than ever that she was right. Their cryptic statements, their mysterious disappearance, their stories about dragons, and Kyuubi's comments—it all made sense. "That's because they aren't."

"True enough, although I never claimed I was." Bo stepped back, unfurling the sides of their cloak. A surge of light washed through the evening dusk, and Imari lifted a hand to shield her eyes. Bo was transforming, shining almost as bright as the sun. They grew larger and larger, billowing toward the top of the mountain like a column of smoke winding up from a bonfire, until they filled the lower half of the sky.

The flash faded and Imari found herself staring at a creature the size of a small hill. Its glittering, blue-scaled body coiled like a snake's, winding in on itself over and over. Stars of silver scattered across its back, leading up in ribbons to its giant lion's head. Flowing whiskers hung down past its enormous jaws, and brilliant azure fur ringed its pointed ears. Its breath washed warm across the hillside, and Imari lost hers. This creature was the most amazing thing she had ever seen, and she couldn't find the words.

Kenta stepped back in surprise, Takeshi sucked in a sharp gasp, and Rin's hackles rose. Only Kaede seemed relatively calm. While Imari struggled to decide what to do, Kaede stepped forward and gave the creature a deep bow.

"It's an honor," she said, without rising. "Please, what is your name?"

The dragon bowed their head in return. Raising, they blinked slowly, regarding them with vivid lilac eyes. "My true name is Suanni of the Endless Sky." Their low, rumbling voice trembled through Imari's bones, but she didn't feel the desire to run or hide. "Forgive me for my deception, but I will make it up to you now. If you allow me, I will take you up the mountain to see Kurogane."

At last, Imari managed to speak. "Why did you leave us before?" she asked, craning her neck to stare up into the dragon's violet irises. "Why are you helping us now?"

Suanni chuckled, streams of silver mist trailing up from their large nostrils. "I left to see whether you would lose your nerve and turn back, or whether you would gather your courage and continue on. Kurogane possesses powerful magic, magic given by my clan only to those who have earned it. You have proven yourselves worthy."

Imari's heart swelled with hope, and a smile spread across her face. "You'll really take us to him?"

"Yes, Imari." Suanni lowered themself to the ground, unfurling their great body. Lying flat on their stomach, they were still taller than Imari, or even Takeshi. "Climb onto my back. I will fly you to the blacksmith's forge."

Imari stepped forward, grinning from ear-to-ear, only to feel a soft hand on her arm. "Imari, wait. Are you sure about this?" Takeshi asked, holding her elbow. "This is a dragon. You're seriously going to ride it?"

Under normal circumstances, Imari would have been annoyed at his interference, but she was far too excited to care. "Yes, I am," she told him, practically laughing. "Takeshi, this is the whole reason I came this far! Are you telling me you don't want to ride a dragon?"

"I—"

"She has a point, Takeshi." Kaede touched Imari's arm, gently brushing his hand aside. "It has the makings of an amazing story."

"I'm in," Kenta said. He hurried over to join them, slinging a friendly arm over Takeshi's shoulder. "Come on, big brother. All the ladies back in Mirai will be all over you when you tell them you rode a dragon up a forbidden mountain."

Takeshi looked at Rin, obviously hoping for some support, but he found none. Now that Suanni was no longer concealing their true form, the wolf seemed much more relaxed and trusting. "I sense no danger," she told him. "I'm inclined to believe our friend."

"So, they're our friend now," Takeshi muttered, but after a while, he sighed and turned back to Imari. "I'm not going to talk you out of this, am I?"

Imari shook her head, still grinning. "Not a chance."

Chapter Sixteen

"HOW ARE YOU DOING, Takeshi?" Kaede called over her shoulder, shouting above the whistling wind. Cold blasts of air whipped her cheeks, making them tingle, and another lock of hair slipped free of her topknot.

Takeshi didn't respond. He had his eyes tightly closed and he clutched at Suanni's spines for dear life.

Just behind him, Kenta seemed to be having the opposite reaction. "We're great, Kaede!" he whooped, stretching his arms above his head and punching the sky. "This is amazing. You can see the whole world from up here. Look!"

He gestured right, and Kaede gasped. In the last light of the fading sunset, she could make out the forest canopy, and beyond, the glittering Jade Sea. It was one smooth surface from their current height, without a single ripple or flaw. It was also enormous, and she couldn't quite believe she had crossed it in only three days—or at all.

"It's beautiful," she said, drinking in the sight. It was the third wonder she had seen today, and she beamed until her chapped lips stung.

"Look the other way," Imari said from in front of her, reaching back to touch her arm. Kaede allowed Imari to point her in the other direction, to where the top of the sun gleamed like the edge of a golden coin against the horizon. A wide river, larger than any she had ever seen, flowed off into the distance. From Imari's maps, she knew what it was: the mighty river Go, the lifeblood of Tsun'i. The stream they had found in the forest probably fed into it.

"It's even better than your maps," she shouted.

Imari tilted her head into the wind, laughing. "I know!" They gazed out at the wide world beyond, and then their eyes met again. The two of them shared a smile, and Kaede didn't feel the chill of the wind anymore.

She continued gazing into Imari's eyes until she felt a peculiar drop in her stomach. Suanni was circling down, diving toward the side of the mountain. Kaede gripped the nearest spine for a little more security, and behind her, she caught Kenta doing the same. For her part, Rin didn't seem worried. Tucked safely between two of Suanni's spines, she kept her muzzle pointed up into the nighttime breeze, jowls flapping and tongue lolling cheerfully from the side of her mouth.

Kaede was so entertained by the sight of her friend's joy she didn't have time to worry about their landing. She didn't flinch until Suanni touched down, and she was fast to recover her sense of balance.

"That was wonderful," Rin barked, still smiling in her wolfish way. "There was so much to see. So much to smell! Is that what tengu feel like when they fly?"

"No," Suanni said. "That is what dragons feel like, noble wolf. It was my pleasure to share it."

"It wasn't my pleasure," Takeshi mumbled. His skin had taken on a distinctly green tinge, and he seemed to be swaying back and forth.

Kenta gave him a friendly slug on the shoulder, one that made Takeshi groan. "Come on, big brother. Let's get you down on solid ground."

"Please." Takeshi allowed Kenta to help him down the slope of Suanni's tail, and Rin offered her assistance as well, nudging cheerfully at his palm.

Meanwhile, Kaede turned to Imari. "Shall we?" she asked, offering her arm.

Imari batted her lashes, accepting her elbow. "Of course." The two of them slid down together, laughing as they came to a stop at the tip of Suanni's tail.

The great dragon turned and peered down at them, whiskers fluttering in what remained of the breeze as the sunset slipped away. "Follow me, friends. Kurogane's forge is in the heart of the mountain. The entrance is not far."

"It better not be," Takeshi mumbled. He had regained some of his footing, although he wove a little as he walked. "We're awfully close to the top."

"Come on, Takeshi," Imari said in a teasing tone. "You shouldn't be afraid of heights. You live near the mountains."

"Yes, near. Not on." Nevertheless, Takeshi was able to keep up as they followed Suanni.

After only a few meters, Kaede caught sight of a shift in the mountain's surface—a dark dip that held a blacker, more prominent shadow than the surrounding purple-blue rocks. She crept toward it, curiosity getting the better of her, with Imari not too far behind. Upon closer inspection, it was the entrance to a tunnel, large enough for a tall man to walk through, and it was smooth and worn as if it had been there for some time. The walls held a strange, flawless glaze that seemed to shine even without light, and Kaede couldn't help wondering where it had come from.

"Suanni," Imari asked, turning back to the dragon, "did you make this?"

"Not me," Suanni said, "but another of my kind. Now, if you don't mind." Once more Suanni transformed, and the tunnel filled with light as they shrank back down to human-size. After a few seconds, Bo stood before them again, wearing the same drab brown robes. "Come with me." They headed down the tunnel, and Kaede followed with Imari on one side, Rin on the other, and the Hibana brothers behind.

Just when Kaede thought the darkness was about to swallow her up, a subtle glow appeared. Veins of metal ore ran along the passage's walls, glowing warm and yellow like burning embers of a young fire. Still, there were enough shadows for Kaede to be surprised when Imari reached out to take her hand. It was an unusually tight grip, and Kaede squeezed back.

Deeper into the heart of the mountain they went, until there was no sign of the entrance they had come through. Gradually, the air grew warmer. Sweat broke out along Kaede's brow, and the scent of burning charcoal tingled in her nose. She looked over at Rin, and realized she wasn't the only one who could smell it. The wolf's muzzle was wrinkled, as though she could taste something bad in the air.

At last, the tunnel came to an end, opening into a wide cave. *No, not a cave,* Kaede realized as she followed Suanni inside. *A forge.* The walls were rough in places, but the overall shape remained smooth and circular, at least a hundred paces wide from one end to the other. Sturdy racks lined the space, each filled with more blacksmithing tools than Kaede had ever seen before—hammers, tongs, hooks, cutters and chisels, and many more she couldn't guess a use for. She also counted at least three anvils of different sizes and shapes.

The centerpiece of the room, however, was the massive forge itself, made of dark stone and metal. A wave of heat from its open mouth washed over them the moment they stepped into the room. A pillar of smoke twisted its way from the top of the forge, floating up toward a hole in the ceiling. Standing in the thick of it was a large, shadowy figure, tinkering with something while their back was turned.

"Ancestors," Imari murmured.

Kaede was similarly stunned. The person before her was large, a good head taller than her, with broad shoulders and heavy muscles. When they turned, Kaede's first instinct was to take a step back. Then the light caught the side of the smith's face, and Kaede gasped in surprise. They had no beard, and their jaw was smooth and round. Kurogane was a woman.

***

"That's Kurogane?" Kenta asked in surprise. His question rose to the ceiling along with the smoke from the forge and out through a blue hole into the night.

Imari let go of Kaede's hand to nudge his side with her elbow. "I don't see any other magical blacksmiths around."

"But—"

She shushed him just in time. The smith headed their way, and Imari was sure she could hear them despite the rush of air and the crackle of flames. Up close, the woman was even more striking. Although she wasn't a person most would call pretty—the smudge of grease across one cheek and the sweaty, tangled state of her hair didn't help—she was impressive. Large and strong, she had a healthy glow and straight white teeth.

She dressed in accordance with Westlands fashion, more practicality than anything else. She wore a simple, sturdy shirt with Tsun'i style knots running up the front and matching plain pants. Both were black without any pattern, and even though Kurogane rolled up her sleeves, her hands and forearms were covered with gloves made of thick hide.

"Welcome to my forge, strangers," the woman said. "If you are friends of Suanni's, you are welcome here."

Imari bowed back, abruptly remembering her manners. "Good day to you, Kurogane-sama. My name is Homura Imari. Thank you for seeing us. The journey here hasn't been easy."

"I expect not." The woman grinned, grabbing a rag draped across her shoulder and using it to clear her gleaming face. "Now, who are your friends?"

"Iori Kaede."

"Hibana Takeshi."

"Hibana Kenta."

They all took turns bowing, until it was Rin's turn. The wolf didn't incline her head after speaking her name, but her tail swished back and forth at a pace that indicated calm interest. A few seconds ticked by as they all regarded each other.

"So," Kenta said with barely contained curiosity and pointedly ignoring the wide-eyed look Imari threw his way, "Blacksteel. A dramatic name, isn't it? How did your parents choose it?"

Kurogane laughed. "They didn't and neither did I. My birth name is Wen Ling, but now I have many names. When you're a hermit who lives up in the mountains, the locals start to call you something. In Tsun'i they call me Tiejiang, the Smith. The people of Xiangsai named me Yuhwa. In the Empire, where I take it you're from, they named me Kurogane. The people who lived around the Jade Sea used to call me that. At least, they did before they all moved away."

Imari's brow furrowed. "But that was a century ago, if not before. Surely you can't be that old? You look..."

"Human?" Wen Ling finished for her. "I am, in a sense. I'm certainly not yokai. But I have become something more than that." She pulled off her gloves, throwing them on the nearest rack.

Imari looked on in surprise. A strange golden light peeked out through Wen Ling's fingers, pulsing into the room. Her right hand and forearm seemed to be made of something other than skin. Light danced over her flesh like the flame against metal, catching the glint of the forge's fire and reflecting it back.

While Imari gaped, Wen Ling explained. "A few centuries back, I was a sailor on the river Go. My ferry took damage during an avalanche from one of the nearby eastern mountains, and my crew and I were trapped beneath the wreckage as it sank."

Imari stared at Wen Ling. She wasn't sure what kind of explanation she had been expecting, but it wasn't a story so similar to her own.

"I was the only survivor. The dragons saved me, but they had to repair the right side of my body." She lifted the hem of her shirt, showing that the same glowing, metallic skin ran all the way along her right side in addition to the scars covering her muscular stomach. "Their magic extends my life, although for how long, I have yet to find out."

Imari wasn't sure what to say. At last, she simply held up her left arm. The sleeve of her kimono slid down, revealing her missing hand. "Put your left half with my right, and we'd have a whole person."

Wen Ling offered a smile of understanding. "You seem fairly whole to me already, Imari. I assume that's why you came to me, though? You want a new hand."

Imari braced herself. This was it: the moment she had spent years planning for, the reason she had come all this way. "After what you've been through, I'm sure you understand. My life hasn't been the same since I lost it. I can't do the same things I used to."

"And yet, you made it all the way here," Wen Ling said. "You crossed the Jade Sea and flew on a dragon. Those are not things a person without courage does." The smith studied her more closely, and Imari felt her skin prickle. "You wear a katana and carry yourself like a samurai. Do you still know how to use that blade of yours one-handed?"

"Yes," Imari said. The question had struck a nerve. It had taken her a long time to re-learn how to complete her kata one-handed, since the katana almost always required a two-handed grip, but she had done it without complaint. Still, she couldn't see what it had to do with her request. Someone who had survived similar trauma had to admit two hands were better than one, no matter what she was capable of.

After a long moment, Wen Ling replied, "I will help you, Imari, but in the method of my choosing. I cannot simply give you back what you had before."

Imari's mouth opened, but she couldn't summon the right words. She was completely confused, unsure whether to thank Wen Ling for the offer of help, or to demand a better explanation. At a loss, she fell back on politeness. "I appreciate your willingness to help me, but—"

"A new hand will do you no good," Wen Ling said. "You aren't the same woman you were before you lost yours."

Imari's heart sank. Wen Ling was reluctant to restore her hand, even though judging by her own repaired limbs, she or the dragons had the capability. Her first instinct was to argue, but before she could blurt out something rude, she thought of her father. *What would he do in this situation?* The answer came to her quickly. *He wouldn't give up. He would stay and convince Wen Ling to change her mind. He would keep pressing, politely, until she saw he was right. I have to do the same.*

"Again, I appreciate the offer of help, as well as your hospitality," Imari said. "Would it be alright if my companions and I troubled you for the night? We wouldn't be able to reach a proper campsite before dark."

Wen Ling nodded. "You're welcome to stay as long as you like. In fact, you'll need to, if you want my help."

Despite her frustration, Imari couldn't help being curious. What kind of gift could Wen Ling possibly have in mind that wasn't a new hand? She added it to her rapidly growing list of questions, resolving to ask tomorrow. Kaede's arm rested on Rin's back for extra support, Kenta's eyes were drooping, and even Takeshi seemed less alert than usual. As magnificent as Wen Ling's forge was, all five of them were exhausted. Imari looked for Suanni as well, but unsurprisingly, they had disappeared again.

"Don't trouble yourselves about them," Wen Ling said, seeming to read her mind. "Dragons come and go as they please."

"I suppose if you're that big, you can do anything you want," Kenta said.

Wen Ling laughed. "Right you are, Kenta. Now, please allow me to show you to your rooms. I do have some prepared for adventurers, although they might be a little dusty. Few make it this far. You should be proud." She headed for a stone opening at the back of the forge, but Takeshi called out in protest.

"Wait. Don't you need to quench the fire in the forge?"

"The fire is ever-burning," Wen Ling explained as they passed. "Dragon fire doesn't go out unless the dragon wills it—another gift they have given me."

Imari shielded her face as they passed the bellows, tilting away and using her shoulder to protect herself. The heat was more intense than she had expected, and the flames were brighter, too. They exited the forge quickly, and she sighed as they stepped into a cooler passage beyond. Like the first tunnel, it was lined with glowing rock, but it was much more inviting, more like a hallway that would be found inside a home. A tatami mat covered the floor, and Imari saw a place to remove her sandals. She did so, catching Kaede's eye as she bent down.

"So?" Kaede whispered, "what do you think?"

"I think I'm going to have to practice my diplomatic skills." Imari glanced over at Wen Ling, who was removing her own shoes on the other side of the hallway. "I also want to find out about that strange skin of hers. Even if she doesn't want to give me a new hand—yet—I think she's capable of making one."

"I think you should hear her offer," Rin said, entering the conversation uninvited. "She has already agreed to help you. Plotting to change her mind before she's explained her plan is rude."

Imari narrowed her eyes. "Are you missing a leg, Rin?"

"No, but a wolf can survive with three, and so can you. Wen Ling wasn't wrong about that."

"I have the utmost respect for you, Rin, but in this situation, you don't get to have an opinion about what I should and shouldn't want. Until you've been in my situation, please don't comment." Without giving Rin a chance to reply, she headed further down the hall, to where Kurogane was waiting for them.

"In here," Wen Ling said, pulling back a door set into the stone. "I have two rooms, so some of you will have to share."

"It's way better than sleeping out in the open," Kenta said, with his usual cheer. "This'll be the best night's sleep we've had in weeks."

Imari had to agree. The rooms were simple, but furnished with comfortable looking futons and low tables. No windows, but just like in the forge, there was a small blue hole in the ceiling to let in fresh air. Despite the opening, the space was warm and cozy. In fact, it was warm enough to make her eyes droop. She bowed. "This is kind of you. My friends and I are grateful."

"Please, if you need anything, don't hesitate to ask," Wen Ling said. "I'll see you all tomorrow for breakfast." She began to exit the room, but before she closed the door, she smiled. "I may come off as rough and brash, but that is not my intent. Living with the yokai tends to dull one's memory of etiquette. The dragons don't see others as above or below themselves, and neither do I. Now, get some rest." With that, Wen Ling shut the screen, leaving the five of them alone.

"What kind of gift do you think she has in mind, Imari?" Kenta asked. "If she isn't going to give you a new hand, what's she going to make?"

"I'm not giving up on the hand yet," Imari told him, full of determination. "I didn't come this far just to be told no."

To her surprise, Takeshi nodded. "I don't think you should give up, either. The dragons gave Kurogane a whole new right half. I don't see why they can't give you a new hand. If anyone's worthy, it's you."

Imari gave him a look of gratitude. "Thanks, Takeshi. So, do you and Kenta want this room or the next one over?"

"We'll take this one," Takeshi said.

"Because it's closer to the door?" Imari asked, amused.

"Of course. Would you expect anything else from me?"

"We'll head next door," Kaede said with a snort. "Sleep well, boys."

Kenta smirked. "Oh, we will, as long as you two keep it down. Don't tire out your lips, Imari. You'll need them tomo…hey!" He winced as Takeshi cuffed him lightly on the back of the head.

"Stop that," he ordered, before giving Imari a short, polite bow. "Good night. We'll see you and Kaede tomorrow."

Imari winked at Kenta, preparing to make a comment of her own, but she refrained when she caught sight of Kaede's cherry red face. It seemed like she was doing her best to hide it, staring pointedly away from them. "Come on," she murmured, taking Kaede's elbow and leading her into the other room. "Don't mind Kenta. He doesn't mean any harm."

"But how did he figure it out?" Kaede whispered, hurrying past the screen door. Once they were safely inside, she let out a long sigh of relief, followed by a low moan of embarrassment. "He didn't see us kissing, did he? Because we only did it that one time under the waterfall and, you know, the next night before bed. And I guess—"

Imari pressed a finger to Kaede's lips, silencing her before she could work herself into a worse fluster. "I'm sure Kenta is just fishing, but if he did see, I don't care." She hesitated, a little worried. "Wait, do you?"

"No!" Kaede blurted out as soon as Imari removed her finger. "I mean, I thought you would. Since, you know, I'm your yojimbo, and Takeshi had a past with you, and I don't know." Her shoulders slumped in despair. "I told you, I really don't know anything about this. I'm pretty hopeless when it comes to girls."

"Well, I wouldn't say hopeless." Imari curled her fingers around the back of Kaede's neck, toying with the soft strands of hair there before leaning up and in for a kiss. It was soft and reassuring, but with just enough of a spark to light up her belly. "In fact," she continued when they broke apart, "I think you're a pretty fast learner."

"You're a pretty good teacher," Kaede said. From her smile, Imari could tell she was much more comfortable now that the two of them were alone.

"Well, I'm afraid I can't do much more teaching tonight. I'm much too tired. Although." She glanced over at the two futons, which had been unrolled several meters apart. "Hold on." She let go of Kaede and headed over to one of them, lifting one end and dragging it across the floor until it pressed snug against the other.

Kaede's face flushed bright red again. "Wait, Imari."

"Don't worry," Imari murmured. "That isn't what I'm asking for. But it's kind of cold in here, with the skylight and all. I thought we could keep each other warm."

It was a complete lie, and Kaede had to know it, but to Imari's delight, she didn't point that out. "I guess that would be okay. We'll have our yukata on, right?"

"Right." Imari sat down on the edge of the futon, patting the space next to her and waiting for Kaede to join her. "Look," she said, placing her hand on top of Kaede's thigh, "this can be whatever you'd like it to be, and it can go as fast or as slow as you want."

"Yes, but why me?"

As soon as the question came out, Imari could tell Kaede had been holding it back for some time—days at least, possibly even weeks. She thought for a moment about her answer. Her first instinct was to compliment Kaede's appearance, but she had a feeling that wasn't the kind of response Kaede was looking for. She wanted something more, and Imari had to admit that when she thought of her reasons, they came one after the other, so fast she could barely keep up.

"I enjoy your company. You're funny and kind, smart and skilled with a sword. You listen to me, and you've never once thought less of me because I'm missing my hand. On top of all that, you're beautiful. I'm not about to let someone like that get away."

She knew she'd answered well when a broad grin spread across Kaede's face. "You really see all that when you look at me?"

"Yes," Imari said. "Do you see those things when you look at me?"

Kaede nodded. "All of them. So...." Her voice trailed off, as though she wasn't sure what else to say.

"So, we probably shouldn't sleep in our kimonos," Imari said. "Get undressed. I promise not to peek unless you want me to."

Kaede blushed and rose from the futon, turning to face a corner of the room. Imari did the same, and just as she had promised, she resisted the temptation to steal a glance over her shoulder for several minutes until Kaede said, "Done."

When she turned, Imari's breath left her once again. Kaede's yukata was snug enough to show the outline of her body, and with her hair down instead of pulled back into a messy topknot, she seemed softer and prettier than usual. Imari liked Kaede's rugged, samurai-warrior look, especially the scar under her eye, but this was a pleasant surprise too. It reminded her of the night back in Yin, when the two of them had shared a room at the inn. But things were different now—more open and serious.

To her delight, Kaede stared at her with similar appreciation. Her dark eyes were wide, as if they couldn't drink in enough, and Imari caught Kaede's tongue peeking out to run over her lower lip. Then Kaede seemed to catch herself, and she snapped out of the intense gaze. "Bed?"

"Bed," Imari agreed.

The two of them settled down together, lying on their sides and facing each other at first. Without speaking, they came together for another kiss. It wasn't deep, but it lasted a long time, and they breathed each other in for several seconds after it ended. "Front or back?" Imari asked.

"Can I take front? I mean, I'd rather..."

Imari resisted the temptation to laugh. In truth, she wouldn't have minded, but she knew Kaede would. "Don't worry, I'll hold you. Turn around."

Kaede did so, and Imari snuggled up against her from behind, draping an arm around her waist and pressing a kiss to the back of her shoulder. "Good night."

"Good night."

That night, with Kaede in her arms, Imari fell asleep faster than she had in months.

Chapter Seventeen

THE NEXT DAY, IMARI woke before the sun. Kaede snored peacefully beside her, and the hint of sky she could see through the hole in the ceiling was still a deep shade of blue. She considered remaining in bed, pressed against Kaede's back and listening to her friend's peaceful breaths until she fell back asleep, but a restless energy got the better of her. She found herself curious about everything that had happened the night before—too curious to simply sleep the morning away.

She removed her arm from Kaede's waist and left their joined futons as slowly as she could, careful not to make a sound. Kaede stirred for a moment, but her eyes didn't open. She turned around, grasping the patch of blanket Imari had been using and bringing it to her face. Imari smiled. It was sweet, watching Kaede search for her scent and her warmth, and she couldn't resist bending over to kiss the top of her head. Kaede was obviously exhausted, because her face didn't even twitch.

Once she was certain Kaede wouldn't wake, Imari rummaged in her bag for one of her cleanest kimonos, a green one with white stitching. The grey haori with the mon of Homura on either side of her chest matched the black hakama. She wanted to look somewhat presentable when she went to speak to Wen Ling. With the morning came fresh hope. She had learned something important yesterday: what she wanted could be done, if not by Wen Ling, then by the dragons themselves. It wasn't that Wen Ling didn't have the ability. She didn't see the need.

Well, I'll make her see, Imari thought as she finished dressing. *I'll ask as many times as I need to.*

She retrieved her swords and left the room, sliding the screen door open slowly and quietly. Takeshi and Kenta were still asleep too, sprawled beneath their blankets, and she crept past them without much difficulty. Rin cracked open one blue eye as she passed, and her tail swished from side to side. Imari lifted a finger to her lips in a gesture for silence. Luckily, Rin remained resting on her paws, and the bright eye closed again.

After she entered the hall, Imari slipped into her sandals and headed for Wen Ling's forge. Dry heat swelled around her, carrying with it the smoky smell of charcoal. As she drew closer, she began to hear the sound of hammering as well. It wasn't particularly loud at first, but nearer to the door, it sounded almost musical, like the chime of bells. She tilted her head to listen. Wen Ling was obviously hard at work on something, even this early in the morning.

Imari listened for a while, waiting rather impatiently, but there was no pause. Eventually, she decided to go in anyway. She entered in time to hear the hiss of steam and watch a billowing cloud surround the area behind the forge itself, where the fire blazed a darker shade of red— much hotter than the day before. She walked around the forge to find the smith standing in the slowly dissipating steam. Behind the forge a wide stone basin filled with water boiled around a pair of tongs. As Imari drew closer, she saw a glowing piece of metal pinched between the tongs, though she couldn't make out the details through all the steam.

"Good morning," Wen Ling said, looking up and taking notice of her. "You have good timing. I just finished folding this billet."

Imari leaned in for a better look at the slab of golden-hot steel rapidly getting darker and covered with black flakes. "What will it become once it's done?" she asked, curiosity getting the better of her. She had come with a clear goal of asking Wen Ling to fulfill her request once more, but she also found the blacksmith's craft quite fascinating.

Wen Ling withdrew the unfinished sword, setting it carefully atop of the anvil to cool. "I don't know. It hasn't told me yet. I'll have to grind it for a few days, then fold it again, and cool it in water. And repeat the process after that. Perhaps it will become clearer then."

Wen Ling shifted the billet until it was perfectly aligned in the middle of the anvil. Then, she started toward the other end of the forge, waving for Imari to follow. On her way, she removed her apron and gloves, setting them on separate hooks on the wall. Then she turned to Imari and regarded her with gleaming eyes.

"I have thought about your situation, Imari," she said slowly. "Would you let me look at your sword?"

Even though the sudden request confused her, Imari withdrew her katana and handed it over. Wen Ling took the weapon carefully, cradling the handle in her palm and letting the back of the blade rest on the other. She looked it over with care, the gleaming fingers of her right hand sliding over the blade. "It's a shame that this blade is such a bad fit for you. The katana is a two-handed weapon."

Imari stiffened. "I can use a katana fine," she said, gesturing to the saya at her hip.

"You misunderstand me, Imari. The determination and effort you must've put into relearning to use a katana only proves your character. However, there are better options for you. I was going to speak to you about it today, in fact."

That got Imari's attention. "What do you mean, better options?"

"The katana is one of the finest blades in existence." Wen Ling turned Imari's sword in her hands, admiring its curve. "But it isn't the only kind of sword there is. The Westlands have their own swordmaking traditions, and there is a particular kind of weapon I think would suit you far better."

"Really?" Imari's annoyance turned at once to breathless anticipation. It wasn't the new hand she wanted, but she had to admit that the prospect of a new sword excited her. Kaede had Mizu-no-Hamon, but she didn't have a named blade of her own. Her katana was serviceable, but surely something made by Kurogane would be worthy of a title. "That's incredibly generous, especially since you only met me yesterday. What do I need to offer you in return? Surely something that valuable—"

Wen Ling waved her off. "I need nothing in return. Outfitting worthy warriors with the swords that compliment them best is what any blacksmith wishes for. It'll bring me great pleasure to know I have helped you find your perfect match." She handed the katana back to Imari and waited until it was sheathed. "Please, come with me." She turned and pulled on the handle of what Imari realized was a door—a metal door so perfectly blended in with the surrounding walls it had was invisible.

With growing excitement, Imari followed Wen Ling through the archway and into a smaller side room. Shafts of golden sunlight poured in from above, and the whole chamber seemed to glitter as she stepped inside. Imari gasped. Stands filled the room, each one housing a weapon. Closest to her was a selection of breathtaking daishō placed upon wooden koshirae. To her left stood a row of spears. To her right, swords she didn't even recognize. No two looked alike, and Imari's eyes darted everywhere at once, trying to take them all in.

"How could you have made so many?" she asked, her awed whisper echoing throughout the chamber.

"I had a lot of time. A good blacksmith in your home country can make a katana in six months, with their team's help. I make one weapon every few years. This room houses almost every weapon I have made in three centuries. " Wen Ling headed to the right side of the room, toward one of the rows Imari didn't recognize. "This is what I wanted to show you."

Wen Ling approached the display and removed a sheathed sword from the nearest stand. She withdrew the blade from its bronze-ringed, wooden scabbard, examining every angle. The sword gleamed, but once Wen Ling removed the oil with the cloth that hung at her side, the steel surface shone brighter still.

Imari approached reverently. The sword was like none she had ever seen before outside of her books. Instead of a single curved edge, it was perfectly straight, sharpened on both sides. The end tapered to a slightly rounded point, and the blade itself seemed thinner and more flexible than what she was used to. Its hilt was more pronounced than that of her katana and shaped differently as well. A spiral of bronze wound up around the grip, ending with the head of a small, intricately carved bronze dragon. Its eyes were sapphires, and each diamond-shaped scale had been scratched into the metal.

"It's amazing," Imari murmured, unable to tear her eyes away.

"It's called a jian," Wen Ling explained. "As impressive as it is that you have learned to fight with a katana using only one hand, it isn't ideal. This sword will suit your style much better. You'll need to stay and train with me for some time to master it, but I have a feeling you'll be a quick learner. It's flexible enough to break past an opponent's guard and agile enough to take advantage of any opening—all with just one arm."

Imari's excitement grew. The longer she looked at the sword, the more enchanted she became. "Thank you," she said, bowing deeply. "It's absolutely beautiful." She rose after several long moments, and then it was to stare at the sword's surface. It twinkled like starlight, but it had the fierce bite of steel. "May I take it now?"

"Take it?" Wen Ling looked up from the blade, her eyes dancing with the same light. The reflection seemed almost mischievous in her dark irises. "It's not yours. I was simply showing one of my jian to you."

"But...but you've said..."

"Again, you misunderstand me. There is an old warrior saying, I'm certain the samurai in your country know it well: the sword always chooses its master, and it only serves one. If I gift you one of my blades, don't you think I ought to make sure it's the right one? For both of you?"

"I've never thought of it that way," Imari admitted. She had heard the saying, but she'd never thought of it so literally.

Wen Ling sheathed the jian, placing it back on its stand. With a few steps, she circled behind Imari. "Relax," she said, placing a calming hand on each of Imari's shoulders, "and close your eyes. Breathe slowly, like you're preparing to meditate. Feel the warmth of the air, smell the oil and metal. Reach out with your ki and say hello."

Imari obeyed without question. This ritual would've seemed silly to her a few months ago, but since then, she had flown on a dragon. She had crossed the Jade Sea. She had seen Kaede fly through the air like an arrow. She had met the legendary Kurogane and was about to be gifted a magical blade. After all that, making friends with a sword didn't seem like such a crazy proposition.

Once her breathing steadied, she began to feel a pull, like the flow of a river or the pressure of the wind. It was an odd feeling, but she let it guide her until a distant voice tugged at her ears.

"Imari, open your eyes."

With a start, Imari snapped back to the present. She stood a few paces away from where she had been before, right in front of a new stand. The blade held was like the first one she'd seen—long and straight, with the same wide guard and dragon-headed pommel. However, its scabbard was green, as were the dragon-scales on its handle.

Imari glanced back at Wen Ling, who gave her a nod. "Go ahead. Take it."

She exhaled slowly, closing her palm around the handle. The blade slid smoothly from its scabbard, and she tilted it into the light, marveling at the perfect balance. While she lost herself in its sheen, Wen Ling appeared at her side with the same cloth in hand. She swiped it along the blade, wiping it clean of oil, and as she did, Imari noticed an inscription close to the hilt. It was in an old variant of Tsun'i script, which she couldn't read, but the characters were beautifully carved.

"What does the inscription mean?"

"Never give up without a fight. Fitting, isn't it?" Wen Ling told her. "I think both of you chose well."

Finally looking away from the sword, Imari bowed deeply. "Thank you. Does it have a name?"

"Not yet," Wen Ling said. "It's certainly deserving of one, but swords generally tell you their own names in time. You'll have to train with it before it comes to you."

"And you can train me?" Imari asked eagerly.

Wen Ling nodded. "I've mastered many different sword techniques, but the jian is one of my specialties. Perhaps it's immodest of me to say, but you won't find a better teacher."

Imari bowed again, even lower than before. "Then I'm at your disposal, Sensei. And please, if you want anything of me in return for the sword and the lessons, ask."

"I ask nothing of you, Imari. Every smith wants their swords to find good homes. I have a feeling this blade will be happy with you."

"You speak about the sword like it's alive," Imari said. As she looked at the way the blade twinkled and glittered, she couldn't help wondering if it was.

Wen Ling laughed. "I do, don't I? But first, one more finishing touch." She headed over to a table on the other side of the room, digging in a small set of drawers Imari hadn't noticed before. She had been so focused on the weapons that she hadn't looked at any of the furniture.

She didn't have long to gawk. A moment later, Wen Ling returned with some brightly colored cord in her hand. It ended in a tassel, and Imari was further impressed when she noticed the colors: white, bronze, and crimson. "How did you know the colors of my mon?" she asked, shaking her head.

"A little dragon told me," Wen Ling joked, "but the tassel isn't only for decoration. Once it's tied to the hilt of your sword, you can sweep it at your opponent's eyes as a distraction."

Imari grinned. "This style of fighting is sounding more and more fun."

"So it is," Wen Ling said. She offered the tassel and the blade, waiting for Imari to take them. "You tie it on."

Carefully, Imari took the sword. The hilt practically melted into her hand, and as she gave a testing stroke, the air seemed to split against the edge of the blade. Already, it felt like an extension of her arm, and she didn't want to put it down again. However, Wen Ling held out the tassel. The strands were rougher than she expected, and she imagined they would hurt lashing across someone's face at a fast speed.

It was a struggle to attach the tassel to the hilt one-handed, and it was with a great deal of fumbling and some embarrassment that she managed the task. "I hate to trouble you after this lovely gift," she said, tugging on the end of the tassel with her teeth to tighten the sloppy knot she had made around the bronze dragon's neck, "and I hate to seem ungrateful, but this would be a lot easier if I had two hands."

Wen Ling snorted. "That was subtle. I stand by what I said before. This blade will serve you well. You'll fight better, and you will have a trophy to show back home to prove you came all this way. I see no reason to give you a hand as well."

"A sword won't help me tie knots," Imari pointed out. "Or turn the pages of a book, or hold chopsticks—"

"You wouldn't hold chopsticks with your left hand anyway."

"That isn't fair." Imari knew she was bordering on rudeness, but she didn't care. She could practically feel her chance slipping away. "I don't understand why you won't help me. The dragons gave you a whole new right half—"

"Because I needed it," Wen Ling said. "Without their magic, I would have died. You are nowhere close to dying. You don't need a new hand. What you need is confidence."

Imari's jaw hardened with anger. "Excuse me, but I have plenty of that already. You said yourself the journey here was difficult."

"And yet, even though you've made it all the way here and been given a beautiful sword, you're still afraid to go back home," Wen Ling said. She watched Imari with interest, although not impatience, her expression thoughtful. "Why? Do you really think the people back in your city will think less of you if you return without a magic hand?"

"No, but I'll think less of myself. I promised myself when I set out that I wouldn't go back without one." She sighed. Arguing with Wen Ling was getting her nowhere—at least, not yet, and a frown formed on the smith's face. "I apologize for my rudeness. You've been incredibly kind to me, and the sword is one of the most beautiful things I've ever seen. It's just that—"

"I know," Wen Ling interrupted. "There are times when I would give up my new body parts to be myself again. But sometimes, we're forced to change, whether we like it or not. It's how we deal with those changes that matters, not the scars they leave on us."

For a while, Imari was silent, considering Wen Ling's words. Sometimes, she thought the smith understood her pain and frustration perfectly. The next moment, she was certain Wen Ling didn't realize how difficult living life without a hand truly was. "I'm not going to stop asking, you know," Imari said at last. "If you don't want to train me because of that, I understand."

"I'll still train you," Wen Ling said. "I wouldn't expect someone as stubborn as you to stop asking—and before you ask, I mean stubborn in a good way."

Imari nodded. "Thank you. And I meant what I said before. If you want me to do anything while I'm here as payment, ask."

"Perhaps we can see about having you and your friends sweep the forge," Wen Ling said. "I do let it get a bit dirty in here sometimes."

Imari glanced around. To her, the forge seemed surprisingly clean, but she bowed nevertheless. "You only have to ask."

"Then we have a deal," Wen Ling said. "Now, come with me. You can help me prepare breakfast for your companions. After we're finished eating, I'll show you some of the new kata you'll need to learn. The jian is quite different than a katana. It will take some adjustment."

"I'm up to the challenge," Imari said at once.

Wen Ling gave her an approving look. "I have no doubt about that."

***

Kaede woke to an empty bed. The sun had risen, and Imari was nowhere to be seen. Disappointed, Kaede sat up, rubbing her eyes. She wasn't sure where Imari had gone, but she wanted to find out. Over the past few months, she had grown used to seeking out other people's company instead of keeping to herself. Besides, her stomach was rumbling. She needed something to eat—preferably something more palatable than the dry rations in her pack.

She rolled her shoulders, pleasantly surprised by how loose they felt. Spending the night in an actual bed had done her a world of good. She felt relaxed and rested, and could summon the energy to stand up quicker than she had during their mornings of travel. She washed the worst of the previous day's dirt away with the bowl of water that had been provided then dressed quickly, finishing by sliding her katana into her obi. Once she was finished, she headed over to the screen that separated her room from Kenta's and Takeshi's.

"Kenta? Takeshi? Are you awake in there?"

A moment later, the screen door folded back, revealing Kenta's grinning face. It was dripping with water, as did the strands of hair framing his cheeks. "Good morning, sleepyhead. You took your time getting up. Where's Imari?" He peered over her shoulder, and Kaede saw the moment he noticed the two futons pushed together. His eyebrows crawled all the way up his forehead, and he gave her a toothy grin.

"She's not with you?" She pushed past him to check their room. "I suppose she left without us."

"Of course she did," Takeshi muttered. He seemed annoyed, but not overly worried. Obviously, he didn't think Wen Ling meant Imari any harm. "One of these days, she'll wise up and start telling people where she's going. That's what I keep telling myself."

"You'll be waiting a long time, but if telling yourself lies is what keeps you sane, go ahead." She caught sight of Rin curled up in the corner. "I suppose you know where she's gotten off to this time?"

"She didn't say," Rin answered, "but I assume she went to see Wen Ling. They were supposed to meet this morning."

"Then we'd better go find her." Kaede wasn't sure she could handle Kenta's ribbing without Imari to help fend him off, good-natured as it was.

"And food," Kenta added. "I'm starving."

"You're always starving," Takeshi said.

The four of them headed out into the hallway together, with the three humans pausing to put their sandals back on before heading back the way they had come. Heat came from the forge, but to their surprise, they found it empty. There was, however, another door in a far corner other than the one they had entered through the night before. Kaede headed in that direction.

Kenta hovered by Kaede's side, looking as if he wanted to say something, but before he started his teasing, Takeshi redirected the conversation. "You know, I can't wait to eat something other than biscuits," he said, musing aloud. "Something hot and fresh-cooked. Maybe some eggs. Even those plums we left back home are starting to sound good."

"I think I smell food," Rin added, trotting past the door and into another hallway lined with lanterns. Its walls were smoother and more polished than some of the others, with more wood and less natural rock.

To Kaede's relief, Kenta seemed to forget all about poking fun at her. He sped up his pace, following both Rin and his nose until he was a short distance ahead of them. Once he was gone, Kaede's nervousness returned. She hadn't considered that without Kenta to act as a buffer, Takeshi might try to speak to her privately about the futons as well.

"Look," she whispered nervously, "about the beds. We didn't—I mean, I'm not trying to cause trouble."

"You aren't," Takeshi said. "I'm not upset with you, if that's what you think. Imari can do what she likes and spend time with whomever she wants." He gave a slight sigh. "Ancestors know she's told me that often enough. Just be careful with her. She thinks she can take on the world."

"For someone so smart, she can be stupid," Kaede said with a laugh. She was happy Takeshi didn't seem to disapprove of her blossoming relationship with Imari and grateful they were on the same page. "Don't worry. I still take my commitment as her yojimbo seriously. I won't let anything happen to her."

"It's not just her safety I'm worried about," Takeshi said with a frown. "Imari doesn't enter into relationships lightly. If you're only in this for a bit of fun or because you're bored—"

Kaede's eyes widened and she shook her head. "No," she interrupted, as loudly as she dared. "I don't take relationships lightly, either. At least, I don't think I do. I've never been in one before."

Takeshi seemed pleased with her answer. "Then I'll stay out of it. Despite my nagging, I do want her to be happy, even if it's not with me."

"That's honorable of you," Kaede said, with a newfound sense of respect. She and Takeshi were getting on better recently, but this was a new step in their relationship. Perhaps he had learned something from his failed engagement to Imari after all.

"Not really," Takeshi said. "If I didn't think you'd be good for her, I'd interfere." He gave her a sidelong look. "Don't tell Imari I said that."

Kaede made a motion of sealing her lips. Soon after, they arrived at the end of the hall to a room that glowed with extra light and the heavenly smell of food. The screen was already open, revealing a kitchen and a table, at which Kenta, Imari, and Wen Ling were already seated. Rin had curled up happily by Imari's feet, her tail thumping on the floor as she gnawed at a piece of raw meat. She looked up from her chewing and slobbering long enough to give them a bark of greeting, and then returned to gulping it down.

"Nice of you to wait for us," Kaede drawled, taking the seat next to Imari.

Imari ignored the quip. Her face glowed like the sun, and she was practically bouncing with excitement. "Kaede, Wen Ling gave me a sword!" She gestured proudly to a scabbard sitting on the edge of the table near her elbow.

"A sword?" Kaede repeated, sidling in closer. "What about your hand?"

"I'm still working on that," Imari said as Wen Ling gave a short sigh.

"But back to the sword." She removed it from its sheath, and Kaede sucked in a breath. The blade was stunning perfectly straight with two sharpened edges, and seemed to glow with its own inner light.

"Is that...?"

"A dragon!" Imari said. "Isn't it beautiful? It's a jian, a one-handed Tsun'i blade. I'll need to stay here a while to train with it. Is that all right with you?" She looked at Takeshi and Kenta too, waiting for their opinions.

"Stay here? Away from my cousin?" Kaede said. "Sounds good to me." Although she was too polite to add it, she was also looking forward to the prospect of sharing a room with Imari for the next few weeks. There would probably be a few awkward moments, but it would be worth it to fall asleep in Imari's arms, and perhaps to steal a few more kisses. Remembering herself, she bowed to Wen Ling. "Thank you for allowing us to stay. If there's anything we can do—"

"Imari has already offered," Wen Ling said. "If you want to help me keep up with the place, I'd appreciate it. Perhaps I can even show you and your friends a trick or two while I'm training her."

Kenta seemed excited by that prospect, but Takeshi remained uncertain. "Are you sure we can afford to stay that long, tono?" He fell back on formal titles, a furrow appearing in the middle of his forehead. "Your father will be missing you."

"Don't try that with me, Takeshi," Imari said. Kaede got the sense that on a worse morning, she would have been annoyed, but her new sword had put her in such good cheer that it outweighed all other feelings. "Father can handle things fine while I'm gone. He doesn't need me."

"It's not about needing you," Takeshi said, but Imari shook her head.

"Come on, Takeshi. There are dragons here. Don't you want to learn from them? How many humans get that opportunity?"

At last, Takeshi seemed to give in. He leaned back in his chair with an expression of defeat. "I suppose I can't talk you out of staying anyway, but I'm not flying on any more dragons unless I absolutely have to."

"Speak fo yosef," Kenta said around a mouthful of eggs over rice. He chewed sloppily then swallowed. "Flying on Suanni is the best thing we've done so far."

Kaede smiled. Flying on dragonback was one of the highlights of their adventure, but she could think of a few others that surpassed it.

"Tell me more about this new sword," she said, ignoring her food in favor of watching Imari.

Immediately, Imari launched into an enthusiastic explanation. "It's folded differently than a katana, first of all..."

Though she tried valiantly to pay attention, Kaede found herself growing distracted by the movement of Imari's lips and the excited sparkle in her eyes. She was lively and cheerful, and beautiful because of it. *I could listen to her talk about anything at all and never get bored*, Kaede realized. She wasn't ready to name the warm feeling in her chest, but she was fairly certain she knew what it was.

After breakfast, Kaede spent the late morning and early afternoon watching Imari and Wen Ling perform kata together in a special room off the forge reserved for that purpose. The forms they passed through were different than the ones she knew, but there was still a familiar rhythm to them: steady breathing, slow heartbeats, and sweeping arcs. They wound from side to side in coiling lines, with Imari standing behind Wen Ling to better copy her movements.

The dance was hypnotic, although Kaede was sure her fascination had almost as much to do with the fluid way Imari moved as it did with the new kata. Kaede had never underestimated Imari's skill with a katana, but after only a few minutes of watching her wield the jian, she knew Wen Ling had been right. It was almost like watching a fresh bud open beneath the rays of the sun, Kaede mused—a beautiful blossoming of confidence.

By the time the exercise was over, Imari's face gleamed with sweat, but her smile was brighter still. She sheathed her blade and made her bows to Wen Ling, but as soon as that ritual was complete, she rushed over for an excited, bone-crushing hug. Kaede accepted it with a laugh, taking a moment to inhale the sweet scent trapped in Imari's hair. Somehow, it still smelled good despite her recent workout.

"You looked great out there," Kaede murmured beside Imari's cheek. She knew she should let go, since Wen Ling was watching, but she couldn't bring herself to unwind her arms from around Imari's waist.

Imari laughed softly. "Great, huh? Are you sure that's the word you want to use?"

Heat washed across Kaede's face, but she didn't argue the point. Imari had looked beautiful, stunning, incredible, but she didn't quite know how to say those things. Instead, she pressed a short kiss to Imari's lips. It was only a peck, but it still sent a jolt through her entire body. This was a special moment, and she wasn't going to let her shyness around public displays of affection or the newness of their relationship stop her from enjoying it.

Once their lips parted, they exchanged sheepish grins and left the embrace. Wen Ling pretended not to pay attention, but Kaede thought she caught a hint of a smirk playing at the corners of the smith's lips. "Am I to assume you saw a difference, Kaede? Imari wields the jian well for a beginner."

Kaede gave an enthusiastic nod. "Definitely. She certainly didn't look like a beginner to me."

"Flatterer," Imari snorted, but her smile widened.

"In a month or so, you'll be even better," Wen Ling said to Imari. "You already have the focus and discipline of a samurai, as well as a surprising amount of flexibility in your technique. I wonder, have you trained with other weapons besides the katana?"

"Yes, I have. I made an effort to learn a bit about every weapon in my father's armory back home. It didn't seem fair to ask the soldiers who followed me to do something I couldn't do."

"A wise attitude to have," Wen Ling said, "although I wonder if perhaps you went through so many weapons because you hadn't yet found the one that suited you best."

That put an even bigger smile on Imari's face. "You might be right about that. So, we've still got a few hours of daylight left. What do you want us to do? We could help you clean the forge like I promised—"

"Actually," said another voice, "I have a suggestion about that."

Kaede turned in surprise. A familiar figure was standing in the doorway to Wen Ling's dojo, dressed in brown robes with the hood pulled up. "Good afternoon, Bo...er, Suanni," she said, making a short bow. "Sorry. I'm still getting used to the new name." She squirmed a little at the self-given reminder that she too was living under a name that wasn't her own.

"It's quite all right," Suanni said. "And I apologize if I startled you."

Wen Ling gave a soft sigh, one that spoke of long but mild suffering. "We need to tie a bell on the end of your tail or something. I never know when you'll show up."

Kaede sighed with relief. "Oh, good, so it's not me. I'm usually good at sensing when there are spirits around me, but I never picked up on Suanni."

"Dragons aren't like other yokai," Suanni explained. "Even those special humans with a connection to the spirits don't always feel our presence." They gave Kaede a long look. "Otherwise, you would probably be rather overwhelmed right now."

"What do you mean?" Kaede asked. "Are there many other dragons who live here?"

"Of course. The mountain isn't called Hongshan for nothing."

"Don't tell Kenta," Imari teased. "He'll want to ride them all."

Suanni chuckled. "I found his enthusiasm refreshing. As for the other dragons, I could show you, if you like. It isn't far."

Kaede looked over to Imari, but she already knew what she would find—an eager grin that spoke of the desire to go on another adventure.

"We'd love to," Imari answered for both of them.

"Should we go and get Kenta and Takeshi?" Kaede asked, although she wanted to keep Imari all to herself for a little longer. The Hibana brothers had seemed grateful for a day to rest, and Kenta especially had been more than content to hole up in the kitchens, close to the food.

"They can go another time," Imari said. "If I'm going to train with Wen Ling, we'll be here a while."

"I'll check on them," Wen Ling offered, perceptive as always. "A good host never neglects their guests." They all exchanged bows, and then Wen Ling exited the dojo, sharing a look with Suanni as she passed.

"Come with me," Suanni said once Wen Ling had left. "As I said, we won't be going far."

Kaede held Imari's hand as they made their way out of the dojo and back through the forge. The fire blazed hot but with less steam and smoke as Wen Ling wasn't working. "I don't know how she finds the time to make all those weapons and run this entire forge by herself," Imari said as they passed by. "It normally takes a team of smiths and apprentices months to make a single sword."

"Wen Ling certainly has a gift," Suanni said, "but more importantly, she has a sense of purpose. I assume she told you she wouldn't require payment for that new sword you carry, Imari?"

"Let me guess," Kaede said. "She never asks for payment, does she?"

Imari nodded. "She told me her greatest joy is matching swords with their perfect partners. She talked about it almost like a marriage bond."

Kaede's eyebrows arched. She snuck a glance at Imari, but then hurried to look away. Still, she was sure she had been caught, because Imari squeezed her fingers a little tighter.

The conversation drifted into silence as they walked back through the glowing tunnel. The distance seemed much shorter than the last time, and soon they were out on the mountainside again, soaking in the sun and fresh air. When there was enough room, Suanni took a step back. Their body began to shift and change, and once more, Kaede found herself witness to one of the most incredible sights she had ever seen.

She couldn't quite understand how Suanni's small human form expanded into the long, coiling body of a dragon. It rippled and stretched and swelled, but it was a process that defied description, and half of it was blurred by a glow that reminded Kaede of the tunnel. Soon, Suanni stood before them in all their glory. They looked even larger in the daylight, with their great lion's head stretching up toward the sky.

"Climb on my back," Suanni said in a great, booming voice. They sounded like thunder, with lightning flashing from their lilac eyes and the sharp points of their teeth. "We're going to the top of the mountain."

Imari let go of Kaede's hand, hurrying over to Suanni's tail and climbed up. Kaede wasn't far behind, and soon they were tucked into the large dip in front of Suanni's forelegs. The dragon reared up, and Kaede's stomach dropped as the dragon leapt from the mountainside, sailing up into the open air.

They circled higher and higher, until Kaede could see all across the countryside. She blinked back dry tears and ducked her head to shield her face from the wind, but she couldn't resist staring out over the forests and plains below. The afternoon sun allowed her to see far more than she had the previous evening, and she followed the river Go all the way to the horizon. That is, until Imari nudged her shoulder.

"Kaede! Kaede, look!"

Imari pointed excitedly in the other direction, up instead of down, and Kaede turned to follow the gesture. She inhaled sharply, staring in awe. Above them, a whole colony of dragons circled around the mountain's peak. They fluttered like bright banners in the sky, all different colors and sizes. It was as if someone had taken a magnificent kite festival and blown it up to incredible size.

"Sun and Moon," Kaede gasped. She started laughing with joy, and behind her, Imari did the same.

"I told you there were other dragons," Suanni said, sounding pleased with themself. "But this isn't the best part. Hold on tight."

They reached the top of the mountain, and Kaede realized with surprise it wasn't a mountain at all. The top dipped down into a large caldera, and steam wafted up from below. Grass and flowers covered the sloping edges, and there were several pools of water at the deepest part of the valley. Kaede could see more dragons gathered around them, swimming about and lounging on the banks. The placement of Wen Ling's forge suddenly made sense. Hongshan seemed to be a dormant volcano.

"It's absolutely beautiful."

Kaede felt Imari's chin tuck over her shoulder and warm arms wrap around her waist. "Yes, it is."

Even when Suanni touched down onto the soft grass that lined the sides of the crater, Imari didn't let go right away. They remained on the dragon's back a few moments longer, until Kaede whispered, "You know, I think I'm going to enjoy staying here a while."

Imari gave her waist another squeeze. "Me too."

Chapter Eighteen

IMARI SWIVELED HER FEET as Wen Ling's sword sliced toward her, dodging out of the way just in time. The air beside her cheek hissed, splitting beneath the blade, but she didn't retreat. She pushed instead, flattening her own sword and thrusting forward.

A clang rang out through the room as steel skidded against steel, and Imari accepted the jolt that ran up her arm. Wen Ling was fast and taking the offensive, but Imari was confident. She had trained hard over the past two months, and there was a warm hum in her muscles that only came over her during the best sparring matches. No longer did she need to hang back and wait for the perfect opening. With her jian, she could create her own.

Wen Ling disengaged, circling several steps back and flicking out with the pommel of her sword. Imari barely managed to avoid the golden tassels that lashed toward her eyes, but she didn't let it distract her. She kept her gaze locked on the edge of Wen Ling's sword, and when it swept in sideways, she was ready. She met the blow with a backhanded twirl, redirecting it off to the side.

"You fight well, Imari," Wen Ling panted as she recovered. "This is the best you've kept up with me so far."

Imari smirked. She brought her elbows back, letting her sword fall diagonally across her chest in a defensive posture and aiming the tip at Wen Ling's throat. "I'm not just fighting well. I'm going to win."

She lunged. Their blades clashed again. Sparks scattered as the sharpened edges scraped past each other. Through sheer force, she recovered first. She struck, and this time, her sword slipped past Wen Ling's guard.

The satisfaction she felt as the edge of her blade touched the padded front of Wen Ling's shirt made her heart swell too big for her chest. She waited, breathless and almost giddy, until Wen Ling lowered her sword and stepped back. She bowed, and Imari bowed in return, unable to hide her grin.

"Excellent," Wen Ling said as she rose. She smiled broadly, and

Imari had never seen someone so pleased to have been defeated. "You've worked hard, and I'm proud to say it shows. You fight as if your sword is a part of you."

Imari gazed down at her blade, still in awe. "It feels like a part of me," she said, gazing into the eyes of the dragon pommel. As she lost herself in the green gems, a sense of peace and understanding came over her. A word whispered in her head, quiet, but strong and true. Characters painted themselves in her mind's eye: inseparable, indistinguishable, whole. "I think I know your name now."

"And what is your sword's name, Imari?" Wen Ling asked, watching with interest.

"Wujian. Unbroken. With this sword, I'm finally whole again." She looked up from the sword and smiled at Wen Ling. "All thanks to you, Sensei."

"Then my job is done." Wen Ling sheathed her own sword, tucking it back into her obi. "It has been my privilege to train you, Imari, and to present you with Wujian. You have been one of my finest students."

In an instant, Imari's good mood vanished. She felt as if the breath had been knocked out of her. This should have been her shining moment, but instead, she felt only a creeping sense of dread. "What do you mean? I can't leave yet."

"Because I still haven't given you a new hand?" Wen Ling asked. "Every day you ask, and every day my answer is the same. You don't need a new hand. You've learned well, and you're a better person than when you arrived here. That should be enough."

A lump rose in Imari's throat. She knew Wen Ling didn't owe her anything—the smith had already given her so much—but disappointment crawled through her like a poison. "Forgive me, Sensei," she said with frost in her voice, "but it's up to me to determine what is enough."

Wen Ling sighed. "You can't continue clinging to what was, Imari. As I've told you, you are a different person now than you used to be."

"And what about you?" Imari snapped before she could think better of it. "You got a whole new arm and leg from the dragons. You can't tell me you don't appreciate them."

"I'm grateful," Wen Ling said softly. "The dragons gave me a second chance, as well as a purpose. But what about your purpose, Imari? You have spent the past several years dreaming of a new hand. What would you do if I granted you one?"

"Go back home," Imari said at once. "I'd return to Mirai and take my father's place as daimyo once he was ready to retire. I want to take care of the city and its people like him."

"And do you need a new hand to do all those things?"

Imari pressed her lips together. The answer was "no," but she didn't want to say the word aloud.

"Wouldn't it be more impressive, more meaningful, if you accomplished all those goals as you are?" Wen Ling approached her, resting a gentle hand on her shoulder. "Like it or not, losing your hand has changed you. It has inconvenienced you, but it has also strengthened you. The loss of your hand is what drove you to travel all this way, to fight battles and ride dragons and train in the way of the jian. You can't tell me you aren't a better person for experiencing all those things."

"Yes, but—"

"How are you to know where else your life will lead? Don't try to change the course of the river. It flows where it does for a reason."

Imari's shoulders slumped in disappointment. They had been through this exact same argument every day since her arrival, but for the first time, she felt truly discouraged. There was a sense of finality in Wen Ling's voice—calm, but harder than the steel of the swords she forged and as unmovable as Hongshan itself.

"I don't know what to say." A hot coal of frustration burned in the middle of Imari's chest, but mostly, she felt sad. It was like losing something important all over again—hope, in addition to her hand.

"You don't need to say anything." Wen Ling removed her hand, taking a step back. "I understand your disappointment. I know you don't understand yet why I won't grant your request, but give it time. You will."

"Then forgive me," Imari murmured, fighting back tears. "I think I want to be alone."

She gave a short bow, the most respectful farewell she could bring herself to make, and slipped out of the dojo. Tears leaked from her stinging eyes as soon as she stepped through the screen door. She felt like a child, crying as she felt her way down the hall, but she couldn't help it. She had been so sure Wen Ling would grow to understand her request and why it was important. Although she had held firm for two months, asking again and again, she couldn't argue with Wen Ling's answer this time. There had been something different about it—a true no. The denial had cracked her heart straight down the middle.

"Kaede," Imari whispered, the name rising to her lips at once.

Kaede would know what to say. What to do. Kaede would hold her until she got a grip on herself and wouldn't think of judging her for her feelings. Kaede was exactly who she needed right now, and so Imari went in search of her, heading toward the bedroom they had shared for the past two months. She only hoped she wouldn't run into Rin or the Hibana brothers on the way.

***

Kaede yawned, closing the book she had been reading and lying back on her futon. It was mid-morning, one of those rare lazy days when she didn't have anything to do, and she had neglected to fold it. She hadn't even bothered to put on a hakama. Kenta and Takeshi had left in search of breakfast, and Imari was long gone, but Kaede felt no particular desire to move. Even the thought of watching Imari train with Wen Ling wasn't quite enough of a draw to make her get up.

Still, the thought was more entertaining than what she had been reading. She appreciated bushio wisdom as much as the next samurai, but Imari captivated her. She let her mind drift back, closing her eyes to better enjoy the memories. She could picture Imari sweeping her blade through the air all too clearly, dark eyes glinting as sharp as the steel in her hand, a few loose strands of hair clinging to the pale curve of her neck.

"Kaede?" The sound of her name, accompanied by a soft knock on the screen door, startled her from the fantasy. "Are you in there?"

It was Imari's voice, but not as it usually sounded. Instead of the cheerful chime of bells, her voice sounded tight and thick with tears. Kaede got up in an instant. "I'm here," she said, hurrying over to the door and pulling it back. Imari was standing by it, cheeks glistening with tear-tracks, lower lip trembling. It was a sight Kaede had never seen before, and it hit her straight in the gut. "Imari, what's wrong?"

Imari didn't answer. She simply opened her arms, and Kaede took the request, wrapping her up in a tight embrace. She held Imari for several moments, rocking her slowly and running a hand along the middle of her back. Tears seeped onto the shoulder of her kimono, making the pale blue a darker shade, but she didn't pay them any mind. "It's okay," she whispered, pressing her lips to Imari's temple.

It took Imari a while to answer, but eventually, her sniffing slowed down. "I'm sorry," she rasped. "I don't usually cry like that. I can't remember the last time—"

"It's all right. I don't mind." Kaede wanted to ask what was wrong, but she knew better. Imari needed comfort more than solutions.

Carefully, Kaede led her over to the bed, urging her to sit down. Imari went without complaint, tucking her heels beneath her and curling into a small, folded ball. The stump of her left hand rested in her lap, and she stared down at it with red-ringed eyes. "Wen Ling says my training is done. She wants me to go back home."

At once, Kaede understood. "And she still won't give you a new hand. Imari, I'm so sorry." She reached out, wrapping an arm around Imari's shoulders.

"Give me a minute." Imari closed her eyes, and Kaede waited until they opened again. "She told me losing my hand made me into who I am. She said I wouldn't be the same person if I still had it."

"I don't think so. You would still be you. Strong and smart and gorgeous."

Imari gave a hoarse laugh. "Flatterer. But I think Wen Ling might be right. Coming from anyone else, I wouldn't have listened, but she knows exactly what I've been through. She isn't speaking from ignorance, but from experience. And she has a point. If I hadn't lost my hand, I wouldn't have gone on this journey." She laced the fingers of her hand through Kaede's, giving them a shaking squeeze. "I wouldn't have met you."

"I like to think we would have met anyway," Kaede said, offering Imari a smile. "The Ancestors work in mysterious ways."

"Maybe." Imari turned to look at her, and Kaede felt the breath leave her chest. Even with red, puffy bags beneath her eyes and messy, smeared cheeks, Imari was beautiful.

Imari must have noticed her gaze, because she turned her face away, wiping it on the sleeve of her yellow kimono. "Please, don't look at me while I'm such a mess."

"Imari," Kaede laughed, "I've seen you covered in dirt and sweat and all sorts of other awful things. At this point, nothing can surprise me." She let go of Imari's hand and reached into the outer fold of her own kimono, producing a handkerchief. "Here, take this."

Imari took it, swiping her eyes and nose clean. When it came away, she looked a little more cheerful. "Wait, this is mine. I recognize the embroidery." She turned the dark crimson cloth over in her hand, running her fingers along the seams. "I gave it to you back in Mirai's marketplace." She laughed, crumpling the handkerchief in her hand. "You got food all over your face. Did you really keep it all this time?"

Kaede flushed. "Yes." A thought occurred to her, and she scooted away, grabbing for the bag at the foot of her bed. "Actually, I have something better to give you than your own handkerchief." She dug in the pack's front pocket, retrieving the small jade teardrop she had taken from beneath the giant wave. "I've been holding onto it for a while, but this might be the right time." She held it in the middle of her outstretched palm, offering it up as a gift.

When Imari caught sight of the gem, her eyes widened. She set the handkerchief in her lap and reached out to take the shining green stone, running her fingertips along its smooth curve. "Kaede, it's beautiful. But why?"

Kaede's voice caught in her throat. There was so much she wanted to share, though she wasn't sure if she should. Imari's face was still tearstained, but a happy glow of hope had blossomed in her eyes. That was what finally gave Kaede the confidence to continue. She curled her hand around the back of Imari's neck, drawing her face close.

The first kiss was a slow, uncertain meeting of mouths. They had done the same many times before over the past two months, but somehow, Kaede sensed this was different. She could taste the salt of Imari's tears as well as the sweetness beneath. The heat made her shiver, but it also made her heart clench. She knew Imari was disappointed. She knew what it felt like to wish you could change yourself only to find out it would be more difficult than expected. It was a wound that always reopened, no matter how well it seemed to have healed on good days. Instead of offering her sympathy with more words, she offered it through touch. She cupped Imari's wet cheek, always gentle, always careful.

To her relief, Imari didn't pull away. She parted her lips, sighing softly—all the permission Kaede needed. Her sigh said, "This is all right." Her sigh said, "Please comfort me."

Kaede ran her thumb across Imari's tear tracks, tenderly wiping them away. "It's okay," she murmured, ignoring Imari's ragged, uneven breaths as they puffed against her mouth. "I'm sorry you didn't get what you wanted, but you still have other things. You have me."

"I know I do," Imari whispered. "I just...I came so far and wished so hard."

Kaede rested their foreheads together, touching Imari's face in little soothing strokes. "Tomorrow, things will look better. You'll remember you spent the last several years without your hand, and it never stopped you before."

"I know," Imari said, but her voice still cracked. "I'll be fine. I just need to be sad for a while."

"Well." Kaede paused to place another soft, closed kiss on Imari's lips. "You can always be sad with me tonight. I don't mind. I've got another clean shoulder for you to cry on."

"No." Imari shifted back a little, and her dark eyes burned with such intensity that Kaede was taken aback. "I can mope and feel sorry for myself on the way home. Right now, I want to feel something else. Something better."

Kaede didn't understand. Her brow furrowed as Imari mirrored her earlier motion, cupping her cheek and drawing her back in. Their second kiss was longer and much deeper. It tasted of hunger instead of sadness, and Kaede suddenly realized what Imari wanted. Imari wanted to forget. Imari wanted to feel emotions other than disappointment. She knew without being told. *But can I do this? Do I want to?*

The answer that came to her was yes. She wanted this for Imari, and most important of all, she wanted it for herself. Imari was the first person she had felt so close to, so comfortable with—comfortable enough to share her body, just as she had already shared her heart. Still, with her decision made, she had to be certain Imari felt the same.

"Are you sure?" she whispered, gazing into Imari's eyes. The sadness in them was already fading, eclipsed by something much brighter. They burned, and Kaede's face bloomed with heat as they focused directly on her lips.

"Kaede," Imari said, her voice no longer hoarse, but low and certain, "you are the one thing in my life right now I'm absolutely sure about. I love you."

The words washed over Kaede like the breaking of the dawn. Her entire body glowed with them, and a wide grin spread across her face until her cheeks could barely hold it. "You love me?" she repeated, almost breathless with joy.

"Yes." Imari's thumb passed gently over the scar on Kaede's cheek, mimicking the way Kaede had wiped her tears away. "I don't care if you're a ronin. I don't care what anyone else will say about us."

At once, Kaede felt a stab of shame—familiar, but sharper than ever before. On the cusp of something so intimate, lying about her identity felt even worse. However, she didn't have time to wallow, because Imari kept going.

"You're the most beautiful person I've ever met. I know what I want, and what I want is you."

Despite her guilt, Kaede believed Imari's words wholeheartedly. During the past few months, she had felt more like herself than ever before. *Maybe I'm becoming better by being Iori Kaede. Maybe I really have grown into the person Imari loves instead of just pretending.* She wanted to be that person, the person Imari had fallen in love with, for as long as possible—forever, if she could. Aozora Kaede was a coward, but Iori Kaede was worthy of this.

She kissed Imari again and the two of them tipped back onto the futon. Kaede wasn't sure what she was doing, but to her relief, it didn't matter. Imari was more than happy to guide her hands. Kaede rested them above the curve of her hips at first, but slowly, Imari coaxed them upwards. Even through the material of Imari's kimono, Kaede could feel warmth radiating from her sides.

"I don't know what I'm doing," Kaede whispered into Imari's lips, "but I want this. I want you."

Imari responded with a low groan. She brought Kaede's hands even higher, until they were resting at the tuck of her waist. Meanwhile, her own hand began to wander. Kaede shuddered as it roamed along her back, her muscles tensing. It felt good to be held like this, even better than the way Imari held her while they slept.

On impulse, she sucked briefly at Imari's bottom lip and then abandoned her mouth entirely, placing a tentative kiss beneath her jaw instead. Imari sighed, tilting her chin to offer more access, and Kaede took the invitation gladly. She placed another kiss against Imari's throat, and then another, until she had made an entire trail down to the crook of Imari's neck. Imari tasted slightly of salt from her training session with Wen Ling, but Kaede didn't mind at all. The subtle taste of sweat clinging to Imari's skin was intoxicating, and her mouth watered for more.

Before she could get too carried away, Imari tugged at the back of Kaede's head, pulling her up for another kiss. This time it was open-mouthed, and their tongues glided together. The taste and heat were distracting, and Kaede didn't notice Imari was reversing their positions until she was flat on her back. Imari straddled her hips, grinning down at her. Several loose strands of hair had escaped her braid to drift around her face, and her eyes shone with something better than tears.

"How about I help you out of those clothes?"

There was clear desire in the request, but Kaede was touched that Imari had phrased it as a question. That eased some of her nerves as she answered, "Yes," and brought Imari's hand to her obi. It was a narrow, simple affair, meant for functionality rather than decoration, and Imari didn't have much trouble with the knot. Kaede lifted up, bracing her weight on her elbows, and Imari's nimble fingers reached around to unfasten the bow.

However, as she shifted, Kaede inadvertently brought their pelvises together. She hadn't thought the motion through, and when their hips met, a powerful jolt passed through her. Heat shot straight between her legs, and she gasped as pressure began to swell there. She could usually handle her erections, especially since Imari had caused quite a few of them over the past several months, but this was different. Imari was directly on top of her, able to feel everything. Surely her yukata wasn't doing much to hide it in their intimate position.

"I...um," she stammered, blushing furiously.

Imari grinned. "I was wondering whether that would happen. I wasn't sure."

"Oh, it happens," Kaede mumbled. "Especially around you. I can't help it."

"Are you all right when it happens?" Imari asked, her amusement softening into concern. "It doesn't upset you to be different than most women?"

"Sometimes," Kaede said, but at Imari's worried look, she corrected herself. "But not right now. You don't have to stop—that is, unless you want to." She swallowed, trying to choose her words more carefully. "Please, Imari, don't stop what you were doing."

Imari's worry vanished. She finished untying Kaede's obi, unwinding the sash from around her waist. Kaede felt a spike of something as Imari's fingertips drifted up along the front of her yukata and the juban underneath, playing with the seams, but it wasn't blind panic. It was nervousness, but also excitement and anticipation. A large part of her wanted Imari to see her naked, wanted Imari to touch her, to know her.

The breathless look of wonder and awe that broke over Imari's face as she opened the front of the yukata was all the reassurance Kaede needed. Imari's gaze started at her face then moved down along her collarbones, disappearing into the shallow dip of her cleavage. Lying flat on her back, Kaede's breasts looked even more modest than usual, but Imari didn't seem to mind. Bracing herself on her other arm, she brought her hand to Kaede's bare side, starting at her waist and stroking up along her ribs.

Kaede's heart hammered. Imari's palm was callused at the edges, but also incredibly gentle. It felt like heaven on her skin, and the peaks of her breasts pulled into stiff points before Imari even reached them. Imari smiled, and the two of them shared a soft laugh. Her fingers trailed higher, caressing the curve of Kaede's left breast and circling the sensitive tip without touching it.

"You're beautiful," Imari said, continuing her teasing outline. She finally took the nipple between her knuckles and gave it a light pinch. It wasn't hard, but it was enough to send another bolt of pleasure straight between Kaede's legs. She swelled a little further, straining beneath the lower half of her yukata. The fabric was still folded over, but she could feel the press of Imari's thighs on either side of her own.

Imari noticed and her eyes sparkled and her smile spread wider. "So, you're sensitive?" She leaned in closer, until Kaede could feel warm breath wash across her chest. "What if I did this?"

The silky heat of Imari's mouth was even more intense than Kaede expected. She bucked as soon as Imari's mouth wrapped around her, stiffening and shivering. Her hand shot up to clutch the back of Imari's head without permission. The soft fire, the swift flicks of Imari's tongue, and the steady suction left Kaede dizzy. It was like nothing she had ever felt before, and she desperately wanted more.

Imari finally released her with a soft pop and Kaede whimpered. "Imari," she murmured, but there was no need to beg. Imari was already kissing across her chest, seeking out the other sensitive peak. She passed the next several minutes, switching back and forth, scattering open-mouthed kisses everywhere.

Imari's hand started at Kaede's stomach, gliding over the quivering muscles there, but gradually moved lower, loosening the edges of her yukata on the way. Kaede was so distracted by the heat of Imari's mouth on her breasts she didn't even notice it peeling open until it was almost too late. She caressed Imari's cheek, urging her to stop. "Wait," she rasped, afraid to be alone in her nakedness. "You too. Please?"

Imari placed a soft, lingering kiss of reassurance on Kaede's lips. "Of course." She rose onto her knees, giving Kaede's lap a little relief, and unfastened her obi.

It fluttered to the floor beside the futon, and Kaede stared in awe as Imari began unfastening her kimono. First her collarbone came into view, then her softly rounded shoulders, and finally her breasts, full and capped with light brown nipples. Every inch of lovely pale skin that came into view made Kaede's tongue grow thick in her mouth. Her eyes widened and a low moan slipped out before she could swallow it down.

Imari beamed at the sound even as Kaede flushed. "I'll take that as a sign of approval," she murmured as the fabric fell down her shoulders. She held her left arm a little further away with a tilt of her shoulders, as if trying to keep it subtly in the background, but Kaede noticed. She folded her fingers around Imari's forearm, gently drawing it back between them.

"Hey, you don't have to keep this out of the way." It was something of a reassurance to realize that Imari was also a little self-conscious of her body despite her greater experience. "It's part of you."

Imari breathed a small sigh. "So, can we make a pact to not worry about how we look for the next few minutes and focus on learning how to make each other feel good?"

Kaede laughed. "A few minutes?" Her eyes dipped back down, admiring the curve of Imari's breasts. They were much larger than her own, and her palms itched to test their weight. "I really hope it lasts longer than that."

Imari noticed where Kaede's eyes had fallen and took her hand, bringing one up to her breast and urging her to cup it. "In that case, let's see how well you can keep up with me."

Confidence swelled in Kaede's chest. She caught Imari's nipple between her fingertips and pulled, testing what kinds of reactions she could get. Imari hummed softly at first, then gasped as she tugged harder. When Kaede sat up and copied what Imari had done to her, pulling the puckered bud past her lips, Imari tilted back.

Once more, Kaede lost herself in the taste of Imari's skin. Her hands roamed along Imari's curves as her mouth explored Imari's chest, seeking out sensitive places. She savored every shiver, every sigh, and the gentle rake of Imari's nails through her hair as signs of success. Soon, sweat had broken out over her own skin as well, and the ache between her legs had become an insistent throb. She would need to do something about it soon, but she wasn't sure how to ask.

In the end, she didn't need to. While she was busy, Imari shifted to open her yukata, letting the front fall open. Kaede broke off from Imari's nipple as the cool air hit her at last, uncertain what to do. She didn't get a chance to ask, because Imari kissed her—hard—and she nearly shook to pieces as the comforting hand stroking along her stomach delved down to the juncture of her thighs, slipping beneath her fundoshi. Then the last barrier was gone, and there was nothing left to protect her.

The moment Imari's soft fingers closed around her and squeezed, Kaede went rigid. No one else had ever touched her there before. Her heartbeat dropped straight into Imari's palm, pounding there. But Imari didn't do anything else. She simply waited, searching Kaede's eyes for something.

"Is this okay?" Imari whispered. "You aren't breathing."

Kaede took in a lungful of air. She hadn't even realized she was short of breath. "Sorry. I just..."

"It's all right. You don't have to talk. Can I try something?"

Kaede chewed nervously at her lower lip. Her eyes flicked down between their bodies, taking in the sight of Imari's hand wrapped around her. The visual was enough to send another stab of desire deep into her belly. Wetness pearled at her tip, threatening to well over and spill onto the tops of Imari's fingers.

"Yes. I trust you."

Imari took Kaede's mouth in yet another slow, exploratory kiss, and once they both relaxed into it, she began to move her hand. She started at the top, drawing her thumb through the clear pool of wetness. Kaede's hips threatened to buck, and she managed to stop herself at the last minute. In a matter of seconds, Imari had found a spot that sent sparks shooting through Kaede's entire body. More slippery heat spilled out, coating Imari's fingers, and Kaede would have been embarrassed if Imari hadn't groaned into her mouth at the exact same moment to show approval.

The extra slickness appeared to be what Imari was waiting for. She began to stroke, setting a slow tempo at first. Kaede had to break away from the kiss and gasp. The feeling of pressure was almost too intense, but she thought she might die if it stopped.

"Good?" Imari asked with a teasing lilt in her voice.

Kaede gave a jerking nod. She had sought relief with her own hand before, of course, but this was different. Imari touched her, toyed with her, showed her an entirely new way to feel. Kaede fought the instinct to buck with everything she had.

She didn't need to seek it out. Imari gave her exactly what she craved. Imari's hand began a steady sliding motion, drawing more pressure from the depths of Kaede's belly to throb through her. The fullness was unbearable, and soon she was groaning along with each pass of Imari's fist.

Part of her wanted to savor this new sensation forever, to enjoy the rush straight to her core, but her poor body couldn't handle something so intense for long. Far before she was ready, her stomach gave a powerful twitch, and the pounding ache within her exploded

Tengoku

outward. She watched as she spilled onto Imari's hand, splashing over the tops of her fingers and running down her fist.

The matching wave of pleasure hit. The sweetness of release was enough to swallow her embarrassment, and Imari's lips swallowed her cries the same way. Kaede had no choice but to ride it out, to surrender to it and Imari as she gave everything she had. She leapt blindly, trusting Imari to catch her.

And catch her Imari did. Kaede was certain she had blacked out for a moment, because the next thing she remembered was Imari raining soft kisses on her face and murmuring sweet words. "Hey, it's all right," she breathed as Kaede let out a groan that was half-satisfaction, half-embarrassment. She had hoped to last a little longer, for Imari's benefit if not her own. "How did that feel?"

At last, Kaede was able to speak. "Amazing. You're amazing."

Imari laughed. "At least the hand I've got is good for something, huh?" Her hand slid down to the base and lower still, cupping the heaviness beneath. Kaede gave a jolt of surprise, crying out as more wetness she hadn't known she possessed spilled free.

Once the last waves passed, Kaede laughed. "Sorry," she mumbled sheepishly, burying her face in Imari's warm, sweet-smelling shoulder.

Imari's other arm wrapped around her, and she held Kaede in the crook of her elbow. "Don't be sorry," she said, still squeezing gently with her hand. "It was a pleasant surprise."

Kaede suddenly realized she could feel Imari's rapid heartbeat as well as the stiff points of her nipples. A different kind of excitement welled within her—an eagerness to learn and explore, to make Imari feel wonderful. "My turn?" she asked, raising her head to give Imari a hopeful look.

"I insist," Imari purred. The last of her tears were gone, and a look of hunger had taken its place. "Do you want me to show you how?"

"Please," Kaede breathed.

"All right, but it's more fun if you figure out at least a little of it for yourself." Imari tipped back, ending their embrace. She removed her fundoshi and spread her thighs, offering a view that grabbed Kaede's attention immediately.

Kaede had seen pictures on woodblock as decoration, but the real thing was miles different. Imari's pink outer lips petaled apart to reveal the deep red inner ones, and both sets shone with wetness. The gleaming folds looked soft as silk, and Kaede found herself reaching out to touch before she was conscious of the choice to do so. Carefully, she sat up and slid the tips of her fingers through the slickness, testing what it felt like.

The heat surprised her, burning even hotter than Imari's mouth when they kissed. She moved her fingers up a little, curious how high she could go. Something round and firm stopped her, and she peeled back Imari's folds to get a better look. Tucked neatly into its hood was a stiff red bud, and to Kaede's joy, it swelled as she touched it. She stroked the tip at first, watching the way Imari's stomach clenched as she did. The soft satin below fluttered, and Kaede watched in wonder a clear stream of wetness slid out.

Kaede followed it with her fingers, searching for the source. To her surprise, they dipped in further than she expected. Imari's entrance grasped at her with strong muscles, trying to drag her in. Kaede's eyes widened, but Imari smiled.

"It's okay if you want to go inside," she said, spreading her knees even wider and tilting her hips up. "You won't hurt me."

Kaede couldn't resist that invitation. She pushed forward with one finger first, surprised by how easily it slid in. As soon as it did, she was taken aback by how tightly Imari's inner walls clung to her. They weren't perfectly smooth as she had imagined, but pleasantly rippled. She began probing forward, trying to feel more, and Imari let out a low groan.

"Forward and up," she gasped, angling her pelvis to demonstrate.

This time, Kaede felt the spot Imari meant. It was a little puffier and firmer than the rest of the softness around her, and she worked a second finger past Imari's opening to feel it better. When she pushed into it, Imari let out an even higher, sweeter sound. Kaede repeated the motion again and again, and every time, Imari gave a sigh of encouragement.

Once, instead of angling forward, she slipped much further in and hit something else soft and round. Imari made a different kind of noise then, still one of pleasure, but she reached down to cup Kaede's hand. "That's nice, but what you were doing before is better. Please, don't stop."

Kaede followed instructions, watching as Imari began rocking urgently onto her fingers. She tried to keep up the curling motion, but Imari was squeezing her so tightly it was difficult to move. The stiff point of Imari's clit was even larger than it had been before, standing proudly beneath its hood and glowing an even deeper red.

Full of enthusiasm and confidence, Kaede brought her other hand between Imari's legs as well. It was awkward using two, but she didn't trust herself to do both tasks with one—yet. She trapped the hard point of Imari's clit between her fingers, pinching lightly to see what would happen.

Imari's reaction was beautiful. She arched, going taut as a bow, and then snapped, shooting up into a sitting position and screaming as her hips went wild. It was more than Kaede could have hoped for. Imari flooded her palm with a rush of liquid heat. The river filled Kaede's hand and dripped down her forearm, but she didn't pull back. Instead, she pushed deeper, hooking against the sensitive spot inside of Imari to see how much more she could get.

Imari kept shivering and spilling for a long time, until her fluttering muscles finally stopped grasping so desperately at Kaede's fingers. They still twitched, but the jolting motions were light and sparse. She went limp and slumped back onto the bed, panting with exhaustion.

"You're a fast student," Imari said after a while, a wide grin stretching across her face.

"You're a good teacher."

Imari pulled Kaede back on top of her, wrapping a hand around her neck and drawing her in for another soft kiss. "Thank you for sharing that with me. I feel better. In moments like this, I don't need more."

Kaede didn't know how to answer, so she simply cuddled closer to Imari, inhaling her scent. It was tinged with the spice of sex, but somehow, that only made it better. "What now?" she whispered. "Do we go to sleep? Clean up?"

Imari arched an eyebrow. "Oh, we aren't finished." Her hand crept down along Kaede's body to cup between her legs again, and Kaede gasped as her shaft swelled to greet the touch. "Let's keep practicing."

***

The mountains of Aozora were not as Hayate remembered them. He had fond childhood memories of playing in the forest at their feet, the same one that connected to the province of Yukimura where he had grown up. Back then, they had been beautiful to behold. The dawn turned them a glowing pink, and the dusk a comfortable purple. He had felt safe in their shadow, protected from the sharp winds that whistled through their snowcapped peaks.

Now, as he rode through the streets of Taiseito toward his uncle's castle, they loomed over him in judgment, a stark, bold black against the sky. The evening noise of the city seemed dim, and he barely took notice of the people he passed. Some, seeing Kaze, stepped aside to let them through, but Hayate couldn't bring himself to acknowledge them as they bowed. He was too focused on what he needed to accomplish.

The castle guards opened the doors, permitting him through without a word. He dismounted just past the inner gates, leaving his horse to be tended to by one of the soldiers. As he entered the courtyard, he noted with some sadness that the garden was going to sleep for the winter. Several flowers had already wilted, the cloud bushes were silver at the edges with frost, and the branches of the trees were close to bare.

"It's going to be all right, Hayate," Kaze said, nudging gently at his hand in a gesture of comfort. "You're doing the right thing."

"I know." He paused before the castle's main entrance, taking a deep breath. "But no one ever said doing the right thing was easy."

He knew the truth in Kaze's words—what he had refused to hear. If he truly loved Setsuna, he needed to ask Lord Aozora to help him reach her. Logically, he understood the decision he was making, but it still felt like a betrayal. Setsuna had taken him in as a child, and though there were moments she had shown a clear preference for Kaede as they grew older, his mother loved him as her own. Underneath all the old hurt, he was certain. *This is what she would expect of me, if she were in her right mind. This is what the woman who raised me would have advised me to do.*

Placing a hand between Kaze's shoulders for moral support, he entered. The halls were the same as he remembered them, decorated with the mon of Aozora: three white mountains against a dark blue background. He passed the banners, making his way through the familiar stone halls from memory. After passing through several outer rooms and startling a few of the servants, he finally arrived at his destination—a painted screen door decorated with a flight of slender cranes. Two guards stood on either side, spears in hand. When they noticed him, both bowed deeply.

"Yukimura-dono," the first said, rising only after several beats had passed. "Our apologies, but you were not expected. Would you like us to inform the daimyo of your arrival?"

"Yes," Hayate said, trying to sound more certain than he actually was. "I have important news to share with him, news that shouldn't wait."

With another bow, the first guard disappeared, leaving him alone with the second. Hayate turned to her and asked, "Has Shogun

Yukimura sent word to Aozora recently? Messengers, perhaps, or soldiers? Anything you can remember would be helpful."

The woman's dark eyebrows furrowed. "No, Yukimura-dono, I'm afraid not. There hasn't been anything aside from the usual letters to the daimyo, from what I've seen."

Hayate dipped his head in thanks. Apparently, his mother still trusted him to bring Kaede home and hadn't sent soldiers here looking for her. That, or Setsuna assumed that Kaede was far too smart to return home, even out of desperation. It also meant his uncle was unlikely to know anything about what had occurred. His stomach churned at the thought of delivering the news. What was he supposed to say? That his mother had gone crazy, Kaede had vanished, experiments were being conducted on wild yokai, and no one had bothered to make mention of it? His uncle would most certainly not be pleased.

Sooner than Hayate wanted, the first guard returned. "The daimyo will see you at once, tono. Please, go through." He and his companion bowed and opened the screen. Hayate squared his shoulders. There would be no putting it off any longer.

When he entered, a wave of warmth washed over him. The irori in the middle of the floor was lit beneath its table, and paper lanterns hung around the room to light it. The walls were stone, but hidden behind decorative screens, and mats covered the floors. At the other end of the room, Lord and Lady Aozora sat on their low platforms. They weren't wearing especially formal clothes, although their blue and white kimonos still befitted their station. Hayate suspected he had interrupted them after formal court hours, and he bowed in apology.

"Uncle, Aunt, it is good to see you. I'm sorry to trouble you."

"It's no trouble," Masaru said with a smile. "We're glad to have you, and Kaze as well, of course." With his dark complexion and his height, he looked like Kaede. Unlike his daughter, though, he was large and broad-shouldered, with a square, blocky chin that ended in a long, tapered beard. "Please, Hayate, sit. You're always welcome, although this is something of a surprise."

Hayate approached the tatami mat before the platforms and took a seat. "Unfortunately, this isn't a friendly visit."

"I assumed as much," Kotone said. Her hair was the same flaming red as Kaede's, and she possessed a similar lean build. "Tell me, is this about Kaede? We haven't heard from her in months. I know she can be forgetful in writing letters, but I'm growing concerned."

Hayate hesitated. He felt as though he had leapt into a freezing stream and didn't know which way to start swimming. Kaze grounded him once more, padding over to take a seat beside him and nuzzling his shoulder. "Tell them, Hayate. It's what's best for everyone."

He took a deep breath. "I'm afraid you're right to be concerned."

More swiftly than he intended, the entire story came spilling out. He told them of Setsuna, of how she came upon the dream of a better society built on the backs of yokai. He told them of how that dream had changed her from a strict but fair leader to a person obsessed without omitting his own complicity. He told them of the way Setsuna had used Kaede's ability to draw the yokai in, and how most of them had gone wild afterward. He told them of the soldiers who had died, and he told them of how Kaede had run.

"At first, I followed her with the intention of bringing her back. I was angry that she had run away from what I considered to be her duty. But as I followed her, it was almost like a fog lifted. The further away I got from Setsuna, the more clearly I saw things. Even so, I didn't want to admit that she was making a mistake. I was stubborn." He turned to Kaze, who looked at him with clear pride. "Kaze was the one who finally convinced me to come to you."

"What about Kaede?" Worry knitted Kotone's brow, and her lips were drawn tight with concern. "Was she all right when you last saw her?"

Hayate nodded. "Yes. She and her new companions left Yin to cross the Jade Sea. I assume she is still with them."

Neither Masaru nor Kotone looked satisfied with that answer. They exchanged a worried look, but they did seem somewhat relieved that, at the very least, Kaede hadn't been in danger the last time Hayate had seen her. "We need to send someone to Tsun'i to look for her at once," Masaru said. "Kaede is a skilled samurai, but crossing the Jade Sea is dangerous for anyone. There's no guarantee she even made it."

"I'm sure she did," Hayate said, compelled to speak up in his cousin's defense. "Kaede knows what she's doing."

"And what about Setsuna?" Kotone asked. "What do you propose to do about her? The situation you've described sounds alarming to say the least. And even if Kaede is found, she won't return until it's dealt with."

"If you're asking my opinion, we need to send soldiers to check on Setsuna at once. I know it could be dangerous, since her station is above yours, but I couldn't think of anyone better to help."

"What about alerting Empress Tomoyo?" Masaru said. "If one of her shogun is conducting dangerous experiments on the yokai, surely she will need to be informed."

Hayate felt a sharp stab of fear. He had hoped to avoid that, but now, he realized he had little choice in the matter. The secret was already out. Setsuna had always said the Empress would be told of their work eventually, when they had succeeded in their quest and the time was right. Hearing Empress Tomoyo's name now made Hayate feel ill. She was only fifteen and relied heavily on her court and the counsel of the shogun under her rule. If they found out what Setsuna had been doing, they would most definitely object. Some might even use it as an excuse to remove Setsuna from power and increase their own standing.

But isn't that why you've come here? To remove her from power, at least until she regains her senses?

"Empress Tomoyo is a merciful and just ruler, but the other shogun might not look on Setsuna's actions as generously," he said at last. "I was hoping we could resolve this quietly, without alerting them."

Masaru didn't look convinced. "I'm afraid my conscience dictates otherwise. Empress Tomoyo must be alerted at once. However, the last thing I want is for Setsuna to fall in disfavor. Everything you've told me makes me suspect she isn't acting entirely of her own will. The sister I know wouldn't take such risks, especially ones that threaten the lives of the people under her rule."

Hayate thought the same, although the suggestion chilled him. "Please, at least try to arrive there first. You'll treat her more fairly than anyone else. It will look better if things are resolved by the time Empress Tomoyo's agents arrive in Yukimura."

"That sounds sensible," Kotone said. "Do you want to go yourself, Masaru, or would you like me to go in your place?"

"I'll go, Kotone." A look of determination hardened Masaru's face, and Hayate felt a little more confident. "Setsuna is my sister. If she and our daughter are in trouble, I want to sort it out."

"I humbly request to accompany you," Hayate said. "This is my responsibility. I've let things alone for too long already."

Masaru nodded. "Of course. We will host you and Kaze for tonight, and I'll gather my most trusted samurai together. We will leave for Yukimura as soon as the preparations have been made."

Chapter Nineteen

THE NEXT MORNING DAWNED pink and rosy. Kaede woke in stages, clinging to the warm blanket of sleep as long as possible. For once, she had enjoyed dreams instead of nightmares, and she wanted to savor them a little longer. It had felt so real—Imari's lips on hers, Imari's hand running all over her body, Imari's warmth.

She blinked, clearing the blur from her eyes to see Imari's face rested a few centimeters away from hers. Her eyes were still shut, and the only covering she had was the thin blanket pooled around her lovely hips.

Kaede sucked in a shocked breath. *It wasn't a dream after all. Did all of it really happen?* She peeled her own side of the sheet down, and her face caught fire. She was naked too, and a visible mark curved along her left breast where Imari had gotten a little too enthusiastic while sucking.

Slowly, a smile spread over her face. Part of her still couldn't quite believe this had really happened, but she didn't have any regrets. Far from it—sharing herself with Imari had been one of the most beautiful experiences of her life.

Growing up, Kaede had often worried about her first time. She had feared no one would want her, or that they would want her for all the wrong reasons. But when she and Imari had come together, she hadn't been afraid. Imari had made her feel treasured. Cared for. Loved.

Her heart swelled, and she reached down on impulse, smoothing some of Imari's hair away from her forehead. Imari stirred, and her lashes fluttered against her cheeks until, at last, her eyes opened. A sleepy smile spread across her face, and she reached out, looping an arm around Kaede's waist. "Let's not get up yet," she murmured, snuggling in closer. "I don't want to leave this bed."

"We have to eventually," Kaede said, although she didn't want to leave either. "We've been locked in here since yesterday afternoon. We're going to need food."

Imari's stomach growled, as if to prove her point. Both laughed, and Imari tucked her face into the crook of Kaede's shoulder. "Oh, fine," she muttered, punctuating the words with a kiss.

Kaede's heart spiked at the feel of Imari's warm lips against her pulse point, but she steadfastly ignored it. If they were going to repeat yesterday's magic, she needed something to eat, or at least some water. Her lips were dry and her muscles felt shaky and weak.

"Breakfast first," Kaede said, stroking the back of Imari's head and gently prying her away before she could start a trail of fresh kisses. "I have a feeling we're going to need our strength."

Imari's eyes glittered. "Well, if you put it like that."

The two of them untangled from the comfortable knot and left the futon, searching for their clothes. They helped each other dress, trading kisses and caresses as they made themselves presentable. It took twice as long, but they couldn't resist. Kaede admired Imari's smooth back and beautiful hips all over again as she fastened the sashes and knots of Imari's kimono, and Imari's fingers grazed her arms and sides in a suggestive way. Pressure swelled between Kaede's legs.

"You're going to make me get hard again," Kaede warned, although she did nothing to remove Imari's wandering hand. Normally, the subject would have been at least a little uncomfortable to discuss, but for once, Kaede wasn't bothered by the reaction. Feeling Imari's hand glide over her skin had made her feel even more at home in it. When Imari looked at her with such love and desire, she forgot all her worries.

"Oh?" Imari smirked, stroking down along Kaede's stomach and stopping short of her hipbones. "What if I do this?"

Kaede caught her wrist, halting the path of her fingers before they could wander into more dangerous territory. The ache had returned, but she tried her best to will it away. "In a few minutes," she said, to soften the rejection. "I don't want to run into Takeshi or Kenta while I'm excited."

Imari withdrew, leaning in for a kiss instead. Kaede could tell she had meant for it to be short, but it lingered by mutual agreement and unwillingness to pull away. "As long as you keep to that promise," Imari murmured when they finally broke apart. "So, food?"

Kaede offered Imari her arm, but the invitation wasn't taken. Instead, Imari snuck in a quick, greedy squeeze of her backside before swaying out of the room. Kaede was left gaping, and it took her several seconds to collect herself before she hurried to catch up. "That wasn't nice," she protested as they entered the hall, but she grinned to make sure Imari knew she didn't really mind.

"If you didn't want me to grope you, you shouldn't look so gorgeous," Imari said. She took Kaede's arm at last, and the two of them headed for the kitchens together, taking a path that led around the forge instead of through. As they passed by, they heard the familiar ring of Wen Ling's hammer. Kaede glanced at Imari's face, waiting to see whether it would fall in disappointment, but to her relief, it didn't. She seemed much more cheerful than she had the day before, and her smile showed no signs of wavering.

Their meal was eaten in privacy and silence, although it wasn't an uncomfortable one. Kaede even found that her food tasted better. Her miso soup and steamed rice disappeared in a flash, and she realized that she was just as hungry as Imari, in no small part thanks to the previous evening's activities. Eventually, though, she and Imari both set down their chopsticks and held hands across the table, simply gazing at each other. Once, Kaede forgot and reached with the wrong one, but Imari didn't mind. "Don't," she murmured, when Kaede realized her mistake and made to pull back. "It's all right. I don't mind."

After a moment of hesitation, Kaede placed her hand on top of Imari's left forearm. She left it there for a minute, stroking the side of Imari's arm through the material of her sleeve. So far, Imari hadn't invited her to touch the old injury. Even through fabric, it was a strangely intimate gesture.

"Does it hurt?" she asked after a while, feeling fairly confident that the question wouldn't ruin Imari's good mood.

Imari shook her head. "Not really. Not anymore. Sometimes I still forget I've lost it, though. I'll try to grab something and…not."

Kaede laughed softly. "At least you have an excuse. I drop things with the two hands I have."

"Could it be because you're distracted, perhaps?" Imari asked, her smirk returning.

Kaede snorted. "I'm going to have faith that you'll remember the graceful moment when I flipped over your head back in Yin or the way I moved last night instead of…other incidents."

Imari leaned further over the table, her eyes half-lidded. "Oh, I was impressed with the way you moved last night."

The sound of the kitchen door opening broke the moment. Kaede turned in surprise, blushing to the roots of her hair when she saw Rin standing in the doorway. The wolf's tail was stiff, angled up toward the ceiling, and judging from her expression, she wasn't pleased. "Rin, how long were you standing there?"

"Long enough," Rin said in a rumbling voice. "Oh, don't look at me like that, Kaede. I'm not upset you and Imari finally spent the night together. It was a long time coming. Anyway, we have a more urgent concern. You have a visitor outside demanding to speak with you both."

Kaede's eyes widened. No other travelers had come to Hongshan in the two months they had spent there, and Wen Ling had given the impression it was an incredibly rare occurrence. "A visitor? What do you mean?"

"Remember your fox friend, Kyuubi? She's hiding outside the cave's entrance. I caught her scent early this morning on my walk and went to see what she wanted. She says she has news about your family."

At once, Kaede's heart sank. She'd thought nothing in the world could bring down her good mood, but apparently, she'd been wrong. All the guilt she had been struggling to suppress for the past several months came rushing back as she remembered the lie she had been feeding all this time.

"Wait, what? How does Kyuubi even know about my family?"

"She's a fox," Rin said, as if that explained everything.

Kaede's shoulders stiffened. "I'm not sure I want to hear it," she muttered, slumping slightly in her chair. Whatever Kyuubi wanted to tell her—and how Kyuubi had found out who her family was still made no sense to her—Kaede knew it couldn't be good. A hundred awful possibilities raced through her head: Setsuna's experiments could have grown larger and more dangerous, Hayate could have found them at last and was about to drag her home again, or perhaps something had happened to her parents.

She was at once both terrified and strangely angry. Her life had been better these past few months than ever before, but it seemed that the past insisted on interrupting her newfound peace and happiness.

"What are you talking about, Kaede?" Imari set her bowl aside, brushing crumbs from the front of her kimono. "If something's happened to your family, we need to find out what it is. I know you aren't on good terms with them."

"That's putting it lightly," Kaede sighed.

Imari's frown deepened. "This isn't like you. You always help people in need. Don't you want to know if something bad has happened?"

I already know something bad has happened. She realized, though, that she didn't have much of a choice. Imari seemed prepared to go and speak to Kyuubi with or without her. Worse still, Imari didn't know the full story of her departure from Yukimura. Time and time and time again, Kaede had wanted to tell her, but she had never found the courage, not even after they had kissed.

Perhaps she had been embarrassed to reveal that she had been lying for so long, or perhaps she had really wanted to be Iori Kaede instead of Aozora Kaede. Aozora Kaede had caused the deaths of several creatures, both human and yokai, and let her power-hungry aunt take advantage of her. Iori Kaede was a brave adventurer, with a beautiful woman who loved her.

"Maybe I should talk to Kyuubi alone," she suggested, but once more, Imari waved her off.

"Of course not," Imari said, taking her hand. "You don't have to deal with these things alone anymore, Kaede. I want to help. Rin, please go and find Takeshi and Kenta, if you don't mind. We'll go outside and meet Kyuubi ourselves."

Kaede's stomach sank like a stone. She tried to stammer an explanation, but there wasn't time. Imari pulled her back through the hall toward the glowing passage that led outside. With each step, Kaede felt as though she were approaching the edge of the mountain itself. She knew she had to say something, anything, but in her panic, she couldn't. A lump of fear had lodged in her throat, and it was all she could do to let Imari drag her outside.

Half of the sun had peeked over the horizon by the time they made it out onto the mountainside. To Kaede's dismay, Kyuubi waited for them behind a boulder nearby, not immediately visible, but not quite hiding either. She was in her fox form, her tails draped elegantly on the ground behind her. Her eyes, however, shifted nervously, and her black nose twitched against the air.

"Kaede, Imari," Kyuubi said, "I'm glad Rin found you. I have urgent news from Aozora."

"What urgent news?" Imari asked before Kaede could say a word.

"It's about your cousin, Hayate," Kyuubi said, speaking to Kaede directly. "He's in Yukimura as we speak, raising an army for a surprise attack on Aozora. He intends to take your parents hostage in order to force you to come home."

Kaede sucked in a painful breath. "What? No, that can't be. I know how badly he wanted to find me, but..." She shook her head, unwilling to believe it. She could understand why Hayate had followed her to the Jade Sea on Setsuna's orders, but taking hostages was a different matter entirely. "You must be mistaken."

"I'm not," Kyuubi insisted. "We foxes have our ways of communicating with each other over long distances. I heard the news from a reliable source in the northern forests. Hayate is gathering an army, and his destination is Taiseito."

"But why?" Imari's eyes narrowed, and her hand drifted toward the hilt of her sword as if preparing to draw it. "Surely the daimyo of Aozora won't allow Hayate's army to invade and take innocent civilians hostage."

Kaede's heart gave a sickening jolt out of rhythm. She opened her mouth, but only pitiful silence came out.

"What do you mean? I'm not mistaken, am I?" Kyuubi turned to Kaede, staring up at her with clever black eyes. "You are Aozora Kaede, aren't you? We spirits do share information."

Imari turned, and the trusting, confused look in her eyes was nearly Kaede's undoing. Imari drew in a soft gasp and stiffened, a wrinkle of hurt appearing in the middle of her brow. "Aozora?" she repeated, shaking her head. "No. You told me your name was Iori."

Kaede couldn't hold Imari's eyes any longer. She looked away, her face burning with shame. There was a long pause, but not a silent one. Kaede could hear the pounding of her own heart in her ears and the ragged, unsteady noise of Imari's breathing. It was unbearable, and her shoulders sagged lower and lower with the weight of guilt.

At last, Kyuubi said, "Please, accept my apologies. I didn't realize."

Kaede didn't bother listening to the rest of the fox's explanation. Everything Kyuubi said was like the roar of the ocean in her ears. Even though she was staring at her feet, she could picture the look of utter betrayal on Imari's face perfectly.

"So, it's true?" Imari said at last. Unlike Kyuubi's voice, hers was perfectly clear, like the slice of a knife. "You gave me a false name? Your parents are the rulers of Aozora? And you haven't told me all this time. . ."

Kaede looked up. She was terrified, but Imari deserved to see her face. It was the least she could do. She tried to explain, to tell Imari all about how her old name had felt like a lingering shadow, to apologize for keeping it a secret for so long, but she knew it wouldn't matter. Imari wouldn't understand. That was why she had kept it to herself, because she hadn't wanted the woman she admired and cared for so much to think less of her.

But she does. And now, on top of everything, I've lied to her too.

"Yes," she said, though it took all her strength just to produce a whisper. My given name is Aozora. My parents rule the province."

At first, Imari seemed wounded. She flinched, her lips slightly parted and quivering as if in pain. "You lied to me, Kaede. Why? After last night, I thought…" Her nose wrinkled, and anger glinted in her eyes. "You didn't trust me, did you?"

"No," Kaede blurted out. "I did…I do! I just—"

"Then why? Why did you keep this from me?"

Kaede felt as if she were free-falling from the top of Hongshan itself. She fumbled, grasping for a hold, for the right words, but all she found was empty air. "Because you would have hated me. And I love you."

Imari began to tear up. She sniffed angrily, swiping at her face with her sleeve and blinking rapidly. "That's the stupidest thing I've ever heard. I would never have hated you for being a noble, but to continue lying?" She took a deliberate step back to find more space. "The Kaede I love would never keep things from me like that."

"You don't understand," Kaede said. Her guilt had been replaced with desperation. She could see her happiness slipping right through her fingers, and her first instinct was to cling tighter with all her might.

"You didn't even give me a chance to understand!" Imari snapped. "So, go ahead. Right now. Explain yourself."

Kaede floundered. In any other moment, she could have rattled off at least ten answers, but in the face of Imari's anger, none of them seemed reasonable. "I can't," she said at last, hanging her head. "All I can say is I'm sorry. My family isn't like yours. I wanted to distance myself from them as much as possible. They've hurt me in ways you can't even imagine."

"How would you know? You never let me try." Imari drew in a deep breath and closed her eyes, letting it out slowly through pursed lips. When she opened them again, the few stray tears that had leaked out were gone. "I don't want to talk about this anymore. We'll deal with it later. Right now, we need to figure out a plan to save your family."

"That would be wise," Kyuubi added, cautiously entering the conversation once more. "You don't have a lot of time—"

"I'm not going," Kaede said. Her answer was automatic, but also firm. She couldn't go back. If she did, Setsuna would use her again. Aozora Kaede might have been content to be such a tool, but Iori Kaede wasn't. The least she could do now was try to be the woman Imari had assumed her to be.

That left Imari stunned all over again. "What? What do you mean, you aren't going? They're your parents!"

"This is why I didn't tell you who I was," Kaede said. Despite the guilt she felt, she wouldn't let herself be criticized either, especially for a decision Imari didn't know the first thing about. "Since it's all coming out now, my aunt is the shogun of Yukimura. Before I left, she was using me to bring in all the yokai she could from the forest near our home. She wanted to control them." Her eyes danced with spots, an imprint of black blood scattered across white snow. "She killed them, and she killed her own samurai."

Imari's anger melted away. The ice in her eyes melted down her cheeks like frost rolling from bare branches. She opened her arms, and Kaede wanted nothing more than to fall into them. She had thought the wound was healed, but telling it now, her heart ached and her cheek stung fresh all over again.

"Kaede, come here," Imari said. "I'm so sorry. I wish you'd told me, but we can fix this—"

Kaede recoiled again. Imari's arms no longer looked inviting, but more like a trap. "There's no fixing it. It's something Aozora Kaede did. Iori Kaede knows better. If I go back, even to save my parents, Setsuna will use me again. I've already watched too many samurai and yokai die because of me. I won't watch more people I love die too." Unbidden, the memory of Hayate's blade pressing into Imari's throat took over Kaede's mind. She imagined blood trickling beneath the sharp edge, pooling in the dip of Imari's collarbone, running in a river down her front. "It could even be you next time! I'm not going to let that happen."

"That isn't your decision," Imari said, lowering her arms.

"And this isn't yours." Kaede squared her shoulders, jutting out her chin. "Don't you remember what happened in Yin? You were acting like Takeshi, stepping in for me when you didn't need to."

"I was trying to protect you," Imari protested. "The Kaede I know would be grateful, and she'd want to do the same for her family, no matter how distant they were."

"This has nothing to do with that."

"How can you say that? You don't even want to help them."

"I do want to help them. What I don't want is to get them killed by going back! See, this is why I was afraid you wouldn't understand. Everything that happened back home is my fault." Kaede began to shake, clenching her fingers into fists. "I ruin everything I touch."

"Kaede, you don't—"

"I'm ruining this right now. The best part of my life." Tears rose in

Kaede's eyes. She couldn't stay any longer. She couldn't listen to Imari's harsh words, or stand to look at the disappointment in her eyes. "I'm going," she said, turning back toward the mouth of the cave. "I just...I have to be alone for a little while."

"So, what?" Imari said, her voice cold and distant. "That's it? You're going to let Hayate take your parents hostage? Refuse to talk to me? Maybe you are the coward you say you are."

Kaede didn't answer. She didn't know what she was going to do, but she needed time and space to figure it out. "I'm sorry," she murmured, but when she headed toward the cave, she didn't look back. She already knew what she would see: Imari's face falling with a heartbroken expression of disappointment.

***

Imari stared after Kaede's retreating form until she disappeared from sight. At first, she wasn't sure what to do. She stood, stunned, reeling with everything that had happened. Part of her still couldn't believe Kaede had deceived her. She had offered her trust only to have it thrown back in her face. It was practically an insult. She had never pushed to learn more about Kaede's past, but this felt like more than an omission. It was a lie, pure and simple. The woman she was in love with had lied to her.

"I'm so sorry, Imari," Kyuubi said, startling her from her thoughts. Imari looked down at the fox. She had been so wrapped up in her own hurt feelings that she hadn't even remembered she wasn't alone. "This is my fault, I'm afraid. I never meant to cause trouble between you and Kaede."

"You didn't." Imari dropped down to her knees, too weary to continue standing any longer. "This is our fault."

"That's the thing about arguments," Kyuubi said. The fox crawled closer, resting her front paws on Imari's lap and staring up at her with her sweet, narrow face. "They're rarely just one person's fault. But if you care at all about my opinion, she shouldn't have lied to you about her family."

"I know that, and she knows it, too." She could still see the look of regret on Kaede's face.

"But her lie isn't what's important right now," Kyuubi continued. "I know it hurts, but you have bigger things to worry about. Right now, Hayate is gathering an army to invade Aozora. You've seen how all those other deaths weigh on Kaede's conscience. How do you think she's going to feel once her head clears? When she realizes she stood by while her family and her entire province were slaughtered?"

Ice flooded Imari's veins. It was true, she was angry at Kaede's deception, but the thought of the woman she loved carrying such a burden was unacceptable. *No matter what she kept from me, she doesn't deserve that.*

"I need to go get her," Imari said, making to rise. "We can work out our problems later. Right now, keeping Aozora safe is more important."

Kyuubi climbed the rest of the way onto her lap, preventing her from standing up. "But will she even come with you? You heard what she said. She's convinced everything that happened back in Yukimura before she left is her fault, and she thinks she isn't good enough for you. You won't be able to convince her to go back with you."

"I have to try anyway," Imari said. "You're right, Kyuubi. When she realizes she could have prevented this, she'll feel guilty all over again."

"And how long will it take her to realize? A day? A week? A month? Kaede is stubborn. By then, it may be too late to fix things."

An idea began to form in Imari's mind. It was vague at first, like a shadow behind a thick layer of fog, but gradually, it started to take shape. "I could go without her," she said slowly, testing the words out. "To Aozora. . ."

"Or," Kyuubi purred, "you could prevent Hayate going even that far. Tackle the problem at its source."

"I'd go to Yukimura then?" At first, the prospect seemed ridiculous. Imari knew there was no way she could stop an invasion all on her own, even with the sword Wen Ling had given her. But the more she thought about it, the more right it felt. Go to Yukimura. Kill Hayate. Protect the family of the woman she loved. It seemed so simple. Of course that was what she needed to do.

"Yes," Kyuubi said, "you should go without her. I'm sure Kaede would be grateful to you for saving her family. It might even make up for the fight you had."

Imari felt a tug of doubt. The plan began to unravel, and she frowned as her head cleared. "No. Kaede doesn't like me stepping in to solve her problems. The only times we argued before now were when I put myself in danger for her."

"But you heard what Kaede said before she left." Kyuubi let her tails drape over Imari's knees. "She thinks she destroys everything she touches. You'll never convince her to go home and fix this, and if you don't, she'll regret it for the rest of her life."

"Yes," Imari repeated. Once more, everything seemed simple and clear. It was as if she'd been lost in a forest, but finally, she had found her way back to the right path. "She'll regret it."

"You don't want the woman you love to lose her parents, do you?" Kyuubi's eyes took on a look of deep concern. The swirls of orange and gold in those deep brown irises were so pretty, Imari completely missed the moment they shifted. When had the color changed? "Think of how devastating that would be for her. Imagine how terrible you would feel if you lost your father."

Imari didn't have to imagine it. A gaping hole of sadness opened in her chest. She felt hollow, too empty even for tears. Her blooming feelings for Kaede aside, her father was the person she loved most in the entire world. The thought of losing him was like losing sunlight or air. The wave of pain was so intense she couldn't breathe.

"No," she said, shaking her head and closing her eyes. "No. I don't want Kaede to feel this."

"That's right. You don't. You need to save Kaede's family so the two of you can mend your relationship and be happy together."

As Kyuubi said those words, Imari felt a surge of relief. Her mind-numbing grief vanished, and a warm, cozy feeling rushed in to take its place. She smiled, then sighed, letting out the heavy breath she had been holding. "Happy." She could be happy with Kaede, if they could get past this. She was certain of it.

"The two of you are meant to be together," Kyuubi purred, cuddling in closer. "I knew it from the first moment I met you. But you can't win true love unless you fight for it. Are you going to fight for your love, Imari, or are you going to let Kaede lose herself in grief and guilt?"

For a moment, Imari's niggling doubts returned. *Kaede can defend herself. I should be fighting at her side, not charging in ahead of her.* But then she remembered the pain, and the relief that had come after, and the train of thought vanished. "I want to fight for her. I'll stop Hayate and Kaede's aunt, no matter what it takes."

"Good." Kyuubi climbed out of Imari's lap and backed away, beginning to ripple and shift. Soon, she was in her human form once more, although the tips of her nine tails still peeked out from beneath the hem of her kimono. "Please, get up, Imari. I have a gift that will help you on your journey."

Imari stood obediently, gazing at Kyuubi's outstretched hand. Within it was one of the most beautiful pearls she had ever seen. It was large enough to fill Kyuubi's entire palm, and mist drifted over its surface, like a nighttime cloud passing over the glowing circle of the moon.

"Sun and Moon," she whispered, staring into its milky surface, "I've never seen anything so beautiful."

"Thank you," Kyuubi said. "We foxes make them, you know. Our pearls allow us to have eyes and ears all over the kingdom, and they make for fast travel too. If you take this pearl, it will carry you to one of its cousins in Yukimura. Then you can stop Hayate and Setsuna."

"Setsuna too?" Imari asked, but she soon forgot the rest of her question. The pearl was too entrancing. Her eyes grew larger and larger the longer she stared into it, and her fingers itched to reach out and take it. It looked smoother than silk, and with the way it was glowing, she was certain it would be warm.

"Yes. Setsuna and Hayate must be dealt with if you want Kaede to love you again, Imari. With them gone and her parents safe, there won't be any barriers left between you anymore."

"No more barriers," Imari agreed. Kyuubi offered her the pearl, and a tingle zipped up her arm as she closed her fingers around it. The living gem was warmer and heavier than she expected, thrumming under her touch.

"Don't forget," Kyuubi said, her voice and figure growing more and more distant, "you're doing this for Kaede. This is the only way."

Imari closed her eyes as the shadows enveloped her, surrendering to a warm, soundless wind that caressed every inch of her skin. *Yes, the only way.* The last thing she saw before she disappeared was a white wolf near the mouth of the cave, turning and running back into the mountain.

Chapter Twenty

KAEDE SAT ON THE edge of the mountainside with her arms around her legs, her back resting against the rough surface of a boulder. It wasn't an ideal spot, with little shelter from the wind and sun, but she didn't care. She didn't want to go back inside the cave and risk running into the Hibana brothers or Wen Ling. Her eyes were too dry to cry and her heart felt battered and bruised.

Everything was falling apart. Her family was in danger, Imari hated her, and she didn't know what to do. The words Imari had thrown at her still cut deep: *Maybe you are the coward you say you are.*

She was a coward. That much was clear from the way Imari had looked at her, first with shock and disappointment, then with anger and disgust. It was so different than the way Imari had looked at her last night, with more love than Kaede had ever seen before shining like stars in her eyes. But none of that had been real. Imari was in love with a fantasy-version of her, one who actually stood and faced her problems. That meant Imari had never really loved her at all.

Kaede shuddered, tucking further in on herself and burying her face in the gap between her knees. It always happened this way. Someone would claim to love her, come close to accepting her without any strings attached, and then it would all fall apart—first with Setsuna, then Hayate, and now, Imari. *Maybe it's my fault that this keeps happening to me. I should have trusted Imari. Maybe I'm not lovable. The only one who doesn't end up disappointed in me is Rin.*

"Kaede!"

The sound of alarmed barking snapped Kaede abruptly from her sorry state. After a few blinks, she saw Rin bounding toward her, a striking white blur against the dull grey-brown of the mountainside. She lifted her head and sniffed, wiping her wind-burned cheeks. "Go away, Rin. I don't want to talk right now."

Rin skidded to a stop without her usual grace, sending small pebbles sliding in a shower behind her paws. "No, you don't understand. Imari's gone, Kaede! Sun and Moon, I told you two not to trust that fox."

Immediately, Kaede refocused. "What do you mean?" she asked, pushing herself to her feet. "Where did Imari go?"

"I don't know. I was waiting for her near the mouth of the cave, keeping my distance. I saw her take something from Kyuubi, and then she disappeared."

Kaede's gut churned. Hearing that Hayate was preparing to march on Aozora had been bad, but this was worse. No matter what they had said to each other, she had sworn an oath as Imari's yojimbo—and another, even stronger oath when the two of them had shared their feelings. If anything happened to Imari, she would never forgive herself.

Kaede drew her katana, folding her fingers tight around the grip. No longer was she despondent, paralyzed with fear and self-loathing. She couldn't afford to be, for Imari's sake. "Where did you last see her?"

Rin took off back down the mountain, and Kaede followed. She slid half the way, but managed to maintain her balance. Less than a minute later, they arrived at the same spot where she and Imari had argued. As Rin had said, Imari was nowhere to be seen, and neither was Kyuubi. There wasn't a trace of them anywhere. All she could see was the empty mountainside and the sharp afternoon glare of the sun.

"Are you sure she disappeared?" she asked Rin, her voice cracking with desperation. "You can't pick up her scent or anything?"

Rin's ears drooped and her tail hung low between her legs. "I'm sorry, Kaede. She's gone. I saw it happen myself."

"We need to tell Wen Ling and Suanni. Maybe they'll know what to do."

It wasn't much of a plan, but it was the only idea Kaede had. She sprinted back for the mouth of the cave with Rin trotting along beside her. "Wen Ling!" she shouted as soon as entered, "Where are you?"

She met Wen Ling at the other end of the passage, nearly bowling the smith over in her hurry. A strong, steady hand reached out to grab her arm, keeping her from tripping over her own feet. "Kaede? I heard you call from the forge. What's the rush?"

"Imari's gone," Kaede blurted out. "She was talking to Kyuubi, and then—"

"Wait, Kyuubi?" Wen Ling's eyes narrowed with what looked like anger, an expression Kaede had never seen before. She grabbed Kaede's elbow, practically dragging her the rest of the way through the hall and into the forge. "Come with me. You need to tell me everything."

"So, you know this fox," Rin growled. "This is looking worse and worse."

"Oh, I definitely know her," Wen Ling said. "Let me summon Suanni. They will need to hear this as well." She let go of Kaede's elbow as they arrived at the forge, striding past the anvils and over to a small alcove. Tucked inside was a drab brown sheet Kaede hadn't noticed before, draped over something tall and thin. It almost looked like an abandoned weapon stand, but as Wen Ling uncovered it, Kaede saw that it wasn't.

Beneath the blanket was a large brass gong suspended on a simple wooden frame, but the surface itself was intricately decorated with raised black lines. Eight symbols were inscribed around the edges, one for each direction, and in the middle, the serpentine silhouette of a dragon coiled in on itself. Kaede barely had time to marvel at the beautiful craftsmanship before Wen Ling removed the mallet from its hook. She struck the center of the gong, and its warm voice rang throughout the forge, echoing up and out through the hole in the ceiling.

They didn't have to wait long for a response. Kaede heard the rush of wind from above, and then a large shadow passed over the opening, blocking out the afternoon sunlight. The forge suddenly became darker, although the ever-burning fires seemed to leap in recognition. A moment later, Suanni swooped down into the cave, slipping their narrow body through the opening and touching gracefully down on the ground.

"We have a problem," Wen Ling said, not bothering with bows. "Imari has disappeared, and Kyuubi is responsible."

"Kyuubi?" Even by human standards, Suanni looked concerned. Their whiskers fluttered with a puff of impatient air, and Kaede could see a glimpse of their gleaming teeth. "So, she's returned then."

Kaede clenched her hands into fists. Every moment not spent searching for her felt like a waste. Her whole chest ached, and her skin crawled with the desire to do something. "We need to focus on Imari, not Kyuubi! She's the one who disappeared into thin air. She could be in danger."

"If Kyuubi is involved, I'm certain she is," Wen Ling said gravely.

Suanni dipped their head, coming closer to eye level. "Kyuubi may present herself as a harmless fox, but she is anything but. She has lived for over a thousand years, and she's spent most of her long life toying with anyone she can, simply for her own amusement. The short lives of humans and most other yokai mean nothing to her. She sees your suffering as a form of entertainment."

"And what about Imari?" Kaede asked. "Is Kyuubi toying with her?"

"Likely," Suanni said. "Kyuubi is a master manipulator. She uses her powers to delve within her victim's mind and convince them to betray their own moral codes. Tell me, what did you and Kyuubi discuss before Imari disappeared? That may tell us where they're headed."

Kaede tried to focus, but her mind was lost in a fearful fog. All she could think about was Imari. "I—I don't know." Her mind flashed from Hayate's sword at Imari's neck, to black dollops of blood dotting upturned mountain snow, to the final words Imari had said to her. *Coward. Coward.*

"Kaede." Rin's cold nose nudged at her shoulder, distracting her from the haunting echo. "I know you're afraid for Imari, but you need to think. What did Kyuubi say to you?"

She brought her hand up to cover her face, raking her nails along the top of her head. "We were arguing. She was angry I hadn't told her about my family. She wanted me to go to Aozora and rescue them from Hayate. Ancestors, I left her. I ran away again. If I'd stayed, I could've done something,"

"You can still do something," Wen Ling said. "Kyuubi uses weaknesses and desires already there to bend humans to her will. You know Imari. With the right push, would she go to Aozora on her own to stop Hayate, despite the danger?"

Kaede dropped her arm. "Absolutely," she said with a laugh of frantic desperation. "She's always trying to step in and fix my problems for me, even though I've told her a hundred times not to."

"Now we're getting somewhere," Suanni said. "I'll fly you to Aozora myself, Kaede."

Kaede didn't even have to consider the offer. She had spent months running as far from home as possible, but if Imari was in Aozora, that was where she would go. Her guilt had hardened into resolve. *Imari needs me. I can't let her down again.*

"Thank you, Suanni. I won't forget this."

"I'll go find Takeshi and Kenta," Wen Ling said, making a swift exit from the forge. "You'll need to bring them with you."

Kaede's heart sank as she realized she would have to explain herself to them too, but she had no other choice. She needed their help to save Imari. If they wanted to hate her afterward for lying to them, that was fine with her, as long as Imari was safe.

"We'll find her," Rin said, nudging gently at her shoulder.

Kaede wrapped her arm around Rin's neck. She tried to say something, but the words wouldn't come. Her heart was missing, and all that remained as an empty hole in her chest.

***

When the rush of wind stopped and Imari opened her eyes, she was no longer standing on the mountainside. Instead, she was in a dim room heated by a square irori sunken in the center of the floor. Aside from the hearth, the room was empty. There didn't appear to be any other furniture—or any other people either.

As her eyes adjusted to the light, Imari realized it wasn't an ordinary room at all. Instead of tatami mats, there was stone beneath her feet. The walls were stone as well, solid and smooth rather than made up of carved blocks. She wasn't in a castle, but a cave.

She looked in the other direction. Through the shadows, she could make out a sliding screen. More light flickered beyond, the only illumination the dark space had aside from the dying embers in the irori. Imari reached to draw her jian from its scabbard only to realize that her hand was already full. She was still holding the large pearl Kyuubi had given her. It was warm to the touch, and she felt a surge of confidence, the same unwavering certainty she had felt while talking to Kyuubi. In fact, she could almost hear the fox's voice. *Keep it safe. I need it to help you.*

She tucked the pearl into her obi then brought her hand to her jian. Step one was simple: look for some indicator of where she was. Yukimura was a large province, one she wasn't familiar with. Step two was slightly more complicated. She needed to find Hayate and kill him before he could march on Aozora.

Wait, kill him? She lowered her sword, feeling a flicker of doubt. *I didn't come here to kill anyone.*

But she had to. Blurred memories flashed through her mind, images of Hayate striking at Kaede with his sword. They grew sharper and sharper until her head ached. There was no other way. Hayate was a threat to Kaede and her family—to the Empire itself. If she truly loved Kaede, she would make sure Hayate could never harm anyone again.

Imari crept toward the screen, listening closely. Aside from the distant drip of water, she couldn't hear anything. She stopped, pressing her ear against the screen, but still, nothing. If anyone was nearby, they were silent as death. She caught the toe of her right foot against the wooden frame and slid the door back.

The room beyond the door was dark as well. The only light came from a low-burning candle, and the soft yellow circle around it highlighted a ghostly face. At first, Imari wondered if she had stumbled across someone dead after all, but as she looked again, she realized she was wrong. The person's eyes were closed, but they were merely asleep.

She peered closer, a sense of recognition passing over her. It was a woman, and a familiar looking one at that. Although the face wasn't an exact match, the resemblance was unmistakable—this person had to be related to Kaede. She had the same dark skin and chiseled features, although her hair was black. At once, Imari knew who this had to be, and she couldn't believe her luck. It seemed she wouldn't have to search for Hayate after all. If anything, he would come running to her.

As she slipped closer, Setsuna's eyes began to twitch behind her closed lids. Her head rolled uneasily across her futon, spreading her dark hair around her head, and a wrinkle formed in her brow. She groaned, and Imari froze, certain she had been spotted. But her fear was for nothing. Setsuna remained trapped in her fitful sleep, lips moving without sound.

Imari stopped beside the bed, aiming the point of her jian at the vulnerable center of Setsuna's throat. She pressed it forward, not enough to draw blood, but enough to make contact. Setsuna's eyes flew open, white and wild. She opened her mouth, and Imari dug the tip of her sword in harder. "Don't scream," she warned, but Setsuna didn't listen. A loud shot of surprise burst from her lips, echoing through the room and beyond.

Imari knew she wouldn't be able to sneak out. Surely a shogun wouldn't be hiding out in a cave without guards nearby. A few moments later, hurried footsteps came from somewhere beyond the bedroom—several people from the sound. She glanced around the room, making certain Setsuna didn't have a weapon within easy reach, and then whirled toward the door. She turned just in time to see three guards burst into the room. They were well-armored and wielding unsheathed swords, and upon seeing her, they charged.

Imari's training with Wen Ling had made her swift and her new sword made her strong. She crossed blades with the nearest soldier, blocking his downward strike and sending him stumbling back. While he reeled, one of his companions came at Imari from the side. She swiveled, sweeping her sword beneath the leather plates of his armor and aiming for his legs above the greaves.

His katana missed her shoulder by an inch, but her jian reached its target. Imari sliced across his thigh and then pulled back, thrusting into the vulnerable gap beneath his right arm. The blow connected. He let out a sharp cry of pain, curling in on himself as blood rushed out to stain the leather plates of his armor.

Imari didn't have time to be shocked by what she had done. The other two guards were upon her again, and she had to sidestep to avoid them. One of them attempted to engage her with a swift circle. She sent his sword wide, bringing her elbow down hard against his shoulder. Her fury gave her strength. Even with his armor protecting him, the guard's knees buckled.

While he hit the ground, Imari whirled to face her third opponent. He had attempted to get behind her, but she sent him scurrying back with a lash of her jian's tassels. He shifted his two-handed grip, knuckles bulging, and launched a flurry of strikes, trying to push her back further into the room and away from the door.

Imari held her ground. She blocked him blow for blow, reacting on instinct. The next time his katana slashed toward her, she brought her jian screaming down. It severed right through his arm above his kote, sending it and the katana falling to the floor. The soldier dropped, crumpled and bleeding.

The final soldier looked at his two companions in terror. He began to back out of the room, but Imari pursued him, blocking his path. Before he could plead or drop his weapon, she engaged. He countered, but not fast enough. His arm faltered. She struck. He let out a rattling sound, a rasp that sent a shiver of doubt racing down Imari's spine. When she looked down, she realized that she had skewered him through a gap in his armor.

She withdrew her sword, wincing at the squelch, and began to come back to herself. A slow, creeping horror consumed her as she looked upon what she had done, and she sucked in a painful breath. The samurai missing his arm wasn't moving. Rivers of blood spilled onto the floor, and her first thought was to crouch down and help. Before she could move, something stopped her.

No. This price needs to be paid. These men are working for Hayate and Setsuna to kill Kaede's family. To overthrow the empire. You can't afford to leave them alive. The thought was repugnant to her, but the voice swelled inside her head until it drowned out her protests. The louder it grew, the more right it seemed. Of course she couldn't stop to help. Better for them to bleed out. She had to focus on Setsuna and Hayate. She had to stop them to save the Aozora and Kaede.

She turned to Setsuna, who had clambered to her feet and was staring at the scene in a sort of paralysis, as if she couldn't process what she had witnessed. Imari lowered her jian, holding it at her side with the point aimed at the floor. Blood dripped from the blade, leaving a thin trail as she approached the shogun. Rage boiled within her, consuming the last of her regret. This was the woman who had chased Kaede away, who had sent her on the run, who had betrayed her and hurt her so deeply. The desire to send her to the floor like the other men was intoxicating. Setsuna wasn't armed. Her jian would pierce that fearfully bobbing throat with ease.

Not yet. She is still useful to you. Kill the other guards and take her as your prisoner. Then Hayate is sure to come to you. You can take care of both of them at the same time without even having to search. The thought of taking revenge upon Hayate, whom she hated even more than Setsuna, was enough. Just thinking of how he had rushed toward her, katana drawn, in the garden of the Zhong An Inn made her tremble with anger.

"Who are you?" Setsuna whispered, snapping Imari out of her memory. The shogun stared at her, wearing the expression of someone trapped in a nightmare.

"Someone who loves Kaede." Imari looked away from Setsuna, glancing around the room for something she could improvise as bindings. "And I'm here to make sure you never hurt her, or anyone else ever again."

In the end, Imari bound Setsuna's arms with the thin ribbons of her own yukata. Tying the knots one-handed was difficult and time consuming, but with some effort, they held firm. Without a weapon, there was no way to slice through them. Through it all, the shogun didn't struggle. She still seemed as if she were in the midst of a horrible dream—that, or she was in a state of shock. Once Setsuna's elbows were tied behind her back and her ankles wrapped together, Imari shoved her onto the futon. Then, she returned to the door and waited. More guards were undoubtedly coming, and when they arrived, she would be ready.

On the way, she picked up the severed arm of the second man she had slain. The rush of blood had slowed, congealing in a sticky pool beside him. If he wasn't dead, he would be soon. Imari removed his kote and placed it over her shortened left forearm instead, ignoring the wet crimson stain it left on the sleeve of her kimono. She had left in such a hurry that she hadn't been able to retrieve her own.

One last time, a small part of her heart rebelled. She had removed someone else's arm, had taken his life. Surely Kaede would react with disgust upon seeing what she had done. But there was no room for guilt within her. The voice in her head was soothing, certain, and filled her with warmth. *You're doing this for Kaede. Once Setsuna and Hayate are dead and her parents are safe, she'll apologize for lying to you and fall into your arms with gratitude.*

✳✳✳

"What do you mean, she's gone?" Takeshi said, staring at Kaede in anger and disbelief. He was dressed more hastily than usual, the folds of his brown kimono rumpled, and he was panting lightly from what Kaede suspected was a rapid sprint down the hallway.

"Just what I said," Kaede said in a strained voice. A knot was stuck in her throat and her chest burned with guilt. "Rin saw her disappear after talking to Kyuubi. She vanished into thin air."

"But people don't just vanish," Kenta protested. He looked even less put together than Takeshi—his hair stuck out every which way and his usual smile was nowhere to be seen. Instead, a worried wrinkle creased his brow. "There has to be some other explanation."

"There isn't," Rin growled, seeming annoyed the Hibana brothers dared to question her. "Wen Ling and Suanni have already told us that this Kyuubi is powerful and manipulative. Wherever Imari is, she must be in terrible danger."

It was the wrong thing to say. "Then we need to get her back," Takeshi declared, drawing his katana even though there were no enemies to face. For a moment, Kaede thought he looked like he actually wanted to use it on her. She took a cautious step back, but there was no need. Kenta put a reassuring hand on Takeshi's shoulder.

"We will, right, Kaede?" he said, giving her a pointed look.

"Yes, we will," she said, with more confidence than she felt. "From our…conversation, Imari seemed determined to go to Aozora to warn them about Hayate."

"She's probably half way across the continent," Takeshi muttered. He shook his head angrily, his frown carving deep grooves in his face.

"That isn't a problem," Suanni said, entering the conversation for the first time since Takeshi and Kenta's arrivals. "I'll fly you there within the day."

"And I'll make sure we ask my parents for help once we get there," Kaede said. "They'll be able to send their soldiers out looking for her."

"Don't think we're going to avoid that topic," Takeshi said, aiming a fresh glare at her. "You lied to us, Aozora-dono. Once Imari is safe, that will be dealt with."

Kaede lowered her head, wincing at the use of her formal title. Her lie was the whole reason Imari had fallen under Kyuubi's influence. *I never should've left the two of them alone. I ran off like an idiot because of my own hurt feelings.*

"This isn't the time, Takeshi," Rin said. "Kaede had her reasons and they aren't yours to judge."

"They are mine to judge," Takeshi insisted, "especially since they're the reason Imari—"

"They aren't the reason Imari was kidnapped," Rin interrupted. "It was Kyuubi's fault. If anything, I blame myself. I suspected the fox was trouble, but I didn't warn you strongly enough."

"Stop!" Kenta said, raising his voice loud enough for it to echo through the forge. Everyone paused and looked at him in surprise. He rarely shouted unless it was with excitement. "This isn't helping. We need to go find Imari. The three of you can bicker with each other until the sun goes down once she's safe, okay?"

Takeshi looked deeply unhappy, but eventually, he nodded. Rin too seemed to accept Kenta's words. She remained silent, although the points of her teeth still showed between her lips.

"For what it's worth, I'm sorry," Kaede murmured. "I never meant for it to turn out this way, and I'm going to do everything I can to make sure we find Imari and bring her back safe."

Even though she hadn't been expecting forgiveness, Kaede was still hurt when Takeshi turned away. He headed toward Suanni, approaching the dragon's tail and preparing to climb on their back. Kenta followed, shoulders slumped. Kaede remained behind until Rin nudged her arm.

"Come on, Kaede," Rin said, licking the side of Kaede's face with her warm tongue. "Be strong. For Imari."

Kaede closed her eyes and took a deep breath. *For Imari.* How her friends felt about her didn't matter right now. Her first priority had to be getting Imari back, wherever she might be. With that goal to latch onto, she began to climb Suanni's tail.

"Wait," a voice called, and she turned to see Wen Ling hurrying toward them with three packs. They were heavy with supplies, and

Kaede took them with some difficulty. "You'll need these. I have a feeling the three of you won't be coming back any time soon, although I suspect we'll meet again."

Kaede bowed. "I hope we do. Thank you, Wen Ling. You've been a generous host and a wonderful teacher for Imari. I know she would love the chance to tell you that herself."

"You're right," Wen Ling said. "I am a wonderful teacher, which means you should have a little faith in Imari. She's strong, and her time here has only made her stronger."

The statement soothed Kaede more than she expected, and she gave Wen Ling a genuine smile. "I'm sure you're right. In fact, she'll probably be annoyed with us for chasing after her like a disobedient child who's run away."

"With any luck. Now, go. Find her. I know you can."

With one last bow of farewell, Kaede grabbed the packs and scurried up onto Suanni's back, taking the rearmost spot in front of their hind legs. Takeshi didn't acknowledge her at all, and Kenta shot her a worried, sad look from over his shoulder. She didn't return it. Despite Rin and Wen Ling's attempts at comforting her, the sting of guilt was too strong.

I'll find her, she told herself, fighting to push those feelings down and gather her courage. *I have to.*

***

Imari stepped over the crumpled body of the last soldier, the spikes of her sandals squelching in the pool of blood that surrounded him. Another dozen had come to try and rescue Setsuna, but Imari had slain them all. Each time fatigue tugged at her muscles, her sword lent her strength, filling her with fresh energy. Each time one of the lucky samurai scored a hit, she thought about Kaede and pushed past the pain. Each time she saw the life leave another man's eyes and doubt took root deep in her heart, the pearl tucked in her kimono scoured the earth before it could sprout.

You're doing the right thing, Kyuubi's voice whispered. *You're helping Kaede. You're helping her parents and the whole Empire. These men are simply part of the price that must be paid.*

Nothing was too steep a price for Kaede's safety. Imari would go to the ends of the earth for her love. Kaede would thank her for this when it was all over. Kaede would be proud of her.

With a careful eye, she scanned the bodies in front of her. They had all been killed in different ways—some skewered, some slit at the throat, others missing limbs. Wujian could cleave through flesh and human bone like it was nothing more than mist. She could feel its power pooling within her, waiting to be unleashed again. But there were no sounds of approaching footsteps. The corridor was still and silent, still and silent except for the sound of soft breathing.

One of the soldiers was still alive. He bled from his nose, his chin bubbling and red, and he looked as though he had just regained consciousness. But his body was otherwise whole. Imari stepped toward him, watching as his hazy eyes grew wide with terror. He looked like a mouse caught in the shadow of a hawk, simply waiting for death to snatch him from above.

Imari didn't kill him like the others. She hooked the tip of her jian into the fabric of his shirt, forcing him to rise onto his knees. "Can you walk?" she asked, holding the point near his nervously bobbing throat.

The man didn't answer, but he did give the slightest of nods.

"You will go to Aozora," she told him. "You will tell Yukimura Hayate he must abandon his attempts to overthrow the daimyo there and come here to face me himself. If he doesn't, I will kill the shogun. Do you understand?"

Once more, the unfortunate man nodded. Imari withdrew her jian, although she kept it trained on him as he rose to his feet. "If you don't, nothing in the whole Empire will protect you. Go. Now."

The man turned and ran at full tilt, scurrying down the corridor and disappearing into the darkness. Imari had no doubt he would follow her orders. She had seen it in his eyes. He was too terrified to resist.

Terrified. He was terrified of me. And why shouldn't he be? He thought I was going to kill him like the others. She looked once more at the corpses that littered the stone corridor. The smell of death was in her nose now, heavy and coppery. *Sun and Moon, what have I done.*

What needed to be done. Your Ancestors would be proud. Your father would be proud. Kaede will be proud.

With each name listed, Imari relaxed and began to smile. She had done well. She was certain of it. Now, all she had to do was watch over Setsuna and wait for Hayate's arrival. There was no doubt in her mind he would come to see what had become of his mother, and when he did—she would be able to make him pay for everything he had done to Kaede..

Chapter Twenty-One

KAEDE DUCKED HER HEAD against the wind, staring down at Suanni's blue and silver scales. Though they were soaring high above the ground, she took no delight in looking at the mountains, forests, and rivers below. Her thoughts were elsewhere, with Imari, and so was her heart. The empty hole in her chest felt even colder than the gales that whipped through her hair and set loose strands of it flying behind her.

Takeshi and Kenta had remained silent since their departure from Hongshan, riding a considerable distance in front of her so they wouldn't have to speak. That left only Rin to comfort her—and Kaede wasn't even sure she deserved to be comforted. Instead of sitting near the top of Suanni's tail, Rin had elected to nestle in the spines where Kaede could reach her. Though she badly wanted to reach out and wrap her arms around Rin's neck, Kaede refrained. She had to focus. To come up with some sort of plan.

She had no idea where Imari was, other than a vague guess that she was probably somewhere in Aozora. The smartest thing to do would be to go to her parents and beg their help. They could provide soldiers to scour the mountains, and the more people out looking for Imari, the better chance they had of finding her.

Normally, the thought of approaching her parents with such a request would've made Kaede sick, but she didn't have the luxury of other options. Imari's life was in danger. Her own family problems didn't matter in comparison.

"Kaede, look," Rin said, turning back to nudge her arm.

Reluctantly, Kaede raised her head. She glanced over Suanni's side, seeing the tops of familiar mountains beneath her. Even from this angle, she could recognize home. *Home.* Her heart didn't leap at the sight of them, and she didn't feel a wave of relief. Aozora wasn't home anymore. Home was Imari.

Hope and fear warred within her as Suanni circled downwards. A black dot appeared against the mountainside, and as it grew larger, Kaede recognized the walls of a city. They were closing in on Taiseto at last. She looked away, resting her cheek against Rin's fur. She would see it soon enough when they landed.

She stirred when she began to hear shouts of surprise from down below. Tiny figures, small as ants, pointed toward the sky, staring up in shock and awe. Kaede realized the sight they must've made, descending into the heart of the city on the back of a giant blue dragon, but she couldn't bear to smile.

"We'll head for the castle," Takeshi said, speaking mostly to Kenta as they flew toward the largest building. It was unmistakably a daimyo's residence, surrounded by stone walls with a blue and white mon fluttering in the cold breeze.

"Good idea." Kenta turned to look over his shoulder. "Kaede, are you ready?" He gave her a weak smile, one that showed genuine concern, and it touched Kaede that Kenta didn't blame her entirely for Imari's disappearance.

"It doesn't matter," she said as Suanni touched down. "It's what needs to be done."

They landed in the garden behind the castle, a beautiful place of snowcapped trees. The river that ran beneath the arched wooden bridge was frozen and the bushes nearby were laced with frost. Normally, she would have appreciated the sight. Unlike the castle, the garden had often been a place of refuge for her. Now, however, it failed to soothe her. It wasn't as beautiful as Mirai's garden. It wasn't as beautiful as Imari.

She didn't have long to brood. More shouts came from the castle and several doors flung open, revealing the shocked faces of the guards. Suanni lowered their tail, offering them a way down. "I suggest you hurry and find your family, Kaede. I shouldn't stay here long. I need to warn the Empress of what has happened."

Kaede stared at the dragon. "Wait, you know Empress Tomoyo?"

Suanni dipped their head. "A story for another time, and that time will come soon. I will wait for you outside the city walls until I know your intentions." They glanced over at the nervous group of guards. "I fear if I stay in the garden, I may cause problems."

Kaede began to protest, but Rin gave her a nudge. Takeshi and Kenta had already climbed down, leaving them behind. With more guards gathering at the edges of the garden, she didn't have much choice. "I'll be quick," she said to Suanni. "Thank you."

She climbed down the dragon's tail and landed softly in the snow. Upon seeing her, the cluster of guards seemed to relax visibly. They made their bows and one of them, a captain Kaede vaguely recognized, stepped forward. "Aozora-dono, your return is most welcome. But..." He glanced over at Suanni with a mixture of fear and amazement, clearly at a loss for words.

"The dragon means you no harm," Kaede assured him. "Where are my parents? I need to speak with them right away."

The captain seemed grateful for the direct question, but he was unable to answer until Suanni had taken off. The dragon's long, coiling body lifted off the ground, swimming up and away through the sky almost like a serpent on water. There were more gasps and murmurs, and Kaede could hear some of the men already questioning what they had seen.

"My parents," Kaede said to the captain. "Where are they?"

The guard snapped back to attention. "Your parents are in the reception hall with Hayate-dono. I will alert them of your arrival at once."

As soon as she heard Hayate's name, Kaede tensed with fear. Perhaps Kyuubi hadn't been entirely dishonest after all. She brushed past the captain, shooting through the curious cluster of guards like an arrow. Bursting into the castle, she took the corridors at a run, not even checking to see whether Kenta and Takeshi followed her. Rin, however, kept pace at her side, blue eyes alight with anger.

Kaede reached the throne room in a matter of minutes. She barreled past the shocked guards standing outside, not even giving them a chance to cross their yari and block her path. When she rushed through the door, she stumbled upon a terrifying sight. Hayate was indeed in the room with her parents, standing right beside them with Kaze at his shoulder.

"Get away from them," she shouted, her hand flying to Mizu-no-Hamon's hilt. She drew her katana and brandished it before her, aiming the point at Hayate's chest.

Identical looks of surprise crossed her parents' faces.

"Kaede?"

"What are you doing here?"

Hayate didn't move to draw his sword. Instead, he took a step away from Masaru and Kotone, holding out his hands in surrender. "Please, Kaede, give me a few moments to explain. I've made mistakes—"

"Your only mistake was coming here." She rushed him, bringing her blade sweeping toward him and ignoring her parents' shouts of protest.

Hayate blocked. Their swords slid awkwardly against each other, and Kaede realized with surprise Hayate hadn't removed his scabbard. Kaze growled. He tried to leap at her, but a white blur blocked him. He and Rin went tumbling onto the stone floor of the castle, locked in a vicious struggle of flashing teeth and kicking paws.

Trusting Rin to hold her own, Kaede focused back on Hayate. She tried to force him back, trading blow after blow. The edge of her blade chipped awkwardly at the hardened wood, but even her anger wasn't enough to split it. "I don't want to fight you, Kaede," Hayate panted. "If you'll just listen—"

Kaede sent him stumbling back with an angry shove. "You almost killed Imari! How is that not wanting to fight? Did you have something to do with her disappearance? Are you working with Kyuubi, too?"

She struck over and over again, but her anger made her sloppy. Hayate easily wove between the strokes of her forms. "I don't know where Imari is, and I've never heard of this 'Kyuubi'. I'm here to ask your parents for help. Setsuna is under some kind of spell."

Kaede froze in mid-strike. Beside her, she saw the two wolves disentangle themselves and perk up their ears, breathing heavily. Neither seemed hurt, much to her relief. She stared at Hayate, lowering her sword. "Wait, a spell?"

Hayate lowered his sheathed katana as well. "I should have seen it sooner. She's changed so abruptly, as if her mind is no longer her own. I feel like a fool for taking so long to realize it."

Everything clicked in Kaede's head. "Kyuubi," she whispered. "It's been her the whole time." Every wrong action Setsuna had ever taken suddenly made sense. For a moment, Kaede felt a wave of dizzying confusion and relief. She had spent months and months feeling betrayed by her aunt, her mentor, her trusted teacher, but really, Setsuna had been another victim all along. "Ancestors, I've been so blind!"

"Who is Kyuubi?" Kaze asked. "I think we need to exchange information, as quickly as possible."

"A clever, evil fox." Rin stepped between Kaede and Hayate, forcing them to separate. "Kyuubi joined our group briefly on the way to Hongshan," she told Hayate. "Later, she came back and told us you were trying to take Kaede's parents hostage."

"Hostage?" Kotone repeated in surprise. She seemed relieved that the fight had ended, and Kaede didn't miss the fact that she removed her hand from her own katana. "No, Hayate came to warn us."

"He told us Setsuna wasn't in her right mind and asked for our help," Masaru said. "We were going to ride out later today."

At that moment, Takeshi and Kenta burst into the room too. The guards had attempted to hold them back, but they hadn't been determined enough in the face of the brothers' clear desperation. Upon seeing Hayate, they both raised their katanas, but Kaede held up a hand to stop them. "Don't. He has information we need."

"He almost killed Imari and you!" Takeshi protested, and the note of genuine concern in his voice on the last word surprised Kaede.

Kaede looked over at her cousin. "Am I right in assuming you've switched sides?" she asked him bluntly, although the words were hard to say. She still remembered the way his sword had gleamed against Imari's neck in the moonlight.

"Yes," Hayate answered at once. "I was wrong to chase you. I was wrong to trust Setsuna blindly without realizing something had changed. I'm trying to make it right now."

Kaede let out a long breath. Under any other circumstances, she might not have forgiven Hayate so easily, or at all. However, the situation was still desperate. She would ally with anyone who could help her find Imari. "It seems like our goals are the same then. We have to help Imari and Setsuna and stop Kyuubi from manipulating anyone else."

"This is more serious than I imagined," Masaru said. "Hayate, I'm afraid we need to send another courier to the Empress at once."

"I don't have time to wait around for couriers," Kaede insisted. "If Imari isn't in Aozora trying to find Hayate, she's in Yukimura. It's the only thing that makes sense."

"And you don't need to contact the Empress," Kenta added. "The dragon who brought us plans to warn her." When Masaru and Kotone stared at him in surprise, he stepped forward, giving them a hesitant, respectful bow. "I apologize, Aozora-dono. I'm Hibana Kenta, and this is my brother—"

"Hibana Takeshi, karo to the Homura family." Takeshi gave a stiff bow to the daimyos as well, but as he straightened, his eyes flicked over to Hayate. "I am honor-bound to warn you, Yukimura Hayate, if you harm Imari or any of my friends again, I won't hesitate to kill you."

Hayate met his stare. "I'll deserve it. Please, let me help you."

After a long, tense pause, Takeshi nodded. "Fine. You said you were about to ride for Kousetsu? How far is it?"

"A week on fast horses," Hayate said.

"Then we'll have to ask Suanni for another ride," Kaede insisted. "We don't have a week to waste."

"Suanni. Is that your…the dragon?" said Masaru, in a tone that clearly showed he doubted it.

Kaede didn't have time to convince him. "Yes. They're waiting outside the city."

Takeshi turned toward Hayate. "Are you coming with us or not?"

Hayate bowed deeply. "You aren't the only person with a loved one in danger. I'll fly with you to Kousetsu immediately."

***

The ride to Yukimura was much shorter than the distance between Hongshan and Aozora. Suanni flew through the sky at incredible speed, moving so fast the snow-capped mountains below became a grey and white blur. However, adding Hayate and Kaze to their party had made things more strained. Takeshi wanted nothing to do with him, forcing Kaede to sit in the middle of Suanni's back in order to separate them

Rin seemed happy, though. She was pleased to be reunited with her brother, and the two of them remained curled up together during the journey, keeping each other warm.

That left Kaede with only Hayate to talk to. At first, neither of them knew what to say, and they listened to the howling voice of the wind. But at last, the tension became too much.

"What made you change your mind?" Kaede asked.

Hayate sighed, although the sound was almost lost. "Kaze had to talk some sense into me. I wish I'd seen it sooner, Kaede. This is all my fault."

Kaede's heart softened. His voice was full of regret—a regret she understood all too well. She had felt it herself ever since running away, and twofold since Imari's disappearance. When he spoke, she heard the words of a man who would give just about anything to go back in time and undo his choices.

"It's as much my fault," she said, an awkward attempt at offering comfort. He was her cousin, after all, and they had been close friends once.

"I don't blame you," Hayate said. "You left because you were afraid. You knew something was wrong. I didn't even see that much."

"I left because I was a coward. If I'd stayed…"

"If I had dared to question her sooner instead of chasing you."

They lapsed into silence again.

"There's no use in this, is there?" Hayate said eventually. "All we can do is try to make up for our mistakes now."

"I hope we can." Kaede looked away from Hayate and down into her lap, tears filling her eyes.

Her response didn't go unnoticed. Hayate's hand moved toward her for a moment, as it had so many times during their shared childhoods, but pulled back after less than a centimeter. Instead, he said, "Imari, the daimyo's daughter I almost killed. You love her, don't you?"

Kaede bit hard at her lip, using the pain to regain some control. "Yes."

"I'm sorry."

Hayate didn't need to say anything else. Kaede knew what he meant. "We'll save them both," she said even though she didn't fully believe it. "Imari and Setsuna."

"Yes. We will."

"Good to see you two getting along again," Kaze said, raising his head to look at them. He wore a clear expression of approval on his face.

Kaede gave him a small smile. As worried as she was about Imari, Kaze was right. It was good to have Hayate back on her side again, and a small portion of the weight on her shoulders had been lifted away.

Hayate smiled back, but then his eyes widened and he pointed down below. "Look," he said, gesturing toward the stretch of forest. "I think we're almost home."

Kaede peered down as well. The forest flying by beneath them was indeed familiar, the same forest she had played in during her summers as a child. The forest where she had met Rin. The forest where she had begged the yokai to transform her. The forest where she had run from Hayate in the dead of night, terrified he would kill her if he caught her.

"We're almost there," Kaede said to herself. "Hold on a little longer, Imari."

Before long, the forest tapered off into a clearing. Tucked beneath the mountain's shadow was a familiar small city. It had high walls surrounding it, but they were hardly necessary. Snuggled comfortably between the trees and the mountain range behind, it was protected on all sides. A shiver of recognition passed through Kaede's body. She didn't want to be here, and she was certain her reception wouldn't be as friendly as it had been in Aozora, even with Hayate to speak for her.

"I'll land a short distance away," Suanni said as they spiraled down toward the forest. "I think it's best if I transform before we encounter any more guards."

"Good idea," Kenta said. "I think a few of them probably had to change their pants after they saw you. Dragons aren't really common around these parts." His humor was forced, but Kaede was grateful for it anyway. It proved a helpful distraction from the worries running through her head.

Takeshi looked as though he wanted to say something, but even he seemed to see the wisdom in Suanni's decision. Suanni broke the canopy of the forest, weaving gracefully between the tree trunks and finding a clear place to touch down. Before Kaede could even climb off Suanni's back, a sharp sound distracted her. She glanced around, checking to see if her companions had heard it too. They all were looking around the forest, and Rin and Kaze's ears were both tilted and alert.

"What was that?" Kenta asked nervously.

Takeshi's brow furrowed. "It sounded like someone screaming. A spirit who lives here?"

"A human," Rin declared.

The wolves slid down Suanni's tail first, trotting off into the snowy forest together.

Kaede was next to the ground. She ran off after them, crunching through the frost and following their footprints, but she didn't have to track them far. She found the pair of wolves only a few meters away, noses pointed at a terrified looking man in the snow. He was dressed in armor, wearing a tattered version of Yukimura's pinecone mon, and both were stained with blood. It looked somewhat old, though the snow had kept some parts of it shiny and wet.

"S...stay back," he shouted, brandishing a pathetic stick and scrambling backwards. He was little more than a boy, seventeen, eighteen at most. There wasn't any hair on his chin, and he looked even younger with his eyes bulging out of his head. He panted harshly, tossing up snow in his effort to get to his feet.

Kaede extended her hand to help him, but he flinched away. "The wolves aren't going to hurt you," she said, motioning for Kaze and Rin to back off. They did so, although Rin didn't look happy about it.

"First her, then a dragon in the sky, now wolves!" the wounded soldier babbled. He seemed on the verge of hysteria, shaking his head as if he expected the visions before him to disappear. "Yukimura-dono. I have to find Yukimura-dono, she said—"

"You mean Yukimura Setsuna?" Kaede asked.

"No—"

"Then you must mean me." Hayate had caught up with her, and at the sight of him, the soldier seemed to calm down. He stopped struggling, and Hayate could pass Kaede and approach him. He offered his hand, and the man took it, although he was still trembling.

"Yukimura-dono, thank the Ancestors! Yukimura-sama is in danger! A woman came and..." His mouth still moved, but all that came out was a terrified moan.

"A woman?" Kaede asked. "This woman didn't happen to have nine tails and say her name was Kyuubi, did she?"

The man shook his head, and Kaede noticed tears leaking from his eyes. "No, but she had one hand. Ancestors, she was terrifying!" He broke down sobbing, unable to answer.

Kaede hardly noticed. "Imari. You saw Imari." She approached the man despite Hayate's warnings, grasping his shoulders and shaking him back to coherence. "Where was she? Is she in danger?"

The man continued sobbing. "The cave." He pointed in a direction Kaede recognized, toward the cave outside the city where Setsuna had conducted her experiments.

Kaede's first instinct was to go at once. She turned, preparing to crash through the branches, but Kenta spoke up. "Wait!" he called from a few meters back, where he and Takeshi stood. "We can't leave him here. He's injured."

"How far are Kousetsu's gates?" Takeshi asked. Clearly, he wanted to go after Imari too. "Can he make it himself? We've all sworn an oath to protect Imari with our lives. This can't wait."

Kaede felt another wave of guilt wash over her. She had failed as Imari's yojimbo, and with every moment that passed, Imari was in more danger.

"Let me go to the cave while you take him back to Kousetsu," Hayate suggested. "Setsuna and her guards won't attack me on sight the way they would Kaede or a stranger. She doesn't even know I went to Kaede's parents for help. I could go in and see what's going on."

Grateful as she was for Hayate's offer, Kaede shook her head. "No. We need to do this together. I need to do this."

"Then let me take him," said another voice. Kaede turned to see Suanni approaching through the trees as Bo, brown hood pulled up to cover their face. They stopped before the soldier, bowing deeply. "How bad are your injuries, friend? Are you able to walk a short distance?"

The soldier seemed surprised but not threatened by Suanni's questions. "Not too bad. I think I could make it to the city. You're all going to sort this out, right? You'll stop her."

"Yes," Kaede promised. "We're going to stop her."

The man breathed a sigh of relief. "Thank you," he said, looking as though the weight of the world had lifted from his shoulders.

"Then come with me," Suanni said, offering a smile from beneath their hood. "I'll make sure you get there safely. Your job here is done."

Before they shepherded the man toward the city, Suanni paused and whispered to Kaede, "I won't be returning after this. The Empress needs to be warned about this situation."

Kaede bowed. "I understand. Thank you for your help, Suanni."

"Be careful, Kaede. I doubt Kyuubi will be at the cave, but if she is, there is only one way to stop her. You need to remove all nine of her tails. Otherwise, your sword can only cause her pain. It won't kill her."

"I hope she's there," Kaede said, fists clenching, "because I intend to deal with her myself."

Moments later, Kaede's hand drifted toward her katana, hovering there as they made their way through the forest. The closer she came to the cave where Setsuna had tried to bring the yokai under her control, the more frightened she felt. This place had a bad feeling, something beyond the terrible memories she carried. Its aura made the hairs on the back of her neck prickle and her gut churn as she crunched over the snow.

The others felt it too. Hayate tensed. The two wolves kept their ears perked. Even Takeshi and Kenta looked wary. "Are we sure this is the place?" Kenta asked, his eyes fixed on the dark, narrow mouth of the cave. There were several spiked footprints leading up to it, but none that Kaede could see leading out.

"It is," Hayate said. "This is where Setsuna conducted all her secret experiments."

"Then we need to go in," Takeshi said. "How many guards can we expect?"

"I don't know. It might be better for me to go in first."

Kaede shook her head. "I'm sworn to protect Imari. We're going in together."

"At least let me go up close and look first," Hayate said. "We don't want to run straight into an ambush."

Kaede ground her teeth. It was a reasonable suggestion, but it went against her instincts. "Fine, but be fast. You aren't going in without us."

"I wouldn't dream of it. Kaze, come on." Hayate and the black wolf slipped off, leaving Kaede waiting restlessly in the brush with Takeshi, Kenta, and Rin.

For a few seconds, silence reigned. All Kaede could hear was the brittle rustling of the ice-covered branches as the wind passed through them.

"I don't like this," Takeshi whispered. He had already drawn his katana, knuckles twitching uncomfortably around the grip. "We should go with him."

"It's going to be okay," Kenta whispered back. "I'm sure he'll give us a signal any second."

Hayate did give a signal, but not the one Kaede expected. Instead of waving them forward, he stumbled back in surprise, letting out a sharp gasp. Then, without even looking toward them, he drew his sword and sprinted straight into the cave. Kaze remained behind, waiting for the others to catch up.

Kaede reached him first. "What happened?" she asked, heart pounding wildly.

"This," Kaze growled, pointing his nose at a lump off to one side. Lying in front of the cave, half-covered in a crimson snowdrift, were three bodies. Everyone had been hacked to pieces, staring skyward with dead, sightless eyes.

Shaking herself free of shock, Kaede drew her katana and rushed into the cave after Hayate. Only one thought burned in her brain. Finding Imari. She had to, before something worse than this happened.

Chapter Twenty-Two

IMARI PACED THE HALL outside Setsuna's rooms, splashing through pools of blood. The longer she waited, the more restless she became. In the darkness, she wasn't sure how much time had passed. Hours? A day? More? She didn't feel hunger or thirst, and she didn't feel exhaustion either. She didn't even feel pain from the minor injuries the soldiers had given her.

All that mattered was the voice.

Just wait, it said. *Hayate will be here soon,* it said. *You can kill him and save Kaede,* it said, *save the Empire.*

Whenever she doubted, it reminded her. Whenever she closed her eyes, it reminded her. Sometimes it praised her, telling her what a heroic thing she was doing and how much Kaede would love her for it afterward. Other times it frightened her, warning her how much pain Kaede would feel if Lord and Lady Aozora were killed. It forced her to relive the night Hayate had attacked Kaede in the garden, threatening to kill them both.

Imari trembled with anger every time she remembered. She remembered the sharp edge of Hayate's katana against her throat. The heavy throb of her heart in her head. The wild fear in Kaede's eyes. She hated him. She hated Setsuna. She hated them for what they had done to Kaede, and for what they had done to her.

Be patient, the voice said. *Your chance is coming.*

The sound of footsteps approaching made Imari snap back to attention. She drew her jian from its scabbard, waiting. Watching. Listening.

The footsteps came closer, heavy and fast. Imari's pulse matched their rhythm. They rounded the corner and Imari finally caught sight of their face. Even in the shadows, she would have recognized it anywhere. Hayate stood before her, clutching his katana.

Upon seeing her, he lowered it. "Homura Imari," he said with a sigh of relief. "Kaede will be so happy—"

"Don't say her name," Imari warned him. She took a defensive stance, kote in front of her and sword drawn behind. "I don't want to hear it from your lips."

Hayate looked at her in surprise. "I know you don't want to see me, but please, listen. We're on the same side now."

With a shout of rage, Imari charged him, sweeping her sword at his throat.

Hayate brought his katana up to block her, but barely. He stumbled back, regaining his balance. "Let me explain!"

She sprang again, knocking his katana aside and going for his stomach. Hayate jumped back. While he retreated, she advanced, raining blow after blow upon him. Her rage gave her strength and speed, but she couldn't break his defense. He moved faster than she did, stopping each of her strikes a moment too soon.

They ran through the cave, Imari pushing, Hayate defending. No matter how fast the point of her sword danced, she couldn't find a way past his defense. He countered with his whole body, able to put more strength behind his weapon than she could match with just her wrist and elbow.

For a moment, her fury made her careless. She thrust too quickly, tipping ever so slightly off balance. But though Imari saw Hayate's eyes catch the mistake and his arms twitch, he didn't bring his katana in through the gap. He merely brushed her blade aside with his. "I don't want to fight," he panted, sweat trickling down one side of his face. "Not anymore."

Imari refused to listen. It was a lie. A trick. She had seen him try to kill Kaede with her own eyes. He was allied with Setsuna. He wanted to overthrow Lord and Lady Aozora. She wouldn't give him the chance. Roaring, she recovered and rushed him again. This time, she went in low, bending her knees and driving the point of her jian forward with all her swiftness and strength. She still wasn't fast enough. She only caught the edge of Hayate's kimono before his katana came down from above in a straight slash, pushing her sword away and sending a shock up along her arm.

Imari gripped the handle harder. She pulled back, flipping the sword around and striking out at his face with the tassels. He reeled, turning his face, and she spun in for another chance. This time, she found his arm. Her jian bit into his shoulder and he grunted, staggering back. Blood blossomed through his sleeve, but still, he didn't retaliate.

"What are you doing?" Imari demanded, spitting through her teeth. "Fight me! Or are you too dishonorable even for that?"

"I told you, we're on the same side. We both want to help Kaede—"

"Liar!"

Imari circled and slashed, feet barely touching the ground as she twirled toward him. Her jian glowed with a dull green light, but she was too focused, to furious to be surprised. She could feel her anger, her strength, her determination flowing through it like a river. It was an extension of her feelings as much as her arm, and she sent it stabbing toward Hayate's heart with everything she had.

Hayate managed to block her once more, but in doing so, he lost his advantage. His double-handed grip on his katana loosened, and Imari sent it flying away from him with a flick of her wrist. His eyes went wide as it clattered to the ground a few yards away, sliding through a sticky pool of blood and coming to rest against the cave wall.

He dove for it, but Imari backed him into the opposite side of the stone corridor, holding her sword against his throat. "How does it feel?" she asked, glaring into his eyes. They had been frightened before, but now, they were simply sad and resigned.

"Imari!"

No other voice could have halted her hand. No other voice could have forced her to look away from Hayate's tortured face. No other voice could have drawn her out of the billowing red fog she was trapped in.

"Kaede," she said, turning and a wide smile spreading across her face. "You came! I knew you would."

But Kaede didn't look happy to see her. Instead, her expression read pure horror. "Imari, what are you doing? Don't kill him! Hayate's on our side now, I promise."

Imari's brow furrowed. Her head began to ache as she fought to understand. "No," she said, shaking her head. Kaede simply didn't understand what the voice had told her. She needed to explain. "No, Hayate tried to kill you! You heard what Kyuubi said. He was going to Aozora to overthrow your parents and use them against you."

"I wasn't," Hayate said. His throat bobbed just above the edge of her blade. "That was all a lie, Imari. A lie Kyuubi told you."

"You can't trust her, Imari," said another voice. It was only then that Imari noticed Kenta and Takeshi standing behind Kaede. Their weapons were drawn too, although aimed at the ground. "Kyuubi is a trickster. Suanni told us."

A stabbing pain pierced Imari's head. The voice spoke at last, louder, and felt like a wave of relief. Surely it would answer her questions. Surely it would make everything clear again, as it had been only moments before.

Kill him. He's the liar and the trickster. Kaede is confused. She doesn't know what she's saying.

"You've done something to her," Imari shouted at Hayate, leaning right into his face. She pushed her sword deeper, not enough to slice his throat, but enough to whiten the flesh around it with pressure. A small drop of blood trickled out around the edge, running down toward his collarbone. "You've made Kaede think you're on her side."

"He is on our side," Kaede insisted. Her voice cracked, close to tears, and Imari heard metal hitting stone. She glanced sideways to see that Kaede had dropped her katana on the ground and stepped forward. "Imari," she whispered, opening her arms. "Come here. I don't want you to kill him."

Don't listen to her, the voice said, but despite its volume, it sounded more distant than before. She looked at Kaede, shaking and unarmed, standing alone in the middle of the corridor.

"I'm doing this for you," Imari whispered, near tears from pain and confusion. "I'm doing this for—"

"You don't need to do anything for Kaede, Imari," Takeshi said urgently. "You always got mad at me for doing things for you. If Kaede wants to kill Hayate, let her do it herself."

The contradiction made Imari waver. She lowered her sword, removing it from Hayate's throat and taking a single step back. He was right. The past several months, she had tried to step in and take care of Kaede's problems—and every time, it had ended up terribly. Yet, here she was, doing the exact same thing again.

That doesn't matter, the voice said. *Kaede wants this. She'll be so grateful.*

"Come here, Imari," Kaede said again, pleading, her face tear-stained. "Put down the sword and come here. It's going to be okay."

Imari groaned, staggering back another few steps. She lowered her sword-arm, bringing the other to her face. Since she couldn't cup her forehead in her hand, she buried it in the crook of her elbow to shield her eyes—anything to get rid of the awful, stabbing spikes of pain driving through her skull.

"No, Kaede doesn't want this. She told me. She's telling me not to."

Don't listen to what she's telling you. She doesn't know her own mind. Kill Hayate. He wants her dead.

But Hayate had made no move to attack anyone. He wasn't even trying to retrieve his weapon. Like Kaede, he was unarmed.

Imari fell to her knees, feeling as if she were being torn in two, ripping apart at the seams. Her thoughts splintered, flying to pieces, and she dropped her sword to the ground. But through the chaos, one thought rang clear. Kaede had asked her to come. She would do what Kaede wanted. The voice couldn't tell her that was wrong.

She started crawling toward Kaede, leaving her sword behind, but she had barely started before Kaede rushed and bent down to meet her. Then Kaede's arms were around her, and suddenly, the pain lessened. Her head still throbbed and her eyes still blurred with tears, but the splitting, unbearable edge was gone. She sagged against Kaede's chest, crying into her kimono.

"It's okay, Imari," Kaede whispered. "It's okay. I've got you."

Imari broke down in sobs. The voice had lied to her. It had been lying all along. All of it, all the things she had done.

"I'm sorry," she cried, still weeping into Kaede's shoulder. "I'm sorry. I'm so sorry."

"Shh," Kaede murmured, kissing her hair. "Don't worry about that now. It doesn't matter."

"But—"

"Imari, how was Kyuubi talking to you? Is she here?"

It took her a while to sniff back enough of her tears to answer. She pulled away slightly, and rummaged in her kimono. She withdrew the milky-white pearl, offering it to Kaede. Before Kaede could take it, however, a searing blaze filled Imari's palm, burning straight into her skin. She yelped and dropped the pearl, and all of them watched it roll across the floor. It began to glow, pulsing with cold, high-pitched laughter.

"Well, that was certainly entertaining," a voice echoed from the pearl. "Congratulations, Imari. You didn't get as far as I'd hoped, but it was still an excellent game. It's a pity you didn't kill Hayate before Kaede arrived. The look on her face would have kept me amused for a long time."

Imari stared at the pearl in disbelief. Her lips moved, but she couldn't speak. Her head swam with feelings and memories, all bleeding together until she couldn't separate them. The voice. Kyuubi. Hayate. Kaede.

"Is that all this was?" Kaede shouted at the pearl. "A stupid game?" She began to rise, but Imari clutched her tighter. She couldn't bear to let go of Kaede again. If she did, she was sure she would slip into madness.

"I wouldn't call it stupid," the pearl said. "Just a little diversion to keep me occupied while I wait for bigger pieces to fall in place. By the way, you should ask Imari about all the bodies in the cave. I'm sure she'll love to explain what happened."

Imari's heart cracked right down the middle. The bodies, the blood. *Oh, Ancestors, when Kaede finds out. When she sees what I've done.*

She tried to pull away, but this time, Kaede tightened their embrace. "Their blood is on your hands, Kyuubi, not hers."

"What? Me?" The voice chuckled. "I didn't wield the sword. Besides, I only encourage people to do what's already in their minds. Coming here was all her idea. And Imari, she would go to the ends of the Roaring Oceans to defend you, Kaede. I suppose that makes this your fault, too."

"Be quiet!" Takeshi yelled. With a look of pure, twisted rage, he charged at the pearl, katana raised above him. It swept down, but as soon as the sharpened tip touched the pearl, it began to glow even brighter. For a moment, it was a brilliant little star, shining so bright it burned Imari's eyes. Then it exploded into a shower of white dust, dust that drifted back to the ground almost like tiny flakes of snow.

Suddenly, Imari felt exhausted. It felt as if a piece of her had been ripped out, leaving a sucking, empty pit behind. She collapsed onto Kaede's lap, shadows creeping in around her eyes. The last thing she remembered before everything went black was Kaede staring down at her, stroking her hair.

***

Kaede sat slumped over beside Imari's bed, shoulders sagging, eyes bleary. Imari was still unconscious and had been since leaving the cave. Kaede had carried her back to Kousetsu herself, rejecting Takeshi and Kenta's offers of help. She was Imari's yojimbo. It was her task.

Hayate had walked beside her the whole time. He carried Setsuna in his arms, although his task was easier. Setsuna was barely a slip of what she had once been a pale, ghostly shadow. They had found her tied up in her bedroom, bound with the silken cord of her own yukata.

Kaede had only needed to take one look at the sloppy knot to realize what had happened. Imari had taken her prisoner. An order from Kyuubi, no doubt. Just thinking about the fox filled Kaede with sickening rage. She had spent months afraid of her aunt, feeling betrayed and hurt, when it hadn't been Setsuna's fault at all.

She blinked, clearing her eyes and staring down at Imari's face. Pained lines creased her brow and sweat had gathered at her temples. Kaede stood and went to lower the fire in the hearth. The least she could do was keep Imari comfortable while they were guests in Hayate's castle.

A soft knock on the door made her pause just as she finished raking away some of the extra coal. She stood and moved to the screen. Takeshi stood there waiting for her, his face as tired and worried as she was sure her own must look. Without saying anything, she bowed and stood aside to let him in.

"How is she?" he asked, carefully approaching the bed. Imari didn't twitch. Her breathing remained steady and rhythmic.

"Normal," Kaede murmured, although she wasn't convinced.

"That's what the healers said when they looked at her." He sighed and took the mat Kaede had abandoned. He stroked back a lock of Imari's hair, but Kaede didn't mind. It seemed like the action of a close friend rather than a lover.

Not that it matters. She might not want to be with me at all after this. I was the one who left her alone with Kyuubi.

"I owe you an apology," Takeshi said, as if she had spoken her thoughts aloud. "I know I was harsh to you back at Hongshan."

"No, I deserved it." Kaede came to join him, sitting at the foot of Imari's futon. Instinctively, she rested a hand on Imari's knee. She hadn't let Imari out of her sight since the cave, and rarely let Imari leave her touch either. "I'm her yojimbo. I shouldn't have left her, even though I was angry."

"You didn't know Kyuubi was a threat," Takeshi said. "We'd been staying at the mountain for two months. Not once in that time did we see any kind of danger. You couldn't have followed her around every minute of every day."

"She would've killed me," Kaede said with a bitter laugh.

"I know I don't always like to admit it, but Imari isn't helpless. She's a good fighter, even better now with Wen Ling's training. It wasn't an unreasonable risk for you to leave her alone so close to the cave, with someone we thought was a friend."

"But Kyuubi wasn't a friend," Kaede said, anger flashing to the surface. "She orchestrated all this, like some kind of puppetmaster. That's all we are to her."

A look of determination settled onto Takeshi's face, hardening his jaw. "And we'll deal with her, but our priority has to be Imari. Things aren't going to be the same when she wakes up, even if she isn't physically hurt."

"What do you mean?" Kaede asked.

Takeshi didn't seem to want to answer her, but eventually, he spoke, keeping his voice even lower than before. "The group of guards Hayate sent to clear out the cave reported back. I was there when he spoke to them. There were fourteen bodies in total scattered throughout the cavern. Some were dismembered."

"Fourteen," Kaede repeated in disbelief. "You think Imari did that?"

"You saw her clothes, Kaede. She was covered in blood. There was no one else alive in those tunnels except for Setsuna, and she was tied up. And why would she kill her own guards? I know it's horrible to think about the other option, but..."

Kaede's first instinct was to protest, to claim that Imari could never do such a thing. But the angry, vengeful warrior who had held her sword to Hayate's throat and the broken, weeping woman who had fallen into her arms hadn't been like the Imari she knew at all. *Because that wasn't the Imari I knew. She was Kyuubi's slave.*

"Should we tell her when she wakes up?"

"I think she already knows. That's why she was weeping when we found her."

"Well, what about the Empress?" Kaede asked. "Surely she won't convict Imari of these deaths when her agents arrive to sort this out. Suanni will tell her about Kyuubi and everything will be fine."

"I'm not worried about Imari being dishonored," Takeshi said. "We all know it wasn't her fault. I'm worried she won't believe it herself."

Kaede closed her eyes. He had a point. They wouldn't hold her responsible, but Imari would have to live with fourteen deaths on her conscience either way. That had been Kyuubi's plan all along. "What about the bodies?"

"The bad-looking ones were cremated at the cave and their ashes collected," Takeshi said. "The guards brought the rest back to the city so their families could see them first."

Tears welled in Kaede's eyes. "She was only trying to protect me," she said in a cracked voice, her chin trembling. "That's what she said. She was trying to protect me."

"Kyuubi used her," Takeshi said. To Kaede's surprise, he put a hand on her shoulder, an unusual gesture of comfort. "But the pearl is gone. It can't hurt Imari anymore. We're going to make sure of that. And when she wakes up, you can't fall apart like this and blame yourself, Kaede. Whatever fight the two of you had, whatever lies you told her and whatever awful things she said to you, it must end. She's going to need you now more than ever. And if you can't be there for her, I really will have a reason to hate you."

Kaede swallowed, regaining control of herself. "You're right. I'll be there for her. I love her. And there won't be any more lies. The truth is already bad enough."

"Aozora, huh?" He gave her shoulder a slight shake. "And here I was, worried you weren't of high enough status for her. Turns out you outrank us all."

Kaede sniffed, wiping away her tears before they could really start, but she gave Takeshi a faint smile. "You know she never cared about ranks and titles. She would've liked all of us even if we'd been peasants. Even Kenta."

Takeshi snorted. "Yes. Even Kenta." He removed his hand and stood up from the mat, brushing the wrinkles out of his kimono. "I'm going to get her some water. You too. Maybe we can get her to drink it."

"All right," Kaede said. "I'll stay with her. In case she wakes up."

"She will," Takeshi said. "The healers said she would. I think she's just exhausted." With one last bow, he left the room, and Kaede turned back to Imari.

To her surprise, Imari's thin eyelids began twitching, as if she were about to awaken. Kaede waited, barely breathing, and at last they opened, revealing Imari's familiar brown eyes. She seemed confused at first, blinking a few times, but then, she smiled softly. "Kaede. You're here."

"Of course, I'm here," Kaede said through a shaking smile. She searched for Imari's hand beneath the thin covers, lacing their fingers together and gripping tight.

Imari gave her palm a weak squeeze. "Don't leave. Please, don't leave again."

"I won't," Kaede promised. "I won't leave you again. I'm so glad you're all right." Imari's lashes began drooping, and Kaede used her free hand to stroke the side of Imari's cheek. "Close your eyes again. It's okay if you need more sleep. I'll be here when you wake up."

"You'll be here." With a sigh, Imari closed her eyes again. Her breathing slowed down as she drifted off, but this time, her face didn't look so pained.

Kaede watched her until she lapsed back into unconsciousness. She was glad to bring Imari comfort, even if it was only for a little while. She knew all too well that the worst of the pain would come later, when she remembered what had happened back in the cave.

***

Blood runs everywhere. At first, it's just the smell—a sickly, coppery scent that clings to the inside of Imari's nose no matter which way she looks. Then it's creeping toward her across the ground, a crimson stain spreading rapidly through the white snow. It's like a vein that's been pierced.

She turns to run, but there's blood coming from that direction too— an entire ocean of blood rushing in waves toward her. Red and thin in some places, black and congealed in others, it eats away the ground beneath her feet.

There is an island of snow to stand on but it shrinks, growing smaller and smaller. The white turns pink, then red, as the blood rises around her feet. It touches her sandals first, seeping through her tabi. She tries sloshing through it, but there's nowhere to run. The sea of blood is endless.

It rises to her calves, then her knees, hot and scalding. She wails, but there's no one around to hear. She's alone. The blood crawls up her thighs, pooling at her hips, forcing her to wade through it. The waves break against her stomach, then her chest, rocking her back and forth, battering her over and over. It reaches her shoulders, her neck.

She tries to scream again, but blood washes into her mouth. It's sweet and salty and disgusting, and she tries to spit it out, but more comes in to take its place. She closes her eyes, but she can still feel it all around her, choking her, drowning her. She flails her arms, trying to swim for the surface, but there is no surface. She's suspended, unable to move as the blood consumes her.

Imari woke with a scream, sucking in great gasps of air. She opened her eyes, expecting to see red, but instead, there was only a small, cozy room. A fire burned in the hearth and there was a mat beside her—a mat with a person on it, pushing themselves up from a huddled position.

"Imari, what happened?" Kaede, tired and with messy hair, but clearly recognizable. She looked as though she hadn't slept in weeks. "Are you all right? I heard you scream."

Imari breathed heavily, unsure what to say. Dimly, she remembered Kaede sitting by her bedside, but then earlier memories came rushing back. They broke over her like the waves of the horrible red ocean, and she recoiled to the other side of the bed, trying to put as much space between herself and Kaede as possible.

"Don't touch me," she said as Kaede reached out a hand, trying to caress her shoulder. "Don't look at me. I don't want you to."

Kaede withdrew her hand, although she looked hurt. "Imari, it's okay," she murmured in a soothing voice. "I think you had a nightmare."

Tears welled in Imari's eyes. The soldiers she had killed were all too real. She remembered now. She could recall in vivid detail everything that had happened. What she didn't understand was how Kaede could bear to look upon her with anything but disgust.

"Why are you here?" she asked, clutching the covers up to her chin. "Why are you looking at me like that?" Kaede's eyes were full of tender concern, and it made Imari want to claw out of her own treacherous skin.

"Because I love you. Because you asked me to stay. Imari, I'm so sorry I left you at Hongshan. I never should have—"

"No." Imari held up her hand, dropping the covers and turning away. "Don't. Don't tell me how this is your fault to make me feel better. I don't deserve it."

"But—"

"I murdered people, Kaede!" Tears leaked from her eyes without warning, and she shuddered through several shaking sobs before she could speak again. "How many?" she asked past the stone in her throat. "How many samurai did I kill?"

Kaede didn't answer.

Imari whirled to face her again, glaring at her. "How many? Tell me."

Kaede still hesitated.

"Tell me!"

Kaede's lower lip trembled. "Fourteen."

Fourteen. Fourteen lives snuffed out. Fourteen soldiers who had fallen beneath her sword. Imari's stomach churned with disgust. She leapt up from the bed, hauling Kaede up and shoving her backwards.

"Get out," she said, pushing frantically at Kaede's shoulders.

Kaede tried to get her footing, but desperation and surprise lent Imari strength. She managed to force Kaede back toward the screen door, shoving her the whole way.

"Imari, wait—"

"Out," Imari said. "I don't want you to look at me. I need…"

She needed to be alone. Nothing else made sense, but she knew that for certain. She needed to be alone.

"Imari—"

With a final surge of strength, Imari shoved Kaede out through the door and yanked it shut. Kaede continued protesting from beyond the screen, but her voice was awash in Imari's ears. She collapsed to her knees on the cold stone floor, burying her face in her arms and weeping. She was broken, and she couldn't bear Kaede's useless attempts at fixing her. At pretending she would be all right. There would be no fixing this. Fourteen samurai were dead because of her. That couldn't be undone.

Chapter Twenty-Three

ONE WEEK PASSED. SEVEN days of grief. Seven days of solitude. Imari spent them alone, refusing to see anyone. Always, her heart longed for kaede, but always, her memories prevented her from calling out. With Kyuubi's fog lifted, she could recall every moment of what she had done in vivid detail.

She remembered the faces of the men she had killed. She remembered the way fresh blood looked on ancient stone and new snow. She remembered how it felt to pull her sword out through someone's stomach, how it felt to draw someone else's blood-soaked kote over her own forearm. She couldn't look at her remaining hand. When she closed her eyes, the sounds were horrible. Screaming, pleading, the last rattling exhale of a soldier breathing his last. Fourteen men, they whispered outside her door. She had killed fourteen men.

She refused to remove Wujian from its scabbard and kept it hidden as far across the room as possible. Just one week before, she had been excited and thrilled to use it. Now, she couldn't bear to touch it, even to strike herself down and end her shame.

Every day at dawn, Kaede came to her door. Always, she stayed and talked, spending hours speaking to the blank screen even when Imari refused to respond.

"It isn't your fault," she said. "Kyuubi was controlling you."

She didn't understand. She hadn't taken fourteen lives.

Imari always waited for Kaede to leave without answering, but later, when she opened the door, she would find a bowl of food and the pink and white blossoms of freshly picked magnolia flowers. They were one of the only buds to bloom in snow. Imari kept them on the table and stared at them when Kaede wasn't there. *How can she bear to be around me? Why does she visit? Why does she still speak to me?*

The last thing a murderer deserved was sympathy. Sometimes, others came. Takeshi and Kenta had tried to gain entrance as well, but she hadn't responded to them either. Even Hayate had come by once, to deliver a soft apology and tell her the Empress was coming to

Kousetsu herself—leaving the Imperial City for the first time in ten years. Imari was grateful. Hopefully, her sentencing and execution would be swift.

Then there were the nights. She barely slept, and when she did, the dreams frightened her. Always, the ocean of blood threatened to consume her. Sometimes the bodies of the dead swam toward her, flailing severed limbs, reaching out to her for help. But she couldn't help them. She couldn't even help herself. Sometimes, she woke to see Kaede's head peeking through the door. She never broached the unspoken boundary and entered the room, but Imari knew Kaede checked on her briefly every night, just to make sure she was still breathing.

On the eighth day things changed. That was the day when, while she rested on her mat and stared listlessly up at the ceiling, Kaede came once more to her door.

"Imari, you need to let me in."

As usual, Imari remained silent. She didn't move from her place on the mat.

"Please. It's important."

At the sound of Kaede's voice, she finally stirred. Guilty as she felt, she hungered for it. She padded over to the screen door and dropped to her knees, closing her eyes and resting her cheek against it to listen.

"Imari, this self-imprisonment isn't doing anyone any good. The Empress will arrive soon, and you need to be ready to talk to her. I know you're listening. I hear you breathing."

Neither of them spoke, but Imari could picture Kaede's face clearly. Even under the threat of the Empress's arrival, Kaede's voice wasn't harsh, rather full of concern, and somehow, that was much worse. Tears of shame welled in Imari's eyes, dripping down her cheeks.

"I don't want to hurt you. I don't want to push past your boundaries. But I need to see you, to make sure you're all right. I'm going to come in, okay? Please, say yes."

Imari's lips trembled. Part of her wanted to, but another equal part fought violently against the thought. Despite the care Kaede had shown for her over the past week, Imari was terrified of finding hatred deep within her eyes.

Still, this couldn't continue. Her guilt and grief accomplished nothing. It certainly wouldn't bring back the dead. It was time to end this. She owed Kaede a goodbye, at least.

"Yes," she whispered, lifting her cheek from the door.

Kaede pulled the screen aside a moment later. She didn't step inside, but instead offered her hand. "Here. Let me help you up?"

Imari swiped at her own face and remained where she was. She didn't look up until Kaede's warm fingers laced with hers, in a touch so tender she nearly cried all over again.

"Why are you here?" Imari asked, blinking rapidly. Kaede peered down at her with such sadness Imari could hardly stand it. "Why are you still here, after I haven't spoken to you in a week other than to tell you to leave?"

"Isn't it obvious?" Kaede drew her up, placing an arm beneath her elbow to steady her. Imari was grateful, her legs felt weak. "I've told you every day. This wasn't your fault. I want to help."

Imari allowed Kaede to lead her back over to the mat. Kaede didn't sit beside her, moving to shut the screen. Part of Imari ached to lose the contact of Kaede's hand, but another part felt relieved. "The only reason I haven't killed myself is because I hoped the families of the soldiers I murdered might take some comfort in my execution. I don't deserve to regain my honor that way."

"Please, don't talk like that." Kaede returned to the mat, sitting down beside her. They didn't touch, but Imari could feel her presence, her warmth. "You haven't brought dishonor on yourself, and I'm sure the Empress isn't going to execute you. Kyuubi—"

"Kyuubi didn't wield my sword." Imari glanced over to the table, where her jian rested within its scabbard. Several times, she had been tempted to take matters into her own hands, but she couldn't bear to draw the blade again.

"Kyuubi wielded your arm, which held your sword. That's enough."

Imari sighed, staring down into her lap. "No, it isn't. It won't bring back the people. There's nothing I can do to fix it."

Warm fingers wrapped around Imari's shoulders, gently turning her sideways until she and Kaede faced each other. "The real Imari wouldn't stop trying," Kaede said, staring straight into her eyes.

Imari faltered. "What?"

"I said, the real Imari wouldn't stop trying to fix it," Kaede repeated, louder and firmer. "She never stopped trying, no matter what. She spent years planning a journey to find Kurogane, even though anyone else would have said she was crazy. She spent two months pestering Wen Ling every single day so she could get a new hand. Every time she lost a sparring match, she studied what went wrong and came back twice as good." Kaede's voice broke, and Imari realized she had started crying, too. "The real Imari survived after a boulder fell on top of her. The real Imari saw through Kyuubi's lies. And the real Imari wouldn't give up now either. She wouldn't talk about killing herself. She would keep trying. You would keep trying."

There was silence for a long time, with Kaede's hands on her shoulders and Kaede's eyes leaking tears. At last, Imari let out a soft, breathy laugh. "You look ugly when you cry," she rasped.

Kaede laughed as well, pulling one of her hands back to wipe at her face. "Yes, well, so do you."

They both hugged each other tight, and in the warmth of Kaede's arms, Imari finally felt as though she could breathe again. Something broke inside her, and all the pain building up in her chest came pouring out. She buried her face in Kaede's shoulder, but she didn't cry anymore. Instead, she inhaled deeply. "So, what do I do?" she muttered against Kaede's neck. "How do I keep trying?"

"It doesn't matter, as long as you do," Kaede murmured into her hair. "It's the trying that counts. But I would start by telling the Empress what happened. Someone needs to stop Kyuubi. She's going to do this again, you know. Suanni told us. This is all a big game to her."

Once more, Imari felt the weight of responsibility settle over her shoulders, but this time, the sense of purpose gave her a flood of strength. "Not someone. Me. Us. We're going to find her and make sure this doesn't happen to anyone else." She shuddered at the memory of the mist, huddling tighter into Kaede's arms. "It's evil, Kaede. The way she gets in your mind. She uses thoughts that are already there and twists them until the opposite make sense. There were these flashes when I realized I was going against my code, but all I could do was watch myself. I was so certain I was doing the right thing." She lifted her head, gazing into Kaede's eyes once more. "You're right. I won't let that happen to anyone else. I can't."

"I know," Kaede said, tucking a crooked finger beneath the point of her chin. "And that's why I love you."

Imari wasn't certain who kissed who, but the moment her lips met Kaede's, they both melted into it. Kaede's mouth was warm and welcoming on hers, and Kaede's fingers felt soft and comforting against her face. Part of her still didn't think she deserved it, but relief overwhelmed her doubts. Kaede still loved her. Kaede didn't hate her. And most important of all, Kaede believed she still had a purpose. Stop Kyuubi. Protect others. Look to the future.

Maybe I can do that, Imari thought. The kiss broke so they could both breathe, and Imari whispered, "Maybe."

"What?" Kaede asked. "Maybe you love me too?"

"No, not that." Imari caressed Kaede's shoulder, massaging it and running her thumb back and forth along Kaede's collarbone. She tried to explain, but words failed her. Instead, she kissed Kaede again, even deeper than before.

Imari wasn't sure how long the two of them stayed there trading kisses. Sometimes, they were light pecks of reassurance. Sometimes they lingered, with a certain slow sureness. But, gradually, they became more heated. It wasn't at all what Imari was expecting, but she welcomed the fire that kindled deep in her belly as Kaede's palm cupped her hip. It was an emotion other than guilt, and she greeted it with open arms.

She brought her hand to Kaede's obi, untying it hesitantly, waiting to be stopped. But Kaede didn't stop her. Kaede smiled instead, a smile full of encouragement and love, and it was like rays of sunlight peeking through the gray wall of clouds after a storm. "I don't know how you can still look at me like that, but I'm grateful. I'm so grateful."

Kaede picked up where Imari had left off, unfastening her obi the rest of the way and unfolding her kimono layer by layer. "So am I." She opened the front, revealing her juban underneath. "I'm grateful I have my Imari back."

"I can't promise she'll stay," Imari said. "These feelings aren't going to go away."

"No, but neither will your hope. Not while I'm around to remind you."

They tipped onto the mat together with Kaede on top. The weight was comforting and Imari wrapped her arms around Kaede's torso, holding her close. Kaede began undoing Imari's yukata. "Is this all right? Are you sure?"

Imari kissed her again. "Yes," she said against Kaede's cheek. "I've missed you."

"Me too." At last, Kaede removed her own juban and fundoshi, leaving Imari to stare at her without any barriers. Imari drank in the sight, the light muscles of Kaede's arms, the tight brown caps of her nipples, the smooth plane of her stomach, and the slight flare of her hips. Her hand shook as she brought it to Kaede's face once more, cupping it sweetly before drawing it slowly down along Kaede's neck.

It wound like a serpent down along Kaede's body, pausing in every dip and valley. She cupped Kaede's breast, thumbing the tip until it was stiff and puckered. Kaede sighed, a sweet sound that soothed Imari more than anything else this past week. Kaede didn't hate her. Kaede didn't think she was a monster. Kaede was responding to her. Kaede had been telling her these things for a week, but it was only now, while Kaede hovered above her and accepting her touch, that she believed it.

Imari moved to Kaede's other breast, repeating the same motions, tugging gently at the brown tip until it hardened. Kaede's panting came faster, and she tilted her head back, exposing her neck. The gesture of implicit trust nearly made Imari cry all over again. Instead, she latched on to Kaede's neck and sucked, not hard, but enough to let Kaede feel the warmth of her lips and tongue. Kaede's hips gave a soft pump, and Imari gasped as their bodies pressed closer together.

Kaede hardened for her. The firmness pressed into Imari's thigh, proof that Kaede was all right with this. Imari drank in the feeling of being wanted. She knew she didn't deserve it, but she let it break over her anyway, allowing it to wash away her tears and her guilt. If Kaede still thought she could be a good person, if Kaede saw something in her worth saving, then maybe there was.

She brought her hand down Kaede's front, leaving her breast and preparing to cup between her legs. Before she could, Kaede caught her wrist, gently urging her to stop. "In another minute," she murmured, gazing into Imari's eyes. "Please, let me touch you first."

Imari tried to protest. If anyone deserved pleasure, it was Kaede for her unwavering loyalty and patience. But there was something in Kaede's eyes, a pleading Imari couldn't ignore. Her broken heart longed for nothing more than Kaede's touch, Kaede's affection, Kaede's love. She needed it, craved it, even though she still questioned whether she was worthy of it.

"Yes." She relaxed, lying on her back and lowering both arms to her sides. Then she waited, trembling and hopeful all at once.

"Thank you." Kaede bent down, pressing one last soft kiss to Imari's lips. "No matter what you think right now, you deserve this."

Imari nodded. She didn't agree, not yet, but she gave her permission anyway. Selfishly, she wanted the tenderness and release Kaede offered.

Kaede's mouth worshiped her body, starting at the crook of her neck and sucking for long minutes as her hands roamed across Imari's chest. They circled around and around her nipples, never quite touching, only to spread out like wings and caress her arms and sides instead. Kaede's warm tongue dragged lower. It followed Imari's collarbone, kissed out to the corner of her shoulder before going back the opposite way.

The kisses finally reached her breasts and Imari's hips rocked instinctively against Kaede's stomach. She couldn't help it, a wordless plea for more. Kaede's hands circled her hips, pinning them ever so carefully to the bed as her mouth wrapped around a stiff peak and sucked. Imari whimpered as the heat finally closed around her. Kaede's mouth was the most beautiful kind of torture, and the silky rasp of her tongue was maddening. She closed her eyes, unable to watch, but she knew Kaede was looking up at her. The gaze burned straight through her.

She lifted her hand from the bed and ran it through Kaede's hair, not pushing, but tangling through the strands and clinging to them in desperation. She felt as though she were on the edge of a cliff, balancing for dear life, afraid and exhilarated at the thought of falling.

At last, Kaede released her nipple, only to kiss her way across to the other. "I love you," she murmured, her warm breath skimming over it before she sealed her lips around the second bud as well. She shifted further down and ran her hands along Imari's thighs, gently coaxing them open.

Imari stiffened. The anticipation had her throbbing, but there was still a lingering shadow over her heart as Kaede's fingers sought out her wetness. When she looked down, Kaede's face was so full of love and forgiveness it almost hurt to look, like staring directly into the sun.

"Imari." She opened her eyes to see Kaede staring down at her. "Stay with me, Imari. Please? I want you here with me, not in your head."

With another slow breath, Imari forced herself to relax. She spread her legs even further, giving Kaede's hand more room to move between them. Kaede's mouth returned to her breast at the same moment Kaede's fingers found her clit. The two sensations set Imari shivering, and she cried out, clutching harder at Kaede's hair. She felt the vibration of a moan against her chest, and she loosened the grip only for Kaede to pull away and whisper, "No. It's okay. I like it."

Imari settled for something in between, not as hard as before, but not soft either. Kaede groaned in approval, and her mouth began a steady trail downward. Not until Kaede's mouth started circling kisses around her navel did the pieces come together. She gasped, torn once more between guilt and longing, but Kaede hushed her worried little noises with a scattering of soft kisses across her stomach. "I want to taste you, Imari. Is that okay?"

Imari shivered. During their one night together, she and Kaede had been so overwhelmed with what their hands could do that they hadn't moved on to the next step. Kaede had never done this for her before—had never done it at all—and the fact that she was offering made Imari feel wonderful. But the feeling that she didn't deserve it rose within her, too.

She shoved that feeling back down with all her remaining strength. "Yes," she murmured, caressing Kaede's cheek. "Yes, it's okay."

But when Kaede's lips trailed down, it was better than okay. Imari put her pain aside, trying to focus on pleasure. She gave a slight jolt as Kaede ducked beneath her knees, then gasped as warmth crept up along her inner thigh, following one of the slick trails there. She dripped with anticipation, inner walls fluttering and heart hammering at full speed.

Imari waited, but nothing happened. Kaede simply stared, a look of awe on her face. "Imari, you're so beautiful."

Kaede had said those words before, but never so close that Imari could feel them whispered against her skin. She had never been ashamed of her body, but she flushed hot as Kaede's wide eyes took her in. With her legs parted and Kaede settled between them, she was completely exposed and vulnerable.

"You just say these things," she laughed, blinking away a fresh round of tears.

"I mean them. Let me show you."

Kaede didn't linger. Moments later, Imari felt the soft, curious tip of a tongue gliding against her. It was tentative at first, but smooth and warm enough to make her shiver. Kaede looked up at her, waiting for guidance or encouragement or both, and Imari gave a soft tug of approval on her hair. "It feels good. Keep going."

A look of determination crossed Kaede's face. "I'll do better than good." She lowered her head again, and this time, Kaede's lips had wrapped around her clit, sucking the sensitive bud free of its thin hood. Imari's hips gave a short jerk.

The stimulation was almost too direct, but her body adjusted. She raked at Kaede's scalp to indicate that she should keep going, drawing in shaking breaths as Kaede's tongue circled her tip. The motions were soft and slow at first, experimental, but Imari managed to show Kaede the right pressure and speed by rocking her hips and moaning when she got it right.

They settled into a rhythm together. The patterns Kaede painted grew more complex as she started to experiment. Occasionally she broke away from the throbbing point of Imari's clit to cover the rest of her in flat, broad strokes—usually when Imari's whimpers grew a little too loud. When Kaede dipped down to taste her entrance, Imari nearly bucked off the mat. The swirl of Kaede's tongue set her aflame, and she wanted to burn.

As Kaede alternated between sucking her and pushing gently at her opening, Imari's vision began to blur. Her muscles clenched with want, and an aching emptiness grew inside her. Kaede's mouth felt wonderful sealed so tight around her, pulling and then relaxing, coaxing the pressure inside of her to build and build. But it wasn't enough. She needed to be stretched, to be filled, to feel the slight edge of pain that came with penetration. Kaede's tongue wasn't firm enough to give the pressure she needed.

"Kaede," she groaned, letting go of Kaede's head and grasping blindly below. "Your hand." Kaede's hand reached up to clutch hers, and at first, Imari could do nothing but squeeze it. Finally, she managed to show what she wanted. She brought Kaede's fingers between their bodies, forcing Kaede to pull her head back.

Kaede looked up in surprise, her chin glistening with wetness, but then a haze came over her eyes as Imari finally guided her fingers to the right place. "Ancestors, Imari, you're so warm." Her fingers started moving, and Imari cried out as they pushed deeper. Kaede had hooked against the sensitive spot along her front wall.

Imari tried to speak, to beg Kaede to keep going, but words failed her. She could only continue rocking her hips into Kaede's palm and make pleading little noises. Luckily, Kaede understood. She brought her mouth back to Imari's clit, trapping the stiff point and lashing it with firm strokes of her tongue.

As Kaede's fingers started to pump, Imari melted. It was all too much—the deep thrusts, the silky glide of Kaede's tongue, the heavy rippling in her belly. She felt herself rushing toward a peak she wasn't prepared for. Tears welled in her eyes, but she let them slide down the sides of her cheeks without wiping them away. She couldn't bear to let go of Kaede's head. She clutched it even tighter to her, barely able to breathe.

Despite the harsh grip, Kaede released her for a moment to the cool air, scattering a few more kisses around the shaft of her clit. "It's okay, Imari. You deserve this."

Imari still didn't believe it, but the conviction in Kaede's voice was enough. The tight knot in her chest loosened at last and a scream tore from her throat. She arched, sobbing with each shudder that rolled through her. Kaede's tongue was liquid fire and her fingers drew an ocean out. She pulsed sticky and hot against Kaede's cupped hand until her thighs and the lower half of Kaede's face were covered in shining ribbons of slickness.

She let out a trembling sigh, dropping her hand from Kaede's head and releasing her tangle of hair, but the steady sucking didn't stop. Kaede lightened up the pressure a little but kept teasing her with feather-light licks. Before Imari's inner walls could even stop twitching, Kaede's fingers started moving within her again, driving back into the same full, pounding spot as before.

Imari had expected Kaede to pull away, grinning and dripping with the proof of her success, but she hadn't been prepared for this. She was even more sensitized the second time around, and her next release swelled within her even faster than the first, crashing right on its heels. She shivered and trembled and came in another spill of slippery heat, choking out Kaede's name with the last of her air.

She wasn't sure how long it lasted. By the time the string of orgasms ended, Imari felt like the edges of a guttering candle, wavering in and out of existence. Her body floated on a cloud of bliss and the only solid, real thing she could feel were Kaede's comforting arms around her waist. Some point during her last peak, Kaede's fingers had slipped out of her.

"Was that okay?" Kaede asked, resting her sticky cheek against Imari's abdomen and gazing up at her. "I mean, I hope you—"

Summoning what was left of her strength, Imari flipped them over, claiming Kaede's former position on top. She covered Kaede's cheeks with kisses, laughing with relief in between. "You're wonderful," she whispered, pressing her lips to every inch of Kaede's face, not caring when she tasted herself. "I don't know what I did to deserve you, but I'm glad to have you."

"You have me," Kaede said with a soft laugh. "You'll always have me, no matter what."

That was something Imari could definitely believe. If Kaede hadn't left her by now, she couldn't imagine anything that would drive her away. "What about you?" she asked, letting her nose brush against Kaede's. "Is there something you need?"

A soft stirring against her hip answered that question. After a brief glance into Kaede's eyes to make sure it was all right, Imari took Kaede in her hand, gasping a little at the pounding she could feel in her palm.

"You don't have to," Kaede said. "This was supposed to be about making you feel loved." But her eyes said something different, her tone uncertain.

"I know I don't have to," Imari breathed, placing another soft kiss against Kaede's lips. Her taste was even stronger there, and she let her tongue swipe along them to gather more salt. "I want to." She began stroking her fist up and down, coaxing a well of warmth from Kaede's tip.

Kaede's body tensed and she let out a sharp groan of surprise. "Imari."

Imari began kissing her way down Kaede's neck, relishing in the taste of sweat clinging to her skin. She wanted more—wanted to discover how Kaede tasted all over. The thought had entered her mind before, but there simply hadn't been time back at Hongshan. Now, she didn't want to wait any longer.

"Let me return the favor," she muttered into Kaede's collarbone. "Please?"

A flash of worry passed across Kaede's face, but it didn't last long before settling into loving trust. She gave Imari a soft smile. "I'd do anything for you, Imari. I trust you."

The words hit home harder than Imari expected. The fact that Kaede trusted her with this, even after everything she had done. It was a gift she couldn't refuse. Slowly, she kissed her way down Kaede's body, making sure to linger in all the sweet spots. She played with the points of Kaede's nipples, taking them in her mouth and holding them there until Kaede's hips started to quiver. Only then did she use her tongue and the edges of her teeth, and it wasn't until Kaede threaded a hand through her hair and pushed her down that she moved on.

Imari spent ages kissing along Kaede's stomach, an eternity trailing ticklish patterns between Kaede's hips. Meanwhile, she kept her hand moving, keeping Kaede close to the edge without pushing her over.

Kaede finally let out a rasping, "Please." Imari's resolve broke. She wanted more of those sounds. She wanted every scrap of pleasure she could draw from Kaede's body. She closed the final gap, placing her open lips against Kaede at last.

Even that small gesture was enough to make Kaede cry out. The fingers in Imari's hair tightened, and a wave of salt washed over her open mouth, spreading along her tongue. Kaede tasted heavy and dark, but not overpowering, and Imari found herself craving more. She stroked her tongue along Kaede's tip, gathering up the next several pulses before they could escape.

Kaede let out a choked sound, and her abdominal muscles flexed. Her lips moved in soundless shapes. She was close already, and Imari couldn't quite comprehend that she was the cause. Kaede was looking upon her as a lover, not a monster. For the first time since the cave, Imari felt close to human again. Imari took Kaede's head into her mouth, wrapping her lips around it and squeezing beneath with her hand.

It was enough. Kaede cried out Imari's name, pouring warmth into the back of her mouth. Kaede's release came in rhythmic pulses, and Imari opened her throat without pulling back. When she swallowed, Kaede let out a little wail. Her hands remained buried in Imari's hair until she emptied herself with a few more weak pulses, twitching against Imari's' tongue.

By the time Kaede finished, her hair clung to her damp face and her eyes were glazed over with a film of happy exhaustion. "Wow," she said, laughing. "Imari."

Imari released Kaede from her mouth with one last kiss, slowly licking up a stream of wetness that had escaped. "Was it what you expected?" she asked, stroking one of Kaede's thighs with her palm.

"Better," Kaede admitted. "I wasn't sure I'd like it...someone's mouth on me, I mean. It's complicated. But not when it's you." She broke out into a grin. "I was thinking about how beautiful you are. How good you made me feel."

Imari smiled. "Are you saying I filled you with so much happiness that you forgot about everything else for a little while? Because that's what you did for me. Thank you, Kaede. I don't know what I would do without you."

"You don't have to find out," Kaede said, taking Imari into her arms. "You're stuck with me. We'll get through this together."

Chapter Twenty-Four

"NO, NO." SETSUNA'S VOICE was a low, murmuring moan, so soft hayate might have missed it if he hadn't been listening. He dipped the cloth into the bowl of cool water beside Setsuna's bed, wetting it and draping it across her forehead.

For the past week, it had been the same. Sometimes Setsuna slept peacefully, but never for long. Fearful fits interrupted her nights, and when she did wake, she remained unresponsive, lost somewhere in her own head. It was all Hayate could do to get her to eat and drink.

He blamed himself each time her nightmares came, and he sat with her through most of them, with Kaze hovering nearby to protect them both. Kyuubi had cursed Setsuna, but he had destroyed the kanzashi she wore in her hair. Perhaps if he hadn't been so quick to get rid of it, she might not be in such an awful state.

"No!" Setsuna shouted, louder this time, and Hayate moved the bowl aside. He knew what was coming next.

"It's me, Mother," he whispered, stroking her damp hair back from her face. His touch didn't soothe the lines of pain around her eyes. "It's Hayate. You're safe here. I promise."

"No, don't—there are others. Friend? Why would you do this? Why?"

Hayate removed the cloth and waited, nothing to do but ride through it. As soon as he pulled his hand back, Setsuna began to thrash. She tossed and turned on the futon, clawing at the covers and flinging her head from side to side. It was such a violent motion it had shocked Hayate the first time he'd seen it, but he knew better than to interfere. Holding Setsuna down would only make it worse.

"No! I'm not the only one! The others. Warn the others. She's whispering." Tears leaked from Setsuna's closed eyes and she screamed.

Then, as suddenly as it started, her fit stopped. She relaxed back onto the bed, her eyes still closed, her neck and chest covered in fresh sweat. Hayate hurried to wipe it away, whispering the whole time. "It's okay now, Mother. It's over. It won't be like this forever. It's going to get better."

But some part of him doubted that. He suspected the worst—that Kyuubi still had some hold over Setsuna. She had owned that pearl for several years, plenty of time for Kyuubi to take root inside her head.

A soft knock at the door startled Hayate. He nearly upset the bowl as he hurried to stand, unwilling to leave Setsuna behind but equally unwilling to have someone intrude. He glanced over to the corner of the room, where Kaze was curled up on a sleeping mat, but the wolf gave a silent nod. Whoever had arrived was a friend.

"Wait a moment," he called out, lighting one of the lanterns on the table. He had kept the room dim for Setsuna's sake. "I'm coming."

Hayate opened the door to see a familiar face. Kenta stood out in the shadowy hallway, holding a lantern of his own in one hand and a bowl of food in the other. He bowed his head before speaking. "Good evening, Yukimura-dono. I'm sorry to interrupt, but I thought I'd bring you some food. I didn't see you at dinner."

After a moment's hesitation, Hayate stood aside, allowing Kenta into the room. "Thanks, Hibana-san," he said, shutting the screen door.

Kenta set the bowl on the table along with his lantern. He caught sight of Kaze in the corner of the room and hurried over, reaching out to scratch his ears. "You might not want to. . ." Hayate began, but to his surprise, Kaze didn't protest. His tail thumped happily on the ground instead.

"Guess a friend of Rin's is a friend of yours too, huh?" Kenta asked.

"A friend of Hayate's is a friend of mine too," Kaze said. "Thank you for looking after him. He doesn't take the time to eat like he should."

"We'll just have to remind him."

With a huff of approval, Kaze settled his chin back on his paws and closed his eyes. Once more, Hayate was surprised. Apparently, Kaze was entrusting his care to Kenta, at least for a couple of minutes.

Kenta turned, aiming a nervous glance toward the bed, and his smile vanished. "So, Yukimura-dono, how is Set...your mother?"

Hayate sighed. "The same, I'm afraid. The healers say it's all in her head."

"You mean Kyuubi's in her head," Kenta muttered. However, he brightened a moment later. "I have good news for you, though. Imari's finally letting people into her room or, well, she let Kaede in. I went to see if Kaede wanted some food too, but she wasn't there."

"But how do you know she was in Imari's room?"

A flush crept across Kenta's face. "Um...I heard them talking, I guess. Yes. Talking." He paused awkwardly. "Anyway, things seem to be better. Maybe that means Setsuna will get better too?"

"Do you want to sit down?" Hayate asked, gesturing at one of the mats on the other side of the table. "I mean, I know you don't have any food."

"It's okay." Kenta took one of the mats while Hayate took the other, making sure to stay as near the bed as possible.

"I don't know if Kaede told you much about my mother," Hayate said after a while, ignoring the bowl of rice in front of him. "She was—she is a good woman. She adopted me as her heir after someone found me in the forest. She didn't need to. I could have been a peasant's child for all she knew, but she never married, and I just turned up."

"She could've named someone else as her heir," Kenta pointed out. "She didn't have to have a child. I guess that means you were really wanted, huh?"

Hayate smiled. "I suppose so, although then one of the distant relatives would have taken over. But my childhood with her was a happy one. It's only in the past few years that things have been…strained."

"Are you talking about you and Yukimura-sama, or you and Kaede?"

"Both," Hayate confessed. "They bonded after Kaede came to Yukimura for training, and I felt left out, I suppose. Looking back, it seems foolish, especially now that I know her actions weren't all her own."

"I'm sure your mother wouldn't have wanted you to feel left out," Kenta said softly. "She loves you. She must have, since you're taking such good care of her now."

"I'm not, really," Hayate said, staring down at his untouched food. Even the warm smell wasn't enough to stir his appetite. "I try, but I wish I could do more. I don't think she'll get better until Kyuubi is dealt with." He looked back over to the bed, where Setsuna was lying peacefully for the time being. "She keeps calling out in her sleep. Something about 'others.' She claims she's 'not the only one.'"

Kenta's brows rose. "What do you think she means?"

"I'm not sure, but I'm afraid. What if the 'others' she speaks of are the other shogun? If Kyuubi could do this to someone as good and strong-willed as Setsuna, there's no telling who else she could influence."

"I see what you mean," Kenta said. He leaned forward, his brow furrowed with concern. "What are you going to do?"

"Tell the Empress when she arrives," Hayate said. "If I'm being crazy, I'm sure she'll tell me."

Kenta's eyes lit up with interest. "You speak as if you've met her before."

"Once, long ago. Kaede and I both did. Setsuna took us to pay our respects on one of her journeys to Asahina. The Empress happened to be there at the time, attending the end of a session. She was only a child then...more of a child than she is now, I mean. I suppose they wanted her to observe before she officially took her father's place on the Kikyo throne. Empress Tomoyo hasn't left the imperial capital since that visit." Hayate closed his eyes again. "I never should have been jealous of Kaede, and I should have realized something was wrong with Setsuna sooner. Her behavior was so out of character."

"It's not your fault," Kenta said. "Sometimes we get a blind spot when it comes to people we love that much."

Hayate took a deep breath. "Yes, I suppose you're right. Thank you, Hibana-san. I feel a little better. You didn't have to come here."

"It's no trouble at all," Kenta said. "But you still have to eat, Yukimura-dono. I insist! How about while you do, I tell you about what Kaede's been up to since she left Yukimura? It's quite an adventure, even the parts where you weren't chasing after us."

***

Another week passed, during which Kaede noticed steady improvements in Imari's behavior. Since the night they had spent in bed together, Imari seemed more willing to accept comfort. She still woke in the middle of the night screaming, and she still stared pensively out through the windows of her room, but there was no more talk of killing herself.

She didn't laugh or joke, but she did give occasional smiles—when Kaede kissed her, when Takeshi brought her a book from Yukimura's expansive library, when Kenta told her a story to occupy her mind. And she was willing to accept touch, too. When Kaede placed a hand on Imari's shoulder, she rarely flinched away.

That was why, when there was a knock on the screen door of Imari's room early one morning, Kaede was pleased to see that her lover didn't start. They had been cuddled up on the futon reading a book together—or rather, Kaede had been reading and Imari had been lost in a light doze. Instead of tensing or shouting, Imari simply opened her eyes, blinking to clear them.

"Who is it?" she asked in a voice thick with sleep.

Near their feet, Rin stirred. She sniffed the air, but the fur on her back didn't bristle with alarm. "Just Takeshi. You'd best go and see what he wants. His breathing is unsettled."

Gently, Kaede disentangled herself from Imari's arms. She tucked Imari in, setting the book within reach in case she wanted it. "Wait here."

Imari looked disappointed at the prospect of her getting up, but she didn't say anything. While she rubbed at her eyes and tried to get her bearings, Kaede slipped on the bath slippers she had abandoned at the side of the bed and straightened the edges of her yukata, heading toward the door. Behind her, she could hear the rustling of sheets. To her surprise, Rin had chosen to remain on the bed beside Imari.

When Kaede pulled back the screen, she did indeed find Takeshi waiting outside, but he wasn't carrying a plate of breakfast as usual. "What is it?" Kaede asked, noting the worried look on his face. His usual frown had returned, one she had not seen in a while. "Imari's just waking up. Last night was a rough one. I decided to let her sleep in a bit."

"I'm afraid she can't," Takeshi said. "The Empress has arrived with her courtiers and a full regiment of imperial guards. After speaking to Hayate about the situation, she's asking to see both of you."

Kaede's stomach clenched. She knew that a conversation with the Empress was inevitable—Imari needed a chance to explain her actions, and they needed to offer a warning about Kyuubi. Still, she didn't want to make Imari feel as though she were on trial. No one else blamed her, but that didn't matter. Imari already blamed herself more than enough.

"I'm not sure she's ready," she whispered, glancing back over her shoulder. Instead of reading the book or falling back asleep, Imari was sitting up beside Rin, clearly waiting to see what was going on in the hallway.

Takeshi sighed. "No one can refuse the Empress. Better to get it over with, don't you think? That's one less worry she has to carry."

"You said both of us," Kaede murmured. "Does that mean I can go with her? She won't interview us separately?"

"I see no reason why not," Takeshi said. "You have Hayate and Suanni on your side, too. Trust me, this won't be so bad."

"Suanni?" Imari asked. "Are they back?"

"Yes," Takeshi said. He turned to Imari and offered a bow. "They're with members of the court. I caught a glimpse of them with Bo in a fine kimono instead of that ratty brown hood they always wear. I don't know if the Empress knows they're a dragon, though."

"Just follow their lead," Rin said. "Don't bring it up unless they do."

"Good idea, but we should hurry," Takeshi explained. "Hayate's already waiting for us. He's acting in place of Setsuna, since she's still out of it."

Kaede hung her head. She felt guilty for not paying more attention to her beloved aunt, especially since she knew Setsuna wasn't responsible for her actions. But keeping Imari stable had required almost all her attention, even with Rin's help. She had trusted Hayate to keep an eye out for Setsuna in her stead, since he was her adopted son.

"I'll make sure the two of us get ready as fast as possible. Thank you, Takeshi." With a bow of farewell, she closed the screen again.

"How long do we have?" Imari asked, rising from the bed. She seemed stiff, resigned, with most of the warmth gone from her eyes.

Kaede reached out to comfort her. She took Imari in her arms, cradling her as she answered. "Not long. The Empress wants to see us as soon as possible."

"To deal with me, of course," Imari said, her voice tinged with bitterness.

Kaede recognized it as self-hatred. "There's nothing to deal with. Hayate and Suanni have already spoken up on your behalf. Apparently, Suanni is one of the Empress's advisers."

"And what about the fact that I killed fourteen samurai?" Imari asked, beginning to shake. "Doesn't that matter?"

Kaede held her tighter. "It matters, but that doesn't mean you're to blame."

Imari was silent for a long time. At last, with a soft kiss to Kaede's lips, she left the hug and straightened her shoulders. "All right. Thank you, Kaede. For everything. No matter what happens, I wanted to…I want you to know." She hesitated, as if she couldn't find the words.

Kaede ran her knuckles along the curve of Imari's cheek until the gesture earned a smile. "I know. I love you, too. Want me to help you get dressed?"

"Please. I don't have the heart for fashion right now. I trust you to make me look…"

"Presentable?" Kaede finished for her.

"I was going to say, 'not like a crazy murderer,' but yes.

Presentable."

Black as the joke was, Kaede took it as a good sign. It was the first time Imari had said anything even slightly humorous since the cave. "Well, I think we have some mon of yours that aren't covered in blood," she said, squeezing Imari's hand. "Hold on. Let me go through your pack."

Once Rin had made a graceful exit into the hallway, it didn't take them as long to dress as Kaede expected. She was able to clean up and put on several layers of formal clothes without much difficulty before suspending her own efforts to help Imari.

"Three hands are better than one, I suppose," Imari mumbled as Kaede finished fastening her obi behind her. "I never really appreciated the servants back home until I had to dress myself during our travels with...you know."

"Well, I'm always happy to help." Kaede placed a kiss on the back of Imari's neck, feeling a bit guilty when she shivered. She had meant for it to be chaste. "Sorry."

"It's fine." With a deep breath, Imari went to stand in front of the copper mirror hanging on the wall. After a moment, she said, "I haven't looked at myself since the cave, you know. I don't know what I was expecting to see, but it wasn't this."

Kaede went to join her at the mirror, resting her chin on Imari's shoulder. "No monsters then?"

Imari shook her head. "No. Just me. A tired me." She poked at the bags beneath her eyes before sighing. "Normally I'd be horrified going before the Empress looking like this, but right now, I don't have the energy to care about the little details." Her eyes drifted away from the mirror, shifting over to her sword and scabbard. Kaede caught the glance at once and went to retrieve it, but Imari shook her head. "No—wait. I don't know if I want it."

Kaede stopped. "That's your choice, Imari."

"But?"

"No but," Kaede said. "Yes, I have an opinion, but it isn't the one that matters. You should be able to do whatever you like."

Imari smiled. "Sometimes, I don't know how you manage to be so perfect. What is your opinion, then?"

Kaede looked at the sword once more. The green stones of the pommel gleamed, as if the dragon carved into the hilt watched them. "I know you're ashamed of what you've done. I would be too, if Kyuubi had taken control of me instead of you. But I don't think you should blame the sword. Think of all you went through to get it. You fought bandits and my cousin, traveled all the way across the Jade Sea, and rode on a dragon. You trained for months to learn how to use it. And, yes, you drew blood with it. But I think it can still do great things. I still think you can do great things. You shouldn't throw it aside as some kind of symbol because you're hurting."

Imari took a long time to digest those words, but at last, she came to a decision. "Kyuubi can stuff her own tails." She strode over to the table and picked up the sword. She tied the scabbard at the back, just as Wen Ling had taught her, and as the sword slid into its proper place, she let out a calming breath. "Wujian is my sword. I'm not going to let her ruin it."

Kaede grinned. "That's my girl," she said, tucking back a lock of hair that had escaped Imari's braid. It wasn't the fancy fan hairstyle most women would choose when seeing the Empress, but it did make Imari look more like herself. "Come on. Let's go before Takeshi comes back to hurry us along."

They exited the room to join Rin only to see a pair of imperial guards waiting beside her, dressed in traditional red and gold. With them was another familiar face. Suanni—or, rather, Bo—wore a fine purple kamishimo befitting the station of the Empress's adviser. Still, Kaede found that their gender remained indiscernible even with their face revealed. They wore the mon of the Empress: a rising golden sun with outstretched rays of light set on a red square.

"Homura Imari, Aozora Kaede," Suanni said, bowing. "It's time we talked."

Kaede took a moment to adjust to hearing her real name, but the awkwardness passed quickly. She distracted herself by looking at the guards, who were acting as though they couldn't hear anything at all. They didn't even seem fazed by Rin's presence. All they did was stand there, still as stone, holding their famous black, steel-tipped spears in their hands.

Suanni noticed her staring. "Don't worry. Empress Tomoyo's imperial guards are used to situations like this. They have sworn oaths under penalty of death not to release any information the Empress deems secret."

"And just how much does the Empress know?" Imari asked.

"Come with me and I'll explain." Suanni started down the hall, motioning for them to follow. Kaede did so, with Imari and Rin on either side and the guards a few paces behind. "When I left you in Yukimura,

Kaede, I headed for the capital to warn the Empress, but there was another reason I didn't go inside the cave with you. A dragon's promise is their honor, and unfortunately, I made a promise to Kyuubi several centuries ago."

Rin growled. "A bad promise, I expect."

"I'm afraid so. Long ago, before I knew her true nature, Kyuubi asked for my protection. She pretended to be injured and afraid and asked me to shelter her. I gave her my word then that no dragon would harm her."

Realization dawned. "You can't touch her," Kaede murmured. "That's why you sent us to the cave alone and flew away."

Suanni nodded. "I have bound myself and my kin to that oath. My time was better spent elsewhere, but I felt I owed you an explanation. I didn't want you to think I would let you and your companions walk into danger casually, without good reason."

"If you can't touch her, what's to be done?" Imari asked. Her voice bordered on angry and Kaede noticed her fists clenching at her sides. "She needs to be stopped. I won't let her do to someone else what she's done to me."

Suanni smiled in approval. "That's exactly how I hoped you would feel, Imari. I fear Kyuubi has bigger plans than this. Toying with one human and forcing them to betray their conscience is a game to her. She has a lust for power, and the fact that she has taken a shogun like Setsuna under her control is deeply disturbing. It makes me wonder if there are others."

"Another shogun?" Kaede asked. "Or other people of power?"

"Both," Suanni said. "But I will let the Empress explain."

With surprise, Kaede realized that they had arrived at their destination: the reception hall. She had been inside many times before to speak with Setsuna, but the doors seemed higher and more intimidating than usual knowing the Empress was behind them. Four more guards were stationed outside to remind her of the fact, all wearing the Empress's golden-red mon.

Kaede turned toward Imari, half-expecting a look of fear on her face, but instead, she found only blankness—perhaps more concerning. "Are you going to be all right, Imari? If you don't think you can go in?"

"I can." Imari's soft voice allowed no room for argument. "I have to."

"I'll be right beside you," Kaede said. "No matter what."

Suanni nodded for the guards, and together, they entered the throne room.

***

The moment Imari entered the throne room, she found it difficult to breathe. Her chest constricted, her throat closing with fear. She had stepped through the door determined, ready to meet the Empress's judgment no matter what, but as she looked toward the raised platform, her courage fled. Even though Kaede and her friends had told her time and time again over the past two weeks that she couldn't be held accountable for her actions, she found herself doubting their words. And part of her believed she should be punished.

After a brief, blind moment of panic, Imari felt a soft nudge at her shoulder. Rin's blue eyes were staring into hers, and then they shifted over toward Kaede. She was remaining perfectly still instead of approaching the platform.

"Move," Rin whispered. "She won't go without you."

That jolted Imari into action. Kaede was risking dishonor and disrespect by remaining with her. With barely a glance at the impressively dressed figure on the platform, Imari moved forward, taking the lowest posture on the long tatami mat as Kaede did the same beside her.

"Please rise, both of you," a voice said, one that sounded high-pitched and youthful to Imari's ears. With permission given, she lifted her head and looked upon the Empress at last.

Empress Tomoyo didn't give the appearance of someone intimidating. Short and slender and through her white makeup, looking no older than the fifteen years Imari knew her to be. Her hair was styled in a large fan, and pinned to one side was a kanzashi of gold and silver. Her kimono was lavish, high-necked, with white blossoms patterned across the plush purple fabric. Seated below her was Hayate, looking much more respectable than Imari had seen him in the past. He seemed uncomfortable, though, and Imari couldn't help wondering if it was because of the Empress, or because Kaze wasn't with him. *Or perhaps it's because of me. I did try to kill him.* His kamishimo concealed most of his neck, and Imari couldn't help glancing toward it, checking to see if any mark was visible. From this distance, she couldn't tell.

"Please, speak," the Empress said.

"We're honored, Heika," Kaede said, inclining her head. "We want to help resolve this situation any way we can."

Empress Tomoyo smiled. "I'm sure you do, Aozora Kaede. My adviser Bo has already told me many of the details, but I need to hear them from both of you."

Imari's mind raced. She didn't want to defend herself. She didn't want to speak of what had happened in the cave. All she wanted was for this to be over, and it wouldn't be while Kyuubi still lived. Kaede had given her strength and a purpose again, but without a goal, she would be adrift in the same sea of blood.

"Please, Your Majesty," Imari murmured, lowering her eyes again, "I must beg one thing of you. I'm willing to answer for my actions however you see fit, but first, please allow me to make amends. Bo has told you of Kyuubi, the fox spirit who put all of this in motion. With your permission, I wish to bring her to justice. Then, you may deal with me as you like."

The Empress was quiet for several moments, and Imari was certain she had overstepped her bounds. But at last, Empress Tomoyo replied, "I'm afraid I must deal with your actions now, Homura Imari. It cannot wait. Do you agree to submit to my judgment, or would you defy it?"

Ice ran through Imari's veins, but she kept her head lowered. "Yes, Your Majesty. I do."

"Heika—" Kaede protested, risking rudeness by interrupting, but Empress Tomoyo held up her hand.

"Wait, Aozora Kaede. You might not find my judgment disagreeable. Homura Imari, it is true that you have taken the lives of fourteen noble samurai. However, you did so in the pursuit of Yukimura Setsuna, one of my shogun, who we have discovered to be a criminal. I have it from several reliable sources that she has been conducting profane experiments on the yokai. These experiments could not continue, and by taking her captive and bringing her here, you helped end them."

Imari raised her head, looking at the Empress in disbelief. "Your Majesty, Yukimura-sama is no criminal. She was manipulated by Kyuubi like I was. She didn't know what she was doing."

The Empress smiled. "Oh? Well then, what would you suggest her punishment be?"

"Nothing. She needs doctors and a long rest under observation, not to be thrown in jail."

"Then wouldn't it make sense for you to receive the same treatment, since you were also manipulated by Kyuubi?" Empress Tomoyo asked, eyes twinkling.

Imari closed her mouth. The Empress had outwitted her. She couldn't ask for her own punishment without demanding that Setsuna suffer the same fate as well. She wasn't certain whether to feel relieved or guilty at the outcome.

"Enough of this nonsense then," Empress Tomoyo said. "Homura Imari, upon the condition that you do your utmost to find and stop the dangerous fugitive Kyuubi, your crimes against Yukimura will be forgiven. Yukimura-dono, is this acceptable to you?"

She turned toward Hayate, who had remained silent on the mat beside the throne. He nodded. "It is, Heika. Through my cousin, I know Homura Imari to be an honorable woman. Yukimura will not demand her blood."

"Very well then," the Empress said. "That business is settled. We have much more to discuss."

Imari let out a breath. The subject of her fate had been settled so quickly and easily she couldn't quite believe it. She was torn between laughing and begging for a harsher punishment. In the end, determination won out. She still had a score to settle with Kyuubi. Her guilt was self-serving at best. It certainly wouldn't help the men she had already killed, or Kyuubi's future victims.

"Bo has told me a great deal about Kyuubi in the past few weeks." The way the Empress emphasized the words "the past few weeks" came as something of a surprise, and Imari's eyes slid over to Suanni. She wasn't quite sure, but she thought their expression looked the slightest bit guilty.

Who would have thought it, a fifteen-year-old girl chastising a dragon?

"The fact that she was able to take control of shogun Yukimura is frightening indeed. It makes me wonder if there were others."

"What makes you think there were others?" Kaede asked.

"My mother, for one," Hayate said. "While you were spending time helping Homura-san recover, I was helping her."

Imari saw a shadow of guilt cross Kaede's face, and it took an effort of will not to reach out and grasp her hand in reassurance. Such a gesture of affection in front of the Empress wouldn't have been proper at all.

"And?" Kaede asked. "How is she doing?"

"Not well," Hayate confessed. "She sleeps fitfully most of the time, and when she wakes, she screams. Sometimes she speaks in broken sentences. She claims Kyuubi is manipulating other people besides her."

Kaede frowned. "Do you think she's talking about the other shogun? You said yourself she was delirious."

"You should listen to her," Imari said. "I remembered a great deal after I was freed from Kyuubi's spell. It started with the pearl she gave me—"

"That has already been removed," Hayate said. "It was set into a hair ornament Setsuna wore. I destroyed it myself."

"Then she might be regaining her senses like I did." She suppressed a shudder, trying not to let her mind drift back to the ocean of blood. "At least, messengers should be sent to check on the other shogun and find out what's going on."

"I agree," Empress Tomoyo said. "However, we have another problem. The shogun are currently in Asahina fortress, gathering for their five-year meeting."

Imari's stomach dropped like a stone. "It's a perfect opportunity. If Kyuubi has taken control of the other shogun, they would be in the best possible position to cause trouble."

"Worse than trouble," Suanni said. "With the shogun under her control, I can't imagine the chaos Kyuubi would be able to cause. A coup, war. This is the sort of thing she lives for. This business with Setsuna reeks of a mere distraction, a way to get the Empress all the way to the north, far from Asahina and the capitol. Normally, she arrives in the middle of the session to hear their proposals."

"But now she's stuck here dealing with Setsuna," Kaede said. "It all makes sense. We need to go to Asahina and find out what's going on."

"I'm glad you think so," Empress Tomoyo said. "Bo recommends I stay here for my own safety, but I can't let this situation go unmonitored." She paused. "Homura Imari, Aozora Kaede, I know both of you have suffered much in the past few weeks. The fact that you have survived at all is admirable. But I need to ask for your help again now. I want you to go to Asahina with Bo—confront Kyuubi if she's there, protect the shogun if she isn't. The Empire cannot fall into chaos, and if we don't act swiftly, I fear that is exactly what will happen."

"Of course, Your Majesty." Imari answered at once. She had already made her decision long before Empress Tomoyo's request, and she wouldn't change it now. "It would be my honor. I see stopping Kyuubi as a way to pay penance for my crimes. I won't let her manipulate anyone else."

"I'll go too," Kaede said, and Imari turned in time to see her smile. "I'm Lady Homura's yojimbo, after all. Someone needs to watch out for her."

"What about your companions?" Hayate asked. "Are they willing to join us?"

"Us?" Kaede asked. "You aren't coming too, are you?"

"Of course, I am," Hayate said. "Kyuubi is the reason Setsuna is…" He paused then rephrased. "I feel it is my duty to Her Majesty."

"It's all right, Yukimura-dono," Empress Tomoyo said. "I know you have a personal reason for going after Kyuubi. You have my permission to join Aozora Kaede and Homura Imari."

"Our companions will come with us," Imari said. "Hibana Takeshi and Hibana Kenta are skilled samurai and loyal friends."

"So will my brother and I." Rin approached the throne as well, and though she didn't lie down, she did recline her head respectfully toward the Empress. "Kaede and Imari are under my protection, and as a yokai myself, I can't allow one of my own people to cause this much devastation. This is not who we are."

Empress Tomoyo smiled. "I would expect nothing less, wolf-clan. Your people have always been honorable. It's reassuring to know we have yokai on our side, too."

"Then we have a plan," Suanni said. "Imari, Kaede, you and your friends will leave with me as soon as possible for a sneak attack. I'll take you myself."

"Meanwhile, regiments of my imperial guard will move in to support you from the eastern shores. However, if you need to return without slaying Kyuubi in order to save the shogun and update me on the situation, you will not have failed."

Imari's jaw stiffened as she gritted her teeth. Though she wouldn't contradict the Empress, in her mind, that wasn't an option. She would kill Kyuubi if the fox was indeed in Asahina, or die trying.

***

"Are you sure Rin didn't want to come with us on our walk?" Imari asked as she and Kaede headed out into the forest. "I wouldn't have minded. This is her home, after all."

Kaede shrugged, picking her way over a few fallen branches. Her raised sandals crunched through the snow, leaving a fresh set of footprints. "I couldn't find her to ask. She's been running wild today with Kaze. I think she's glad to have her brother back, and to be home." She hesitated, seeming to consider her words before continuing. "She might have also wanted to give the two of us some space. You know, since it's our last night here and we don't know what's going to happen tomorrow."

Imari bit her lip, finding it puffier than expected. The cold and damp was seeping into her bones even though the trees sheltered her from the worst of the wind. "You don't think she's jealous, do you? I'm not trying to steal you away from her or anything."

Kaede waved her off. "No, not jealous. She knows I'm not going to stop being her best friend. We've been together too long for that." After the next snowdrift, she paused, waiting for Imari to catch up. "Actually, the place I'm taking you is kind of special. It's where I found her."

"Only you would take me trekking out in the forest the night before we're set to leave on our mission," Imari laughed, "looking for the place where you found a wild spirit wolf."

"Hey," Kaede said, sounding slightly hurt. "I just...I don't know when the two of us will be back here again."

Or if the two of us will ever be back here again. Such depressing thoughts had begun creeping into Imari's mind with unhappy regularity during her recovery.

"Remember when you showed me the shrine behind your father's castle? Well, this is my special place. I want you to see it. "

Imari took Kaede's hand, shushing her softly. "I understand. You don't have to explain yourself anymore."

The two of them stopped speaking as they walked deeper into the woods, but the forest around them wasn't quiet. Without the distraction of conversation, Imari could hear songbirds chirping despite the snow. Rustling in the bushes told her that small animals were nearby, and in the distance, she thought she could hear the gurgling sound of a river.

"I'm surprised it isn't frozen," she said, turning her head in that direction.

"Not quite cold enough," Kaede said. "Come on. We're close."

A few minutes later, Kaede swept aside the branches of a thin, wispy pine tree to reveal a clearing beyond. Imari stepped forward, spotting the river she had heard at last—but not just the river. To her surprise, it fed into a beautiful pool, almost perfectly round. Smooth rocks dotted its outer edge, and though the surface of the river beyond eddied and flowed, the top of the pool almost looked like smooth glass.

"It's beautiful," she murmured, stepping past Kaede for a closer look.

Kaede stepped past the branches to join her, letting them fall back in place beside the tree. "It is," she said with a small smile. "I found Rin here when I was a child visiting my aunt. She'd lost her pack, so I kept her warm until they came for her. Her mother was grateful." She gazed out over the pool, seemingly lost in memories. "Years later, I came back here again. I was only twelve, but I was already changing. I was getting taller, and my voice had started to drop. I cried until the wolves found me."

Imari remained silent, waiting for Kaede to continue. "Haruna, Rin's mother, told me to bathe in the pool when the moon came out. She said Tsukine would bless me for my kindness to the spirits. I didn't believe her." She smiled again, tears glistening in her eyes. "But I did see some changes after that. My voice didn't drop anymore, and my beard never came in. I checked in the mirror every day, dreading when it would." She looked down at the front of her kimono, which had a slight swell. "And I got these, of course. Once, I asked Haruna why the pool didn't change everything. She just said that when the time comes, I'll know why."

"And?" Imari whispered. "Were you satisfied with that answer?"

Kaede shrugged. "Not at first. Now, I don't know. I'm happy with myself. I'm content." She turned, and her eyes reminded Imari of the moon. "I'm glad I met you. There are lots of things in my life that haven't gone as planned but I'm lucky you're one of them."

Imari stepped closer to Kaede's side, folding an arm around her waist. "We leave for Asahina tomorrow morning," she whispered, resting her cheek against Kaede's shoulder. "Are you ready for that?"

"Are you?"

"I am," Imari said. "I need to do this." She laughed into Kaede's kimono. "Takeshi would yell at me for saying that. He would say I didn't have anything to make up for and tell me risking my life was stupid."

"Give him some credit," Kaede said, chuckling a bit. "He's gotten a lot better, hasn't he? I think he would understand."

"Maybe." Imari looked at the pool once more. The stars had come out, leaving tiny white pinpricks on its dark blue surface. "What about Rin? She won't mind you showing me this place, will she?"

"No, she won't." It wasn't Kaede that answered, but another voice a short distance away. Imari raised her head from Kaede's shoulder, whirling around in time to see a shadow approach from the underbrush. Rin stepped out into the clearing, blinding white against the dark silhouettes of the trees.

"Rin," Kaede said, smiling broadly. "I assume you heard us and decided to come sniffing around?"

Rin huffed, silver trails of steam drifting up from her black nose. "Didn't need to sniff. You two were loud enough to track with my nose plugged and my eyes shut." Then, to Imari's surprise, the wolf's blue eyes fixed on her. "I'm not upset with you, Imari. If anything, I admire you more now than I did before."

Imari looked at Rin in confusion. Though the wolf had spent a great deal of time in her room over the past few weeks, she had assumed that was only because of Kaede. Now, she wondered if Rin had been watching over her as well. "You admire me?" She shook her head, narrowing her eyes. "After killing fourteen people?"

Rin huffed. "For escaping from Kyuubi's influence and for recovering afterward. That sort of torment would have broken a weaker woman, but here you are, about to go to Asahina. You're trying to put things right even though you're still broken inside."

Imari flinched. It felt as though Rin's eyes peered straight through her. "What are you trying to say?"

"That I misjudged you." Rin trotted forward through the snow, sitting regally before her. "When I first met you, I didn't think you were good enough for Kaede. I thought you were going to use her like everyone else. But you've proven me wrong. You're brave and strong. You've given Kaede a reason to stop running and start fighting. And I'm glad you're going to Asahina with us. Even though Kaede is your yojimbo, I trust you to protect her, too. She deserves a mate who will defend her to the death."

A wide smile spread across Imari's face. "That...that might just be the kindest thing anyone's ever said to me," she said, laughing with a cold stream of breath. "Thank you, Rin. Could I—can I hug you?"

She half-expected the wolf to say no, but instead, Rin nodded. Imari wrapped her arms around Rin's neck, burying her face in the wolf's thick fur. Flakes of snow clung to the outer layer, but she was remarkably warm and soft. "We're all going to stop Kyuubi together," she said near Rin's ear. "No more running away for any of us."

Rae D. Magdon

Chapter Twenty-Five

IMARI WOKE THE NEXT morning and was alone. Two bags were neatly packed at the foot of the futon, but she couldn't find Kaede. Her half of the futon was cold. Quietly, Imari crept out of bed, glancing about the room. Only a hint of misty grey sunlight was visible through the window. Kaede should have been asleep beside her, at least for a few more minutes.

She dressed as quickly as her single hand allowed, picking out her warmest, most comfortable traveling clothes. Suanni had said the journey south would take less than a day, but flying on dragonback was cold, and the fortress that held Asahina stood on the peak of a tall mountain, just as high as the northern mountain ranges of Yukimura and Aozora. This time of year, there was bound to be snow.

Opening the screen and peering out into the hallway didn't reveal any signs of Kaede either. Imari thought for a moment, then headed right on a hunch—not toward the castle gates but deeper into the private quarters.

She reached Setsuna's door. The guards were positioned some distance away to offer privacy, but Imari could hear a familiar voice just beyond. "I need to find Aozora-dono," she told them. "It's almost time for us to leave."

The guards waved her past, and she approached the door, sliding it open without knocking. She found exactly what she expected. Kaede sat next to Setsuna's bed, holding her aunt's hand in hers and speaking to her softly. At the sound of the door opening, she looked up, jolting a little until she realized who had interrupted.

"Oh, Imari. It's you. I was just…saying goodbye."

Imari approached the bed as well, resting her hand on Kaede's shoulder and looking down at Setsuna. The shogun looked frail and thin amidst the thick covers, but for the moment, she seemed to be sleeping peacefully. "You feel guilty for letting Hayate watch over her these past two weeks, don't you?"

Kaede nodded. "I know I needed to be with you and he was doing a fine job on his own." She closed her eyes, exhaling deeply. "But she was there for me at an important time in my life. She opened her home to me when my parents made me anxious. She trained me in the ways of bushido and taught me what it meant to be a woman. About caring for other people, about being strong without losing your empathy, about the women in our family that came before me."

"Then I have her to thank for the wonderful woman you've become." Imari gave Kaede's shoulder a comforting squeeze. "I'm doing better, Kaede. I'm not the same, but I'm standing here. Setsuna could recover, too."

"She had Kyuubi's pearl for years. If two days did that to you—"

"You said Setsuna was strong," Imari said, interrupting Kaede before those negative thoughts could spiral any further. "Have faith in her and focus on dealing with Kyuubi. That might be the way to save her."

That seemed to help. Kaede sat up straighter, letting go of Setsuna's hand and placing it on top of Imari's. "You're right. I'm not going to help her sitting here. I just wanted to see her before we left." She placed a kiss on Setsuna's forehead and rose from the mat. "I'll come back. Hayate won't have to take care of you alone."

Imari helped Kaede to her feet, and when she saw tears glistening in her lover's eyes, she opened her arms. Kaede stepped into them, and Imari held her for several seconds, waiting for the storm to pass. It moved on quickly, and after a few moments, Kaede left the embrace, her face hardening. "All right. Let's go find the others. We want to get an early start."

***

Kaede watched the ground whip by beneath them in a blur obscured by wisps of white clouds. Perched high on Suanni's back, she could see far into the distance, but there wasn't much to look at. The jagged mountains and the silver, snow-dusted forest faded quickly behind them, and in front of them stretched the wide plains she had crossed on her way to Mirai, an even patchwork of brown and green.

Further ahead, growing larger with each minute, was a lone mountain: not unlike Hongshan, although not so tall as to pierce the clouds. It was mostly shadow thanks to the glare of the sun to their right, but Kaede could see its silhouette. Asahina would be near the top, a heavily defended mountain fortress where the shogun met to discuss the future of Akatsuki Teikoku. She had been there only once before, but remembered it as a grim place without much sunlight or laughter.

Getting in would be a problem. They couldn't simply fly over the walls on Suanni, or Kyuubi would be alerted to their presence and use one of her magic pearls to escape. A sneak attack was imperative if they wanted to catch her—and Kaede wanted to catch her. She knew her priority should be to look after the shogun as the Empress had asked, but her heart felt differently. Kyuubi had hurt Imari, and Imari wouldn't be able to finish healing until the fox was dealt with.

Her thoughts spun in circles as the day passed on. Plains and rice paddies turned to low, rolling hills. Mirai was off a fair distance to the west, but not so far that the view was different. She thought she even caught a glimpse of the city once, a tiny smudge of smoke against the horizon. She reached behind her, grasping Imari's hand, and Imari squeezed back.

Their fingers remained linked until much later, when the mountain began to loom over them and Suanni tilted down toward the ground. The sun dipped behind the horizon, leaving only a red and orange stripe to mark its place. No moon rose on the other side of the sky—only a deepening shade of blue. Even the stars seemed faint and distant.

Suanni finally landed between two rocky hills some distance away from the mountain itself. Kaede was surprised at how far away they had chosen to touch down. "Suanni, why here? Asahina's still pretty far away."

"Because all of you need rest before you sneak inside the fortress, and we need to talk." Suanni lowered their tail, offering a way down. Since she was in front, Kaede waited for Hayate, the Hibana brothers, and the wolves to descend first. She and Imari went last, finally letting go of each other's hands.

Once they were all on the ground, Suanni began to ripple and change. A few moments later, they took their human form once again, wearing their usual dark brown hood. "I won't be able to fly you into the fortress itself," Suanni said, repeating Kaede's earlier thoughts. "Kyuubi will sense my ki and escape before we can catch her, possibly with the shogun she has enslaved. I will need to stay in my human form for as long as possible, unless the worst happens."

"Then how are we going to get in?" Kenta asked. "The fortress has to be full of guards. Sneaking past them isn't going to be easy."

"We have to try," Hayate said. "None of us came into this thinking it would be simple."

"Kaze and I could go first to get a sense of the place," Rin offered. "We might be able to pass for mountain wolves."

"Maybe," Imari said, "but what we really need is someone who's familiar with this place. Kaede, Hayate, you've been here before, haven't you?"

Kaede sighed. "I was a child. All I remember is that the walls were high and thick and there were lots of soldiers in uniform."

"I can't recall much more," Hayate added with a disappointed frown. "We might not be able to come up with a plan until we get a closer look, and that's going to involve climbing the mountain and trusting our luck."

Takeshi's brow furrowed. "I don't like going in without a plan. This might be our only chance to stop Kyuubi and save the shogun. We don't want to ruin it by rushing in unprepared."

"Then perhaps a compromise," Suanni suggested. "Sleep on it for a few hours. You're going to need your strength, as well as clear heads. Coming up with a plan of action will be easier."

Once more, Kaede got the distinct impression that Suanni wasn't telling them everything. They had a familiar twinkle in their eye. Still, Kaede had learned pushing would get her nowhere. Suanni's advice hadn't led them astray before.

"I vote for a few hours of rest," she said, cutting off the protests she knew would come from Imari. "We all want to end this as fast as possible, but Takeshi's right. We can't rush in without a plan, and so far, we've got nothing."

"If we put it to a vote, I'd lose, wouldn't I?" Imari huffed.

"Aren't you the one who said that we didn't need to vote, because you were going to do what you wanted anyway?" Takeshi asked. "I'm surprised you aren't putting up more of a fight."

A shadow passed across Imari's face. "I've learned that doing what I want right away doesn't always work out for the best."

Immediately, Takeshi seemed to regret his words. "Imari, I—"

"It's all right," Imari said, stopping him before he could bow. "Let's get something to eat and set up camp. A few hours of sleep won't do us any harm. Kyuubi isn't going to run before she even knows we're coming."

They set up camp quickly, doling out the rations they had brought and eating in a mutually agreed upon silence. Kaede observed everyone's faces over the fire, noting that they all looked the same. Her companions' expressions were wary but determined, resigned to what they needed to do.

After a short meal, everyone went to bed. Kaede spread out her pallet next to Imari's. Lying on her side, she was able to wrap her arm around Imari's waist. Back at Hongshan, Imari had taken the rear position more often, but since Yukimura, they had reversed. Kaede didn't mind the change. She was happy to offer any comfort she could.

The others fell asleep quickly, much to Kaede's surprise. Kenta started snoring, and Takeshi and Hayate made no movements. Imari's breathing was even and steady, and Kaede could tell that she had drifted off too. Even the wolves were dozing side by side instead of watching over the camp, and even Suanni had shut their eyes. Tucked between the hills, there was little chance of danger.

Kaede tried to join them, but too many thoughts and fears swirled around in her head. Imari and Setsuna's faces were foremost in her mind, but whenever she tried to focus on them, Kyuubi's cold laugh shattered them. Her mind was dragged to memories of blood hissing on top of the snow and dead eyes staring up at a pale grey sky.

A soft scraping sound jolted her out of the memory. She opened one eye without lifting her head, pretending to remain asleep. So far, there had been no nighttime noises aside from Kenta's snoring. But the sound didn't come again, and her heartbeat slowed down once more. Kaede began to relax until she noticed Rin's gaze lock with hers. The wolf's blue eyes were cracked open, and although she hadn't moved from her position, her ears perked.

Kaede understood the signal. The next time the sound came from somewhere behind and to her left, she rolled off the sleeping mat and into a crouch, grabbing for her wakizashi instead of her katana as she went. In close quarters, she would probably need it.

She landed on the balls of her feet just in time to see a slender shadow on the other side of camp. They tried to break away and run, but found themselves face to face with Rin. They whirled around but Kaze bounded out of the shadows and blocked them. With no other way left to go, the stranger rushed straight for Kaede, reaching for their obi.

She didn't give them a chance to draw their blade. She lunged, grunting as she collided with the intruder. Her shoulder met their chest, and the two of them tumbled onto the ground, locked in a fierce struggle. The stranger fought desperately, but Kaede had the advantage. She brought her wakizashi to her opponent's throat, letting them feel the sharp edge. "Don't move. I'd rather not spill blood tonight."

The intruder stopped struggling and placed their hands above their head in surrender. By that time, the entire camp had awoken. The others came rushing over, blades drawn and eyes wide.

"What happened?" Hayate panted, staring down at the pinned stranger in surprise.

"It seems Rin and Kaze have caught a thief," Takeshi said.

Kaede took another look at the person beneath her, a woman and a familiar one at that. She hadn't noticed before in the dark, but she recognized the stranger's features. She was indeed a thief—one they had encountered before. "Ishikawa Gin?"

***

"Oh, great," Gin groaned, rolling her eyes. Despite having a sword at her throat, she didn't seem appropriately frightened. "The Ancestors must despise me. Of all the camps in the Empire, I had to stumble into yours. Look, I was just trying to score some food and a few pouches. I didn't know it was you lot. Trust me, I don't want to fight any of you again."

"That's because you lost," Imari said, approaching the pinned woman and stopping at her side. She was surprised by Gin's arrival, but she doubted the thief would be much of a threat this time. Her heart rate had already slowed down. "Let her up, Kaede. She isn't going to run—not when our friends can chase her down."

Kaede removed her wakizashi from Gin's neck, and the thief rubbed sulkily at the spot even though it hadn't broken skin. "What are you going to do to me?"

"That depends on why you're here," Imari said.

"Wait," Hayate said, sounding confused, "you know this person?"

"Kind of," Kenta said, putting away his sword. "She runs a small gang of thieves a few miles beyond the Homura border. What are you doing all the way over here?"

"The same thing I was doing there," Gin said. "I couldn't stay so close to Homura after almost killing the daimyo's daughter, so I headed east before someone came after me. I know this area pretty well."

The beginnings of an idea stirred in Imari's head. "You do? Explain."

"Well, it's in the name, isn't it?" Gin said, as if it were obvious. "Ishikawa. My ancestors served the daimyos of Asahina centuries ago. We were here even before Mirai was."

Imari's brows lifted. "Ishikawa is your real name? I thought you were being dramatic."

"Nope, it's real," Gin sighed, as if she was already weary of explaining. "The 'legendary' Ishikawa was one of my ancestors. He came from my village, too, you know. Iga was a thriving town back then, of course, and now I'm just trying to keep the place afloat."

"Even if it means robbing travelers?" Hayate asked, clearly skeptical.

"Only the rich ones," Gin said. "I'm not about to rob some poor sap with nothing. Even thieves have standards."

Imari gave Gin a scrutinizing look, and then glanced over at Suanni, who was hanging back from the rest of the group and observing quietly. "You knew this was going to happen, didn't you? I don't know how, but you knew."

Suanni merely smiled.

"I know what you're thinking, Imari, and it's not a good idea," Rin growled. Her hackles were still raised, and she glared at Gin with her lips peeled back. "This woman almost killed Kaede last time."

"I wasn't going to kill her," Gin protested, edging away from the wolf. Rin seemed to be the only member of the group who made her truly nervous.

"And ransoming Imari is better?" Rin said.

"Don't dismiss the idea yet, Rin," Kaze said in a calm voice. He held his tail much lower than his sister. "We needed a way into the fortress, and now we have one. This is all to the good."

"Wait, fortress?" Gin did a double take. "You mean Asahina? The top-of-the-mountain, crawling-with-shogun-and-samurai fortress? Not to mention it's the seat of power of the Toyotomi clan! Do you know how many times they tried to kill the original Ishikawa? No way am I going up there, even if you try and make me. I'm not stupid enough to risk my neck."

Despite Gin's words, Imari jumped on the opportunity. "What if I gave you a really good reason to say yes?"

"No way. There's nothing in the world you could give me to make me go up there."

"What if I relayed how dire the situation in Iga is directly to the Empress?" Gin snorted, but Imari continued. "No, it's true. I had an audience with her yesterday. I'm sure she'll want to help you, but if she doesn't, I'll personally make sure every member of your village has enough food and supplies to last them for the next ten years. I'll even get my father to repair the roads so more travelers come through."

Gin's eyes narrowed. "Why are you trying to bribe me, anyway? Why do you want to get into that fortress so badly?"

Imari sighed. The truth would be best. "We think an evil fox spirit is there right now, trying to manipulate the shogun."

"What?" Gin let out a bark of laughter, shaking her head. "Now I know you're crazy. Fox spirits and seeing Empress Tomoyo. Sun and Moon, I never should've come here."

"Look, we're telling the truth," Kaede said. "Kyuubi has already possessed one shogun. The others could be in danger. Her Majesty has ordered us to sneak in and find out what's going on as soon as possible."

"You're all crazy," Gin repeated, but Imari could see that her resolve was weakening. The thief was chewing thoughtfully at her lip, and her eyes were cautious, but not mistrustful. Against her better judgment, she was starting to listen to them.

"This story is too crazy to be made up," Imari said. "That's what you're thinking right now. But you should be thinking about all the people in your village. I give you my word as a samurai that I'll restore it to its former glory, even if it requires emptying all of Mirai's coffers to do it."

Gin hesitated, clearly wavering.

"Besides, if Kyuubi is controlling the shogun, where will her eye turn next? Homura and Toyotomi lands, which includes Iga. We can't let anything happen to our homes." She stepped forward. "Come on, Gin. Just show us how to get in. There has to be a way, right?"

At last, Gin gave a loud groan. She shook her head, pinching her brow for a moment, and then stood up, brushing the dust from her threadbare kimono. "Fine, I'll help you. But if you go back on your word—"

"We won't," Kenta interrupted, barging into the conversation with a grin. "I'll put on a hat and build those roads myself if I have to."

"Cool it with the enthusiasm," Gin said, holding up a hand. "You've convinced me for now. There's only one way into Asahina that doesn't involve the front gate. My father told me about it. It's a tiny path up the steeper side of the mountain, and it's usually snowed over. I hope you all brought tall sandals, because you're going to need them."

"I still don't like this," Rin muttered.

Imari prepared to argue, but Kaede put a hand on Rin's back, reassuring her instead. "Well, it's the best option we've got. So, are you in?"

"She'll get over it," Kaze said. "All right, Gin. Lead the way."

Rin and Kaze were forced to take the lead as they made their way up the winding, snowy mountain trail. Imari did her best to keep up, but she found it difficult even though she had dressed for snow. The trail Gin had spoken of was hardly a path at all. At best, it was a series of barely-connected patches along the mountainside where the rocks didn't reach up to a person's shoulders.

"Are you sure this is the right way?" Gin raised her voice to be heard above the wind as it barreled down the mountainside, whipping painfully past her face and lashing through her hair.

Gin turned back, glaring over her shoulder. "Do you see any other way up? I know what I'm doing."

Imari doubted it, but she didn't have much of a choice. Gin had little to gain by taking them the wrong way, at least. She slipped over a patch of ice, and she would have fallen into a snowbank if Kaede hadn't caught her elbow.

"Careful," she whispered, and for a moment, Imari felt the heat of Kaede's breath against her cheek.

"You, too."

After that, Imari made more of an effort to step in Rin's pawprints. They were large enough to hold most of her sandals, and at least that way, she could be sure of her steps.

"Should have...taken the stairs." Kenta panted behind them. Imari couldn't blame him. He was carrying the only pack they had decided to bring with them. "I'd rather fight guards than this."

"You wouldn't," Takeshi said darkly. "Besides, it's not much further."

Imari raised her hand to shield her face from the spray of fallen snow the wind had picked up from the ground, looking up at the top of the mountain. Takeshi was right. They were approaching what looked like a large square shadow from one side. The rear walls of Asahina were hard to make out from below in the dark, but she could at least tell that they were getting closer.

"I see why no one tries to come up this way. Look," Hayate said from a few paces back, pointing.

Imari followed his gesture. Instead of a steep slope, the section of mountain behind the fortress was a sheer drop down, almost like the face of a cliff. Beneath, gales of wind howled at them and the drop ended in a sea of sharp rocks below.

"You've got that right," Gin said. "That's why Ishikawa Goemon managed to escape this way without getting caught. All the guards assumed he slipped out the front. This is before the part where they tried to boil him and his daughter alive, of course."

"Of course," Suanni said. Though they were at the rear of the group, they had no trouble climbing the icy slope, just as they hadn't struggled to cross the Jade Sea.

"What are you going to do when we get to the top?" Imari asked them.

Suanni gave their usual cryptic answer. "That depends entirely on what we find when we arrive."

Kyuubi. We need to find Kyuubi. Though Imari knew the shogun needed to be her priority, the desire for justice burned brightly within her. It kept her warm and strong against the snow, and she picked up her pace, catching up with Rin and Kaze. Without speaking, they closed ranks in front of her, shielding her from the worst of the wind.

The path leveled off a few minutes later. Up close, Asahina was even more impressive. A thick wall of solid stone climbed up into the sky. Only a hundred meters of empty space sat between the foot of the wall and the cliff, all covered in fresh, undisturbed snowfall.

"How do we get through?" Kenta asked, craning his neck.

"Through the door," Gin said, as if it were obvious. She pointed toward a small wooden door set into the wall, one Imari had completely missed in the dark. "You didn't think I'd take you up a treacherous mountain path that didn't lead anywhere, did you?"

Imari approached the door for a closer look. Thick bars of iron were set across its front, but it didn't look as though it had been opened in years. "So, do we break it down?"

Gin snorted. "You're welcome to try. Don't come to me expecting me to pop your shoulder back in."

"I think there's a better way." Hayate glanced over at Kaede. "Do you want to, or me?"

"You go ahead," Kaede said. "You're better at it."

"All right." Hayate rolled his shoulders, standing back several paces and stretching. He broke into a run, and quick as a flash, he was up and over the wall, practically hovering in midair as he scaled its side.

Even though she had seen the same feat before, Imari gaped. The way Hayate defied gravity was incredible, and she blinked in case her eyes were playing tricks on her. But it was no trick. Gin sputtered in a satisfying way, and Kenta grinned.

"Did he just climb straight up a wall?" Gin asked, glancing from face to face as if looking for confirmation.

Kenta nodded. "He sure did. Just wait."

They waited, only to hear a muffled thud followed by a soft crunch. Imari guessed that Hayate had removed the wooden bar keeping the gate shut from the inside. A moment later, it swung open, revealing the inside of a courtyard as well as Hayate's pale face. "Come on, let's go in before anyone sees us."

Together, the nine of them crept into the fortress courtyard. From their new vantage point, Imari saw that they were at the top of the castle itself. A pyramid of tiered squares built directly into the mountainside lay beneath them, each larger than the last and holding its own buildings. They led down like a giant set of stone steps, and Imari realized that coming through the front would have been a terrible mistake. Climbing through all those floors without giving themselves away was surely impossible.

"Thank you, Gin," she whispered, half to herself.

"I try," Gin said, overhearing the comment. "So, I'll head back down now, okay?"

"Wait." Takeshi stepped in front of her, blocking her path back to the door. "I don't think so. You aren't leaving until we find the shogun."

Gin backed away from him, reaching for her sword. "Hey! The deal was that I get you up here. I did that. I never promised anything about helping you fight."

"She's right, Takeshi," Imari said. She stepped between the two of them, placing a hand on his arm. "Gin never said she was going to come with us."

"Well, she should. If we don't stop Kyuubi, her village is right in the line of fire." He ignored Imari, looking past her toward Gin. "I thought you were a thief with principles, like Ishikawa Goemon. Now's your chance to prove it."

Gin groaned, casting her eyes skyward. "Sun and Moon, the stupid things I do. Fine. I'll stick around, but I'm not making any promises as to how long."

They turned back to the smaller building on their level. In the daylight, it would be grand indeed. The slanted roof was trimmed with what looked like black and yellow, the Toyotomi colors, and wide, impressive steps led up to it. The mon of Toyotomi, a black symbol indiscernible at night on a pale-yellow field, waved back and forth eerily on their poles lining both sides. "This says 'throne room' to me," she said, gazing up the steps. "Should we start here?"

"You should." Suanni peered up the steps, concentrating heavily, and Imari caught Kaede shuddering beside her, as if she had felt something stir in the air. "I cannot tell you where the shogun are, but I sense Kyuubi's ki nearby."

Imari didn't need to hear anymore. She started up the stairs without waiting for the others, already reaching for her jian.

"Imari, maybe we should come up with a plan first?" Kaede asked, jogging to catch up and whispering beside her. "You know, stake out the place or something."

"We have a plan," Imari said. "Find Kyuubi and kill her."

"You'll need to chop off all nine of her tails," Suanni reminded them. They had taken the stairs at a run as well, although they weren't out of breath. "That's where she keeps her power."

"Okay. Find Kyuubi, chop off her tails, kill her."

Kaede sighed. "At least there aren't any guards—"

Fast footsteps came from behind them, followed by several loud shouts of alarm. Imari whirled around to see a band of guards approaching, clad in armor with their swords drawn. They headed straight for the foot of the stairs, where Takeshi, Kenta, Hayate, Gin, Rin, and Kaze met them. The guards drew back at the sight of the two wolves, but not for long. After a moment to get over their shock, they charged forward. Rin and Kaze lunged for one while Takeshi engaged another, his katana a flash of silver against the night.

Kaede made to run back down the steps, her own katana already in hand, but Imari grabbed her arm, pulling her to a stop. "No, don't! We have to keep going up. This might be our only chance."

"She's right," Suanni said. "Kyuubi won't stay long once she hears this."

With one last desperate look at their friends, Kaede shrugged off Imari's hold on her arm and started up the stairs. They covered the distance in record time. The tall set of double doors to the throne room weren't locked or guarded, and Imari shouldered past them, bursting into the room with Kaede and Suanni at her heels.

Sitting between a set of painted screens, Kyuubi perched on the red and gold platform reserved in honor of the Empress.

Chapter Twenty-Six

"SUANNI," KYUUBI SAID, STANDING up and striding toward the edge of the platform. "I'm not all that surprised to see you here after my little game in Yukimura, but I wasn't expecting you to bring company. And what interesting company it is."

Kaede gripped her katana tighter as the fox's gaze shifted to her. "You won't find the rest of the shogun here, Aozora Kaede. Setsuna was only the first. I've already sent the others down the mountain with an army at their backs. They're marching on the capital as we speak."

"It doesn't matter," Suanni said. "The Empress isn't there."

"Exactly. That was the plan." Kyuubi licked her lips. "The dragon magic that makes Seinarukyo impregnable is conditioned upon the Empress actually being there. Just imagine the chaos on the streets of a city that has not been touched by strife in centuries? Whether the shogun succeed or fail in dethroning little Tomoyo in the end doesn't even matter. I'll get the chaos I want, and there's always plenty to keep me busy during a war. Lots of pain and death to drink in. I'll be able to gorge myself for years."

A shudder of fear raced down Kaede's spine. "Suanni, there has to be something we can do."

Kyuubi smirked at Imari. "And Homura Imari, I certainly wasn't expecting to see you here. I thought you'd have done the honorable thing and taken your own life by now. Isn't that the way you humans atone for your disgrace? Tell me, how have you been sleeping with the eyes of the dead on you?"

"Oh, I'm still alive and well," Imari spat. "I thought about killing myself, but the thought of killing you was much more satisfying."

"Don't let her draw you in, Imari," Suanni said. "Even without her pearls, she can draw on the weaknesses of your mind."

"Weakness." Kyuubi chuckled. "You're one to talk about weakness, Suanni. You can't even touch me. After all, I'm only a poor, defenseless little fox, aren't I?"

For the first time, she could remember, Kaede saw a flicker of anger cross Suanni's face. "I might not be able to touch you, but they can. And I can stop the shogun from marching down the mountain."

"Better hurry, little dragon," Kyuubi drawled. "Good luck turning around an entire army."

In a flash, Suanni had vanished back through the double doors, departing without another word. Kaede barely had time to register that they were gone.

"Oh, don't mind them," Kyuubi said. "I like it better this way—just the three of us, like it was back at Hongshan." She brought her clenched fist in front of her, not holding a weapon, but seeming to draw on the air around her. Blue threads of lightning danced at the tips of her fingers, hissing and sparking. "This little game has been amusing, but I think it's time to claim my victory. I have a war to start, empires to destroy. You understand, don't you?"

"People and yokai are dead because of your game," Imari snarled. She held her sword in front of her, pointing the tip at Kyuubi.

Kyuubi laughed. "I didn't kill anyone. People are dead because you slaughtered them. It's a pity history will remember you this way after I kill you, isn't it? The Butcher of Yukimura. Your father would be so proud."

With a shout of rage, Imari threw herself at the fox. Wujian struck like a bolt from the heavens, but before she could connect, Kyuubi unleashed the lightning at her fingertips. Kaede rushed toward them, but there was nothing she could do. The blue sparks collided with Imari's sword, shooting down the blade.

To Kaede's relief, the hilt swallowed them. The lightning vanished without so much as a puff of smoke. Imari stopped and stared in similar amazement, but Kyuubi didn't seem concerned. "Not a bad sword," she drawled, blowing the smoke from her fingertips. "It's one of Wen Ling's better models, I suppose. Too bad your flesh isn't lightning-proof as well."

"She's just toying with us," Kaede said, stopping short at Imari's side. She turned to the fox, drawing Mizu-no-Hamon back in a defensive stance. "Don't let her get to you."

"Me? Toy with someone?" Kyuubi shook her head in mock amazement, her nine tails swishing tauntingly behind her. "I would never. But I can see why you would think that. You've always been a liar, haven't you, Kaede? You're lying even now, pretending like you're going to jump in front of Imari and save her the next time I strike. But you're too much of a coward. When I kill Imari, it's going to be all your fault."

Kaede didn't respond to the taunts. Instead, she caught Imari's eye, and the two of them dove in together, moving as one. More lightning gathered in Kyuubi's hand, shooting toward them in a blazing column of blue. Kaede ducked left, and through the flash, she caught sight of Imari diving right. They charged from both sides, closing in on the platform.

Kaede swept for Kyuubi's shoulder, but she wasn't quick enough. The fox was gone, moving so fast Kaede could barely keep track of her. She reappeared a few yards away, her own katana bared and pulsing with blue fire. "Meet Rakurai," she laughed, her eyes gleaming almost as bright as her blade.

"Lightning strike?" Imari snorted. "How original."

"It's not the name that matters," Kyuubi said in a singsong voice. "It's the body count attached. But you'd know all about that, wouldn't you?" She launched herself into the air, her sword sparkling over her head.

Kaede leapt to meet her. They clashed above the platform, swords screaming. Kaede could feel the sparks from Kyuubi's blade wash over her forearms, but she ignored the blistering heat. She tightened her grip on Mizu-no-Hamon and pushed with all her strength. Kyuubi's katana slipped off to the side, and the two of them landed back on the ground less than a meter apart.

Kyuubi struck again, but this time, Imari blocked it. She twirled, braid whipping around her head, and struck at Kyuubi's face with the tassels on the hilt of her jian. For a moment, Kyuubi was stunned, and Kaede seized the opportunity. She brought her katana down, aiming for middle of the closest tail.

Her sword sliced straight through it. Kyuubi screamed, jumping out of the way, but it was too late. The white, brushy tip of the fox's first tail fell limp to the ground. There was no blood, and after a moment, it vanished completely, dissolving into the stone.

"All right," Kyuubi snarled, truly angry for the first time. Her eyes gleamed wickedly and her lips peeled back to show sharpened teeth. "Playtime is over. It will take me another hundred years to grow that back!"

"You're assuming you'll live that long," Imari said.

Kyuubi shifted the handle of her sword to one hand, gathering another ball of blue lightning in the other, but a sound from the other end of the hall startled all three of them. The door burst open, and Rin and Kaze barreled into the room, with Hayate, Takeshi, Kenta, and Gin hot on their heels. Two dangerous growls rumbled through the room.

"Ah, I see the cavalry's arrived," Kyuubi said with a sarcastic toss of her head. Her remaining eight tails swished angrily along the ground, like a cat's just before it pounced. "All the better. You two lovebirds can watch all your friends die before I kill you."

"Hey, I'm not one of their friends," Gin said, taking a step back. She took in the scorched stones of the floor and the glowing lightning in Kyuubi's hand. "I'm the hired help, and—Sun and Moon, is that lightning? Nobody told me the fox had lightning!"

"Nobody told us either," Kenta said. "Come on, be brave. There's a war on the line here!"

"Oh, fine," Gin huffed. "But if the rest of you rush in and die, I'm out of here."

"Enough!" Kyuubi yelled, raising her sword over her head with both hands. "At this point, all of you are just a nuisance." She brought it sweeping down in a straight line, and a wall of blue fire shot out with it, heading straight for the ragtag group in the doorway.

Takeshi and Gin dove one way, Hayate and Kenta the other, but Rin and Kaze didn't flinch. They leapt straight over the flames, running for Kyuubi. The three of them crashed together, fox and wolves, sword and fangs. Kaede's heart lurched with fear. She circled around them, trying to find an opening, but they were locked together. She could barely see what was happening through the blur of white, black, and orange.

At last, the fray erupted with a brilliant surge of blue and an ear-splitting howl. Kaze stumbled back, bleeding from several crimson slices along his pelt, and Rin staggered the other way, the edges of her fur singed black. But as Kaze panted and heaved in pain, Kaede saw that he was holding something orange and white in his mouth. Another of Kyuubi's tails and it vanished from his dripping jaws just as the first had.

With fresh courage, everyone else charged. Gin and Takeshi went low, while Hayate and Kenta went high. Kyuubi struggled to fend them all off together. She twisted and swiveled to avoid each blade that sailed her way, always remaining out of reach.

Kaede ran back in as well with Imari at her side. She swept for Kyuubi's back, hoping to catch another of the seven tails whisking through the air, but they waved tauntingly out of the way. "Circle her!" she heard Imari call out. "At least one of us will get a chance."

Hearing this, Kyuubi broke free of the brawl, summoning more lightning. Kaede prepared to dodge, but the fox never aimed it at her. Instead, there was a thunderous boom, the nearby wall blasted open in a shower of stone and dust. Kaede shielded her eyes with her hand to avoid the spray.

When the dust settled, Kyuubi was already disappearing over the rubble. Kaede ran after her, tapping into her ki and sprinting as fast as she could. She ran as the wolf runs, eyes locked onto her prey, never flagging despite the cold stabs of ice in her lungs as she burst out into the snowy courtyard. As Kyuubi scaled the wall surrounding the castle, she did as well, running up and over without a second thought. She sailed down with outstretched arms, landing mere moments after Kyuubi did.

"You're fast," Kyuubi said, whirling on her again, "but not fast enough."

They circled each other, swords darting out. When Kaede struck, Kyuubi slid sideways at the last moment. When Kyuubi lashed out at her with another channeled bolt of lightning, Kaede sidestepped. It hurtled past her, blasting into one of the garden doors.

The flare illuminated another figure jumping down from atop the wall. Hayate had followed her over, and he landed, heading straight for Kyuubi with his sword outstretched. Kaede's heart swelled with pride. Finally, she and her cousin were fighting on the same side. Together, the two of them forced Kyuubi back, trading off blows. While Kaede kept Kyuubi's attention on her, meeting Rakurai strike for strike, Hayate danced around behind her. He brought his sword down, and once more, Kyuubi yowled in anger and pain. A third tail fluttered to the ground, bright orange against the pale white snow.

Kyuubi responded with rage. She whirled around and struck at Hayate. Her blade connected with his arm and sent him staggering backward. Hayate's shrill scream chilled her bones and the smell of burning flesh hit Kaede's nose. She pushed through her fear, hurrying to help him.

There wasn't much she could do. Hayate had fallen to his knees, clutching at his shoulder as blood poured out from between his fingers. "Go," he hissed through gritted teeth, his breath exhaling like steam. "I'll come after you."

"No," Kaede protested, but there wasn't time. Kyuubi was vanishing into the night. The rest of her friends came running through the door Kyuubi's lightning strike had burned. Kaze was with them, although he was limping rather badly. Blood dotted the snow in a trail behind him as he stumbled.

"Hayate!" he barked, picking up his pace, but he almost stumbled with the effort. Rin tucked her head beneath his, helping him stay steady until he reached them. He collapsed against Hayate's chest, flicking his pink tongue out to caress his friend's wounded shoulder.

"Leave us," Hayate said again. "We'll look out for each other. You've only got six more tails to go."

"Good," Rin growled. "One left for each of us." Satisfied that her brother was safe for the moment, she lifted her nose to the nighttime wind. It blew fiercely, stinging Kaede's cheeks and spraying her face with cold flecks of snow from the ground. "She went this way," Rin said, "behind the castle."

"But there's nothing that way," Kenta said. He didn't look happy about the idea of leaving Hayate, and his lower lip trembled. "No road, and no more buildings. It's an empty cliff. I saw it when Suanni was flying us in."

"That's where she's headed," Rin insisted. "Let's go."

With one last apologetic look at Hayate and Kaze, Kaede headed in the direction Rin had indicated. There was a faint set of footprints in the snow, although they were rapidly disappearing. She followed them through the dark, stumbling over jagged rocks until she heard Rin let out a howl. There in front of them, she could just see the tips of Kyuubi's remaining six tails disappearing around the distant edge of the wall.

She picked up her pace, skirting around the corner in time to see Kyuubi heading toward the cliff. With a final burst of speed, she planted herself squarely in the fox's path. Kyuubi split the air with Rakurai, but Kaede had Mizu-no-Hamon ready. They danced through their forms, spinning to avoid each other's swords.

"Do you want to know how much your deception hurt Imari? With her heart broken, it was so easy enter her mind." Suddenly, Kyuubi squalled in surprise and agony, hopping through the snow almost comically.

Kaede looked behind the fox in surprise, expecting to see Imari, but instead it was Gin who met her gaze. She waved the tail she had lopped off teasingly through the air, giving Kyuubi her most impudent grin. "Caught you monologuing. You've got no one but yourself to blame for this one."

"You rotten thief!" With a growl, Kyuubi rounded on Gin, her sword a dazzling streak of blue against the night sky. Gin managed to deflect her first few blows, but she couldn't keep up. The next time they clashed, Kyuubi's blade glided past hers, slicing along her side. Gin groaned, swaying dangerously, but Kyuubi didn't have time to follow up on the wounding strike. Takeshi's blade blocked Kyuubi's, and Gin could scramble away on her hands and knees, bleeding through her kimono.

With a roar, Kyuubi engaged Takeshi, only to find he wasn't alone. Imari and Kenta were there too, meeting her at every turn. Kaede hurried to join them, and together, the four of them backed Kyuubi further and further toward the cliff. Several times, the fox attempted to dart past one of them, but they closed ranks, refusing to let her through.

"What about you?" she said, sneering at Kenta. He stood closest to her, with two steaming craters on either side of him where Kyuubi's lightning had melted the snow. "Do you want this to be your big, shining moment? Do you think it will make your friends finally respect you? Do you think they'll laugh with you as you tell the tale instead of at you for a change?"

For once, Kenta wasn't smiling. Kyuubi's glowing blue sword brought out the shadows in his face, making his round face look more angular. "There's only one tail I'm interested in." He charged, but instead of meeting Kyuubi head on as she expected, he feinted, weaving to the left. His sword came down, severing Kyuubi's fifth tail.

In doing so, he opened himself up. Kyuubi sent him flying with a spinning kick. He sailed backwards, colliding with one of the large boulders near the edge of the cliff.

Kaede felt the jolt herself. "Kenta!" she yelled, only to realize someone else was shouting his name too. Takeshi had turned with her, and the wide eyes read fear.

Kenta didn't move, slumped at the base of the rock.

Takeshi started toward him, and Kyuubi took the opening. She struck at Takeshi's exposed back, and only Imari's swiftness managed to save his life. She inserted herself between them, sending Kyuubi's blade off-target with a block from her kote. She brought her jian in from the other side, striking at the side of Kyuubi's leg, but it didn't land. Kyuubi jumped backwards, and Kaede took over, dodging another flash of lightning and meeting the fox's crackling katana with her own.

"That's four of your friends gone," Kyuubi said.

"And five of your tails," Imari shot back, charging in again. "Who's winning?"

"Wonderful. You can count." Kyuubi's upper lip peeled back. "Since we're discussing missing body parts, how's that hand of yours holding up?" She aimed her next strike at Imari's left elbow.

Once more, Imari swept Kyuubi's sword aside. "One hand is more than enough to beat you."

"Then why do you make him fight for you?" Kyuubi aimed another lightning strike at Takeshi, and he barely ducked in time. "You're cruel, letting him follow you around like a loyal dog, using his feelings for you to get what you want. You're as manipulative as I am."

"That's a lie," Takeshi shouted. He rushed back in, flashing through his forms, forcing Kyuubi to retreat.

"Well, she did leave you for the first lying coward that came into her life after she cast you aside. Good luck finding anyone else to care for you."

Takeshi's response was a swift, perfectly executed spiral that took him around to Kyuubi's other side. When he emerged, the fox's sixth tail went fluttering away.

"Then enjoy dying alone," Kyuubi shrieked, striking at Takeshi. Kaede tried to get between them, but she couldn't move fast enough. Takeshi cried out, collapsing into the snow.

While Imari hurried to help him, Kaede launched herself at Kyuubi again. She grunted, lashing at Kyuubi with a backhanded strike, putting all her strength behind the blow. Her anger made her sloppy. The edge of Kyuubi's katana sank into the side of her arm, slicing through her skin. It was a shallow cut, but it burned like cold fire and brought tears to her eyes. Her grip on her sword loosened, and by the time she caught herself, Kyuubi was already holding another bright ball of lightning.

She braced herself, waiting for the pain, but it never came. Instead of blue, she saw white as Rin dashed in front of her. The lightning hit Rin, and Kaede screamed as the wolf's body jolted and shook with the impact. When Rin fell, it was on top of Kyuubi, still biting and clawing even as her muscles spasmed and blue fire raced along her fur.

There was a scream, and then Kyuubi squirmed out from under Rin's bulky frame, dashing away and leaving the wolf limp on the ground. The snow hissed, still dancing with sparks, and when Kaede crouched down, she saw Rin's eyes were closed. Tiny little puffs of silver air trailed from her black nose. But she had Kyuubi's seventh tail trapped within her teeth, pulled out by the root.

Tears welled in Kaede's eyes. She stroked Rin's head, waiting for her friend's eyes to open, but they didn't. The only thing that kept her from sinking into despair was the subtle rise and fall of Rin's side.

"Rin," she whispered, sniffing back the river that ran from her eyes and nose. "Please, wake up."

A firm hand grasped her shoulder, and she looked up to see Imari standing over her. "Takeshi's alive and Kenta's unconscious. What about

Rin?"

Kaede couldn't answer. She wasn't sure what would happen, and she didn't want to leave Rin. But Imari was pulling her up by the elbow, forcing her to stand, and she didn't have the strength to protest. "We have to go, Kaede. Kyuubi's getting away."

Even though she knew Imari was right, she hesitated. All their friends were injured or worse. *But what would they want you to do?* She stared down at Rin, who was laying deathly still. *What would Rin want you to do?*

She squared her shoulders and stood apart from Imari, finding her own footing without support. "Let's finish this." She swallowed hard. "I don't want it to be for nothing."

Imari nodded. They ran off into the night, following Kyuubi's tracks through the softly falling snow. It didn't take them long to catch sight of her. Kaede felt as though it had taken her an eternity to leave Rin's side, but it had been a few moments. Kyuubi had only gotten as far as the other side of the cliff. As Kaede watched, she came to a stop, searching for something within the folds of her kimono. When she withdrew her hand, she was clutching a milky white pearl.

"Look who's the coward now," Kaede shouted, full of rage. "You're the one running away!"

Kyuubi ignored her. The pearl began to shine with magical light, and Kaede put on a burst of speed. She collided with Kyuubi, sending them both sprawling. The pearl sank into a nearby snowdrift. Kyuubi dove after it, but Imari caught up. She brought her sword down at the perfect moment, and Kyuubi's eighth tail fell away.

Enraged, Kyuubi abandoned her search and turned on them. She leapt several feet in the air, her entire body glowing blue as a brilliant beam of fire burst from the end of her sword. To Kaede's relief, Imari managed to dodge it. The ground exploded where she had been standing a breath before, leaving a steaming crater behind.

When Kyuubi landed, the two of them met in a storm. They crashed together like thunder and lightning, swords flashing, blue sparks scattering into the night. Kaede picked herself up, hurrying to Imari's side and helping her push Kyuubi back toward the cliff. Soon, they were balanced on the edge, tilted into the fierce wind battering the mountainside. Through sharp flecks of snow and strands of her own hair whipping about her face, Kaede saw the black drop beyond. They were only a few meters away. Almost too close.

Kyuubi rushed at her with a snarl, reversing their positions.

Suddenly, Kaede found her back to the cliff. She fell into a defensive form, but Kyuubi forced her back, tipping her over the edge.

Kaede dropped Mizu-no-Hamon and grabbed out in desperation. She clawed at Kyuubi's kimono, clutching the fabric for dear life. Her fingers slipped off the fabric, but she found a hold—right in the middle of Kyuubi's final tail. With a jolt, she stopped falling, and she heard a pained cry from above her. Kyuubi grasped the edge of the cliff with both hands, struggling to pull herself back up. The fox kicked out, trying to force Kaede to let go, but she held on tighter.

"Not a chance," Kaede growled. "If I'm going down, you're going with me."

"Neither of us has to go down!" Kyuubi said, speaking quickly. "Imari, pull us up!"

Kaede peered up past Kyuubi and caught sight of Imari standing at the edge of the cliff. She looked panic-stricken and she held her sword limp at her side, as if she wasn't sure what to do. After a moment, she seemed to come to a decision. She reached for Kyuubi's hands, preparing to grasp them.

"Don't!" Kaede shouted

"I'm not letting you fall," Imari called back above the roaring wind, her face frighteningly pale against the night sky above her and her eyes wide.

Kaede shifted her grip until she was clinging to Kyuubi's tail one-handed. Her arm burned from holding the entire weight of her body, and Kyuubi squealed above her, but she ignored it all. With her free hand, she reached for her obi, drawing her wakizashi from its saya. She fumbled in her hurry, and the grip almost slipped from her numb, shaking hand, but she managed to wrap her fingers around it.

Imari must have seen the glint of silver, because she shook her head. "Kaede, no!" Her voice sounded faint and distant, and Kaede could barely hear it above the deafening throb of her own heartbeat in her ears. She gazed at Imari one last time. In her mind, she replaced Imari's look of agony with one of love.

"I love you," she said, bringing up her blade. "May we meet again across the Roaring Ocean."

She cut through Kyuubi's final tail with one swipe. As soon as it was severed, she fell, hurtling down into the darkness.

Chapter Twenty-Seven

A SCREAM SHATTERED THE air, shaking the mountainside, primal and desperate. The scream of a lost soul, of a breaking heart. Imari's ears ached with the sound, but it wasn't until sharp fire lit up her throat that she realized she made the noise.

She barely saw Kyuubi's expression of shock and dismay, or the life leaving her eyes. She barely noticed the fox tumble into the void after Kaede, dead before she could hit the ground far, far below. Her mind couldn't process it, because she was stuck on a single thought: Kaede was gone.

She dropped her sword and scrambled to the edge of the cliff, peering down in desperation, but there was nothing. All she could see was inky blackness. With a wail, Imari collapsed to her knees, unable to do anything but weep. The wind lashed at her face, freezing her tears half way down her cheeks.

It was over, and Kaede was gone.

Even though it broke her heart all over again each time, she replayed Kaede's final words in her head over and over. *"I love you May we meet again."* She didn't want to meet Kaede in some other life, or across the Roaring Ocean in the place of Last Resort. That wasn't good enough. She wanted her lover back. Her best friend. Her heart.

"I didn't mean it," she sobbed, burying her face in her hands. "You aren't a coward, Kaede. You're the bravest person I know."

"Really?"

Imari blinked away her tears, letting her hands fall away. She looked up, certain she was seeing some kind of hysterical hallucination. Kaede stood before her, floating as if on the air.

"Go away," she shouted at the specter, lashing out in anger. "I know you're not real."

Kaede didn't go away. She stepped back onto the cliff, offering Imari her hand. "I'm sorry, I didn't mean to make you cry."

That was the moment Imari realized Kaede had survived. Only Kaede would worry more about making her cry than almost dying. "You idiot," she cried, shoving Kaede gently in the middle of the chest. "You stupid, awful, wonderful—"

Kaede cut her off with a kiss, and Imari sagged into her embrace. The warmth of Kaede's arms kept off the cold and thawed out her heart once more. "I thought you were dead," she muttered between kisses, shaking terribly. Kaede's lips were rough and chapped, and her own weren't any better, but she didn't care. "You fell off the cliff."

"Yes, but I fell onto a dragon. Look."

Imari looked over Kaede's shoulder to see Suanni floating beside the cliff. It was difficult to tell on their large lion's face, but Imari thought they looked pleased with themselves. "Thank the Ancestors," she breathed, tucking her face into Kaede's shoulder again. She didn't know how Suanni had managed to arrive at exactly the right moment, but she didn't care. Kaede was alive, and that was all that mattered.

"Hey," Kaede said, gently trying to extract herself from the embrace, "I love you and I'm really sorry for almost sacrificing myself, but we have to go."

"No," Imari said. "I don't think I can let go."

"We need to check on Rin and the others."

Imari knew Kaede was right, but it was still difficult to unwind her arms from around Kaede's waist. She was still overwhelmed with emotion even though her tears were happy ones. It wasn't until Kaede bent to pick up their fallen swords and offered her Wujian that she felt able to move on her own.

Once she regained control of her limbs, she faced Suanni, bowing deeply. "Thank you," she said, hoping her sincerity would come through in her voice. She wasn't sure what else to say. What could she say to the one who had saved her lover's life?

Suanni lifted their head, peering at her with lamp-like yellow eyes. "It wasn't Kaede's day to pass to the other shore. I'm only glad I arrived in time."

"Did you stop the shogun?" Kaede asked, sheathing Mizu-no-Hamon.

"I did. I was able to disturb some of the rocks on the pathway down. It was more than enough to stall them."

"And Kyuubi? Is she?"

"The fox is dead," Suanni said. "I will go and retrieve her body. It needs to be disposed of properly. Despite all she has done, she is yokai. We have our customs."

Imari thought Kyuubi could rot on the mountainside until next spring for all she cared, but she didn't say so. Instead, she took Kaede's hand. "We'll go and check on the others. Hopefully everyone made it."

"That is my hope, too. Kyuubi has already caused enough death and suffering." With a final bow, Suanni flew off into the night, disappearing from view.

Still holding Kaede's hand tight, Imari headed over to where they had last seen Takeshi and Kenta. To her relief, the Hibana brothers were up and moving when she arrived. Kenta had regained consciousness, and though the back of Takeshi's kimono was stained with blood, he sat upright.

Kaede, however, only had eyes for Rin. She dropped Imari's hand, running to kneel beside her friend. "How is she?" she asked Kenta, who was crouched near Rin's haunches.

"Still alive for now," Kenta said. "I don't know, Kaede. It doesn't look good."

Imari hurried over to join them. Rin was still breathing, but her eyes remained closed. "It was a bad hit," she said, flinching at the memory. She was sure a human would have been killed instantly. Kaede brought Rin's head into her lap, petting between her ears. "You have to wake up, Rin. I survived falling off a cliff. You're not going to let a little lightning stop you, right?"

"Back up," Kenta said, "you survived falling off a cliff?"

"Not important right now," Takeshi groaned. His face was a mask of pain. "Kyuubi's dead, right?"

Imari crawled over to sit beside him. "Yes. She won't be bothering us anymore."

Takeshi began to say something else, but he lost his words. Instead, he turned, looking back toward the castle. Imari followed his gaze, a big smile spreading across her face. Stumbling toward them through the snow were three familiar figures, two humans and one wolf.

Imari raised her hand and called out, but to her surprise, it was Kenta who jumped up and rushed over to greet their friends first. He took Hayate's weight from Gin, who seemed the least injured and was doing her best to support him. With a little limping, the four of them made it back to Rin.

"What happened?" Hayate panted, kneeling beside Kaede with Kenta's help.

Kaze sniffed around Rin's face, smelling her breath and nudging her with his nose. "She's badly injured."

"What should we do?" Kaede asked.

"Move her somewhere safe and warm," Kaze said. "I'll carry her on my back."

"You can't," Hayate protested, but Imari cut him off, taking control of the situation.

"If Kaze says he can carry her, I believe him. We'll all help. We can't stay out here, and we can't leave her alone."

Together, they managed to lift Rin onto Kaze's back, standing three on each side. Hayate and Takeshi weren't much help with their injuries, but Kaede seemed to have the strength of ten people all on her own. Imari was half-certain she could have carried Rin alone if she'd had to. Slowly, they trudged off through the snow, making their way back to the castle.

"Nearly getting killed by a fox with magic lightning, playing doctor to a spirit wolf," Gin muttered from her place on the line. "Ancestors, the things you've all dragged me into." Despite her complaining, she carried Rin the same as the rest of them, holding one of the wolf's hind legs steady.

"Think of it this way," Kenta said, "you'll be a hero to your village. I'm sure Empress Tomoyo herself will take a special interest in revitalizing the town when she hears what you've done."

"She's the Empress. She should have taken an interest before things got bad." But through Gin's grumbling, Imari noticed her smile. "As annoying as you all are, I'm glad everyone made it out."

Imari saw Kaede stiffen in front of her, and she could almost hear her beloved say, *Not everyone.*

***

The next morning dawned cold and grey. Kaede was awake to see it break in muted colors through the window, because even though she was tired to the point of shaking, she hadn't been able to sleep. She had remained at Rin's side all through the night, waiting for her to wake up. Thankfully, she hadn't been alone in her vigil. Imari, Kaze, Hayate, both Hibana brothers, and even Gin had insisted on remaining with her in the room the Toyotomi guards had shown them to upon their return to the castle.

Doctors were by during the first part of the night to bandage their wounds, dressing the worst with poultices to prevent infection and soothe their burns. Rin, however, was a difficult case. Except for a small burn on her chest, she had no visible injuries. The doctors had been reluctant to examine her, and Kaze's insistence on curling up next to her and fixing his yellow eyes on anyone who came near hadn't helped matters.

Still, one of the doctors had tried to offer some hope. He claimed that the longer Rin's condition remained stable, with no change in her heartbeat or breathing and no rapid movements of her muscles, the more likely she was to recover. That was why Kaede had stayed awake even while every muscle in her body screamed and her eyes ached with exhaustion.

The others hadn't been so stalwart. One by one, they had drifted off into healing sleeps, stretched out on pallets the doctors had brought. Imari had lasted the longest, but even she had eventually rested her head in Kaede's lap, claiming she only needed to close her eyes for a moment. Kaede hadn't minded. Stroking Imari's hair gave her worried hands something to do as she greeted the morning alone.

As strips of pale sunlight stretched across the floor, Kaede listened to the sound of everyone's breathing. It was hard to hear Rin's ragged sips of air beneath the thunderous sound of Kenta's snoring and Takeshi's low moans of pain, but it was there, faint and reassuring. As long as there was breath, there was hope.

"Kaede?"

The whispered sound of her name made her turn and blink in surprise. After a few moments of bleary confusion, she realized Hayate had woken up. He held himself awkwardly, with his shoulders at a tilt, but he had managed to sit up on his own.

"Go back to sleep," she murmured. "Nothing's changed."

"I was about to tell you the same thing," Hayate said, "but you haven't been to sleep at all, have you?"

"I can't." Kaede gazed back at Rin. "What if I close my eyes, and a few minutes later, she…" She couldn't say the word "dies," but she thought it loud enough for Hayate to hear.

"I'm sorry," he said. "If I had been stronger and kept going, maybe she wouldn't have gotten hurt."

Kaede shook her head. "No, Hayate. You did your part and claimed one of Kyuubi's tails. I was proud to fight by your side again, and I always will be. I'm glad you're alive."

Hayate remained silent for a long time, as if considering her words. After a while, he said, "That isn't the only thing I need to apologize for. My jealousy is why we're here in the first place. I was so wrapped up in proving myself to Setsuna, proving she should love me more than you, I didn't see the warning signs. If I'd realized Kyuubi was manipulating her sooner, we could've done something before now."

"Hayate, you've already apologized for this. We could play this game forever. If I'd given you more time with your mother instead of clinging to her, you wouldn't have gotten jealous. If I hadn't run away from home, things would've played out differently, too." Kaede looked down at Imari, still fast asleep in her lap. "Assuming Rin makes it, I don't have any regrets. And if she doesn't, you're the last person I'd blame."

"I know," Hayate said. "I just look at Kaze and wonder, what if it had been my best friend?"

They lapsed into silence again, gazing at the two wolves. They were still curled up together on the largest of the mats.

"So," Hayate spoke up again, his voice still a whisper. "Change of topic. Your friend, Hibana-san. He's really something, huh?"

For the first time since her reunion with Imari on the edge of the cliff, Kaede smiled. "Which one?" she whispered back wryly, "because they're both single, but only one of them is a member of our court."

Hayate gave her a sheepish smirk then nodded subtly over at Kenta. He was still snoring away, his mouth hanging agape. He wasn't exactly the picture of handsomeness, but perhaps Hayate saw something she didn't.

"Lucky pick," Kaede said, her heart lifting a little. "I'll drop a hint in his ear, if you're prepared to hear him talk yours off. If you two get to know each other better, maybe something good can come out of this."

"Something good already has," Hayate said. He glanced pointedly at Imari, who let out a soft sigh and shifted position, as if she knew she was being observed. "I'm happy for you, Kaede, even though she almost killed me."

Kaede gave a quiet laugh. "She's normally sweet, I promise. You'll see once you get to know her."

Imari yawned and lifted her head, blinking sleepily. "Kaede? How's Rin?"

"The same." Kaede's heart sank once more and her stomach turned into a sucking pit of worry.

"But that's good, isn't it?" Imari said. "The doctors said to give her time."

Kaede didn't answer. With Imari awake, she stood up, shifting over to Rin's pallet. As she had done countless times throughout the night, she stroked the soft space between Rin's ears. Her movements woke Kaze, who cracked open his yellow eyes and snuggled in closer to his sister. His tongue flicked out to clean the side of Rin's cheek.

"She smells better," he said, trying to offer reassurance.

Kaede gave him a weak smile. She appreciated what Kaze was trying to do, but she wouldn't feel better until Rin was awake. She hunkered down next to the wolves, closing her eyes and resting her cheek on one of Rin's paws. From her new place, she could feel the soft puff of Rin's breath every few seconds.

"If I open my eyes, will you stop staring at me and get some sleep?"

At first, Kaede thought she had imagined things. She looked at Rin again and her heart leapt with joy. The wolf's blue eyes were open—glazed with exhaustion and pain, but open.

"Rin!" she shouted. She threw her arms around Rin's neck, squeezing tight and burying her face in her best friend's fur. "Ancestors, I thought we were going to lose you."

Rin snorted softly. "No fox can stop a wolf. But please, softer. You're hurting me."

Kaede pulled back at once. "I'm sorry. Are you okay? What can I do for you?"

By that time, the rest of the room had woken up. All of them crowded around Rin, Imari and Hayate first, then Kenta and Gin, who had been woken by Kaede's shouting. Takeshi was the slowest, but he too dragged himself off his mat to come and greet Rin.

"It's so good to see you awake, Rin." Imari reached down to stroke her fur.

"It's good to see you, too," Rin said, "but please, tell me what I heard you say about Kaede going over a cliff was a bad dream."

"Suanni caught me," Kaede replied.

Imari shook her head. "Don't worry, Rin. Kaede and I will be having words about that later."

"What about everyone else?" Rin lifted her head weakly, gazing at the crowd gathered by her mat. "Glad to see you all made it, although if I'm the worst off, that's just embarrassing." She huffed in Gin's direction. "Even the thief held up better than me."

"I think I remembered why I don't like you," Gin mumbled, but she gave Rin a small smile to show she was joking.

Kaede barely noticed. Her eyes welled over with tears, and she had to wipe them away with her sleeve.

"Don't do that," Rin said, resting her head on Kaede's knee and caressing her hand with a warm tongue. "I hate it when you cry."

"I can't help it," Kaede sniffed. "You almost died for me."

"You would have done the same. I was just in the right place at the right time."

Kaede tried to say that it was more than that, but she was distracted by Imari passing over her handkerchief. She took it and swiped the rivers from her face while Imari rubbed circles on her back. "Try and get some sleep," she murmured. "You need it."

"I'll look after Rin if you want to rest," Takeshi offered. "My shoulder isn't going to let me sleep again now that I'm awake anyway."

"Me too," Kenta added. "I only got a little knock on the head. I'm fine to sit up for a while."

Kaede remained uncertain, but it was Kaze who finally convinced her. "She's going to be fine, Kaede. You don't have to watch over her alone."

A great weight lifted from Kaede's shoulders. Kaze was right. She didn't have to look out for Rin alone anymore—or do anything alone, for that matter. She had Imari, and she had Hayate back, and more friends than she had ever dreamed of. With relief came exhaustion, and she yawned loud and long before covering her mouth with her hand and cuddling up beside Rin. "Just for a few minutes," she said, draping an arm around the wolf's midsection. She smiled when she felt Imari drag her mat closer and settle down behind her.

"Thank you," she whispered to Rin as her eyes drifted shut. "You'll always be my best friend."

Rin didn't say anything, but Kaede fell asleep to the soft, happy thump of her tail against the floor.

***

The following days passed quickly for Imari. Between looking after her injured friends and helping to direct temporary repairs to the castle, she kept busy. Empress Tomoyo arrived on the second day with a full complement of soldiers, and her first order of business was to interview the imprisoned shogun, who were being temporarily housed in the dungeon. She requested Imari's presence, claiming she had "first-hand experience" with Kyuubi's manipulation.

As they were brought before the Empress, each shogun told the same story: they had come across a large pearl at some point in the past few years and it had started whispering to them. They were horrified to learn exactly what they had done, and there had been a few dramatic requests for executions to end their shame. Empress Tomoyo had dismissed those requests decisively, reminding the samurai that it was their duty now to restore their own honor. She stripped them of their ranks as punishment for being deceived, with the promise to return their positions if they proved themselves wiser in the future.

Imari had to admit, under the circumstances, the Empress was displaying both mercy and foresight. However, she took a more sympathetic view toward their requests for an honorable death. She remembered how disgusted she had been with herself after breaking free from Kyuubi's spell. The violation still lingered, casting a shadow over her whenever she remembered how it felt.

"You'll have to be careful, Imari," the Empress said after dismissing yet another green-looking shogun from the southern provinces. "If you keep being this helpful, I'll have to make you a shogun yourself."

Imari bowed deeply. "You flatter me, Your Majesty, but perhaps my father would be better suited to that title."

"And this has nothing to do with you wanting to take over Mirai from him when you return there?" Empress Tomoyo asked with a knowing smile.

"Maybe," Imari admitted. "It would be strange, going back home after adventuring all over Tengoku only to help him with his extra correspondence."

"I'm sure we can find something much more useful for you and your friends to do. You all deserve to be rewarded for what you've done for the Empire."

"Ishikawa Gin will be happy to hear that, Heika," Imari said. "Her village could certainly use a helping hand from the royal court to get it on its feet again. Oh, and a pardon for her previous crimes wouldn't go unappreciated either, if that would be your will."

"Ishikawa-san...you mean the other woman who helped you into the castle?" Empress Tomoyo frowned. "I wasn't aware she had previous crimes that needed pardoning."

"The weight of her crimes isn't heavier than the heroism she showed," Imari said. "She was only stealing to feed her village, and she risked her life to help us. She even cut off one of Kyuubi's tails."

Empress Tomoyo nodded. "Consider it done. Considering her actions, I will grant her an audience to discuss the problems in her village. What about Yukimura Hayate? As I understand it, he was a great deal of help as well."

Imari thought for a moment. "Well, Yukimura is going to need a new daimyo, at least while Setsuna recovers. It only seems right that her son should take over for her."

"Another reasonable request. Hayate is next in line anyway, and he has proven himself. If he does well in the position, perhaps I can consider lifting his family's punishment in a few years and make him a shogun. What about your other friends, Hibana Kenta and Takeshi? As Homura samurai, it is your place to reward them."

"It is, Your Majesty, and I already know what I'm going to do for one of them," Imari said with a laugh. "I'm going to send Hibana Kenta on a little vacation to the northern provinces. You know, to make sure things settle down properly." She gave the Empress a small smile. "He and Yukimura Hayate have been getting along well recently."

The Empress laughed. "It seems the universe decided to reward him instead of waiting on his master."

Imari laughed as well, but then her brow furrowed in thought. "Hibana Takeshi is harder," she mused aloud. "It's strange. I've known him since I was a child, and we were even engaged for a little while, but I still don't have a good grip on what he might want."

That wasn't entirely true. *The two of us are going to have to have a talk,* she thought to herself, her heart sinking at the prospect.

"Well, you have time to ask him," Empress Tomoyo said. "It's only been a few days. What about Aozora Kaede? I plan to commission a scroll of her deeds for the Library of the New Moon, of course."

Imari looked at the Empress in astonishment. Having one's deeds recorded in the Library of the New Moon was one of Akatsuki Teikoku's highest honors, one only bestowed on national heroes. There had only been two such scrolls awarded in the last century, and none in the past fifty years. Then again, she shouldn't be surprised. Kaede had defeated Kyuubi, prevented a civil war, and saved countless lives. If anyone deserved such an honor, it was her.

"I'm sure she'll accept it humbly," Imari said, bowing deeply. "I can't think of a more fitting reward, Heika."

Empress Tomoyo smirked. "I'm sure you can, but my advisers tell me I'm too young to speculate about such things."

Imari's cheeks flushed. It wasn't so much that the Empress was fifteen—she remembered what it had been like to experience those tumultuous years—but the fact Empress Tomoyo had been bold enough to say so. Apparently, the Empress was offering the honor of her trust and friendship. "Actually," she said, lighting up with an idea, "there might be one more thing you can do for us, if you would be so kind."

The Empress leaned in closer. "Tell me. I'll see what I can do."

***

Imari didn't get a chance to speak to Takeshi until later that evening. He had tried his best to help her organize over the past several days, but aside from Rin, he had suffered the worst injuries. When she didn't see him at dinner, she gathered a bowl of steamed rice and cooked chicken and returned to the room he and Kenta had been given, hoping to find him there instead.

She wasn't disappointed. When she nudged the screen with her foot, still carrying the bowl in her hand, and called out his name, he responded almost immediately.

"Come in, Imari. I'm sorry, I was resting."

Imari shouldered her way in. Takeshi rested on his futon, although it didn't look as though she had disturbed him from as deep sleep. His hair was in place, and he seemed to be fully dressed.

"Are you sure I'm not bothering you?" she asked, setting the steaming bowl on the table in the middle of the room. "I got worried when I didn't see you at dinner, so I brought you something."

Takeshi gave her a smile. "Thank you. I appreciate that. I'm afraid I haven't had much appetite lately."

"You still need to eat," Imari insisted. She sat on one of the cushioned mats beside the table, about a yard away from Takeshi's bedding. "I'm not going to let you die of starvation after everything you managed to survive so far."

At the mention of his injury, Takeshi rolled his shoulders. "I'm doing fine. See? My back isn't bothering me as much anymore."

Imari sighed. From the tension that stretched between them, she knew Takeshi knew the real reason she had come. Never one to dance around important subjects, she took a deep breath and plunged into uncertain waters. "Was what Kyuubi said that night true, Takeshi? Are you afraid of being alone?" When his forehead wrinkled, she coaxed him further. "Come on. After everything we've been through, you can talk to me."

Takeshi didn't answer right away, but he didn't avoid her eyes either. For once, he met them straight on instead of averting them politely. "Sometimes," he said at last. "I know the two of us didn't work together, but part of me isn't sure I'll ever find someone else."

Imari smiled. She felt sympathy for Takeshi's pain, but the truthful answer he had given gave her hope as well. Back during their relationship, he had rarely been so open and honest. She took one of his hands. "Takeshi, I know you will find someone. You've already changed so much since we were engaged, all for the good. You're a better man than you were even a few months ago, and I'm not the only one who's able to see it."

Takeshi stared into her eyes, some of the worried lines smoothing from his face. "That's kind of you to say. . ."

"I'm not just saying it to make you feel better. I mean it. The next woman who comes into your life is going to be so lucky."

Takeshi laughed softly. "Well, you've always been truthful with me, even when it hurt. I believe you. I have to say, it's going to be hard to find someone as wonderful as you."

"Hard, maybe, but not impossible," Imari said.

"No, not impossible," Takeshi agreed. "I think watching you and Kaede has been good for me. It gives me hope. That isn't strange, is it?"

"Not at all." Imari hesitated, weighing her options. The more she thought about it, the more she felt like this was the right time to tell Takeshi of her intentions. He was her best friend, after all. "I'm going to ask Kaede to marry me. That's one of the reasons I wanted to clear the air between us."

To her joy, Takeshi smiled genuinely. "Normally, I would question your judgment and tell you it was too soon to think about marriage but not after everything the four of us have been through together."

Imari chuckled in agreement. "We have faced down much more frightening things, haven't we? But even though we've suffered together, it wasn't all bad. Those two peaceful months at Hongshan were some of the happiest of my life. Kaede and I worked well even when the world wasn't threatening to collapse around us."

Takeshi seemed to understand. "I won't be presumptuous enough to offer my blessing, because I know you don't need it, but you're welcome to it anyway. I'm happy for the two of you and I think you're making the right decision."

Imari's heart swelled with love, both for Kaede and for Takeshi. "I know I am, but I'm glad you approve. As much as I complain, I care what you think. You're my best friend and the most honorable man I know."

"What about your father?" Takeshi teased. "Although I'm sure he'll be thrilled when you tell him the news."

"You and he are tied for first," Imari said. "Now come over here and eat. I'm not leaving until you finish the rice in that bowl."

Carefully, Takeshi drew himself up from the futon, walking over to the table. Once he was close enough, she wrapped him in a tight hug, careful not to put pressure on his bandages. "Thank you," she murmured, kissing him lightly on the cheek.

Takeshi wrapped his arms around her as well. "You don't need to thank me. Seeing you and Kaede happy is enough."

Chapter Twenty-Eight

THE NEXT WEEK DRAGGED by. Imari's lips quivered with the question she wanted to ask, but she had made up her mind to wait until her father arrived. She had sent for him with the empress's permission, thinking it best to bring him up to speed before rumors of her battle with Kyuubi reached him. If Imari's guess was right, he was on his way to Asahina as fast as he and his samurai could travel.

Although she was certain he would approve of Kaede once she told him of their adventures together, Imari wanted his blessing. It stunned her to think that while she had gotten to know Kaede intimately over the past six months, her father knew almost nothing about the woman she loved. It was a problem Imari wanted to fix, but in the meantime, she was stuck waiting. *And that's assuming Kaede says yes.*

Imari prayed she would. Kaede had been incredibly affectionate since her near-death experience; the two of them spent their days together and every night wrapped in each other's arms. Still, there was a niggling sense of doubt. Despite all they had been through, theirs had been something of a whirlwind romance. They hadn't had a traditional courtship at all. Imari was certain of her decision, but she couldn't assume Kaede felt the same, no matter how high her hopes were. Though she saw at least a hundred chances to tell Kaede what was in her heart, she bit her tongue instead. She needed to wait for the perfect moment.

That was why, as dawn's rosy fingers crept in through their window one morning, Imari lost herself staring at Kaede's sleeping form. The covers pooled around Kaede's hips, and the sleeves of her yukata had rolled up during the night, revealing her tanned forearms. Her lips curved in a soft, sweet smile and she breathed steady and peaceful.

On impulse, Imari scooted closer. She wrapped her right arm around Kaede's midsection, pressing a light kiss to her shoulder. For a moment, she simply inhaled Kaede's warm sleep-scent. During moments like this, her heart was so full of love her chest ached with it.

Kaede sensed the shift, or at least Imari's movements. She groaned and opened her eyes, blinking slowly. "Were you watching me again?" she mumbled, her voice still low and throaty with sleep. "You know, coming from anyone else, it would be creepy."

Imari gave Kaede a guilty grin, although she wasn't the least bit repentant. "I'm sorry. You're beautiful. Sometimes I look at you and I'm so overwhelmed. I don't know what I did with myself before I met you."

"You probably got in a lot less trouble," Kaede chuckled.

"True," Imari admitted, "but it hasn't all been the bad sort of trouble." She moved her hand down along the curve of Kaede's side, stopping at her hip and squeezing lightly.

Her teasing produced the desired result. In a flash, Imari found herself flat on her back with Kaede's weight on top of her. One of Kaede's thighs pressed between her legs, not quite a demand, but not an accident either.

"You can't keep your hands to yourself, can you?" Kaede teased, kissing the point of her chin.

Imari gave Kaede a look, waiting for her to realize what she had said. When she finally did, she groaned and tucked her head in embarrassment. "Sorry. A figure of speech. I'm tired."

"It's okay, it was funny. And no, I can't keep my hand to myself." To prove it, she brought her hand down to Kaede's backside, giving it a firm squeeze and sitting up to try and catch her lips in a kiss.

"You could at least let me brush my teeth first," Kaede snorted, only half pulling away.

"I don't care." Imari took her mouth just to prove it, running her tongue along Kaede's full lower lip. It didn't taste any different than usual—and Kaede's taste was always enough to drive Imari wild.

They broke apart, Kaede breathing heavy and ragged. "Sometimes I think I could kiss you forever," she murmured. Her eyes had become dark pools of desire, and heat blossomed between Imari's legs as she gazed into them. Kaede's knee wasn't quite riding against her yet, but it was close enough to cause some delicious friction.

"I couldn't." With their bodies pressed flush, Imari could feel Kaede stirring. "Looks like you couldn't, either," she purred, hooking her knees around Kaede's hips. They gave a short pump in response, enough for Imari to feel her outline. It was a surprisingly bold gesture, and Imari laughed softly to show she appreciated it. She began to loosen Kaede's yukata, doing her best to untie the obi backwards and one-handed.

Kaede wasn't much help. Her mouth wandered down along Imari's neck, making it even more difficult to concentrate. "This gets easier the more we practice," she sighed, going to work on Imari's yukata as well. She was faster, and soon Imari felt Kaede's hands running along her bare stomach.

"And what do you want to practice, Kaede?"

A look of uncertainty passed over Kaede's face, as if she was considering something deeply. Eventually, without coaxing, she spoke. "I want to learn how you feel, Imari," she said, choosing her words with great care. "From the inside. I mean, if you want to."

Imari's eyes widened, but after a few seconds, a broad grin spread across her face. "Of course, I want to." She finally managed to get Kaede's yukata open, and she brought her palm up to Kaede's left breast, caressing the subtle curve. "I was hoping you would ask."

"I've thought about it," Kaede admitted. Her voice shook, but with what sounded like excitement rather than nerves. "A lot. With you, I want to try."

"Not because you think I'm unhappy with the way things are, I hope," Imari said.

Kaede looked horrified. "Not at all. I just." She flushed, averting her eyes. "You feel so good around my fingers. You're one of the warmest, softest things I've ever touched." The length of Kaede's shaft gave a throb of need against Imari's hip. Her own inner walls rippled in response, and a soft stream of warmth spilled down along her inner thigh at the suggestion.

"What?" she whispered, twining the fingers of her right hand through Kaede's and guiding their linked hands between her legs. "You mean this?" She cupped her palm over Kaede's, urging her to squeeze.

Kaede's fingertips glided through Imari's wetness before she even let go of them. She sought out the sensitive spots she had learned before, and Imari's breath hitched as two of Kaede's fingers swirled around her entrance. Instead of pressing inside, they slid through the pool of slickness there and spread it higher, coating the tip of Imari's clit.

Imari's hips jolted at the light contact. She gasped Kaede's name, bracing herself on her left elbow and using her right hand to claw at the back of Kaede's yukata. She managed to pull it down to Kaede's forearms, but couldn't manage to get the sleeves all the way off. Kaede's hand was too busy working between her legs, and she didn't seem inclined to stop.

"I...thought you wanted..." Imari panted, but she couldn't finish her sentence. She could barely keep her eyes open. Kaede's face was a beautiful blur hovering above hers. A simple touch had never made her come undone so rapidly before.

"In a minute." Kaede abandoned the aching point of her clit and slid two knuckles along the root instead, teasing the shaft through its thin hood. "I want this first. I love watching you. Is that okay?"

Imari nodded, the only answer she could manage. Soon, the swift circles of Kaede's fingers had Imari throwing her head back and moaning to the ceiling. She suspected what was coming when Kaede took over the motion with her thumb, but the press of a finger at her opening still set her shivering. The first push was smooth, without a hint of resistance. Her hips hovered off the bed as Kaede's finger hooked forward, searching for the special spot inside her.

When Kaede found it, colors flashed before Imari's eyes. "More," she begged, rocking harder into the palm of Kaede's hand. "Please."

Kaede added a second finger and began kissing down the slope of her chest. Imari felt a hot mouth seal around the peak of her breast as both of Kaede's fingers curled up, and she saw stars. A loud cry tore from her chest, breaking in her throat, and she was certain she would shudder to pieces.

But Kaede didn't give her the release her body craved. She kept up the pressure, keeping her fingers in place and pushing. Imari trembled, raking her nails down along Kaede's back, but there was nothing she could do. Somehow, Kaede had found precisely the right angle to keep her balanced on the edge.

"Kaede."

Kaede kissed over to her other breast, sucking the stiff bud deep into her mouth and grazing it with the edges of her teeth. Her dark eyes darted up, and Imari could tell that Kaede was drinking in the expression on her face. She didn't know what Kaede was looking for—approval, perhaps, or maybe just her pleasure—but Imari didn't care. She fisted Kaede's hair with her right hand, dragging her up for a hard, deep kiss.

Kaede's fingers pushed even deeper inside her, and Imari finally crossed the Roaring Ocean to find heaven. She spilled into Kaede's palm, shaking the entire time, giving sharp cries into Kaede's mouth with each wave that broke over her. Through it all, Kaede kept moving within her, carrying her safely back to shore.

As her crest faded and their kiss broke, Imari gazed dreamily up into Kaede's eyes. There were moments she couldn't quite believe Kaede had never done this with anyone but her before, and this was one of them. "What did I do to deserve you?" she sighed, collapsing backwards onto the bed. Her limbs were limp and heavy, and her entire body tingled.

Kaede's face glowed with pride. "You stole the words out of my mouth." She removed her fingers carefully, placing a soft parting kiss on Imari's lips.

After a slight shake to clear her head and a luxurious stretch, Imari reached down to take Kaede's sticky hand in hers. She brought it to her mouth, folding her lips around the first two shining fingers and running her tongue between them. Her own taste spread across her tongue, and though she found it pleasant, it wasn't quite satisfying. She would have preferred tasting her lover far more.

But Kaede had asked for something else, and Imari hadn't forgotten. She gathered her second wind, releasing Kaede's fingers with a soft pop and reversing their positions. "Now it's your turn," she murmured, placing her hand in the center of Kaede's chest and tipping her over. "Lie back for me and close your eyes."

***

Kaede wanted to ask why, but she resisted the temptation. She trusted Imari wholeheartedly, and so she obeyed, reclining the opposite way on the futon and closing her eyes. She even stretched her arms above her head, surrendering herself to whatever Imari wanted to do. Her heart hammered in her chest and she swallowed hard, barely breathing.

Warm lips skated along Kaede's collarbone, and she felt the futon beneath her dip as Imari moved on top of her. As Imari's knees settled on either side of her thighs and Imari's hand slid up to cup the swell of her left breast, Kaede suddenly understood why Imari had asked her to close her eyes. Without the benefit of sight, even the subtle sensations were more intense.

"You made me feel so good, Kaede," Imari said, twirling around and around the hard point of her nipple. She gave it a light pinch, and the breath Kaede had been holding rushed out. "I want to make you feel the same way."

"You do." Kaede's voice trailed off as Imari dusted feathery kisses along her neck, working back up toward her jaw. "Sun and Moon, you do."

The edges of Imari's teeth sank into Kaede's pulse point, not quite biting, but tugging and holding for a moment. When she let go, Kaede could still feel their impression. "It's about to get even better. Are you ready?"

Kaede's head spun, but she managed to rasp out an answer. "Yes."

As soon as Kaede gave her permission, Imari began a slow, thorough exploration of her entire body. With her eyes closed, Kaede wasn't sure what was coming next. One moment, Imari's hand ran along her arms, admiring the lean muscles. The next, it caressed the plane of Kaede's stomach, lighting up the ticklish skin there. Her mouth explored every inch of Kaede's shoulders, and she wasn't afraid to use liberal amounts of tongue and teeth.

By the time Imari's hand reached her thighs, stroking them from knee to hip and coaxing them open, Kaede was shaking and short of breath. Fire crawled everywhere Imari had touched and the dull ache between her legs had become a desperate throb. She almost gave in to the temptation to open her eyes, but before she could, Imari's fist found her. It folded around the middle of her shaft, slowly drawing up toward the tip.

Kaede bucked into Imari's hand on instinct. She couldn't help herself. She already felt full, and Imari's soft palm was inviting.

But it's not where I want to be.

The thought was exhilarating. Every time she imagined how it would feel to be buried to the hilt inside Imari, her desire doubled. It wasn't something she had thought about often before. If anything, the idea had made her slightly uncomfortable. But with Imari, she felt wanted. Treasured. Safe. Safe enough to consider things she never would have dreamed of before.

Most of all, she felt safe enough to speak her needs aloud. "Imari," she muttered, rolling her head to the side. She was afraid that if she didn't, the temptation to look would be too great. "Imari, I want you. I want to feel you."

"Like this?" Imari's fist began to stroke her, working her from base to tip. At the top of each stroke, Kaede's muscles tensed and her heart thudded harder. Imari's thumb rolled over her, and Kaede bit her lower lip every time it happened.

"No," she said at last. That one word was all she could manage.

Imari's hand stopped, pulling away completely, and Kaede immediately regretted her decision. She twitched as it skated along her stomach instead, teasing the sensitive strip of skin between her hipbones. "What about this?"

Kaede guessed what was coming next when Imari's hot breath

washed over her, but she still wasn't prepared for the moment Imari's tongue flicked out to taste her. It started with a lick, then a kiss, and finally, soft lips sealed around her. Kaede let out a hoarse groan, grabbing blindly for Imari's hair. Fortunately, Imari didn't seem to mind. If anything, it encouraged her further. She started to suck, and it was all Kaede could do to urge her away.

"N...no," she stammered. "I want...I want."

"Tell me," Imari said, placing another kiss on her tip. "Tell me what you want and I'll give it to you."

Kaede summoned what little will she had. It was difficult to form an answer while Imari's fingertips trailed back and forth along her belly and Imari's lips were hovering so close to her, but she finally blurted out, "Inside you. I want to be inside you."

"That's my girl," Imari said with a note of pride in her voice. "I want you inside me too. Just be patient for one more minute." Before Kaede could protest, the futon dipped and she felt Imari shift away from her. The loss of skin was devastating, and Kaede sighed unhappily until Imari stroked her knee in comfort. "Keep your eyes closed. I'm not leaving, I promise. I just have to get some bamboo tissue paper, unless you want a bunch of little Kaedes running around."

Kaede suddenly understood. She had been so caught up that she hadn't remembered. At first, it made her sad. Yet another reminder of how she was different. But after thinking about it for a few more seconds, her heart lifted. She definitely didn't want any little Kaedes running around any time soon. *But a little Imari a few years down the road might not be such a bad thing.*

That put ideas into Kaede's head. Despite her best intentions, she couldn't resist peeking. She cracked open one eye and was treated to the glorious sight of Imari's rear a few yards away, as well as a backwards view of Imari's fingers delving between her legs. They were buried part way inside her, and Kaede couldn't help remembering the way Imari's tight inner walls had clamped down around her own only a few minutes earlier.

Imari chose that moment to look back over her shoulder. "I thought I said no peeking."

Kaede shut her eyes again. "I'm impressed that you're so prepared. I didn't even think about it. It doesn't hurt putting it in, does it?"

"No. I don't even feel it once it's in, and you won't either."

Kaede's heart gave another uneven thud. The thought of how Imari would feel around her, slick and hot and tight, had her leaking wetness of her own.

Imari came back over to the futon. Her thighs pressed on either side of Kaede's, and they gasped as their bodies came back into contact. "You're so beautiful," Kaede murmured, smiling up at where she assumed Imari was.

"You can't even see me," Imari pointed out.

"It doesn't matter. It's still true, but when can I look again?"

"In a moment," Imari said. "First, I just want you to feel."

Kaede took a deep breath. "Okay."

Imari's hand closed around her again, but this time, it was with a different purpose. Kaede felt it guide her into a different angle, and then something warm touched her tip. For a split second, she couldn't breathe, couldn't make a sound, couldn't think. Every nerve concentrated on the part of her that was touching Imari. She had never felt such softness.

Then, slowly, the silky heat began to swallow her. Just the head at first—and that was almost enough to make her empty herself early. She pounded with heavy pressure, and the fullness grew worse. Imari's entrance was clinging to her, grasping her, trying to suck her in.

Her first instinct was to push upward, to bury herself in heaven, but she held herself back. She gripped the edges of the futon instead, quivering with the effort of remaining still. Imari rewarded her patience. Little by little, she began to sink down. The tight ring of liquid fire moved lower.

Imari started moaning, soft groans at first, ones that Kaede mistook for discomfort. She opened her eyes in concern, letting go of the bed and preparing to reach out, but instead, she was greeted with one of the most beautiful sights she had ever seen: Imari sliding onto her, taking her all the way inside.

Imari noticed her open eyes and blushed. "I didn't want you to see that," she said softly. "I thought it might upset you to watch."

Kaede didn't answer at first. She simply stared in awe, gazing down between their bodies at the place where they were joined. Imari's outer lips petaled apart around her, holding her in. She could even see the base of her shaft stretching Imari open. The bright red button of Imari's clit stood proud beneath its hood, pleading to be touched.

"No," Kaede whispered, shaking her head. "No, it doesn't upset me. It looks...you feel—"

Imari bent down to kiss her, and Kaede forgot everything she had been trying to say. All that mattered was Imari's lips on hers and the way Imari's muscles squeezed her. She could feel every flutter of Imari's inner walls, each shared pulse that passed between their bodies.

But Kaede wanted more. She needed to move, to glide through the slippery heat surrounding her. Even though she was already embedded within Imari, she gave her hips a gentle push, asking for permission without words. Imari took over, rising a few centimeters before lowering herself back down again.

Kaede gasped. The movement was maddening. Imari felt even better than she imagined, so hot and smooth she could barely stand it. The sensations overwhelmed her, but they were also addictive. She began to pump her hips, not at all sure what she was doing, but completely unable to remain still.

Imari placed her hand in the middle of Kaede's chest, letting it rest between her breasts. "Don't force it," she said, tugging at one of Kaede's hard nipples. "Let me get a rhythm going."

Once more, Kaede surrendered herself to Imari's experience. The slow, rocking rhythm Imari picked was both blissful and torturous, and she eased her impatience by running her palms along Imari's legs, feeling the tight muscles there. They tensed as Imari rose, and then relaxed as she sank down. Each time Imari enveloped her again, Kaede twitched. Her peak was building much faster than she had expected, and she knew she wouldn't be able to hold it off for long.

"Imari," she said, trying to offer a warning. "I can't."

To Kaede's amazement and delight, Imari removed her palm and tilted back, adjusting their positions. The new angle put her on even more prominent display, and Kaede watched with wide eyes as Imari took her hand and brought it between their bodies. "Bring me with you," she said, a clear note of desire in her voice. From the way Imari clutched at her, Kaede could tell that she wasn't alone in her need.

"Always." She found the tip of Imari's clit, rubbing it in time with their rolling hips. The moment she touched it, Imari sped up, and Kaede realized she did have some control over the rhythm after all. She started stroking in earnest, and Imari quivered above her, tilting her head back to the ceiling and letting out short little cries.

The sounds were wonderful, but not as blissful as the rest of her reactions. Imari's lips were slightly parted, sucking in shallow sips of air, and her eyes were half-lidded, threatening to close. Kaede throbbed at the sight. She needed release, but part of her was unsure of coming this way. It was new and different, and she didn't want to leave Imari unsatisfied.

Right before Kaede could beg for mercy, Imari went stiff above her. Her entire body lit up with a fierce tremble, and her inner walls went wild, rippling with deep, powerful contractions. While Imari mouthed soundlessly to the ceiling, Kaede shouted. More wetness spilled out around her, burning silk squeezed her, and each shiver through Imari's body shot straight to her core.

Kaede fell over the edge gazing into Imari's eyes, burying herself as deep as possible. She gave Imari everything she had, clasping tight to her hip to keep their bodies together. The flood that poured out of her was stronger than anything she had ever felt before, and Imari's pulsing muscles drew out more. She whimpered as Kaede emptied herself, falling into another round of shudders.

They soared for a long time before coming to land safely on the ground. Kaede didn't realize it was over until Imari collapsed on top of her, panting heavily beside her ear. She folded her arms around Imari on instinct, cradling her. "Thank you," she said as soon as she could speak again. "That was…so much more incredible than I imagined it could be."

"Why are you thanking me?" Imari laughed. "You're the one who carried me across the ocean three times. Sometimes I still can't believe you're new at this."

Kaede smirked. "A student is only as good as her teacher. And I wouldn't want lessons from anyone else."

Imari raised her head, surprising Kaede with the serious look on her face. "Do you mean that, Kaede?" she asked, no longer laughing, but speaking sincerely. "This is your first relationship, and I know it hasn't always been easy."

Kaede ran her hand up and down Imari's back in soothing lines. "I mean it. I might not know much about relationships, but I know my own mind, and I know you. I could search the whole Empire and beyond and I wouldn't find a more wonderful woman."

"There's at least one," Imari said, "because she's lying right beneath me."

Kaede gave a happy sigh. Holding Imari's weight on top of her was comforting. "I don't want this moment to end."

"It doesn't have to." Once more, Imari's expression had become serious—though it was still glowing with love. "I promised myself I wouldn't ask until I had a chance to talk to my father, but I can't keep it in anymore. Kaede, when I think about my future path, I can't imagine walking it without you. I want you with me every day and every night."

She gave a slight shudder, her smile falling. "When you went off the edge of that cliff, I felt like I was falling as well. You're a part of me."

Understanding dawned and Kaede sucked in a small gasp of surprise. "Imari." A smile broke across her face, so wide it hurt her cheeks. "Are you asking me—"

"Yes," Imari said. "I want to marry you. If you'll have me, of course."

At first, Kaede couldn't answer. Her relationship with Imari had developed quickly and intensely—perhaps a little too quickly—but in some ways, it felt as if they had known each other for their entire lives. She had grown to know Imari better in the past months than anyone else. Her heart and her mind were at odds, but eventually, they came to a compromise.

"You're not saying anything," Imari said, a small wrinkle marring her forehead.

"Yes," Kaede blurted out before Imari could worry any longer. "Yes, I'll marry you, but on one condition."

"Name it," Imari said breathlessly. "Anything you want."

"We wait a year." At Imari's look of confusion, Kaede explained herself. "We never got the chance to court each other properly. Those two months of getting to know each other at Mount Hongshan were wonderful. There wasn't any pressure to save the world—it was the two of us together. I want more of that. I don't want us to get married in a rush and cheat ourselves out of a courtship. Is that okay?"

Imari beamed. "It's more than okay. It's perfect."

With a long breath of relief, Kaede tucked her face into Imari's shoulder, pressing a kiss there. The gesture made Imari's muscles clench around her, and she began to stir again. "So…again?" she whispered, placing another kiss in the same spot and sucking briefly. "To celebrate our engagement?"

Imari lifted her weight up, tipping onto her back and bringing Kaede with her until their positions were reversed. "Of course. But this time, you get to set the pace."

***

Hayate watched the snow fall through the slats in his bedroom window, letting his mind drift. Kaze had curled up in the corner to sleep, leaving the room silent and giving him plenty of space to think.

The past week had been a whirlwind of change, but not all the developments had been bad. Through Imari, he had learned that Empress Tomoyo intended to make him the new daimyo of Yukimura. It was an awesome responsibility, one he had not expected to inherit for several years, if at all.

He still wanted the position, but not because it was a prize to be won. It was a heavy burden, one he wanted to carry for Setsuna's sake more than his own. Before her fall, she had been a wise and kind leader. Hayate only hoped he could carry on the way she would have if Kyuubi hadn't interfered. People depended on him, including Setsuna herself.

He planned to leave for Yukimura in the next few days once things in Asahina were more settled. While Lord Aozora would certainly do his best to take care of Setsuna, Hayate couldn't help worrying about her. He wanted to be there during her recovery, to help her if he could. Despite everything that had happened, she was still his mother.

A rap against his door interrupted his thoughts.

"Yukimura-dono? It's me, Hibana Kenta. Can I come in?"

A small smile tilted the corners of Hayate's lips. "Yes," he said, rising from his mat.

Kenta entered the room wearing his usual cheerful smile. He bowed briefly, and then immediately hurried over to crouch beside Kaze. When Kaze's tail started thumping against the floor, Kenta reached out to scratch his ears. "I was just going to ask you both if you wanted to come to dinner. I didn't see you at lunch, so I'm guessing you didn't have any."

Hayate felt a stab of guilt. He and Kenta had taken many of their meals together over the past few days, but he hadn't realized his company would be missed. "I'm sorry, Hibana-san. I was...lost in thought."

Kenta straightened up again, turning to face Hayate with a look of concern. "Is it about Yukimura-sama? From the second-hand news I've heard, Lord Aozora is taking good care of her."

"Yes, but I'm the one who should be taking care of her," Hayate said after a moment of hesitation. He wasn't quite sure why he trusted Kenta enough to discuss the subject with him, but it would be a relief to get some of his worries off his chest. A burden shared was a burden halved. "She took care of me for my entire life and asked for nothing in return but my love. I hope I can do the same for her."

Kenta seemed to understand. His expression softened, and when he spoke, it was more quietly than usual. "Takeshi and I lost our parents when we were young. Lord Homura took us in and trained us himself.

We weren't his children, but he treated us like family. If he was in Lady Yukimura's situation, I know I'd want to help him."

"Do you plan to return to Mirai once the situation here is resolved?" Hayate asked. "I'm sure you must be eager to go back home." He could certainly empathize, although the thought left him a little bit sad as well.

"Yes, for a few weeks," Kenta said. "After that...well, I think I've gotten a taste for adventuring. Kaede and Imari will probably make a trip to the Northern Provinces to see Kaede's parents, and they've asked me to come along with them."

Hayate's brows rose in surprise. "And? What was your answer?"

"I said yes," Kenta said, his grin slightly sheepish. "That is, if you don't mind, Yukimura-dono."

"Not at all," Hayate said, perhaps a little too quickly. His stomach did a nervous flip and warmth began to creep into his face. "You're welcome in Yukimura as well, you know, not just Aozora. I mean, I'm sure Kaede will want to check on how things are going there." His voice trailed off, and the two of them stared at each other in awkward silence.

To Hayate's surprise, it was Kaze who broke the stalemate. "Would the two of you just admit that you want to spend more time together? Honestly, Rin is right. Humans act so foolish when they're looking for a mate."

Hayate and Kenta shared a horrified look, but after a moment, they both burst out laughing. "I was hoping to visit Yukimura for a little while," Kenta said once he caught his breath, "but if I did, it would be to see you. I've enjoyed your company since we met."

Hayate grinned. "Even the parts where we were almost killed?"

"Yes, even those parts," Kenta said. "And even the part where your wolf embarrassed us."

"I'm not his wolf," Kaze protested. "If anything, Hayate is my human. I picked him out."

"Then it seems both of us have excellent taste," Kenta said while Hayate groaned softly to himself. "So, Yukimura-dono? Will you let me trouble you for a while when I make my trip? Or is that too forward?"

Hayate smiled, feeling much lighter than he had in several days. "It's no trouble at all. In fact, the honor will be mine."

***

Kaede sat outside on the garden bench she had brushed clear of snow, drawing the crisp air deep into her lungs and staring up at the pale sky. It was bright and cheerful, as winter days went, but her skin prickled anyway and her stomach had twisted itself into knots.

Imari's father was due to arrive any minute and Kaede had no idea what to say. Lord Homura had always treated her with respect, even when he'd thought she was nothing but a ronin, but that didn't do much to ease her nerves. She had gone from being Imari's yojimbo to her prospective wife—and that made all the difference.

"Stop worrying about it, Kaede," Rin said from beside her feet. The wolf had curled up on top of them to keep them warm, although it wasn't really helping. She had rolled around in the clean garden snow upon venturing outside—one of the first times she'd managed the trip since the battle with Kyuubi—and now the top layer of her white fur was wet with melted snowflakes.

Kaede sighed, wiggling her wet toes inside of her tabi. Thanks to Rin's "protection," her sandals hadn't done much to keep off the damp, raised as they were.

"I can't help it," she said to Rin. "Imari loves her father. She'll be so hurt if he disapproves."

"And who's to say he'll disapprove?" Rin raised her head, giving Kaede a reproachful look. "You'll make a fine mate for Imari and would for anyone else."

Kaede smiled. "Things have changed a lot since Mirai, huh? Back then, you wouldn't stop warning me to have nothing to do with Imari."

"I think she deserves you." Rin turned her head, resting her chin on Kaede's knee and gazing up at her with soft eyes. "That's high enough praise."

Kaede reached down to scratch the matted fur between Rin's ears. "You always know just what to say, don't you?"

"I simply state the truth," Rin said. "I still say you humans could learn from us wolves on that subject."

The opening of the garden door several yards away interrupted their conversation. A thin, cloaked figure slipped past the screen and Kaede made to get up.

"Don't bother," Rin said, refusing to move from her comfortable place. "It's only Gin."

As the figure moved closer, Kaede saw Rin was right. Gin had indeed snuck into the garden, although she didn't seem surprised to find others there. "Aozora-dono," she said, approaching the bench and

Tengoku

bowing briefly. "Glad I found you. I was about to slip out, and I figured I should give you a goodbye, at least."

Kaede's brow furrowed with concern. "You're leaving? Why? Surely the Empress hasn't ordered you to?"

"No, but I know better than to overstay my welcome," Gin said. "Toyotomi and Ishikawa don't mix—there's just too much bloody history there—and Asahina isn't the place for a thief."

"A former thief," Kaede insisted. "I thought Empress Tomoyo pardoned you of your past crimes?"

Gin gave a genuine smile. "She did, and she promised to help rebuild Iga. I'm sure a lot of that was Homura-dono's doing. Please, tell her thank you for me."

"You should stay and tell her yourself," Kaede said, trying to convince Gin one last time. "I'm sure she wouldn't want you to leave yet."

"Oh, I'm sure I'll see her again," Gin said. "She's promised to check on the relief efforts to my village herself, since Mirai is so close by. But until then, I need to get back. My people need me, and I'd rather avoid Lord Homura's arrival, to be honest. I did try to kidnap and ransom his daughter. It'd be awkward. You know how it is."

That Kaede could relate to. "At least you're not marrying his daughter," she mumbled, although she grinned as well.

Gin snorted. "Marry Homura-dono? No thank you. I'll leave that to you, Kaede. Who knows what insane quest she'll drag you on next?"

"Hopefully one with more dragons and less foxes," Kaede said cheerfully. She finally managed to nudge Rin off her feet and stand, and once she did, she gave Gin a deep bow. "Thank you for everything you've done, Ishikawa-san. You're the most honorable thief I've ever had the pleasure of meeting."

"Honorable thief." Gin laughed softly to herself. "I like that. Until next time, Aozora-dono. I'm sure we'll see each other again." With one more bow of farewell, Gin slipped over to the far garden wall and out through one of the wooden doors. Kaede had no doubt she would blend easily into the crowd outside the fortress, and she also suspected the Empress's stable would be missing a horse soon.

"I'm sure she won't mind," she said to herself. "After everything that's happened, Gin's earned it as part of her reward."

"What are you talking about?" Rin asked.

Kaede shook her head. "Oh, nothing. I suppose we should go and find Imari, shouldn't we? She'd appreciate a hand to hold while she waits for her father."

Rin picked herself up out of the snow, shaking the flakes from her coat. "Very well. Lead the way."

Together, they left the garden and entered the castle again. There were few people in the hall during the middle part of the day. She headed to Imari's room, sliding back the screen to find her lover in her juban, fretting over her choice of kimono.

"Problems?" she asked, arching both eyebrows.

Imari sighed. "Always." She held up the dark crimson kimono she had chosen, holding it up to her front. "Does this say: I know I've been away on an adventure for half a year, but I'm fine, I promise?"

"While I respect your fashion choices, maybe you should just tell him that?" Kaede suggested. "I'm not sure your father speaks kimono."

Beside her, Rin huffed in approval.

"I know," Imari said. "So, should I show him my jian right away, or later? It's impressive, but then I'll have to tell him about how I used it to fight an evil nine-tailed fox spirit."

Kaede considered it. "Show him Wujian. I'm sure he's already heard bits and pieces of what happened."

"Or, I could tell him we're engaged first," Imari suggested slyly. "That might take his mind off the fact we all almost died."

"Oh no," Kaede said, shaking her head. "That's what I'm nervous about. Don't throw me under the horse's hooves to save yourself."

"I was going to tell him sooner rather than later." Imari approached her, taking her hand and giving it a reassuring squeeze. "Don't worry so much, Kaede. He's going to be so happy for me. For us. I love you, and that's all that matters to him."

Kaede let out a slow breath. "All right. I trust you. When is he arriving?"

Imari glanced over at the corner of the room, where an incense stick was burning. She looked mildly alarmed and hurried to put on her kimono. Without being asked, Kaede helped, straightening out edges and smoothing down folds. Finally came the katiganu, which Kaede placed upon Imari's shoulders before circling around to admire the view. She placed a kiss at the nape of Imari's neck as she finished the bow.

"You look beautiful. This will be fine."

"I know. I'll be glad to see him. I've really missed him since I left home."

"I'm sure you have." After a pause, Kaede added, "Perhaps I'll follow your example and try to form a closer relationship with my own family. If there was ever a time to mend broken bridges, now would be one."

Imari glanced over her shoulder, giving Kaede a look of approval. "Good." She stepped away to grab her sword, tucking it securely into her obi. "Now, let's go see if my father has arrived. The messenger said his party would reach Asahina around midday."

They exited the castle and arrived at the fortress's front gates in time to see a good-sized group of samurai wearing the colors of Homura making their way up the mountain path. They were on horseback, but Kaede could still pick out Lord Homura in the middle of the group. With his mon displayed prominently across his kimono, he was instantly recognizable.

Kaede swallowed nervously, but Imari grinned and bounced beside her. "He's never going to believe everything I've done when I tell him."

"I still don't believe everything we've done," Kaede said.

A pair of guards opened the gates, and Lord Homura's party entered. As soon as he caught sight of them, he pulled his horse to the side, dismounting and offering the reins to one of his men. "Imari," he murmured, hurrying over to them at a brisk pace.

To the surprise of several onlookers—but not Kaede—Imari didn't give her father a respectful bow. Instead, she threw her arms around him, hugging his neck. He seemed a little surprised, too, but he returned the gesture, ignoring the whispers.

Kaede smiled. It was sweet that Imari was so affectionate with her father, even in public. She waited until the embrace ended and the two of them made their bows before stepping forward to join them.

"And what prompted such an enthusiastic greeting?" Lord Homura asked Imari. "You act as if you thought you might never see me again." Imari gave a guilty wince, and Lord Homura's eyes widened. "It seems you have a lot to tell me."

"I do, Father, but don't worry." Imari reached back, taking Kaede's hand with her own and pulling her forward. "It's a story the Moon will smile upon."

The End

Glossary of Terms and Places

Kimono: every-day clothing; differentiates in material and cut to show status.

Hakama: skirt-like garment worn over the kimono by samurai.

Kataginu: sleeveless jacket with wide shoulders worn by samurai for formal occasions.

Kamishimo: formal samurai attire that includes a kimono, hakama and kataginu.

Tatsuki: a white cord used to keep the sleeves of one's kimono up and out of the way.

Karo: trusted advisers to the daimyo.

Bushido: the philosophy and mindset of the samurai, the code of conduct.

Akatsuki Teikoku: the Empire of the Dawn, the most eastern country on Tengoku; ruled by the Empress through the individual daimyo-landlords and shogun military leaders.

Kingdom of Tsun'i: ancient kingdom to the west of the Jade Sea; ruled by the Twin Kings and guarded by the Iron Golems.

Kingdom of Xiangsai: a younger kingdom to the south of Tsun'i and Akatsuki; ruled by the mysterious Jheong dynasty, mistrustful of outsiders and fiercely protective of its lands.

Jade Sea: a massive inland sea that had been turned to jade in a cataclysm some hundred years before.

Yin: a dying city on the shore of the Jade Sea that once was a thriving center of trade.

Mirai: the crown jewel of Homura province, known for its hot springs as well as steel and textile manufacturers.

Mount Aka: "Red Mountain", *see Hongshan*.

Hongshan: the mysterious mountain on the borders of Tsun'i, surrounded by the rumors of dragons.

Taiseito: a city in the shadow of the Northern Mountains, capital of Aozora province.

Kousetsu: a city in the far north, capital of Yukimura province.

River Go: a massive river that flows through Tsun'i from north to south-west, known as the Lifeblood of Tsun'i.

Hyewang: a Tsun'i city at the north most tip of the Jade Sea, important trade and travel center between Tsun'i and Akatsuki.

Asahina: a mountain fortress, place where the shogun meet to share information and celebrate their victories.

Seinarukyo: the Imperial City, Akatsuki Teikoku capitol from which the Empress and her court rules, impenetrable in two hundred years.

Irori: a sunken, square hearth mainly used for heat and cooking.

Katana: two-handed long sword of the samurai; it is curved and slender, with a single edge.

Saya: lacquered wooden scabbard.

Wakizashi: a shorter companion sword to the katana.

Daishō: the pairing of katana and wakizashi, symbol of the samurai class.

Daimyo: powerful, hereditary feudal lords who rule over large provinces.

Yokai: supernatural spirits. In Tengoku, they are typically large, sentient animals.

Ki: energy within living things. Can be translated to mean "breath" or "air".

Yari: a straight-headed spear.

Kote: gauntlets

Mon: family and ruling clan crest, displayed on banners, clothing and armor.

Ronin: a samurai with no lord or master, "one who wanders".

Yamayuri: mountain lily, famous for its striking white-golden colored blooms.

Saya-ate: a duel of honor fought when one samurai deliberately bumps their scabbard against another samurai's scabbard

Ume: plum trees

Kanzashi: traditional hair ornament worn by women, often but not always in the shape of flowers

Shogun: military leaders one step above the daimyo landowners, but fewer in number.

Otou-san: father (informal).

Okaa-sama: mother (formal).

Obi: sash worn around the middle. The sash is also used to hold daishō.

Yukata: a casual summer kimono, often used as sleepwear.

Fundoshi: loincloth undergarment.

Juban: a thin, lightweight undergarment; similar to an undershirt.

Jian: a double-edged straight sword held in one hand; oftentimes colored tassels are attached to the hilt or pommel of this sword.

Heika: Your Majesty.

-dono: way of address towards a person of superior station.

-danna: master, a respectful way of addressing a skillful person.

-san: way of address towards a person of equal station.

-sama: a way of address towards a person showing them great respect and admiration.

About Rae D. Magdon

Rae d. Magdon is a writer and author specializing in sapphic romance and speculative fiction. When she felt the current selection of stories about queer women were too white, too strictly gendered, and far too few in number, she decided to start writing her own. From 2012 to 2016, she has written and published ten novels with desert palm press, won a rainbow award in the 2016 science fiction category, and was runner up in 2015 for the golden crown literary award in the fantasy category. She wholeheartedly believes that all queer women deserve their own adventures, and especially their own happy endings.

Connect with Rae online:

Website: http://raedmagdon.com/
Facebook: https://www.facebook.com/RaeDMagdon
Tumblr: http://raedmagdon.tumblr.com/
Email: raedmagdon@gmail.com

Other Books by Rae D. Magdon

Amendyr Series

The Second Sister
ISBN: 9781311262042
Eleanor of Sandleford's entire world is shaken when her father marries the mysterious, reclusive Lady Kingsclere to gain her noble title. Ripped away from the only home she has ever known, Ellie is forced to live at Baxstresse Manor with her two new stepsisters, Luciana and Belladonna. Luciana is sadistic, but Belladonna is the woman who truly haunts her. When her father dies and her new stepmother goes suddenly mad, Ellie is cheated out of her inheritance and forced to become a servant. With the help of a shy maid, a friendly cook, a talking cat, and her mysterious second stepsister, Ellie must stop Luciana from using an ancient sorcerer's chain to bewitch the handsome Prince Brendan and take over the entire kingdom of Seria.

Wolf's Eyes
ISBN: 9781311755872
Cathelin Raybrook has always been different. She Knows things without being told and Sees things before they happen. When her visions urge her to leave her friends in Seria and return to Amendyr, the magical kingdom of her birth, she travels across the border in search of her grandmother to learn more about her visions. But before she can find her family, she is captured by a witch, rescued by a handsome stranger, and forced to join a strange group of forest-dwellers with even stranger magical abilities. With the help of her new lover, her new family, and her eccentric new teacher, she must learn to gain control of her powers and do some rescuing of her own before they take control of her instead.

The Witch's Daughter
ISBN: 978131672643

Ailynn Gothel has always been the perfect daughter. Thanks to her mother's teachings, she knows how to heal the sick, conjure the elements, and take care of Raisa, her closest and dearest friend. But when Ailynn's feelings for Raisa grow deeper, her simple life falls apart. Her mother hides Raisa deep in a cave to shield her from the world, and Ailynn must leave home in search of a spell to free her. While the kingdom beyond the forest is full of dangers, Ailynn's greatest fear is that Raisa will no longer want her when she returns. She is a witch's daughter, after all—and witches never get their happily ever after.

The Mirror's Gaze
ISBN: 9781942976196

In the final sequel of the Amendyr series civil war has broken out in Amendyr. With undead monsters ravaging the land, an evil queen on Kalmarin's white throne, and the kingdom's true heir missing, Cathelin Raybrook and Ailynn Gothel must join forces to protect their homeland. They hope to gain the aid of the Liarre, a reclusive community of magical creatures, but some of their leaders are reluctant to join a war that isn't theirs. Meanwhile, Lady Eleanor of Baxstresse thinks she's safe across the border in Seria, but when a mysterious girl in white arrives in an abandoned carriage, she finds herself drawn into the conflict as well. Together, they must find the source of the evil queen's power, and discover a way to destroy it before it's too late.

Desert Palm Press

Death Wears Yellow Garters
ISBN: 9781942976011
Jay Venkatesan's life was going pretty great. She had Nicole—her perfect new girlfriend—and her anxiety was mostly under control. But when Nicole's grandfather dies under mysterious circumstances at his 70th birthday party, Jay is thrown into a tailspin. Her eccentric Aunt Mimi is determined to solve the mystery no matter what she thinks about it, and the police are eyeing Nicole as one of their prime suspects. No matter how often Jay insists that real life isn't like one of her aunt's crime novels, she finds herself dragged along for the ride as the mystery unravels and the shocking truth comes to light.

Written with Michelle Magly

Dark Horizons Series

Dark Horizons
ISBN: 9781310892646
Lieutenant Taylor Morgan has never met an ikthian that wasn't trying to kill her, but when she accidentally takes one of the aliens hostage, she finds herself with an entirely new set of responsibilities. Her captive, Maia Kalanis, is no normal ikthian, and the encroaching Dominion is willing to do just about anything to get her back. Her superiors want to use Maia as a bargaining chip, but the more time Taylor spends alone with her, the more conflicted she becomes. Torn between Maia and her duty to her home-world, Taylor must decide where her loyalties lie.

Starless Nights
ISBN: 9781310317736
In this sequel to Dark Horizons Taylor and Maia did not know where they would go when they fled Earth. They trusted Akton to take them somewhere safe. Leaving behind a wake of chaos and disorder, Coalition soldier Rachel is left to deal with the backlash of Taylor's actions, and soon finds herself chasing after the runaways. Rachel

quickly learns the final frontier is not a forgiving place for humans, but her chances for survival are better out there than back on Earth. Meanwhile, Taylor and Maia find themselves living off the generosity of rebel leader Sorra, an ikthian living a double life for the sake of the rebellion. With Maia's research in hand, Sorra believes they can deliver a fatal blow against the Dominion.

Desert Palm Press

All The Pretty Things
ISBN: 9781311061393
With the launch of her political campaign, the last thing Tess needed was a distraction. She had enough to deal with running as a Republican and a closeted lesbian. But when Special Agent Robin Hart from the FBI arrives in Cincinnati to investigate a corruption case, Tess finds herself spending more time than she should with the attractive woman. Things get a little more complicated when Robin begins to display signs of affection, and Tess fears her own outing might erupt in political scandal and sink all chances of pursuing her dreams.

Cover Design By : Rachel George
www.rachelgeorgeillustration.com

Note to Readers:

Thank you for reading a book from Desert Palm Press. We have made every effort to edit this book. However, typos do slip in. If you find an error in the text, please email **lee@desertpalmpress.com** so the issue can be corrected.

We appreciate you as a reader and want to ensure you enjoy the reading process. We would like you to consider posting a review on your preferred media sites such as Amazon, Smashwords, Bella Books, Goodreads, Tumblr, Twitter, Facebook, and/or your blog or website.

For more information on upcoming releases, author interviews, contest, giveaways and more, please sign up for our newsletter and visit us as at Desert Palm Press: **www.desertpalmpress.com** and "Like" us on Facebook: **https://www.facebook.com/DesertPalmPress/?fref=ts**.

Bright blessing.

CPSIA information can be obtained
at www.ICGtesting.com
Printed in the USA
LVHW030453040522
717858LV00011B/815